Totally Bound Publishing books by Cerise DeLand:

Swords of Passion
At Her Service
For Her Honour
With Her Kiss

Tough Texas Hombres
One Tough Hombre
Two Tough Hombres

Anthologies
At Your Service: His Delectable Cook
Sharing the Billionaire: Cuffed to Him

Hard Drivin' Man

I0634598

Sense and Sensibility

A Clandestine Classic

JANE AUSTEN and CERISE DeLAND

Sense and Sensibility
ISBN # 978-1-78184-665-0
©Copyright Cerise DeLand 2013
Cover Art by Posh Gosh ©Copyright December 2013
Interior text design by Claire Siemaszkiewicz
Totally Bound Publishing

This is a work of fiction. All characters, places and events are from the author's imagination and should not be confused with fact. Any resemblance to persons, living or dead, events or places is purely coincidental.

All rights reserved. No part of this publication may be reproduced in any material form, whether by printing, photocopying, scanning or otherwise without the written permission of the publisher, Totally Bound Publishing.

Applications should be addressed in the first instance, in writing, to Totally Bound Publishing. Unauthorised or restricted acts in relation to this publication may result in civil proceedings and/or criminal prosecution.
The author and illustrator have asserted their respective rights under the Copyright Designs and Patents Acts 1988 (as amended) to be identified as the author of this book and illustrator of the artwork.

Published in 2013 by Totally Bound Publishing, Newland House, The Point, Weaver Road, Lincoln, LN6 3QN, United Kingdom.

No part of this book may be reproduced, scanned, or distributed in any printed or electronic form without permission. Please do not participate in or encourage piracy of copyrighted materials in violation of the authors' rights. Purchase only authorised copies.

Totally Bound Publishing is an imprint of Total-E-Ntwined Limited.

If you purchased this book without a cover you should be aware that this book is stolen property. It was reported as "unsold and destroyed" to the publisher and neither the author nor the publisher has received any payment for this "stripped book".

Sense and Sensibility

Dedication

For my very best friend, mentor, lunch buddy and
critique partner, Desiree Holt. A fabulous writer,
dedicated to her art and her profession, she is an
inspiration and a joy to work, travel and drink with!

Chapter One

The family of Dashwood had long been settled in Sussex. Their estate was large, and their residence was at Norland Park, in the centre of their property, where for many generations they had lived in so respectable a manner as to engage the general good opinion of their surrounding acquaintance.

The late owner of this estate was a single man, who lived to a very advanced age, and who for many years of his life had a constant companion and housekeeper in his sister. But her death, which happened ten years before his own, produced a great alteration in his home, for to supply her loss he invited and received into his house the family of his nephew Mr Henry Dashwood, the legal inheritor of the Norland estate and the person to whom he intended to bequeath it.

In the society of his nephew and niece and their children, the old gentleman's days were comfortably spent. His attachment to them all increased. The constant attention of Mr and Mrs Henry Dashwood to his wishes, which proceeded not merely from interest but from goodness of heart, gave him every degree of solid comfort which his age could receive, and the cheerfulness of the children added a relish to his existence.

By a former marriage, Mr Henry Dashwood had one son—by his present lady, three daughters. The son, a steady respectable young man, was amply provided for by the fortune of his mother, which had been large, and half of which devolved on him on his coming of age. By his own marriage likewise, which happened soon afterwards, he added to his wealth. To him therefore the succession to the Norland estate was not so really important as to his sisters, for their fortune, independent of what might arise to them from their father's inheriting that property, could be but small. Their mother had nothing and their father only seven thousand pounds in his own disposal, for the remaining moiety of his first wife's fortune was also secured to her child and he had only a life interest in it.

The old gentleman died—his will was read, and like almost every other will, gave as much disappointment as pleasure. He was neither so unjust nor so ungrateful as to leave his estate from his nephew, but he left it to him on such terms as destroyed half the value of the bequest. Mr Dashwood had wished for it more for the sake of his wife and daughters than for himself or his son, but to his son and his son's son, a child of four years old, it was secured in such a way as to leave to himself no power of providing for those who were most dear to him, and who most needed a provision by any charge on the estate or by any sale of its valuable woods.

The whole was tied up for the benefit of this child, who in occasional visits with his father and mother at

Norland had so far gained on the affections of his uncle—by such attractions as are by no means unusual in children of two or three years old, an imperfect articulation, an earnest desire of having his own way, many cunning tricks and a great deal of noise—as to outweigh all the value of all the attention which for years he had received from his niece and her daughters. He meant not to be unkind, however, and as a mark of his affection for the three girls, he left them a thousand pounds apiece.

Mr Dashwood's disappointment was at first severe, but his temper was cheerful and sanguine, and he might reasonably hope to live many years, and by living economically lay by a considerable sum from the produce of an estate already large and capable of almost immediate improvement. But the fortune which had been so tardy in coming was his only one twelvemonth. He survived his uncle no longer, and ten thousand pounds, including the late legacies, was all that remained for his widow and daughters.

His son was sent for as soon as his danger was known, and to him Mr Dashwood recommended with all the strength and urgency which illness could command the interest of his mother-in-law and sisters.

Mr John Dashwood had not the strong feelings of the rest of the family, but he was affected by a recommendation of such a nature at such a time, and he promised to do everything in his power to make them comfortable. His father was rendered easy by such an assurance, and Mr John Dashwood had then leisure to consider how much there might prudently be in his power to do for them.

He was not an ill-disposed young man, unless to be rather cold-hearted and rather selfish is to be ill-disposed—but he was in general well respected, for he conducted himself with propriety in the discharge of his ordinary duties. Had he married a more amiable woman, he might have been made still more respectable than he was — he might even have been made amiable himself, for he was very young when he married, and very fond of his wife. But Mrs John Dashwood was a strong caricature of himself, more narrow-minded and selfish.

When he gave his promise to his father, he meditated within himself to increase the fortunes of his sisters by the present of a thousand pounds apiece. He then really thought himself equal to it. The prospect of four thousand a year in addition to his present income, besides the remaining half of his own mother's fortune, warmed his heart and made him feel capable of generosity. Yes, he would give them three thousand pounds — it would be liberal and handsome! It would be enough to make them completely easy. Three thousand pounds! He could spare so considerable a sum with little inconvenience. He thought of it all day long and for many days successively, and he did not repent.

No sooner was his father's funeral over than Mrs John Dashwood, without sending any notice of her intention to her mother-in-law, arrived with her child and their attendants. No one could dispute her right to come — the house was her husband's from the moment of his father's decease — but the indelicacy of her conduct was so much the greater, and to a woman in Mrs Dashwood's situation, with only common feelings, must have been highly unpleasing. But in her mind there was a sense of honour so keen, a generosity so romantic, that any offence of the kind, by whomsoever given or received, was to her a source of immovable disgust. Mrs John Dashwood had never been a favourite with any of her husband's family, but she had had no opportunity till the present of showing them with how little attention to the comfort of other people she could act when occasion required it.

So acutely did Mrs Dashwood feel this ungracious behaviour and so earnestly did she despise her daughter-in-law for it that on the arrival of the latter she would have quitted the house forever, had not the entreaty of her eldest girl induced her first to reflect on the propriety of going. Her own tender love for all her three children determined her afterwards to stay, and for their sakes avoid a breach with their brother.

Elinor, this eldest daughter whose advice was so effectual, possessed a strength of understanding and coolness of judgement which qualified her, though only nineteen, to be the counsellor of her mother, and enabled her frequently to counteract to the advantage of them all that eagerness of mind in Mrs Dashwood which must generally have led to imprudence. She had an excellent heart, her disposition was affectionate and her feelings were strong, but she knew how to govern them—or so she had concluded, though in truth, she had not yet been severely tested by any unfortunate incident. It was a knowledge which her mother had yet to learn, and which one of her sisters had resolved never to be taught.

Marianne's abilities were in many respects quite equal to Elinor's. She was sensible and clever, but being younger and eager in everything, her sorrows, her joys could have no moderation. She was generous, amiable, interesting—she was everything but prudent. The resemblance between her and her mother was strikingly great. Many in the Dashwoods' company noted this privately, but had no occasion or reason to consider it of any import.

Elinor saw with concern the excess of her sister's sensibility, but excused it as well because of her youth. But by Mrs Dashwood it was valued and cherished. They encouraged each other now in the violence of their affliction. The agony of grief which overpowered them at first was voluntarily renewed, was sought for, was created again and again. They gave themselves up wholly to their sorrow, seeking increase of wretchedness in every reflection that could afford it, and resolved against ever admitting consolation in future. Elinor too was deeply afflicted, but still she could struggle, she could exert herself. She could consult with her brother, could receive her sister-in-law on her arrival and treat her with proper attention, and could strive to rouse her mother to similar exertion and encourage her to similar forbearance.

Margaret, the other sister, was a good-humoured, well-disposed girl, but as she had already imbibed a good deal of Marianne's romance without having much of her sense, she did not, at thirteen, bid fair to equal her sisters at a more advanced period of life.

Chapter Two

Mrs John Dashwood now installed herself mistress of Norland, and her mother and sisters-in-law were degraded to the condition of visitors. As such, however, they were treated by her with quiet civility and by her husband with as much kindness as he could feel towards anybody beyond himself, his wife and their child. He really pressed them with some earnestness to consider Norland as their home, and as no plan appeared so eligible to Mrs Dashwood as remaining there till she could accommodate herself with a house in the neighbourhood, his invitation was accepted.

A continuance in a place where everything reminded her of former delight was exactly what suited her mind. In seasons of cheerfulness, no temper could be more cheerful than hers, or possess in a greater degree that sanguine expectation of happiness which is happiness itself. But in sorrow she must be equally carried away by her fancy, and as far beyond consolation as in pleasure she was beyond alloy.

Mrs John Dashwood did not at all approve of what her husband intended to do for his sisters. To take three thousand pounds from the fortune of their dear little boy would be impoverishing him to the most dreadful degree. She begged him to think again on the subject. Indeed, she appealed to him as only a wife may, using not only all her logic but also all the physical assets which her husband so admired—especially, as on this occasion, when she employed them so frequently and lavishly. In their marriage bed, in his dressing room, after tea upon the Turkish carpet, she led him to consider the issue over and over again.

How could he answer it to himself to rob his child, and his only child too, of so large a sum? And what possible claim could the Miss Dashwoods, who were related to him only by half blood, which she considered as no relationship at all, have on his generosity to so large an amount? It was very well known that no affection was ever supposed to exist between the children of any man by different marriages, and why was he to ruin himself and their poor little Harry by giving away all his money to his half-sisters?

"It was my father's last request to me," replied her husband one morning as he buttoned his flies and attempted to regain his composure as well as his authority over his wife, "that I should assist his widow and daughters."

"He did not know what he was talking of, I dare say. Ten to one but he was light-headed at the time."

"Perhaps," he allowed, narrowing his gaze on her pebbled nipples that he had been so generously offered—and so heartily sucked. "Although I daresay the man could not have had his wits about him had he ever seen you in your natural splendour, Madam."

"You do compliment me too much, my dear man." She winked at him, naughty as ever in their play.

"Come here quickly." He crooked a finger at her.

Mrs Dashwood approached him, smiling and naked, allowing him to savour the view of her pendulous breasts and her swollen cunny, wet from his tongue and his emissions.

"Had he been in his right senses, he could not have thought of such a thing as begging you to give away half your fortune from your own child."

"He did not stipulate for any particular sum, my dear Fanny, he only requested me in general terms to assist them and make their situation more comfortable than it was in his power to do." He bent to nip one of her areolas. She did so like the bite of his teeth, waspish witch that she was. "Perhaps it would have been as well if he had left it wholly to myself. He could hardly suppose I should neglect them. But as he required the promise, I could not do less than give it, at least I thought so at the time. The promise therefore was given, and must be performed. Something must be done for them whenever they leave Norland and settle in a new home."

"Well then, let something be done for them, but that something need not be three thousand pounds. Consider," she added as she brushed against him purring like a crafty cat and stroked his manly length, a last assault this morning to gain his final agreement to her plea, "that when the money is once parted with it never can return. Your sisters will marry, and it will be gone forever. If indeed it could be restored to our poor little boy —"

"Why, to be sure," said her husband very gravely, his cock hardening once more at her manual persuasion, "that would make great difference. The time may come when Harry will regret that so large a sum was parted with. If he should have a numerous family, for instance, it would be a very convenient addition."

"To be sure it would, my dearest." Her lips curved in a small delight as his manhood stiffened even more so under her ministrations. He had always been so virile, randy and ready for her repeatedly. If she used his attraction to her as a tool, who could fault her? After all, was she not the most alluring, agreeable wife, meeting all his needs and opening her quim for him, especially whenever she thought the moment useful to her purposes?

"Perhaps then it would be better for all parties if the sum were diminished one half. Five hundred pounds would be a prodigious increase to their fortunes!"

"Oh! Beyond anything great! What brother on earth would do half so much for his sisters, even if really his sisters! And as it is—only half blood! But you have such a generous spirit!" She sank to her knees before him, opening the buttons he had sought to close too early to give them any resolution to this testy matter. She fished out his cock from his trousers and small clothes, then rubbed her cheek against the soft fine flesh of his private member. She did so love licking him, and certainly when it brought her not only his manly essence down her throat but a good fucking on the floor.

"I would not wish to do anything mean," he replied, panting, driving one hand into her hair and holding very, very still so that she might do him the honours he so craved and well deserved. "One had rather on such occasions do too much than too little. No one, at least, can think I have not done enough for them — even themselves, they can hardly expect more."

"There is no knowing what they may expect," said the lady between hearty licks along his rigid length, "but we are not to think of their expectations — the question is what you can afford to do."

"Certainly — and I think I may afford to give them five hundred pounds apiece." He shoved his hips forward, permitting her to show her gratitude by taking the whole of him into the cavern of her throat. "As it is, without any addition of mine, they will each have about three thousand pounds on their mother's death — a very comfortable fortune for any young woman."

His wife, nearly delirious with her conquest and desirous of his full ejaculation into her mouth, caressed his large balls with one hand while she anchored his cock with the other, pausing only to secure the negotiation. "To be sure it is, and indeed, it strikes me that they can want no addition at all. They will have ten thousand pounds divided amongst them. If they marry, they will be sure of doing well, and if they do not, they may all live very comfortably together on the interest of ten thousand pounds."

"That is very true, and therefore I do not know whether, upon the whole, it would not be more advisable to do something for their mother while she lives, rather than for them — something of the annuity kind I mean." He stilled, waiting for her opinion of this newest idea — and hoping that his wife had not yet finished her attentions to his very healthy cock. "My sisters would feel the good effects of it as well as herself. A hundred a year would make them all perfectly comfortable."

His wife hesitated a little, however, in giving her consent to this plan.

"To be sure," said she, her fingers motionless upon his member, "it is better than parting with fifteen hundred pounds at once. But then, if Mrs Dashwood should live fifteen years we shall be completely taken in."

"Fifteen years! My dear Fanny, her life cannot be worth half that purchase."

"Certainly not, but if you observe, people always live forever when there is an annuity to be paid them. And she is very stout and healthy, and hardly forty." She tickled the underside of his sack, a manoeuvre she reserved for her most intricate negotiations with him. He gasped. She grinned. She dared say he swayed in ecstasy, and so he should, because she now had to deliver her *coup de grâce*.

"An annuity is a very serious business. It comes over and over every year and there is no getting rid of it. You are not aware of what you are doing."

At her harshness, her husband froze.

"I have known a great deal of the trouble of annuities, for my mother was clogged with the payment of three to old superannuated servants by my father's will, and it is amazing how disagreeable she found it. Twice every year these annuities were to be paid, then there was the trouble of getting it to them, then one of them was said to have died, and afterwards it turned out to be no such thing. My mother was quite sick of it. Her income was not her own, she said, with such perpetual claims on it. And it was the more unkind in my father because otherwise the money would have been entirely at my mother's disposal, without any restriction whatever. It has given me such an abhorrence of annuities that I am sure I would not pin myself down to the payment of one for all the world." She laid her cheek against the curve of his groin, tempting him to counter her and deny her her fond wish in this matter.

"It is certainly an unpleasant thing," replied Mr Dashwood with temperate tone, as he ran his fingers through her curls, "to have those kind of yearly drains on one's income. One's fortune, as your mother justly says, is not one's own. To be tied down to the regular payment of such a sum on every rent day is by no means desirable — it takes away one's independence."

She kissed the tip of his cock, oozing beautifully with the pearly drops that told her he would do all to please her. "Undoubtedly, and after all you have no thanks for it. They think themselves secure, you do no more than what is expected, and it raises no gratitude at all. If I were you, whatever I did should be done at my own discretion entirely. I would not bind myself to allow them anything yearly. It may be very inconvenient some years to spare a hundred, or even fifty pounds from our own expenses."

He shivered as she rewarded his words with a hearty suck on his thick, blue-veined helmet. "I believe you are right, my love. It will be better that there should be no annuity in the case. Whatever I may give them occasionally will be of far greater assistance than a yearly allowance, because they would only enlarge their style of living if they felt sure of a larger income, and would not be sixpence the richer for it at the end of the year. It will certainly be much the best way. A present of fifty pounds now and then will prevent their ever being distressed for money, and will, I think, be amply discharging my promise to my father."

Ah, indeed. She pulled at his trousers, the better to get
her fingers to his asshole and insert one knuckle of her
thumb. "To be sure it will. Indeed, to say the truth, I
am convinced within myself that your father had no
idea of your giving them any money at all. The
assistance he thought of, I dare say, was only such as
might be reasonably expected of you. For instance,
such as looking out for a comfortable small house for
them, helping them to move their things, and sending
them presents of fish and game and so forth whenever
they are in season. I'll lay my life that he meant
nothing farther. Indeed, it would be very strange and
unreasonable if he did."

"Oh, my dear woman," he whispered in throaty
recompense for her service to his balls, his cock and
ass.

She reeled, eager to have him spurt his essence into
her mouth, then at the last to be offered the finer
morsel of his hole to lick. This finale was always her
reward to him for his agreement to her plans for them.
To spur him onward, she gave him another hardy
suck of his cock. "Do but consider, my dear Mr
Dashwood, how excessively comfortable your mother-
in-law and her daughters may live on the interest of
seven thousand pounds—besides the thousand
pounds belonging to each of the girls, which brings
them in fifty pounds a year apiece—and of course they
will pay their mother for their board out of it.

"Altogether they will have five hundred a year
amongst them, and what on earth can four women
want for more than that? They will live so cheap!
Their housekeeping will be nothing at all. They will
have no carriage, no horses and hardly any servants.
They will keep no company and can have no expenses
of any kind! Only conceive how comfortable they will

be! Five hundred a year! I am sure I cannot imagine how they will spend half of it, and as to your giving them more, it is quite absurd to think of it. They will be much more able to give you something, as they should for your thoughtfulness in their regard."

"Upon my word," said Mr Dashwood, pleased and proud of his wife's beautiful turn of phrase in praise of him, "I believe you are perfectly right. My father certainly could mean nothing more by his request to me than what you say. I clearly understand it now, and I will strictly fulfil my engagement by such acts of assistance and kindness to them as you have described. When my mother removes into another house, my services shall be readily given to accommodate her as far as I can. Some little present of furniture too may be acceptable then."

"Certainly," returned Mrs John Dashwood. "But, however, one thing must be considered. When your father and mother moved to Norland, though the furniture of Stanhill was sold, all the china, plate and linen was saved and is now left to your mother. Her house will therefore be almost completely fitted up as soon as she takes it."

"That is a material consideration undoubtedly. A valuable legacy indeed! And yet some of the plate would have been a very pleasant addition to our own stock here."

"Yes, and the set of breakfast china is twice as handsome as what belongs to this house. A great deal too handsome, in my opinion, for any place they can ever afford to live in. But, however, so it is. Your father thought only of them. And I must say this — that you owe no particular gratitude to him, nor attention to his wishes. For we very well know that if he could, he would have left almost everything in the world to them."

This argument was irresistible, as was his generous wife, who now tugged him to the floor once more, rolled him over and spread his cheeks so that she might offer him the just reward of his earnest deliberations. She tenderly lapped at his arse and had him sighing like a schoolboy, gleefully allowing the sensuous pleasure of her rasping organ upon his dark hole to wash through him. As he rolled over once more to present her with his still-rigid cock, she ooed and ahhed as ever she did when given the chance to admire his manly accoutrements. This organ, he knew, she would now relish with her tongue and teeth and jaws so that when he gave up his precious fluids to her care, he would shout with joy.

Truly, in so many fine ways, this morning's discussion had been useful. It had given to his intentions whatever of decision was wanting before, and he finally resolved that it would be absolutely unnecessary, if not highly indecorous, to do more for the widow and children of his father than such kind of neighbourly acts as his own wife pointed out.

Chapter Three

Mrs Dashwood remained at Norland several months, not from any disinclination to move, when the sight of every well-known spot ceased to raise the violent emotion which it produced for a while. When her spirits began to revive, and her mind became capable of some other exertion than that of heightening its affliction by melancholy remembrances, she was impatient to be gone and indefatigable in her enquiries for a suitable dwelling in the neighbourhood of Norland. To remove far from that beloved spot was impossible. But she could hear of no situation that at once answered her notions of comfort and ease and suited the prudence of her eldest daughter, whose steadier judgement rejected several houses as too large for their income which her mother would have approved.

Mrs Dashwood had been informed by her husband of the solemn promise on the part of his son in their favour, which gave comfort to his last earthly reflections. She doubted the sincerity of this assurance no more than he had doubted it himself, and she thought of it for her daughters' sake with satisfaction, though as for herself she was persuaded that a much smaller provision than seven thousand pounds would support her in affluence. For their brother's sake too — for the sake of his own heart — she rejoiced, and she reproached herself for being unjust to his merit before in believing him incapable of generosity. His attentive behaviour to herself and his sisters convinced her that their welfare was dear to him, and for a long time she firmly relied on the liberality of his intentions.

The contempt which she had very early in their acquaintance felt for her daughter-in-law was very much increased by the further knowledge of her manipulative character, which half a year's residence in her family afforded intimately. The means by which the woman manoeuvred her husband into new and startling opinions on every matter, from the abundance and use of candles to the number of servants and the type of linens they used when dining *en famille,* astonished Mrs Dashwood. On many occasions she heard the cries and sighs of the married couple — and she could all too readily envision the scenes which engendered them. Mrs Dashwood had never used such wiles on her own husband — or, well, not as often — certainly not as often as her daughter-in-law employed them on her own spouse.

She did not begrudge the woman the tools to make her life more...amenable. But it was embarrassing finding the couple *in flagrante delicto.* Such discoveries added to Mrs Dashwood's distress, and perhaps in spite of every consideration of politeness or maternal affection on the side of the former, the two ladies might have found it impossible to have lived together so long had not a particular circumstance occurred to give still greater eligibility, according to the opinions of Mrs Dashwood, to her daughters' continuance at Norland.

This circumstance was a growing attachment between her eldest girl and the brother of Mrs John Dashwood, a gentlemanlike and pleasing young man who was introduced to their acquaintance soon after his sister's establishment at Norland and who had since spent the greatest part of his time there.

Edward Ferrars had arrived at Norland for a visit not two weeks after their wedding. How he had come so quickly or why had always bemused Mrs Dashwood and she had often asked her eldest daughter, Elinor, if she had any idea why that was so. Elinor was too polite to ask and so they continued to speculate the cause.

But all else about Edward seemed an open book to Elinor. In fact, Mrs Dashwood found them so much in each other's company that others in the household no longer asked where either Elinor or Edward were. They could be found in the library or the garden, reading, talking, laughing quietly. As weeks passed and the young couple spent morning until night together, often to the exclusion of others, Mrs Dashwood noticed a change however slight in their demeanour. They would close the library doors instead of leaving them open. They would drift toward the deepest corners of the garden maze. Or they would take tea early and alone together, the front parlour doors left only slightly ajar, their last propriety against ridicule.

On three occasions Mrs Dashwood had burst in upon them, not intending to surprise them, only to discover Edward's mouth upon Elinor's or his hand upon her breast. Then one stormy day she had found them pressed together, Elinor beneath Edward on the map table in the library, her skirts rucked up, his flies open and his cock hidden firmly between her virginal folds.

Though Mrs Dashwood had concealed her shock and had not mentioned any dismay at her discovery, the couple had broken apart with cries of surprise. As Edward had stood, hastening to conceal his manly attributes, Mrs Dashwood had had the joyous delight of gazing upon his long blunt cock. One hand rising to her throat, Mrs Dashwood had fought down her impulse to praise his length and girth and commend him to her daughter then and there. Instead, she had made polite banter, covering her own physical reaction to his prowess and reminding herself that she should be concerned with the state of her daughter's virginity. She wished to discuss the matter with Elinor, knowing it would be her duty to enquire. She girded herself to charge courageously into the subject, yet found herself tilting at the windmill of her own reluctance to discuss her daughter's intimate relations.

Some mothers might have encouraged the intimacy from motives of interest, for Edward Ferrars was the eldest son of a man who had died very rich. Some might have repressed it from motives of prudence, for except a trifling sum, the whole of his fortune depended on the will of his mother. But Mrs Dashwood was alike uninfluenced by either consideration. It was enough for her that he appeared to be amiable, that he had a physical passion for her daughter evidenced by his physical ardour, and above all, that he loved her daughter. That Elinor, by her openness to his company and his intimate advances, returned the partiality further allowed Mrs Dashwood to accept their relationship. It was contrary to every doctrine of hers that difference of fortune should keep any couple asunder who were attracted by resemblance of disposition, and that Elinor's merit should not be acknowledged by everyone who knew her was to her comprehension impossible.

Edward Ferrars was not recommended to their good opinion by any peculiar graces of person or address. He was not handsome by some people's standards. Yet, if one considered that his face was long, his body lean, his shoulders broad, he could appeal to many young women. Add to that the marvellous asset that his thighs showed to advantage in tailored breeches, as did the wealth of his cock and balls. His voice was mellow, a baritone that brushed the senses. His laugh was polite, yet when he laughed with Elinor, his tone was deep and hearty. Quiet, almost retiring as he was, he seemed too refined to compare to the rogues of the day, and yet his manners required intimacy to make them pleasing. He was too diffident to do justice to himself, but when his natural shyness was overcome, his behaviour gave every indication of an open, affectionate heart.

Indeed, he took up a noble habit of surprising Elinor each day with a gift. A sprig of rosemary from a bush in the garden or a poem he had penned the night before endeared him to Elinor, and all noted how congenial they were together. His understanding was good, and his education had given it solid improvement. But he was neither fitted by abilities nor disposition to answer the wishes of his mother and sister, who longed to see him distinguished as — they hardly knew what.

He spoke of this to Elinor at length, and to Mrs Dashwood only haltingly. His mother and sister haggled with him about his future prospects. They wanted him to make a fine figure in the world in some manner or other. His mother wished to interest him in political concerns, to get him into parliament, or to see him connected with some of the great men of the day. Mrs John Dashwood wished it likewise, but in the meanwhile, till one of these superior blessings could be attained, it would have quieted her ambition to see him driving a barouche. But Edward had no turn for great men or barouches. He did not look the part of rogue nor act it. Nor could he pretend such a ruse. All his wishes centred in domestic comfort and the quiet of private life. Fortunately he had a younger brother who was more promising.

Edward had been staying several weeks in the house before he engaged much of Mrs Dashwood's attention, for she was at that time in such affliction as rendered her careless of surrounding objects. Until that period when she discovered him in the library with Elinor upon the map table, Mrs Dashwood had taken his interest in Elinor as the ordinary meeting of like minds and temperaments, foretelling of no particular engagement. She saw only that he was quiet and unobtrusive, and she liked him for it. He did not disturb the wretchedness of her mind by ill-timed conversation. She was first called to observe and approve him farther only after the library incident, by a reflection which Elinor chanced one day to make on the difference between him and his sister. It was a contrast which recommended him most forcibly to her mother.

"It is enough," said she, "to say that he is unlike Fanny is enough. It implies everything amiable. I love him already."

"I think you will like him," said Elinor, "when you know more of him."

"Like him!" replied her mother with a smile. "I feel no sentiment of approbation inferior to love."

"You may esteem him."

Wishing to learn more of her daughter's implication, she stated, "I have never yet known what it was to separate esteem and love."

Realising that Elinor regarded him more highly than any other man, Mrs Dashwood now took pains to get acquainted with him. Her manners were attaching, and soon banished his reserve. She speedily comprehended all his merits. The persuasion of his regard for Elinor perhaps assisted her penetration, but she really felt assured of his worth — and even that quietness of manner, which militated against all her established ideas of what a young man's address ought to be, was no longer uninteresting when she knew his heart to be warm and his temper affectionate.

No sooner did she perceive any symptom of love in his behaviour to Elinor than she considered their serious attachment as certain and looked forward to their marriage as rapidly approaching.

"In a few months, my dear Marianne," said she, not revealing all that she knew of the intimate attachments of Elinor and Edward to her innocent younger daughter, "Elinor will in all probability be settled for life. We shall miss her, but she will be happy."

"Oh! Mama, how shall we do without her?"

"My love, it will be scarcely a separation. We shall live within a few miles of each other and shall meet every day of our lives. You will gain a brother, a real, affectionate brother. I have the highest opinion in the world of Edward's heart. But you look grave, Marianne. Do you disapprove your sister's choice?"

"Perhaps," said Marianne, "I may consider it with some surprise. Edward is very amiable, and I love him tenderly. But yet he is not the kind of young man—there is something wanting—his figure is not striking, it has none of that grace which I should expect in the man who could seriously attach my sister. His eyes want all that spirit, that fire, which at once announce virtue and intelligence."

"Oh, Marianne, my dearest, I assure you that—" Mrs Dashwood paused, aghast at her own intemperate words. She surely could not, indeed must not, reveal what she knew of Elinor and Edward's pleasures taken in the library. In fact, how many other places and how many other times had they cast their scruples to the wind and enjoyed themselves?

"Assure me of what, Mama?"

"He has a fire in him, dearest. Men do."

"How could you know? I do not see it. And I see people as they are, Mama. You know I do. Say you do."

At this, Mrs Dashwood could only demur. Then too she did not wish to nay-say her charming daughter.

"There. I am pleased you agree with me about him. And besides all this, I am afraid, Mama, he has no real taste. Music seems scarcely to attract him, and though he admires Elinor's drawings very much, it is not the admiration of a person who can understand their worth. It is evident, in spite of his frequent attention to her while she draws, that in fact he knows nothing of the matter. He admires as a lover, not as a connoisseur. To satisfy me, those characters must be united. I could not be happy with a man whose taste did not in every point coincide with my own. He must enter into all my feelings. The same books, the same music must charm us both. Oh, mama, how spiritless, how tame was Edward's manner in reading to us last night!"

Mrs Dashwood bristled at that reference, for she had watched him as he read and discovered that he had had a raging erection. Mrs Dashwood could only conjecture that before he and Elinor had entered the drawing room, they had engaged in some pleasurable caresses.

Marianne rattled on about his reading while Mrs Dashwood became outrageously and inordinately excited at the idea of physical intimacy. Truly, she was a woman of a certain age and had not enjoyed a man's fucking in a long time. Once she had been a lusty woman with her husband, welcoming his advances, taking his balls into her mouth, his long hard cock into her hand and yes, oh yes, into her cunt. Shifting on the chair as she listened to her daughter drone on about Edward, Mrs Dashwood felt her *chat* flood with hot wet cream, a joyous declaration that she was not herself dead to the wonders of sexual conversation! Her nipples—God, she yearned to leave her daughter and go upstairs to pluck and twist them, to part her female flesh and please herself until she sighed in an abandoned orgasm.

"Are you listening to me, Mama?"

"Yes. Yes, dear," she managed, promising herself a sumptuous treat tonight in her bed. She would pleasure herself exactly the way Mr Dashwood had so enjoyed watching her do it—naked, her thighs splayed open, her heavy breasts cupped in her own hands. Then slowly, slowly, she would let her fingers descend to play within her swollen folds, then circle and pinch her wondrous clitoris. Oh, tonight, she would begin again the habit that she had once employed to entertain her husband in his illness and herself since she had been a chit of sixteen. "I am listening to you. Go on, Marianne."

"I felt for my sister most severely. Yet she bore it with so much composure she seemed scarcely to notice it. I could hardly keep my seat. To hear those beautiful lines which have frequently almost driven me wild, pronounced with such impenetrable calmness, such dreadful indifference!"

"He would certainly have done more justice to simple and elegant prose. I thought so at the time, but you *would* give him Cowper."

"Nay, Mama, if he is not to be animated by Cowper—but we must allow for difference of taste. Elinor has not my feelings, and therefore she may overlook it and be happy with him. But it would have broken my heart, had I loved him, to hear him read with so little sensibility. Mama, the more I know of the world, the more am I convinced that I shall never see a man whom I can really love. I require so much! He must have all Edward's virtues, and his person and manners must ornament his goodness with every possible charm."

Mrs Dashwood smiled at the carefree notions of youth. "Remember, my love, that you are not nineteen. It is yet too early in life to despair of such a happiness." *Yours will come. And like me, you will discover with time and practice the joys of self-gratification to enhance and intrigue your chosen lover. Then may you bring to your life a full happiness.* "Why should you be less fortunate than your mother? In one circumstance only, my Marianne, may your destiny be different from hers!"

Chapter Four

"What a pity it is, Elinor," said Marianne the next day, "that Edward should have no taste for drawing."

"No taste for drawing!" replied Elinor. "Why should you think so? He does not draw himself, indeed, but he has great pleasure in seeing the performances of other people, and I assure you he is by no means deficient in natural taste, though he has not had opportunities of improving it. Had he ever been in the way of learning, I think he would have drawn very well. He distrusts his own judgement in such matters so much that he is always unwilling to give his opinion on any picture, but he has an innate propriety and simplicity of taste which in general direct him perfectly right."

Marianne was afraid of offending and said no more on the subject, but the kind of approbation which Elinor described as excited in him by the drawings of other people was very far from that rapturous delight which, in her opinion, could alone be called taste. Yet, though smiling within herself at the mistake, she honoured her sister for that blind partiality to Edward which produced it and wondered at what action of Edward toward Elinor had engendered it. *Could he be effusive in private?* Marianne dared to hope for her sister's sake that this was true.

"I hope, Marianne," continued Elinor, "you do not consider him as deficient in general taste. Indeed, I think I may say that you cannot, for your behaviour to him is perfectly cordial, and if that were your opinion, I am sure you could never be civil to him."

Marianne hardly knew what to say. She would not wound the feelings of her sister on any account, and yet to say what she did not believe was impossible. At length she replied, "Do not be offended, Elinor, if my praise of him is not in everything equal to your sense of his merits. I have not had so many opportunities of estimating the minuter propensities of his mind, his inclinations and tastes as you have, but I have the highest opinion in the world of his goodness and sense. I think him everything that is worthy and amiable." *Dare I think him ardent, as well?*

"I am sure," replied Elinor with a smile, "that his dearest friends could not be dissatisfied with such commendation as that. I do not perceive how you could express yourself more warmly."

Marianne was rejoiced to find her sister so easily pleased.

"Of his sense and his goodness," continued Elinor, "no one can, I think, be in doubt who has seen him often enough to engage him in unreserved conversation. The excellence of his understanding and his principles can be concealed only by that shyness which too often keeps him silent. You know enough of him to do justice to his solid worth. But of his minuter propensities, as you call them, you have from peculiar circumstances been kept more ignorant than myself. He and I have been at times thrown a good deal together, while you have been wholly engrossed on the most affectionate principle by my mother."

Marianne nodded, for Elinor's statement was true, but the very reminder that Edward and Elinor had been alone together often brought new fantasies to her mind. She leant forward, her examination of Elinor's blush proof that she and Edward had done more than simply converse.

Flustered, Elinor rushed onward to answer more fully. "I have seen a great deal of him, have studied his sentiments and heard his opinion on subjects of literature and taste, and, upon the whole I venture to pronounce that his mind is well-informed, enjoyment of books exceedingly great, his imagination lively, his observation just and correct and his taste delicate and pure. His abilities in every respect improve as much upon acquaintance as his manners and person. At first sight his address is certainly not striking, and his person can hardly be called handsome till the expression of his eyes, which are uncommonly good, and the general sweetness of his countenance is perceived. At present, I know him so well that I think him really handsome, or at least almost so. His...his features are even and pleasing. He is comfortably taller than I and...and his shoulders very broad. His hands are well formed and his skin warm. I do like him. What say you, Marianne?"

Overjoyed that her calm, sensible sister could offer such praises to the man she favoured, Marianne smiled. "I shall very soon think him handsome, Elinor, if I do not now. When you tell me to love him as a brother, I shall no more see imperfection in his face than I now do in his heart."

Elinor started at this declaration, and was sorry for the warmth she had been betrayed into in speaking of him. Had she given too much away by her eagerness to respond to Marianne? Had she praised his physical attributes too highly? She did admire his face and form, his shoulders that seemed like a haven to her, his hands that were eloquent as they touched her throat and plucked her nipples. Oh, to think of what he had done to her! How he had made her senses soar with just a caress of his fingertip to her inner thigh and her nether folds. He was a master of silent ardour and she swooned to be near him, have more of his careful adoration.

Yes. She felt that Edward stood very high in her opinion. She believed the regard to be mutual, but she required greater certainty of it to make Marianne's conviction of their attachment agreeable to her. She knew that what Marianne and her mother conjectured one moment, they believed the next—that with them to wish was to hope and to hope was to expect. She herself was more prudent, more circumspect, knowing full well that in a society built on status and financial agreements, a melding of minds between a man and woman was a private joy to be savoured and not necessarily a foundation for an engagement. She tried to explain the real state of the case to her sister.

"I do not attempt to deny," said she, "that I think very highly of him—that I greatly esteem, that I like him."

Marianne here burst forth with indignation. "Esteem him! Like him! Cold-hearted Elinor! Oh, worse than cold-hearted! Ashamed of being otherwise. Use those words again, and I will leave the room this moment."

Elinor could not help laughing. "Excuse me," said she, "and be assured that I meant no offence to you by speaking in so quiet a way of my own feelings. Believe them to be stronger than I have declared. Believe them, in short, to be such as his merit, and the suspicion—the hope of his affection for me may warrant without imprudence or folly. But farther than this you must not believe. I am by no means assured of his regard for me. There are moments when the extent of it seems doubtful, and till his sentiments are fully known, you cannot wonder at my wishing to avoid any encouragement of my own partiality by believing or calling it more than it is.

"In my heart I feel little—scarcely any doubt of his preference. But there are other points to be considered besides his inclination. He is very far from being independent. What his mother really is we cannot know, but from Fanny's occasional mention of her conduct and opinions, we have never been disposed to think her amiable. And I am very much mistaken if Edward is not himself aware that there would be many difficulties in his way, if he were to wish to marry a woman who had not either a great fortune or high rank."

Marianne was astonished to find how much the imagination of her mother and herself had outstripped the truth. She had seen the passion in Elinor's gaze as she considered Edward when his attentions were elsewhere. How could her sister live—nay, *breathe*—and not have any resolution from Edward of their future bliss?

"And you really are not engaged to him!" said she. "Yet it certainly soon will happen. But two advantages will proceed from this delay. I shall not lose you so soon, and Edward will have greater opportunity of improving that natural taste for your favourite pursuit which must be so indispensably necessary to your future felicity. Oh, if he should be so far stimulated by your genius as to learn to draw himself, how delightful it would be!"

Elinor had given her real opinion to her sister. She could not consider her partiality for Edward in so prosperous a state as Marianne had believed it. There was, at times when they were in the company of others, a want of spirits about him which, if it did not denote indifference, spoke of something almost as unpromising. A doubt of her regard, supposing him to feel it, need not give him more than inquietude. It would not be likely to produce that dejection of mind which frequently attended him.

A more reasonable cause might be found in the dependent situation which forbade the indulgence of his affection. She knew that his mother neither behaved to him so as to make his home comfortable at present, nor to give him any assurance that he might form a home for himself without strictly attending to her views for his aggrandisement.

With such a knowledge as this, it was impossible for Elinor to feel easy on the subject, no matter his rapturous attentions to her person when they were alone and caught up in the fascination of each other. She was far from depending on that result of his preference of her which her mother and sister still considered as certain. Nay, the longer they were together the more doubtful seemed the nature of his regard, and sometimes for a few painful minutes when she discounted his ardent demeanour towards her, she believed it to be no more than friendship.

But whatever might really be its limits, it was enough, when perceived by his sister, to make her uneasy, and at the same time — which was still more common — to make her uncivil. She took the first opportunity of affronting her mother-in-law on the occasion, talking to her so expressively of her brother's great expectations, of Mrs Ferrars' resolution that both her sons should marry well and of the danger attending any young woman who attempted to "draw him in" that Mrs Dashwood could neither pretend to be unconscious nor endeavour to be calm. She gave her an answer which marked her contempt and instantly left the room, resolving that whatever might be the inconvenience or expense of so sudden a removal, her beloved Elinor should not be exposed another week to such insinuations.

In this state of her spirits, a letter was delivered to her from the post which contained a proposal particularly well timed. It was the offer of a small house on very easy terms belonging to a relation of her own, a gentleman of consequence and property in Devonshire.

The letter was from this gentleman himself, and written in the true spirit of friendly accommodation. He understood that she was in need of a dwelling, and though the house he now offered her was merely a cottage, he assured her that everything should be done to it which she might think necessary, if the situation pleased her. He earnestly pressed her, after giving the particulars of the house and garden, to come with her daughters to Barton Park, the place of his own residence, from whence she might judge herself whether Barton Cottage—for the houses were in the same parish—could by any alteration be made comfortable to her. He seemed really anxious to accommodate them and the whole of his letter was written in so friendly a style as could not fail of giving pleasure to his cousin, more especially at a moment when she was suffering under the cold and unfeeling behaviour of her nearer connections.

She needed no time for deliberation or enquiry. Her resolution was formed as she read. The situation of Barton, in a county so far distant from Sussex as Devonshire—which but a few hours before would have been a sufficient objection to outweigh every possible advantage belonging to the place—was now its first recommendation. To quit the neighbourhood of Norland was no longer an evil, it was an object of desire, it was a blessing in comparison of the misery of continuing her daughter-in-law's guest, and to remove forever from that beloved place would be less painful than to inhabit or visit it while such a woman was its mistress. She instantly wrote Sir John Middleton her acknowledgement of his kindness and her acceptance of his proposal, then hastened to show both letters to her daughters, that she might be secure of their approbation before her answer were sent.

Elinor had always thought it would be more prudent for them to settle at some distance from Norland than immediately amongst their present acquaintance. On that head, therefore, it was not for her to oppose her mother's intention of removing into Devonshire. The house too, as described by Sir John, was on so simple a scale and the rent so uncommonly moderate as to leave her no right of objection on either point. And therefore, though it was not a plan which brought any charm to her fancy, though it was a removal from the vicinity of Norland beyond her wishes, though she knew she chanced a complete break with Edward, she made no attempt to dissuade her mother from sending a letter of acquiescence.

Chapter Five

No sooner was her answer dispatched than Mrs Dashwood called Elinor to accompany her to the drawing room and indulged herself in the pleasure of announcing to her son-in-law and his wife that she was provided with a house and should incommode them no longer than till everything were ready for her inhabiting it. They heard her with surprise. Mrs John Dashwood said nothing, but her husband civilly hoped that she would not be settled far from Norland. She had great satisfaction in replying that she was going into Devonshire.

Edward turned hastily towards her and Elinor on hearing this and, in a voice of surprise and concern which required no explanation to her, repeated, "Devonshire! Are you indeed going there? So far from hence! And to what part of it?"

She explained the situation. It was within four miles northward of Exeter.

Elinor blanched, fearful to lose Edward now that the departure seemed not only certain but imminent. She stared at Edward, mourning drawing down her features.

Mrs Dashwood marvelled at her daughter's composure.

"It is but a cottage," she continued, "but I hope to see many of my friends in it. A room or two can easily be added, and if my friends find no difficulty in travelling so far to see me, I am sure I will find none in accommodating them."

She concluded with a very kind invitation to Mr and Mrs John Dashwood to visit her at Barton, and to Edward she gave one with still greater affection. He thanked her for it and as he gazed upon Elinor, he promised in eloquent terms so uncharacteristic of him to visit them very soon. Appearing as down-hearted as Elinor, he attempted to say more. Yet, with glances at his sister, he dared not continue. Mrs Dashwood silently praised his discretion, even if she would have preferred he declare himself then and there as to his relationship to Elinor.

Though her late conversation with her daughter-in-law had made her resolve on remaining at Norland no longer than was unavoidable, it had not produced the smallest effect on her in that point to which it principally tended. To separate Edward and Elinor was as far from being her object as ever, and she wished to show Mrs John Dashwood, by this pointed invitation to her brother, how totally she disregarded her disapprobation of the match.

Mr John Dashwood told his mother again and again how exceedingly sorry he was that she had taken a house at such a distance from Norland as to prevent his being of any service to her in removing her furniture. He really felt conscientiously vexed on the occasion, for the very exertion to which he had limited the performance of his promise to his father was by this arrangement rendered impracticable.

The furniture was all sent around by water. It chiefly consisted of household linen, plate, china and books, with a handsome pianoforte of Marianne's. Mrs John Dashwood saw the packages depart with a sigh—she could not help feeling it hard that as Mrs Dashwood's income would be so trifling in comparison with their own, she should have any handsome article of furniture.

Mrs Dashwood took the house for a twelvemonth. It was ready furnished and she might have immediate possession. No difficulty arose on either side in the agreement, and she waited only for the disposal of her effects at Norland and to determine her future household before she set off for the west. And this, as she was exceedingly rapid in the performance of everything that interested her, was soon done. The horses which were left her by her husband had been sold soon after his death, and an opportunity now offering of disposing of her carriage, she agreed to sell that likewise at the earnest advice of her eldest daughter. For the comfort of her children, had she consulted only her own wishes, she would have kept it, but the discretion of Elinor prevailed. Her wisdom too limited the number of their servants to three—two maids and a man—with whom they were speedily provided from amongst those who had formed their establishment at Norland.

The man and one of the maids were sent off immediately into Devonshire to prepare the house for their mistress's arrival, for as Lady Middleton was entirely unknown to Mrs Dashwood, she preferred going directly to the cottage to being a visitor at Barton Park. She relied so undoubtingly on Sir John's description of the house as to feel no curiosity to examine it herself till she entered it as her own.

Her eagerness to be gone from Norland was preserved from diminution by the evident satisfaction of her daughter-in-law in the prospect of her removal, a satisfaction which was but feebly attempted to be concealed under a cold invitation to her to defer her departure. Now was the time when her son-in-law's promise to his father might with particular propriety be fulfilled. Since he had neglected to do it on first coming to the estate, their quitting his house might be looked on as the most suitable period for its accomplishment. But Mrs Dashwood began shortly to give over every hope of the kind, and to be convinced from the general drift of his discourse that his assistance extended no farther than their maintenance for six months at Norland. He so frequently talked of the increasing expenses of housekeeping, and of the perpetual demands upon his purse which a man of any consequence in the world was beyond calculation exposed to, that he seemed rather to stand in need of more money himself than to have any design of giving money away.

In a very few weeks from the day which brought Sir John Middleton's first letter to Norland, everything was so far settled in their future abode as to enable Mrs Dashwood and her daughters to begin their journey.

Many were the tears shed by them in their last adieus to a place so much beloved. "Dear, dear Norland!" said Marianne, as she wandered alone before the house on the last evening of their being there. "When shall I cease to regret you! When learn to feel a home elsewhere! Oh, happy house, could you know what I suffer in now viewing you from this spot, from whence perhaps I may view you no more! And you, ye well-known trees! But you will continue the same. No leaf will decay because we are removed, nor any branch become motionless although we can observe you no longer! No, you will continue the same, unconscious of the pleasure or the regret you occasion and insensible of any change in those who walk under your shade! But who will remain to enjoy you?"

The following morning Elinor stood at the drawing-room window watching as the wagons pulled up to the front door and the servants secured the last bag to the boot. Kneading her hands together, she prayed Marianne would finish her farewell to Edward as quickly as Mama had done minutes ago.

"I do repeat our mother's invitation to you, Edward, to visit us soon," Marianne offered.

"I will," he promised with urgency in his tone. "Goodbye."

Behind her Elinor heard Marianne step towards the door. "I will leave it ajar, shall I, Elinor, so that you may hear us as Mama and I take our final leave?"

"Please. Thank you," Elinor said and watched her sister leave them.

"Elinor," Edward whispered, as he cupped her shoulders and drew her backwards against his virile body.

Elinor swooned, welcoming the heat and ardour of his passion. His cock—that high, hard rod—branded her buttocks with declaration of his affection. She rubbed her arse against him, a sigh escaping her.

Murmuring his own crude delight, Edward settled her securely in her stance then—*dear God*—he left her!

Undone, nigh unto screaming at the loss of his body, Elinor thrust her hand to her mouth and bit violently on her knuckle as he made for the door.

Suddenly, he spun, caught Elinor by her shoulders, and embraced her again. "I cannot leave you like this. How will I do without you?" He whirled her about and led her to the far corner where Elinor was certain no one in the hall might see them.

He backed her to the wall, his firm torso against hers, one leg intruding between hers as he curled an arm around her waist and dipped one hand into the bodice of her day gown. Her eyelids fell closed in the ecstasy of his touch. He was warm and gentle, all perfect attributes of a lover as he kissed her brows, her ears, her throat and fondled the aching nub of her nipple.

"My darling friend, my dearest companion, how will I face each day without you? I awaken and welcome the sun knowing you will shine brighter than any of its rays. I come to breakfast, longing for the sweet look in your eyes, the bow in your sensuous mouth. I yearn to kiss you as I do now." He rubbed his generous lips over hers, teasing, tasting, testing her response. When she flung her arms around his wide shoulders and clung to him, he responded with a groan. "You must remember me when we are parted."

"Oh, yes. Most of all, what would you have me recall?"

"This." He took one of her hands and astonished her when he pressed her hand to his enormous erection. "For you. Only for you am I engorged, bursting, eager to die inside you."

Elinor could scarcely catch her breath, she was so enamoured of his actions and his words. Her breasts swelled and she yearned to rip off her dress and let him have every inch of her body to suckle and bite. Her quim filled with such a gush of hot liquid she ached to ride his thigh and have his rigid manhood invade her, have him take all of her and keep her for his own.

Her hunger shocked her. She was wise, prudent, sensible in all things save this. He had caressed her breasts before, plucked them and twisted them when they had been alone—he had lifted her skirts and palmed her mound, exclaiming over her frothy nether hair and her juicy cunt—but never had he been so violently ardent, and she craved him this way. Mad and bad, he was a creature that appealed and delighted. She needed more of him. "Come inside me, if you wish it. I do."

He pulled back, his dark eyes smouldering with wicked want. She grinned at him, a witch to his warlock.

"You do not know what you say."

"Let me learn it then."

"You undo me with your passion for me, Elinor, my dear." He lifted her, his fingers trailing up the smooth expanse of her thigh. "I am overjoyed to press your sweet flesh into the welcome, happy fullness of my palm. Oh, my darling friend, you are so wet. Drenched. My God, your ardour coats my fingers and I am at sea in your luscious cunt. How I wish to drown there. May I?" he asked as he inserted one finger high inside her chat and followed it with two.

She undulated on his elegant fingers, her hips prodding him to work her, work her, work her as instinct told her he should. "You may do all to me."

He rammed three fingers up inside her so artfully that she came up off her toes in delight. "I will fuck you in the only way I might."

She sobbed in joy, lost to any reason and rejoicing in her freedom. "Give me all, Edward. I need all."

He choked on his own ardour, but discovered a nub of flesh inside her chat that he fondled. The circular caresses drove her wild with wanting until she gasped, her world splintering into a thousand pieces.

"My dear friend, my all," he crooned and crushed her to him while she regained ever so slowly her ability to think. "Remember this and all we were to each other. Another time, a better place, we shall resume with more bliss than we can summon in this hasty moment."

Then, with a lingering kiss to her mouth and a pained look of remorse, he pressed her against the wall and left her yet again.

"Edward?" Marianne asked. "Is Elinor ready?"

Elinor heard him say nothing. Straightening her skirts, and pushing her tender nipple back inside her bodice, she waited until she breathed more steadily and emerged into the foyer.

Elinor allowed one fat tear to wend its way down her feverish cheek, sorrowing for the decadent rapture so cruelly ended by necessity.

Chapter Six

The first part of their journey was performed in too melancholy a disposition to be otherwise than tedious and unpleasant. But as they drew towards the end of it, their interest in the appearance of a country which they were to inhabit overcame their dejection, and a view of Barton Valley as they entered it gave them cheerfulness. It was a pleasant fertile spot, well wooded and rich in pasture. After winding along it for more than a mile, they reached their own house. A small green court was the whole of its demesne in front, and a neat wicket gate admitted them into it.

As a house, Barton Cottage, though small, was comfortable and compact. But as a cottage it was defective, for the building was regular, the roof was tiled, the window shutters were not painted green nor were the walls covered with honeysuckles. A narrow passage led directly through the house into the garden behind. On each side of the entrance was a sitting room about sixteen feet square and beyond them were the offices and the stairs. Four bedrooms and two garrets formed the rest of the house. It had not been built many years and was in good repair.

In comparison of Norland, it was poor and small indeed! But the tears which recollection called forth as they entered the house were soon dried away. They were cheered by the joy of the servants on their arrival, and each for the sake of the others resolved to appear happy. It was very early in September, the season was fine and from first seeing the place under the advantage of good weather, they received an impression in its favour which was of material service in recommending it to their lasting approbation.

The situation of the house was good. High hills rose immediately behind and at no great distance on each side, some of which were open downs, the others cultivated and woody. The village of Barton was chiefly on one of these hills and formed a pleasant view from the cottage windows. The prospect in front was more extensive — it commanded the whole of the valley and reached into the country beyond. The hills which surrounded the cottage terminated the valley in that direction. Under another name and in another course, it branched out again between two of the steepest of them.

With the size and furniture of the house Mrs Dashwood was upon the whole well satisfied. For though her former style of life rendered many additions to the latter indispensable, yet to add and improve was a delight to her, and she had at this time ready money enough to supply all that was wanted of greater elegance to the apartments.

"As for the house itself, to be sure," said she, "it is too small for our family, but we will make ourselves tolerably comfortable for the present, as it is too late in the year for improvements. Perhaps in the spring, if I have plenty of money, as I dare say I shall, we may think about building. These parlours are both too small for such parties of our friends as I hope to see often collected here. I have some thoughts of throwing the passage into one of them with perhaps a part of the other, and so leave the remainder of that other for an entrance. This, with a new drawing room which may be easily added and a bedchamber and garret above, will make it a very snug little cottage. I could wish the stairs were handsome. But one must not expect everything, though I suppose it would be no difficult matter to widen them. I shall see how much I am beforehand with the world in the spring, and we will plan our improvements accordingly."

In the meantime, till all these alterations could be made from the savings of an income of five hundred a year by a woman who never saved in her life, they were wise enough to be contented with the house as it was. Each of them was busy in arranging their particular concerns and endeavouring, by placing around them books and other possessions, to form themselves a home. Marianne's pianoforte was unpacked and properly disposed of, and Elinor's drawings were affixed to the walls of their sitting room.

In such employments as these they were interrupted soon after breakfast the next day by the entrance of their landlord, who called to welcome them to Barton and to offer them every accommodation from his own house and garden in which theirs might at present be deficient.

Sir John Middleton was a good-looking man about forty. He had formerly visited at Stanhill, but it was too long for his young cousins to remember him. His countenance was thoroughly good-humoured and his manners were as friendly as the style of his letter. Their arrival seemed to afford him real satisfaction and their comfort to be an object of real solicitude to him. He said much of his earnest desire of their living in the most sociable terms with his family, and pressed them so cordially to dine at Barton Park every day till they were better settled at home that, though his entreaties were carried to a point of perseverance beyond civility, they could not give offence.

His kindness was not confined to words, for within an hour after he left them a large basket full of garden stuff and fruit arrived from the park, which was followed before the end of the day by a present of game. He insisted moreover on conveying all their letters to and from the post for them, and would not be denied the satisfaction of sending them his newspaper every day.

Lady Middleton had sent a very civil message by him denoting her intention of waiting on Mrs Dashwood as soon as she could be assured that her visit would be no inconvenience, and as this message was answered by an invitation equally polite, her ladyship was introduced to them the next day.

They were of course very anxious to see a person on whom so much of their comfort at Barton must depend, and the elegance of her appearance was favourable to their wishes. Lady Middleton was not more than six or seven and twenty. Her face was handsome, her figure tall and striking and her address graceful. Her manners had all the elegance which her husband's wanted. But they would have been improved by some share of his frankness and warmth, and her visit was long enough to detract something from their first admiration by showing that, though perfectly well-bred, she was reserved, cold and had nothing to say for herself beyond the most commonplace enquiry or remark.

Conversation however was not wanted, for Sir John was very chatty and Lady Middleton had taken the wise precaution of bringing with her their eldest child – a fine little boy about six years old – by which means there was one subject always to be recurred to by the ladies in case of extremity. They had to enquire his name and age, admire his beauty and ask him questions, which his mother answered for him while he hung about her and held down his head, to the great surprise of her ladyship, who wondered at his being so shy before company, as he could make noise enough at home. On every formal visit a child ought to be of the party by way of provision for discourse. In the present case it took up ten minutes to determine whether the boy were most like his father or mother, and in what particular he resembled either, for of course everybody differed and everybody was astonished at the opinion of the others.

An opportunity was soon to be given to the Dashwoods of debating on the rest of the children, as Sir John would not leave the house without securing their promise of dining at the park the next day.

Chapter Seven

Barton Park was about half a mile from the cottage. The ladies had passed near it in their way along the valley, but it was screened from their view at home by the projection of a hill. The house was large and handsome and the Middletons lived in a style of equal hospitality and elegance. The former was for Sir John's gratification, the latter for that of his lady. They were scarcely ever without some friends staying with them in the house and they kept more company of every kind than any other family in the neighbourhood. It was necessary to the happiness of both, for however dissimilar in temper and outward behaviour, they strongly resembled each other in that total want of talent and taste which confined their employments, unconnected with such as society produced, within a very narrow compass.

Sir John was a sportsman, Lady Middleton a mother. He hunted and shot, and she humoured her children, and these were their only resources. Lady Middleton had the advantage of being able to spoil her children all the year round, while Sir John's independent employments were in existence only half the time. Continual engagements at home and abroad, however, supplied all the deficiencies of nature and education, supported the good spirits of Sir John and gave exercise to the good breeding of his wife.

Lady Middleton piqued herself upon the elegance of her table and of all her domestic arrangements, and from this kind of vanity was her greatest enjoyment in any of their parties. But Sir John's satisfaction in society was much more real. He delighted in collecting about him more young people than his house would hold, and the noisier they were the better was he pleased. He was a blessing to all the juvenile part of the neighbourhood, for in summer he was forever forming parties to eat cold ham and chicken out of doors, and in winter his private balls were numerous enough for any young lady who was not suffering under the insatiable appetite of fifteen.

The arrival of a new family in the country was always a matter of joy to him, and in every point of view he was charmed with the inhabitants he had now procured for his cottage at Barton. The Miss Dashwoods were young, pretty and unaffected. It was enough to secure his good opinion, for to be unaffected was all that a pretty girl could want to make her mind as captivating as her person. The friendliness of his disposition made him happy in accommodating those whose situation might be considered, in comparison with the past, as unfortunate. In showing kindness to his cousins therefore he had the real satisfaction of a good heart, and in settling a family of females only in his cottage, he had all the satisfaction of a sportsman. For a sportsman, though he esteems only those of his sex who are sportsmen likewise, is not often desirous of encouraging their taste by admitting them to a residence within his own manor.

Mrs Dashwood and her daughters were met at the door of the house by Sir John, who welcomed them to Barton Park with unaffected sincerity and as he attended them to the drawing room repeated to the young ladies the concern which the same subject had drawn from him the day before at being unable to get any smart young men to meet them. They would see, he said, only one gentleman there besides himself, a particular friend who was staying at the park, but who was neither very young nor very gay. He hoped they would all excuse the smallness of the party and could assure them it should never happen so again. He had been to several families that morning in hopes of procuring some addition to their number, but it was moonlight and everybody was full of engagements. Luckily Lady Middleton's mother had arrived at Barton within the last hour, and as she was a very cheerful agreeable woman, he hoped the young ladies would not find it so very dull as they might imagine. The young ladies as well as their mother were perfectly satisfied with having two entire strangers of the party, and wished for no more.

Mrs Jennings, Lady Middleton's mother, was a good-humoured, merry, fat, elderly woman who talked a great deal, seemed very happy and rather vulgar. She was full of jokes and laughter, and before dinner was over had said many witty things on the subject of lovers and husbands, hoped they had not left their hearts behind them in Sussex and pretended to see them blush whether they did or not. Marianne was vexed at it for her sister's sake and turned her eyes towards Elinor to see how she bore these attacks, with an earnestness which gave Elinor far more pain than could arise from such commonplace raillery as Mrs Jennings'.

Colonel Brandon, the friend of Sir John, seemed no more adapted by resemblance of manner to be his friend than Lady Middleton was to be his wife or Mrs Jennings to be Lady Middleton's mother. He was silent and grave. His appearance however was not unpleasing. Elinor thought him dashing but quietly inscrutable, in spite of his being in the opinion of Marianne and Margaret an absolute old bachelor, for he was on the wrong side of five and thirty. But though his face was not handsome, his countenance was sensible and his address was particularly gentlemanlike.

There was nothing in any of the party which could recommend them as companions to the Dashwoods, but the cold insipidity of Lady Middleton was so particularly repulsive that in comparison of it the gravity of Colonel Brandon and even the boisterous mirth of Sir John and his mother-in-law was interesting. Lady Middleton seemed to be roused to enjoyment only by the entrance of her four noisy children after dinner, who pulled her about, tore her clothes and put an end to every kind of discourse except what related to themselves.

In the evening, as Marianne was discovered to be musical, she was invited to play. The instrument was unlocked, everybody prepared to be charmed and Marianne, who sang very well, at their request went through the chief of the songs which Lady Middleton had brought into the family on her marriage and which perhaps had lain ever since in the same position on the pianoforte. For her ladyship had celebrated that event by giving up music, although by her mother's account, she had played extremely well and by her own was very fond of it.

Marianne's performance was highly applauded. Sir John was loud in his admiration at the end of every song, and as loud in his conversation with the others while every song lasted. Lady Middleton frequently called him to order, wondered how anyone's attention could be diverted from music for a moment, and asked Marianne to sing a particular song which Marianne had just finished.

Colonel Brandon alone of all the party heard her without being in raptures. He paid her only the compliment of attention, and she felt a respect for him on the occasion which the others had reasonably forfeited by their shameless want of taste. His pleasure in music, though it amounted not to that ecstatic delight which alone could sympathise with her own, was estimable when contrasted against the horrible insensibility of the others, and she was reasonable enough to allow that a man of five and thirty might well have outlived all acuteness of feeling and every exquisite power of enjoyment. She was perfectly disposed, she told Elinor, to make every allowance for the colonel's advanced state of life which humanity required.

Chapter Eight

Mrs Jennings was a widow with an ample jointure. She had only two daughters, both of whom she had lived to see respectably married, and she had now therefore nothing to do but to marry all the rest of the world. In the promotion of this object she was zealously active, as far as her ability reached, and missed no opportunity of projecting weddings among all the young people of her acquaintance. She was remarkably quick in the discovery of attachments and had enjoyed the advantage of raising the blushes and the vanity of many a young lady by insinuations of her power over such a young man. This kind of discernment enabled her soon after her arrival at Barton decisively to pronounce that Colonel Brandon was very much in love with Marianne Dashwood.

She rather suspected it to be so on the very first evening of their being together, from his listening so attentively while she sang to them, and when the visit was returned by the Middletons' dining at the cottage, the fact was ascertained by his listening to her again. It must be so. She was perfectly convinced of it. It would be an excellent match, for he was rich and she was handsome. Mrs Jennings had been anxious to see Colonel Brandon well married ever since her connection with Sir John first brought him to her knowledge, and she was always anxious to get a good husband for every pretty girl.

The immediate advantage to herself was by no means inconsiderable, for it supplied her with endless jokes against them both. At the park she laughed at the colonel and in the cottage at Marianne. To the former her raillery was probably, as far as it regarded only himself, perfectly indifferent. But to the latter it was at first incomprehensible, and when its object was understood she hardly knew whether most to laugh at its absurdity or censure its impertinence, for she considered it as an unfeeling reflection on the colonel's advanced years and on his forlorn condition as an old bachelor.

Mrs Dashwood, who could not think a man five years younger than herself so exceedingly ancient as he appeared to the youthful fancy of her daughter, ventured to clear Mrs Jennings from the probability of wishing to throw ridicule on his age.

"But at least, Mama, you cannot deny the absurdity of the accusation, though you may not think it intentionally ill-natured. Colonel Brandon is certainly younger than Mrs Jennings, but he is old enough to be my father, and if he were ever animated enough to be in love must have long outlived every sensation of the kind. It is too ridiculous! When is a man to be safe from such wit, if age and infirmity will not protect him?"

"Infirmity!" said Elinor. "Do you call Colonel Brandon infirm? I can easily suppose that his age may appear much greater to you than to my mother, but you can hardly deceive yourself as to his having the use of his limbs!"

"Did not you hear him complain of the rheumatism? And is not that the commonest infirmity of declining life?"

"My dearest child," said her mother, laughing, "at this rate you must be in continual terror of my decay, and it must seem to you a miracle that my life has been extended to the advanced age of forty."

"Mama, you are not doing me justice. I know very well that Colonel Brandon is not old enough to make his friends yet apprehensive of losing him in the course of nature. He may live twenty years longer. But thirty-five has nothing to do with matrimony."

"Perhaps," said Elinor, "thirty-five and eighteen had better not have anything to do with matrimony together. But if there should by any chance happen to be a woman who is single at seven and twenty, I should not think Colonel Brandon's being thirty-five any objection to his marrying her."

"A woman of seven and twenty," said Marianne after pausing a moment, "can never hope to feel or inspire affection again, and if her home be uncomfortable or her fortune small, I can suppose that she might bring herself to submit to the offices of a nurse, for the sake of the provision and security of a wife. In his marrying such a woman therefore there would be nothing unsuitable. It would be a compact of convenience, and the world would be satisfied. In my eyes it would be no marriage at all, but that would be nothing. To me it would seem only a commercial exchange, in which each wished to be benefited at the expense of the other."

"It would be impossible, I know," replied Elinor, "to convince you that a woman of seven and twenty could feel for a man of thirty-five anything near enough to love to make him a desirable companion to her. But I must object to your dooming Colonel Brandon and his wife to the constant confinement of a sick chamber merely because he chanced to complain yesterday—a very cold damp day—of a slight rheumatic feel in one of his shoulders."

"But he talked of flannel waistcoats," said Marianne, "and with me a flannel waistcoat is invariably connected with aches, cramps, rheumatisms and every species of ailment that can afflict the old and the feeble."

"Had he been only in a violent fever, you would not have despised him half so much. Confess, Marianne, is not there something interesting to you in the flushed cheek, hollow eye and quick pulse of a fever?"

Soon after this, upon Elinor's leaving the room—"Mama," said Marianne, "I have an alarm on the subject of illness which I cannot conceal from you. I am sure Edward Ferrars is not well. We have now been here almost a fortnight, and yet he does not come. Nothing but real indisposition could occasion this extraordinary delay. What else can detain him at Norland?"

"Had you any idea of his coming so soon?" said Mrs Dashwood. "I had none. On the contrary, if I have felt any anxiety at all on the subject, it has been in recollecting that he sometimes showed a want of pleasure and readiness in accepting my invitation when I talked of his coming to Barton. Does Elinor expect him already?"

"I have never mentioned it to her, but of course she must."

"I rather think you are mistaken, for when I was talking to her yesterday of getting a new grate for the spare bedchamber, she observed that there was no immediate hurry for it, as it was not likely that the room would be wanted for some time."

"How strange this is! What can be the meaning of it! But the whole of their behaviour to each other has been unaccountable! How cold, how composed were their last adieus! How languid their conversation the last evening of their being together! In Edward's farewell there was no distinction between Elinor and me — it was the good wishes of an affectionate brother to both. Twice did I leave them purposely together in the course of the last morning, and each time did he most unaccountably follow me out of the room."

"You did not tell me this, Marianne. Now I am concerned. What can be the matter between them?"

"I am as confounded as you, Mama, by both their actions that morning. Edward was more agitated than sorrowful as he strode past me. And Elinor, in quitting Norland and Edward, cried not as I did. Even now her self-command is invariable. When is she dejected or melancholy? When does she try to avoid society, or appear restless and dissatisfied in it?"

Chapter Nine

The Dashwoods were now settled at Barton with tolerable comfort to themselves. The house and the garden with all the objects surrounding them were now become familiar, and the ordinary pursuits which had given to Norland half its charms were engaged in again with far greater enjoyment than Norland had been able to afford since the loss of their father. Sir John Middleton, who called on them every day for the first fortnight and who was not in the habit of seeing much occupation at home, could not conceal his amazement on finding them always employed.

Their visitors, except those from Barton Park, were not many. In spite of Sir John's urgent entreaties that they would mix more in the neighbourhood and repeated assurances of his carriage being always at their service, the independence of Mrs Dashwood's spirit overcame the wish of society for her children, and she was resolute in declining to visit any family beyond the distance of a walk. There were but few who could be so classed, and it was not all of them that were attainable.

About a mile and a half from the cottage along the narrow winding valley of Allenham, which issued from that of Barton as formerly described, the girls had in one of their earliest walks discovered an ancient respectable-looking mansion which, by reminding them a little of Norland, interested their imagination and made them wish to be better acquainted with it. But they learnt on enquiry that its possessor, an elderly lady of very good character, was unfortunately too infirm to mix with the world and never stirred from home.

The whole country about them abounded in beautiful walks. The high downs which invited them from almost every window of the cottage to seek the exquisite enjoyment of air on their summits were a happy alternative when the dirt of the valleys beneath shut up their superior beauties. Towards one of these hills did Marianne and Margaret one memorable morning direct their steps, attracted by the partial sunshine of a showery sky and unable longer to bear the confinement which the settled rain of the two preceding days had occasioned. The weather was not tempting enough to draw the two others from their pencil and their book, in spite of Marianne's declaration that the day would be lastingly fair and that every threatening cloud would be drawn off from their hills, and the two girls set off together.

They gaily ascended the downs, rejoicing in their own penetration at every glimpse of blue sky, and when they caught in their faces the animating gales of a high south-westerly wind, they pitied the fears which had prevented their mother and Elinor from sharing such delightful sensations.

"Is there a felicity in the world," said Marianne, "superior to this? Margaret, we will walk here at least two hours."

Margaret agreed and they pursued their way against the wind, resisting it with laughing delight for about twenty minutes longer, when suddenly the clouds united over their heads and a driving rain set full in their face. Chagrined and surprised, they were obliged, though unwillingly, to turn back, for no shelter was nearer than their own house. One consolation however remained for them to which the exigence of the moment gave more than usual propriety — it was that of running with all possible speed down the steep side of the hill which led immediately to their garden gate.

They set off. Marianne had at first the advantage, but a false step brought her suddenly to the ground, and Margaret, unable to stop herself to assist her, was involuntarily hurried along and reached the bottom in safety. She cried out at the sight before her, her sister quite in disarray upon the ground and moaning.

Margaret calmed her sister then called out into the forest for help. "I will not leave you, dearest, until someone comes."

A gentleman carrying a gun with two pointers playing round him was passing up the hill and within a few yards of Marianne when her accident happened. He put down his gun and ran to her assistance. She had raised herself from the ground, but her foot had been twisted in her fall and she was scarcely able to stand. The gentleman offered his services, and perceiving that her modesty declined what her situation rendered necessary, took her up in his arms without farther delay and carried her down the hill.

"Good sir," said Marianne to her handsome champion, "you are most kind to aid me."

"It is the least I may do for you, Miss—?"

She told him her name and her situation—that she and her mother and siblings were now in residence so close by. Her haste to tell him all was in hope he might reciprocate and tell her his own situation. She discovered as they talked that he was articulate, funny and wise. In truth, he was the most dashing creature she had ever met. Taller than she by many inches, with sinewy arms, he possessed a beauty of proportioned features such that had she not already been in his arms, she would have swooned at his feet to hasten his possession of her. With a perfect mouth, manly and wide, he had a vibrancy to his countenance that struck Marianne as more than pleasing.

His appearance had indeed a remarkable unsettling effect upon her, her body tingling as it never had before, her nipples hardening and her nether regions flooding with urgent hot juices. Though she had never known such raptures other than those she had read about or dreamt about, Marianne dared to fantasise that this man was not merely her rescuer—he was a man fated to become much more. So she conversed with him, her arms around him, wishing to never let him go. They spoke of so much that as she saw the house in her sights, she wished she had feigned ignorance of their locale when first he had assisted her. She resigned herself to gain all she could from these few moments, laughing with him and luring him on down the path. Then passing through the garden, the gate of which had been left open by Margaret, he bore her directly into the house whither Margaret was just arrived, and quitted not his hold till he had seated her in a chair in the parlour.

Elinor and her mother rose up in amazement at their entrance. While the eyes of both were fixed on him with an evident wonder and a secret admiration which equally sprang from his appearance, he apologised for his intrusion by relating its cause in a manner so frank and so graceful that his person, which was uncommonly handsome, received additional charms from his voice and expression. Had he been even old, ugly and vulgar, the gratitude and kindness of Mrs Dashwood would have been secured by any act of attention to her child, but the influence of youth, beauty and elegance gave an interest to the action which came home to her feelings. She thanked him again and again, and with a sweetness of address which always attended her, invited him to be seated. But this he declined, as he was dirty and wet.

Marianne shivered, blushing and turning her eyes to her hands, wishing to feel his strong arms about her again, pressing her to his hot firm chest. Indeed, he must have wished the same, because Marianne saw the proof of it as her gaze travelled to his trousers and saw there an impressive bulge. She smiled to herself, a knowing affirmation on her lips. *You desire me in an ardent way, do you, kind sir? Your cock gives evidence of your aspirations. My desire matches yours. Try me. Come back to test me, taste me. Come to me tomorrow and tomorrow.*

Mrs Dashwood then begged to know to whom she was obliged. His name, he replied, was Willoughby, and his present home was at Allenham, from whence he hoped she would allow him the honour of calling tomorrow to enquire after Miss Dashwood. The honour was readily granted, and he then departed, to make himself still more interesting, in the midst of a heavy rain.

His manly beauty and more than common gracefulness were instantly the theme of general admiration, and the laugh which his gallantry raised against Marianne received particular spirit from his exterior attractions. Marianne herself had seen less of his person than the rest, for the confusion which crimsoned over her face on his lifting her up had robbed her of the power of regarding him after their entering the house. But she had seen enough of him to join in all the admiration of the others, and with an energy which always adorned her praise.

His person and air were equal to what her fancy had ever drawn for the hero of a favourite story, and in his carrying her into the house with so little previous formality, there was a rapidity of thought which particularly recommended the action to her. Every circumstance belonging to him was interesting. His name was good, his residence was in their favourite village, and she soon found out that of all manly dresses a shooting jacket was the most becoming. Her imagination was busy, her reflections were pleasant and the pain of a sprained ankle was disregarded.

Sir John called on them as soon as the next interval of fair weather that morning allowed him to get out of doors, and Marianne's accident being related to him, he was eagerly asked whether he knew any gentleman of the name of Willoughby at Allenham.

"Willoughby!" cried Sir John. "What, is he in the country? That is good news however. I will ride over tomorrow and ask him to dinner on Thursday."

"You know him then," said Mrs Dashwood.

"Know him! To be sure I do. Why, he is down here every year."

"And what sort of a young man is he? Not married yet, is he?"

"Not yet, no. As good a kind of fellow as ever lived, I assure you. A very decent shot, and there is not a bolder rider in England."

"And is that all you can say for him?" cried Marianne indignantly. "But what are his manners on more intimate acquaintance? What his pursuits, his talents and genius?"

Sir John was rather puzzled.

"Upon my soul," said he, "I do not know much about him as to all that. But he is a pleasant, good-humoured fellow and has got the nicest little black bitch of a pointer I ever saw. Was she out with him today?"

But Marianne could no more satisfy him as to the colour of Mr Willoughby's pointer, than he could describe to her the shades of his mind.

"But who is he?" said Elinor. "Where does he come from? Has he a house at Allenham?"

On this point Sir John could give more certain intelligence. He told them that Mr Willoughby had no property of his own in the country, that he resided there only while he was visiting the old lady at Allenham Court, to whom he was related and whose possessions he was to inherit, adding, "Yes, yes, he is very well worth catching, I can tell you, Miss Dashwood. He has a pretty little estate of his own in Somersetshire besides, and if I were you, I would not give him up to my younger sister in spite of all this tumbling down hills. Miss Marianne must not expect to have all the men to herself. Brandon will be jealous, if she does not take care."

"I do not believe," said Mrs Dashwood with a good-humoured smile, "that Mr Willoughby will be incommoded by the attempts of either of my daughters towards what you call 'catching' him. It is not an employment to which they have been brought up. Men are very safe with us, let them be ever so rich. I am glad to find, however, from what you say, that he is a respectable young man, and one whose acquaintance will not be ineligible."

"He is as good a sort of fellow, I believe, as ever lived," repeated Sir John. "I remember last Christmas at a little hop at the park, he danced from eight o'clock till four without once sitting down."

"Did he indeed?" cried Marianne with sparkling eyes, delighted at the news but wondering with whom the man had danced. "And with elegance, with spirit?"

"Yes, and he was up again at eight to ride to covert."

"That is what I like, that is what a young man ought to be. Whatever be his pursuits, his eagerness in them should know no moderation and leave him no sense of fatigue."

"Aye, aye, I see how it will be," said Sir John, "I see how it will be. You will be setting your cap at him now, and never think of poor Brandon."

The mention of Brandon quite irked Marianne who wished only to speak of Willoughby. "That is an expression, Sir John," said Marianne warmly so as not to insult Sir John too badly, "which I particularly dislike. I abhor every commonplace phrase by which wit is intended, and 'setting one's cap at a man' or 'making a conquest' are the most odious of all. Their tendency is gross and illiberal, and if their construction could ever be deemed clever, time has long ago destroyed all its ingenuity."

Sir John did not much understand this reproof, but he laughed as heartily as if he did then replied, "Ay, you will make conquests enough, I dare say, one way or other. Poor Brandon!"

Marianne pouted, her sensitivities wounded by Sir John's outburst. "Poor, upon my word. If he cares for me, it is his own doing. I did not encourage him, for I have a finer constitution than that."

"Indeed, poor Brandon! He is quite smitten already, and he is very well worth setting your cap at, I can tell you, in spite of all this tumbling about and spraining of ankles."

Chapter Ten

Marianne's preserver — as Margaret, with more elegance than precision, styled Willoughby — called at the cottage early the next morning to make his personal enquiries. He was received by Mrs Dashwood with more than politeness, with a kindness which Sir John's account of him and her own gratitude prompted, and everything that passed during the visit tended to assure him of the sense, elegance, mutual affection and domestic comfort of the family to whom accident had now introduced him. Of their personal charms he had not required a second interview to be convinced.

He smiled to himself, assured of his welcome, and by such charming creatures. Miss Elinor Dashwood had a delicate complexion, regular features and a remarkably pretty figure. Marianne was still handsomer. Her form, though not so correct as her sister's, in having the advantage of height was more striking and more curvaceous and appealing to his senses. Her face was so lovely, her cheeks so round, so well-proportioned, her forehead high and showing such intelligence that when in the common cant of praise, she was called a beautiful girl, truth was less violently outraged than usually happens. Her skin was sadly very brown, but from its transparency her unblemished complexion was uncommonly brilliant. Her features were all good. Her smile was sweet and attractive, and in her eyes, which were very dark blue, there was a life, a spirit, an eagerness which could hardly be seen without delight.

From Willoughby their expression was at first held back by the embarrassment which the remembrance of his assistance created. But when this passed away, when her spirits became collected, when she saw that to the perfect good-breeding of the gentleman he united frankness and vivacity, and above all when she heard him declare that of music and dancing he was passionately fond, she gave him such a look of approbation as secured the largest share of his discourse to herself for the rest of his stay. He declared himself enchanted.

It was only necessary to mention any favourite amusement to engage her to talk. She could not be silent when such points were introduced, and she had neither shyness nor reserve in their discussion. This he took as her natural exuberance for him, and most promising for their future relationship, which he hoped to deepen and enrich by all means at his disposal.

They speedily discovered that their enjoyment of dancing and music was mutual, and that it arose from a general conformity of judgement in all that related to either. Encouraged by this to a further examination of his opinions, she proceeded to question him on the subject of books. Her favourite authors were brought forward and dwelt upon with so rapturous a delight that any young man of five and twenty must have been insensible indeed not to become an immediate convert to the excellence of such works, however disregarded before.

Their taste was strikingly alike. The same authors and poets, the same books, the same passages of Coleridge's *Kubla Khan* and Lord Byron's *When We Two Parted* were idolised by each — or if any difference appeared, any objection arose, it lasted no longer than till the force of her arguments and the brightness of her eyes could be displayed. He acquiesced in all her decisions, caught all her enthusiasm and his own desires to encourage her unfettered displays of emotion, and long before his visit concluded they conversed with the familiarity of a long-established acquaintance.

With more pleasure than he had felt in weeks, he took his leave. As he wended down the path from the Dashwoods' home he exulted in the excitement of meeting a like mind in Marianne. How he hungered for more of her company. His body quaked with the expectation of what they might find together as they conversed. He took heart that Marianne's mother and older sister had left them together alone for a few moments. In that space, he had moved to Marianne's side, took her soft hand and stroked her elegant fingers to the tips. She had shivered in her coy response to him, and he, ever so attuned to a young lady's physical displays of attraction to him, had bent to press his lips to the fold of her delicate ear. He had nipped her, then whispered of how he wished to put his lips on her mouth, her throat, her nipples. *Yes.* He grinned. She had quivered in ripe anticipation of his forays into sensuous adventures. Marianne, he decided as he secured his hat on his head, was a marvellous new joy for him to explore. She welcomed him and he would not turn away without rewarding her for her boldness.

"Well, Marianne," said Elinor, as soon as he had left them, "for one morning I think you have done pretty well. You have already ascertained Mr Willoughby's opinion in almost every matter of importance. You know what he thinks of Cowper and Scott, you are certain of his estimating their beauties as he ought, and you have received every assurance of his admiring Pope no more than is proper. But how is your acquaintance to be long supported under such extraordinary despatch of every subject for discourse? You will soon have exhausted each favourite topic. Another meeting will suffice to explain his sentiments on picturesque beauty and second marriages, then you can have nothing farther to ask."

"Elinor," cried Marianne, "is this fair? Is this just? Are my ideas so scanty? But I see what you mean. I have been too much at my ease, too happy, too frank. I have erred against every commonplace notion of decorum. I have been open and sincere where I ought to have been reserved, spiritless, dull, and deceitful — had I talked only of the weather and the roads, and had I spoken only once in ten minutes, this reproach would have been spared."

"My love," said her mother, "you must not be offended with Elinor — she was only in jest. I should scold her myself, if she were capable of wishing to check the delight of your conversation with our new friend." Marianne was softened in a moment.

Willoughby, on his side, gave every proof of his pleasure in their acquaintance which an evident wish of improving it could offer. He came to them every day, bearing a small handful of flowers he had picked from the hillside. Meagre as they were, the posies stood as an example of his romantic nature, as if he were pure and untouched by convention or ruse. To enquire after Marianne was at first his excuse, but the encouragement of his reception, to which every day gave greater kindness, made such an excuse unnecessary before it had ceased to be possible by Marianne's perfect recovery.

She was confined for some days to the house, but never had any confinement been less irksome. Willoughby was a young man of good abilities, quick imagination, lively spirits and open, affectionate manners. He was exactly formed to engage Marianne's heart, for with all this he joined not only a captivating person but a natural ardour of mind which was now roused and increased by the example of her own, and which recommended him to her affection beyond everything else.

His society became gradually her most exquisite enjoyment. They read, they talked, they sang together. His musical talents were considerable, and he read with all the sensibility and spirit which, according to Marianne, Edward had unfortunately wanted.

In Mrs Dashwood's estimation he was as faultless as in Marianne's, and Elinor saw nothing to censure in him but a propensity, in which he strongly resembled and peculiarly delighted her sister, of saying too much what he thought on every occasion without attention to persons or circumstances. In hastily forming and giving his opinion of other people, in sacrificing general politeness to the enjoyment of undivided attention where his heart was engaged and in slighting too easily the forms of worldly propriety, he displayed a want of caution which Elinor could not approve in spite of all that he and Marianne could say in its support. His ideas about others verged on offensive to Elinor, but she held her tongue, ascribing his sharpness and lack of tact to his youth, his station and his encouragement by Marianne.

Marianne began now to perceive that the desperation which had seized her at eighteen of ever seeing a man who could satisfy her ideas of perfection had been rash and unjustifiable. Willoughby was all that her fancy had delineated in that unhappy hour and in every brighter period as capable of attaching her, and his behaviour declared his wishes to be in that respect as earnest as his abilities were strong.

Her mother too, in whose mind not one speculative thought of their marriage had been raised by his prospect of riches, was led before the end of a week to hope and expect it, and secretly to congratulate herself on having gained two such sons-in-law as Edward and Willoughby. In such conclusions Elinor cautioned them to no avail and eventually gave up the cause of trying to inject reason into their unbridled joy.

Colonel Brandon's partiality for Marianne, which had so early been discovered by his friends, now first became perceptible to Elinor when it ceased to be noticed by them. Their attention and wit were drawn off to his more fortunate rival, and the raillery which the other had incurred before any partiality arose was removed when his feelings began really to call for the ridicule so justly annexed to sensibility. Elinor was obliged, though unwillingly, to believe that the sentiments which Mrs Jennings had assigned him for her own satisfaction were now actually excited by her sister, and that however a general resemblance of disposition between the parties might forward the affection of Mr Willoughby, an equally striking opposition of character was no hindrance to the regard of Colonel Brandon.

She saw it with concern, for what could a silent man of five and thirty hope when opposed to a very lively one of five and twenty? And as she could not even wish him successful, she heartily wished him indifferent. She liked him for his moderation — in spite of his gravity and reserve, she beheld in him an object of interest. His manners, though serious, were mild, and his reserve appeared rather the result of some oppression of spirits than of any natural gloominess of temper. Sir John had dropped hints of past injuries and disappointments, which justified her belief of his being an unfortunate man, and she regarded him with respect and compassion.

Perhaps she pitied and esteemed him the more because he was slighted by Willoughby and Marianne, who, prejudiced against him for being neither lively nor young, seemed resolved to undervalue his merits.

"Brandon is just the kind of man," said Willoughby one day when they were talking of him together, "whom everybody speaks well of and nobody cares about, whom all are delighted to see and nobody remembers to talk to."

"That is exactly what I think of him," cried Marianne.

"Do not boast of it, however," said Elinor in haste, "for it is injustice in both of you. He is highly esteemed by all the family at the park, and I never see him myself without taking pains to converse with him."

"That he is patronised by you," replied Willoughby, "is certainly in his favour, but as for the esteem of the others, it is a reproach in itself. Who would submit to the indignity of being approved by such a woman as

Lady Middleton and Mrs Jennings that could command the indifference of anybody else?"

To Elinor this seemed especially cruel of him to say, maligning now not merely Brandon but the two ladies as well. "But perhaps the abuse of such people as yourself and Marianne will make amends for the regard of Lady Middleton and her mother. If their praise is censure, your censure may be praise, for they are not more undiscerning than you are prejudiced and unjust."

"In defence of your protégé you can even be saucy."

Saucy? Ha! "My protégé, as you call him, is a sensible man, and sense will always have attractions for me. Yes, Marianne, even in a man between thirty and forty. He has seen a great deal of the world, has been abroad, has read and has a thinking mind. I have found him capable of giving me much information on various subjects, and he has always answered my enquiries with readiness of good-breeding and good nature."

"That is to say," cried Marianne contemptuously, "he has told you that in the East Indies the climate is hot and the mosquitoes are troublesome."

"He would have told me so, I doubt not, had I made any such enquiries, but they happened to be points on which I had been previously informed."

"Perhaps," said Willoughby, "his observations may have extended to the existence of nabobs, gold mohrs and palanquins."

"I may venture to say that his observations have stretched much further than your candour. But why should you dislike him?"

"I do not dislike him. I consider him, on the contrary, as a very respectable man who has everybody's good word and nobody's notice, who has more money than he can spend, more time than he knows how to employ, and two new coats every year."

"Add to which," cried Marianne, "that he has neither genius, taste nor spirit. That his understanding has no brilliancy, his feelings no ardour and his voice no expression."

"You decide on his imperfections so much in the mass," replied Elinor with distaste, "and so much on the strength of your own imagination, that the commendation I am able to give of him is comparatively cold and insipid. I can only pronounce him to be a sensible man, well-bred, well-informed, of gentle address and, I believe, possessing an amiable heart."

"Miss Dashwood," cried Willoughby, "you are now using me unkindly."

Elinor stared at him, astonished at his accusation.

"You are endeavouring to disarm me by reason and to convince me against my will. But it will not do. You shall find me as stubborn as you can be artful. I have three unanswerable reasons for disliking Colonel Brandon. He threatened me with rain when I wanted it to be fine, he has found fault with the hanging of my curricle, and I cannot persuade him to buy my brown mare. If it will be any satisfaction to you, however, to be told that I believe his character to be in other respects irreproachable, I am ready to confess it. And in return for an acknowledgement which must give me some pain, you cannot deny me the privilege of disliking him as much as ever."

Realising any effort to improve Willoughby was hopeless, Elinor excused herself. Thereafter, she suffered mightily to witness such critiques of others in the company of her sister and her sister's beau.

Chapter Eleven

Little had Mrs Dashwood or her daughters imagined when they first came into Devonshire that so many engagements would arise to occupy their time as shortly presented themselves, or that they should have such frequent invitations and such constant visitors as to leave them little leisure for serious employment. Yet such was the case.

When Marianne was recovered, the schemes of amusement at home and abroad which Sir John had been previously forming were put into execution. The private balls at the park then began, and parties on the water were made and accomplished as often as a showery October would allow. In every meeting of the kind Willoughby was included, and the ease and familiarity which naturally attended these parties were exactly calculated to give increasing intimacy to his acquaintance with the Dashwoods, to afford him opportunity of witnessing the excellencies of Marianne, of marking his animated admiration of her and of receiving in her behaviour to himself the most pointed assurance of her affection.

Elinor could not be surprised at their attachment. She had seen them together in the most passionate embraces which had shocked her at first, then brought forth vivid memories of Edward's attentions toward her. The manner in which Willoughby had backed Marianne to a far wall in a tiny closet in the village assembly hall during a ball, his hand under her skirts, his mouth on her bare breast, recalled the incident the day her family had departed Norland. On another occasion, Elinor had excused herself from a tea party to find the ladies' reclining room only to discover Marianne in one of the parlours seated in Willoughby's lap, her thighs spread wide, her head flung back as the two of them rubbed their lower bodies together.

Worse still was the couple's frequent tendency to escape the public venues for the shadows of a room or garden and not care who noted their haste to depart. Certainly she understood their passion. She quite recalled, all too often and with hot wet evidence of it, her own excesses. She did not wish it less. She only wished that it were less openly shown, and once or twice did venture to suggest the propriety of some self-command to Marianne. But Marianne abhorred all concealment where no real disgrace could attend unreserve, and to aim at the restraint of sentiments which were not in themselves illaudable appeared to her not merely an unnecessary effort, but a disgraceful subjection of reason to commonplace and mistaken notions. Willoughby thought the same, and their behaviour at all times was an illustration of their opinions.

When he was present she had no eyes for anyone else. Everything he did was right. Everything he said was clever. If their evenings at the park were concluded with cards, he cheated himself and all the rest of the party to get her a good hand. If dancing formed the amusement of the night, they were partners for half the time, and when obliged to separate for a couple of dances, were careful to stand together and scarcely spoke a word to anybody else. Such conduct made them of course most exceedingly laughed at, but ridicule could not shame and seemed hardly to provoke them. Elinor marvelled at them and questioned her own conclusion that their behaviour was beyond the pale. She herself had experienced similar passion, had she not? Yet she did not excuse Edward everything, for such would be extreme, even in the name of love.

Mrs Dashwood entered into all their feelings with a warmth which left her no inclination for checking this excessive display of them. To her it was but the natural consequence of a strong affection in a young and ardent mind.

This was the season of happiness to Marianne. Her heart was devoted to Willoughby, and the fond attachment to Norland which she brought with her from Sussex was more likely to be softened than she had thought it possible before by the charms which his society bestowed on her present home.

Elinor's happiness was not so great. Her heart was not so much at ease, nor her satisfaction in their amusements so pure. They afforded her no companion that could make amends for what she had left behind, nor that could teach her to think of Norland with less regret than ever. Neither Lady Middleton nor Mrs Jennings could supply to her the conversation she missed, although the latter was an everlasting talker, and from the first had regarded her with a kindness which ensured her a large share of her discourse. She had already repeated her own history to Elinor three or four times, and had Elinor's memory been equal to her means of improvement, she might have known very early in their acquaintance all the particulars of Mr Jennings' last illness and what he said to his wife a few minutes before he died.

Lady Middleton was more agreeable than her mother only in being more silent. Elinor needed little observation to perceive that her reserve was a mere calmness of manner with which sense had nothing to do. Towards her husband and mother she was the same as to them, and intimacy was therefore neither to be looked for nor desired. She had nothing to say one day that she had not said the day before. Her insipidity was invariable, for even her spirits were always the same. Though she did not oppose the parties arranged by her husband, provided everything were conducted in style and her two eldest children attended her, she never appeared to receive more enjoyment from them than she might have experienced in sitting at home. So little did her presence add to the pleasure of the others by any share in their conversation that they were sometimes only reminded of her being amongst them by her solicitude about her troublesome boys.

In Colonel Brandon alone of all her new acquaintance did Elinor find a person who could in any degree claim the respect of abilities, excite the interest of friendship or give pleasure as a companion. With increasing ease of manner and address he would appear at her side at teas, assemblies, at homes and smaller gatherings. He brought her punch, danced with her, conversed in mild and civil tones. His discourse was informative, his years in India a novel topic, his views on politics moderate and yet complex. His maturity suited her natural tendency towards reason in all things. And over time, Elinor began to admire the curve of his mouth as he laughed, the half-smile he offered when rueful, the elegance of his hands as he gestured and the tautness of his muscular lean form. Yes, on many levels now that she knew him better, Brandon appealed to Elinor.

Willoughby was out of the question. Her admiration and regard, even her sisterly regard, was all his own, but he was a lover. His attentions were wholly Marianne's, and a far less agreeable man might have been more generally pleasing. Colonel Brandon, unfortunately for himself, had no such encouragement to think only of Marianne, and in conversing with Elinor he found the greatest consolation for the indifference of her sister.

Elinor's compassion for him increased, as she had reason to suspect that the misery of disappointed love had already been known to him. This suspicion was given by some words which accidentally dropped from him one evening at the park, when they were sitting down together by mutual consent while the others were dancing. His eyes were fixed on Marianne, and after a silence of some minutes he said with a faint smile, "Your sister, I understand, does not approve of second attachments."

"No," replied Elinor, acknowledging that Brandon still considered Marianne the most desirable of the two of them, "her opinions are all romantic."

"Or rather, as I believe, she considers them impossible to exist."

"I believe she does." Elinor's jealousy flared uncontrollably, causing her to blurt out words that were quite unforgiveable. "But how she contrives it without reflecting on the character of her own father, who had himself two wives, I know not. A few years however will settle her opinions on the reasonable basis of common sense and observation, then they may be more easy to define and to justify than they now are by anybody but herself."

"This will probably be the case," he replied, oblivious it seemed to Elinor's green-eyed envy, "and yet there is something so amiable in the prejudices of a young mind that one is sorry to see them give way to the reception of more general opinions."

"I cannot agree with you there," said Elinor. "There are inconveniences attending such feelings as Marianne's which all the charms of enthusiasm and ignorance of the world cannot atone for. Her systems have all the unfortunate tendency of setting propriety at nought, and a better acquaintance with the world is what I look forward to as her greatest possible advantage."

After a short pause he resumed the conversation by saying, "Does your sister make no distinction in her objections against a second attachment? Or is it equally criminal in everybody? Are those who have been disappointed in their first choice, whether from the inconstancy of its object or the perverseness of circumstances, to be equally indifferent during the rest of their lives?"

"Upon my word, I am not acquainted with the minutiae of her principles. I only know that I never yet heard her admit any instance of a second attachment's being pardonable."

"This," said he, "cannot hold, but a change, a total change of sentiments—No, no, do not desire it, for when the romantic refinements of a young mind are obliged to give way, how frequently are they succeeded by such opinions as are but too common and too dangerous! I speak from experience. I once knew a lady who in temper and mind greatly resembled your sister, who thought and judged like her, but who from an enforced change—from a series of unfortunate circumstances—"

Here he stopped suddenly, appeared to think that he had said too much, and by his countenance gave rise to conjectures which might not otherwise have entered Elinor's head. The lady would probably have passed without suspicion had he not convinced Miss Dashwood that what concerned her ought not to escape his lips. As it was, it required but a slight effort of fancy to connect his emotion with the tender recollection of past regard. Elinor attempted no more. But Marianne, in her place, would not have done so little. The whole story would have been speedily formed under her active imagination, and everything established in the most melancholy order of disastrous love.

Chapter Twelve

As Elinor and Marianne were walking together the next morning the latter communicated a piece of news to her sister which, in spite of all that she knew before of Marianne's imprudence and want of thought, surprised her by its extravagant testimony of both. Marianne told her with the greatest delight that Willoughby had given her a horse, one that he had bred himself on his estate in Somersetshire and which was exactly calculated to carry a woman.

"Oh, Marianne, how can you approve of this?"

Without considering that it was not in her mother's plan to keep any horse—that if she were to alter her resolution in favour of this gift she must buy another for the servant and keep a servant to ride it and after all build a stable to receive them—she had accepted the present without hesitation, and told her sister of it in raptures.

"He intends to send his groom into Somersetshire immediately for it," she added, delight suffusing her features, "and when it arrives we will ride every day.

You shall share its use with me. Imagine to yourself, my dear Elinor, the delight of a gallop on some of these downs."

Most unwilling was she to awaken from such a dream of felicity to comprehend all the unhappy truths which attended the affair, and for some time she refused to submit to them. As to an additional servant, the expense would be a trifle. Mama, she was sure, would never object to it. And any horse would do for him—he might always get one at the park. As to a stable, the merest shed would be sufficient.

Elinor then ventured to doubt the propriety of her receiving such a present from a man so little, or at least so lately, known to her. This was too much.

"You are mistaken, Elinor," said she warmly, "in supposing I know very little of Willoughby. I have not known him long indeed, but I am much better acquainted with him than I am with any other creature in the world except yourself and Mama. It is not time or opportunity that is to determine intimacy, it is disposition alone."

"Certainly more, Marianne, than disposition. I have seen you both in each other's embrace. You in the throes of passion."

"Willoughby as well, dear Elinor. He as well! Seven years would be insufficient to make some people acquainted with each other, and seven days are more than enough for others. I should hold myself guilty of greater impropriety in accepting a horse from my brother than from Willoughby. Of John I know very little, though we have lived together for years, but of Willoughby my judgement has long been formed."

In wild frustration, Elinor ran a hand through her hair and thought it wisest to touch that point no more. She knew her sister's temper. Opposition on so tender a subject would only attach her the more to her own opinion. But by an appeal to her affection for her mother, by representing the inconveniences which that indulgent mother must draw on herself if—as would probably be the case—she consented to this increase of establishment, Marianne was shortly subdued. She promised not to tempt her mother to such imprudent kindness by mentioning the offer, and to tell Willoughby when she saw him next that it must be declined.

She was faithful to her word, and when Willoughby called at the cottage the same day, Elinor heard her express her disappointment to him in a low voice on being obliged to forego the acceptance of his present. The reasons for this alteration were at the same time related, and they were such as to make further entreaty on his side impossible. His concern however was very apparent, and after expressing it with earnestness, he added in the same low voice, "But Marianne, the horse is still yours, though you cannot use it now. I shall keep it only till you can claim it. When you leave Barton to form your own establishment in a more lasting home, Queen Mab shall receive you."

This was all overheard by Miss Elinor Dashwood, and in the whole of the sentence, in his manner of pronouncing it and in his addressing her sister by her Christian name alone, she instantly saw an intimacy so decided, a meaning so direct as marked a perfect agreement between them. From that moment she doubted not of their being engaged to each other, and the belief of it created no other surprise than that she or any of their friends should be left by tempers so frank to discover it by accident.

Margaret related something to her the next day which placed this matter in a still clearer light. Willoughby had spent the preceding evening with them, and Margaret, by being left some time in the parlour with only him and Marianne, had had opportunity for observations which with a most important face she communicated to her eldest sister when they were next by themselves.

"Oh, Elinor!" she cried. "I have such a secret to tell you about Marianne. I am sure she will be married to Mr Willoughby very soon."

"You have said so," replied Elinor, "almost every day since they first met on Highchurch Down, and they had not known each other a week, I believe, before you were certain that Marianne wore his picture round her neck, but it turned out to be only the miniature of our great uncle."

"But indeed this is quite another thing. I am sure they will be married very soon, for he has got a lock of her hair."

"Take care, Margaret. It may be only the hair of some great uncle of his."

"But indeed, Elinor, it is Marianne's. I am almost sure it is, for I saw him cut it off. Last night after tea when you and Mama went out of the room, they were whispering and talking together as fast as could be, and he seemed to be begging something of her, and presently he took up her scissors and cut off a long lock of her hair. He removed her pins and it all tumbled down her back, and he kissed it and folded it up in a piece of white paper and put it into his pocketbook. Then he picked up her hand and held it to his heart. I left them alone, Elinor, and know I should not have. Yet my senses told me it would be best. I was not even out of the room when Willoughby had Marianne in his arms. They were kissing, Elinor. I heard him moaning and Marianne panting quickly so that I—"

"Yes, yes, my dearest, thank you. You of course did well to leave them."

"Will you tell Mama? She will scold me for leaving. I would hate that."

"I understand your dilemma, dearest." Elinor left the matter unanswered for Margaret as she promised herself to deliberate the matters at hand. If Margaret's words were true, the relationship between Willoughby and Marianne was progressing at such a pace that a final agreement must come soon.

For such particulars, stated on such authority, Elinor could not withhold her credit. Nor was she disposed to it, for the circumstance was in perfect unison with what she had heard and seen herself.

Margaret's sagacity was not always displayed in a way so satisfactory to her sister. When Mrs Jennings attacked her one evening at the park to give the name of the young man who was Elinor's particular favourite, which had been long a matter of great curiosity to her, Margaret answered by looking at her sister and saying, "I must not tell, may I, Elinor?"

This of course made everybody laugh, and Elinor tried to laugh too. But the effort was painful. She was convinced that Margaret had fixed on a person whose name she could not bear with composure to become a standing joke with Mrs Jennings.

Marianne felt for her most sincerely, but she did more harm than good to the cause by turning very red and saying in an angry manner to Margaret, "Remember that whatever your conjectures may be, you have no right to repeat them."

"I never had any conjectures about it," replied Margaret, "it was you who told me of it yourself."

Elinor's gaze shot to Marianne's. Why had she told Margaret this? She did not wish to be the object of discussion.

This increased the mirth of the company, and Margaret was eagerly pressed to say something more.

"Oh! Pray, Miss Margaret, let us know all about it," said Mrs Jennings. "What is the gentleman's name?"

"I must not tell, ma'am. But I know very well what it is, and I know where he is too."

"Yes, yes, we can guess where he is, at his own house at Norland to be sure. He is the curate of the parish I dare say."

"No, that he is not. He is of no profession at all."

"Margaret," said Marianne with great warmth and Elinor perceived some guile, "you know that all this is an invention of your own, and that there is no such person in existence."

"Well, then he is lately dead, Marianne, for I am sure there was such a man once, and his name begins with an F."

Most grateful did Elinor feel to Lady Middleton for observing at this moment that it rained very hard, though she believed the interruption to proceed less from any attention to her than from her ladyship's great dislike of all such inelegant subjects of raillery as delighted her husband and mother. The idea however started by her was immediately pursued by Colonel Brandon, who was on every occasion mindful of the feelings of others — especially Elinor's — and much was said on the subject of rain by both of them. In a surprising move that Elinor found welcome and rather out of character, Willoughby winked at her, then opened the piano-forte and asked Marianne to sit down to it, and thus amidst the various endeavours of different people to quit the topic, it fell to the ground. But not so easily did Elinor recover from the alarm into which it had thrown her.

A party was formed this evening for going on the following day to see a very fine place about twelve miles from Barton, belonging to a brother-in-law of Colonel Brandon without whose interest it could not be seen, as the proprietor, who was then abroad, had left strict orders on that head. The grounds were declared to be highly beautiful and Sir John, who was particularly warm in their praise, might be allowed to be a tolerable judge, for he had formed parties to visit them at least twice every summer for the last ten years. They contained a noble piece of water, a sail on which was to a form a great part of the morning's amusement. Cold provisions were to be taken, open carriages only to be employed and everything conducted in the usual style of a complete party of pleasure.

To some few of the company it appeared rather a bold undertaking considering the time of year and that it had rained every day for the last fortnight, and Mrs Dashwood, who had already a cold, was persuaded by Elinor to stay at home.

Chapter Thirteen

Their intended excursion to Whitwell turned out very different from what Elinor had expected. She was prepared to be wet through, fatigued and frightened, but the event was still more unfortunate, for they did not go at all.

By ten o'clock the whole party was assembled at the park where they were to breakfast. The morning was rather favourable though it had rained all night, as the clouds were then dispersing across the sky, and the sun frequently appeared. They were all in high spirits and good humour, eager to be happy and determined to submit to the greatest inconveniences and hardships rather than be otherwise.

While they were at breakfast the letters were brought in. Among the rest there was one for Colonel Brandon. He took it, looked at the direction, changed colour and immediately left the room.

"What is the matter with Brandon?" said Sir John.

Nobody could tell.

"I hope he has had no bad news," said Lady Middleton. "It must be something extraordinary that could make Colonel Brandon leave my breakfast table so suddenly."

In about five minutes he returned.

"No bad news, Colonel, I hope," said Mrs Jennings as soon as he entered the room.

"None at all, ma'am, I thank you."

"Was it from Avignon? I hope it is not to say that your sister is worse."

"No, ma'am. It came from town and is merely a letter of business."

"But how came the hand to discompose you so much, if it was only a letter of business? Come, come, this won't do, Colonel, so let us hear the truth of it."

"My dear madam," said Lady Middleton, "recollect what you are saying."

"Perhaps it is to tell you that your cousin Fanny is married?" said Mrs Jennings without attending to her daughter's reproof.

"No indeed, it is not."

"Well then, I know who it is from, Colonel. And I hope she is well."

"Whom do you mean, ma'am?" said he, colouring a little.

"Oh, you know who I mean."

"I am particularly sorry, ma'am," said he, addressing Lady Middleton, "that I should receive this letter today, for it is on business which requires my immediate attendance in town."

"In town!" cried Mrs Jennings. "What can you have to do in town at this time of year?"

"My own loss is great," he continued, "in being obliged to leave so agreeable a party, but I am the more concerned, as I fear my presence is necessary to gain your admittance at Whitwell."

What a blow upon them all was this!

"But if you write a note to the housekeeper, Mr Brandon," said Marianne eagerly, "will it not be sufficient?"

He shook his head.

"We must go," said Sir John. "It shall not be put off when we are so near it. You cannot go to town till tomorrow, Brandon, that is all."

Fidgeting in her chair, Elinor glanced up at Brandon, alarmed for him. She could not countenance the audacity of her companions. How bold were Mrs Jennings, Sir John and even Marianne to go so far as to argue with Colonel Brandon in such a very familiar manner?

Her friend met her gaze, his demeanour all composure and determination. "I wish it could be so easily settled. But it is not in my power to delay my journey for one day!"

"If you would but let us know what your business is," said Mrs Jennings, "we might see whether it could be put off or not."

"You would not be six hours later," said Willoughby, "if you were to defer your journey till our return."

"I cannot afford to lose one hour."

Elinor then heard Willoughby say in a low voice to Marianne, "There are some people who cannot bear a party of pleasure. Brandon is one of them. He was afraid of catching cold I dare say, and invented this trick for getting out of it. I would lay fifty guineas the letter was of his own writing."

"I have no doubt of it," replied Marianne.

Elinor glared at Marianne. As for Willoughby, she had no power to chastise him or influence him to finer manners.

"There is no persuading you to change your mind, Brandon, I know of old," said Sir John, "when once you are determined on anything. But, however, I hope you will think better of it. Consider, here are the two Miss Careys come over from Newton, the three Miss Dashwoods walked up from the cottage and Mr Willoughby got up two hours before his usual time on purpose to go to Whitwell."

Colonel Brandon again repeated his sorrow at being the cause of disappointing the party, but at the same time declared it to be unavoidable.

"Well then, when will you come back again?"

"I hope we shall see you at Barton," added her ladyship, "as soon as you can conveniently leave town, and we must put off the party to Whitwell till you return."

"You are very obliging. But it is so uncertain when I may have it in my power to return that I dare not engage for it at all."

"Oh, he must and shall come back," cried Sir John. "If he is not here by the end of the week, I shall go after him."

"Ay, so do, Sir John," cried Mrs Jennings, "then perhaps you may find out what his business is."

"I do not want to pry into other men's concerns. I suppose it is something he is ashamed of."

A muscle in Brandon's cheek ticked. Elinor saw his irritation and applauded his restraint, though at the same time she also wished to box Sir John's ears.

Colonel Brandon's horses were announced.

"You do not go to town on horseback, do you?" added Sir John.

"No. Only to Honiton. I shall then go post."

"Well, as you are resolved to go, I wish you a good journey. But you had better change your mind."

Oh, insufferable man!

"I assure you it is not in my power." He then took leave of the whole party. "Is there no chance of my seeing you and your sisters in town this winter, Miss Dashwood?"

"I am afraid none at all."

"Then I must bid you farewell for a longer time than I should wish to do."

To Marianne, he merely bowed and said nothing.

"Come, Colonel," said Mrs Jennings, "before you go, do let us know what you are going about."

He wished her a good morning, and attended by Sir John, left the room.

The complaints and lamentations which politeness had hitherto restrained now burst forth universally, and they all agreed again and again how provoking it was to be so disappointed.

"I can guess what his business is, however," said Mrs Jennings exultingly.

"Can you, ma'am?" said almost everybody.

"Yes, it is about Miss Williams, I am sure."

"And who is Miss Williams?" asked Marianne.

"What, do not you know who Miss Williams is? I am sure you must have heard of her before. She is a relation of the Colonel's, my dear, a very near relation. We will not say how near, for fear of shocking the young ladies." Then, lowering her voice a little, she said to Elinor, "She is his natural daughter."

"Indeed!"

"Oh, yes, and as like him as she can stare. I dare say the Colonel will leave her all his fortune."

When Sir John returned he joined most heartily in the general regret on so unfortunate an event, concluding however by observing that as they were all got together they must do something by way of being happy. After some consultation it was agreed that although happiness could only be enjoyed at Whitwell, they might procure a tolerable composure of mind by driving about the country. The carriages were then ordered. Willoughby's was first, and Marianne never looked happier than when she got into it. He drove through the park very fast and they were soon out of sight, the entire party save Elinor laughing at their departure.

Marianne exulted in Willoughby's dashing act. Curling her arm through his as he worked the reins, she settled against him.

"I daresay, my dear girl, I feel your body purring like a cat's."

Gazing up at his striking face, she admired his roguish beauty and the fact that he was hers. "When I am with you, I am a cat."

He reined the horses to a halt and caught her against him. "I like you wild and clawing at me. Shall I encourage you to do that?"

She tossed him a saucy glance, her shoulder up, her chin to one side. "Do as you will, Willoughby. I am yours."

Capturing her hand, he pressed it to his chest. But she was not satisfied with so staid a sample of his charms. She trailed her hand downward to his flies where her fingers cupped his swollen flesh and kneaded his manly attributes.

"I say," he gasped, his hand covering hers, "you are a minx. I lose my breath, my mind."

She arched a brow. "But not your erection."

"Never. Not with you in my reach."

"I pray you, show me this proud declaration of your regard for me."

"No. You are but a girl."

"Your girl, you rogue." She massaged his cock and balls. "This package must be unwrapped." She worked at his buttons and soon his cock stood straight up, the helmet bold and proud, droplets of delights oozing from his slit. "Oh, this is quite perfect, Willoughby. I have never seen anything so tall and thick. Oh. And he moves! He jerks for me. Shall I reward him?"

"Do, do," Willoughby encouraged her, sighing and biting his lower lip. "He awaits your fine touch."

She rubbed her thumb over his essence dribbling from his seam. "He gives more and more. I am enchanted, Willoughby. What more can I do to show him my enthusiasm?"

"Kiss him."

"Oh," she enthused and bent to the act. "He is luscious. Hot and hard, the skin soft and yet so malleable. How do you *do* this, Willoughby?"

Laughing, he collapsed backward to the seat and let her have her way. "It is natural, my pet. I give all to you. That is my fondest pleasure."

"Do you, dear sir?" Teasing him, she kissed his cock once more, licking her lips between her blessings to his member. "Show me your aunt's house then." She took all of his fine manhood down her throat, hearing him groan his approval of her act.

"Shall I?" he seemed to ask himself more than her.

"Of course. We need more...*room* for our pleasures, would you not say?" She let her eyes dance at him. The merry idea of a couch, a bed, a carpeted floor to lay him down and suck on his marvellous member filled her heart with rapture.

"I do, I do." He pushed her up from him, fumbling to button his flies. "I need to have your mouth on me until completion."

"Completion?" She sat back, allowing him his haste and preening that she had led him to it, even though her breasts ached and her lower body pulsed with need of him. "What is that?"

He caught her chin. "Heaven."

"Take me there," she entreated him. "Now."

With a shout of joy, he seized the reins and off they went through the woods, down a lane, round a bend to turn at last into a drive fit to hold three carriages abreast. Marianne opened her mouth, the taste of his musky member still on her tongue, and gasped her delight.

"Built when George the Second sat the throne," Willoughby said as he whipped the horses faster down the lane. "Two parlours, two dining rooms, a grand ballroom, ten bedrooms. At last count, eight staff."

"Oh, marvellous," she praised the site of the divine little house as she grasped his arm. "But will they intrude on us? I hope not. I wish to have you to myself, dear Willoughby."

"I shall instruct them to stay well away." He gathered her close and set the whip across the horses' backs once more. "Total and utter abandon, we shall have."

"As we always do," she encouraged him in their mutual agreement to enjoy all to the last degree.

He urged the horses to a halt before the main door, but when he helped her down, he led her towards a side door so that the servants might not note where they went inside the house. Then up the side stairs he led her to a charming yellow sitting room where the sun shone invitingly upon all the furnishings, the linens and the carpet.

Marianne stood at the opened doorway, delighted with the view. Willoughby drew her inside and shut the door softly, the latch clicking quietly in the lock. He turned her to him, his hands shaking as he unbuttoned her bodice.

"Let me see my two beauties. How I have hungered to taste them today." He took her heavy breasts from her chemise, her nipples, she proudly noted, hard as diamonds from the expectation of his tongue and teeth upon them. "Oh, how luscious you are, my pet."

"Nibble on them, Willoughby." She thrust her breasts forward, the better for him to suckle and bite.

He did her the honours lavishly, making such ravenous lewd noises as he feasted that she arched backward, mewling, lost in his touches.

"Shall I offer you my cock now, dearest? Are you ready to have me to completion?"

She swayed, rubbing her hips against his and feeling the power of his attraction to her. "Let me have you. I will do you proud, good sir."

On a shout, he tugged her to the thick Turkish carpet. There, rolling on his back, he undid his own flies so quickly and efficiently that his member shot out from his breeches, tall and red and ready for her.

She giggled, palming him. "How long he is. Weeping in anticipation of me."

"I beg you," he growled, thrusting his hand into her hair and scattering her pins to the rug as he pulled her face to his cock, "do this now before I die for want of you."

She surveyed his impressive cock and his very heavy balls. He smelled of musk and his own good self. She could eat him alive and still not get enough of him, he was so dear, so fiercely dear to her. Yet to honour him and ensure he never forgot this fine hour when she serviced him, she took her time. She licked his tip. She savoured his pearls. She dropped again to surround him with the pleasure of her delicate lips. She held him at his thick root and laved his entire length. At this, he thrust up a hand to his forehead and begged for more of her care.

Smiling, she lapped at his cock, beneath, around, swirling, taking, giving, pulling at him gently until he gasped and held her head to his member. Instinctively understanding that this was that mysterious completion he discussed, she let him lead her now and she sucked him, all of him, all the way down and up, quickly, more quickly, until he bucked his hips at her and into her mouth she felt the gush of hot thick seed. And she milked him, sucked him, drained him dry with such gusto and aplomb that he groaned and rolled back and forth, his beautiful cock slick and glistening from her ministrations.

At once, he grabbed her, kissing her furiously on the forehead and cheeks. Why did he not kiss her on the mouth, she wondered as she tried to influence him to do that. But he won then pushed her to the carpet herself.

"Your reward, my pretty pet, is the same delight."

"You mean —?"

"Completion for you? Of course," he said chuckling. "Come, do not be shy now as I have wanted to see you flower for me. I have felt your dew. Now I wish to be the honey bee and drink as I should from your petals. Lie back. That's right. Let me lift your skirts. Oh, my pet. No drawers today? How prescient of you to be naked. What a jewel you are. There, how does that feel?"

She let her thighs splay open wider, the touch of his fingers to her chat so comforting, so natural, so romantic and right.

"Tell me, dear girl. You must encourage me."

She arched a brow at him. "I think you know what you are about, Willoughby. You have stroked my cunny so often these past weeks. You know what I like."

"Ah, yes," he crooned and threw up her skirts higher so that she could not see his face as he looked at her female flesh. "I do like your labia." He squeezed one. "Fat and coated with juice to welcome me. I like your hair, too." He combed it and she sighed, drifting, dreaming and swelling at his touch.

"What do you like about it, sire?"

"How thick it is. I wish to shave it one day soon."

"Shave it. Really? But why?"

"The better to suck your sweetness into my mouth."

"Try now anyway." She encouraged him, her hand going to his hair and her fingers sinking in the soft wealth of it. "I want your lips on me."

He obliged her, nestling down between her legs and putting his mouth to her quim with such force that she screamed in delight. With no reprieve, he sucked her and licked her, getting his mouth and cheeks and chin so wet with her desire for him that she whimpered in exquisite need, clutching at his shoulders. He sent one, two, three fingers up inside her virgin's passage and when she bucked, he calmed her saying no one would know what they did. He promised to be careful, gentle so that her innocent barrier would be intact. Then, by

God, he would eat her so that he wore the scent for the rest of his life. And he did.

She railed at him to bring her some relief and so as he came up to rise above her and paint her lips with the cream from her own cunt, he told her he would never hurt her, but treasure her. "And here is how, my pet." At that, he sank down once more between her legs and found a portion of her cunny that he had often pinched and twisted. But now he circled and plucked and licked and bit her there until she once more screamed like a banshee and throbbed, dear God, as if the whole world pulsed with her!

She clutched him, crying, exclaiming as she shook, and he laughed and laughed as he held her and rejoiced at his success.

At last, she returned to some sensible state of mind and cuddled closer into his embrace. "My word, Willoughby, that was incredibly wonderful. This completion of yours is a state I wish to visit often."

He pushed back her hair and kissed her lips, the musk of her own cream ripe upon his swollen mouth. "I will take you there again and again. Of course, you must do the same for me."

"I will. You do know I will. For how could I not want that daily? Nay, hourly?"

He roared in laughter now.

"What? Can this not be done on the hour?"

"For you? I shall be a shell of a man."

She harrumphed, triumphant and preening. "I shall keep you well fed."

"With your cream? And your outrageous screams of delight? You shall, pet of mine. You shall."

Cuddling close, she was at last assured that after today, she could amuse him and enchant him for a very long time.

* * * *

Elinor could scarce believe that Willoughby had driven off with her sister in such short fashion and nothing more of them was seen till their return, which did not happen till after the return of all the rest. They both seemed delighted with their drive, but said only in general terms that they had kept in the lanes while the others went on the downs.

It was settled that there should be a dance in the evening, and that everybody should be extremely merry all day long. Some more of the Careys came to dinner, and they had the pleasure of sitting down nearly twenty to table, which Sir John observed with great contentment. Willoughby took his usual place between the two elder Miss Dashwoods. Mrs Jennings sat on Elinor's right hand, and they had not been long seated before she leant behind her and Willoughby and said to Marianne loud enough for them both to hear, "I have found you out in spite of all your tricks. I know where you spent the morning."

Marianne coloured, and replied very hastily, "Where, pray?"

"Did not you know," said Willoughby, "that we had been out in my curricle?"

"Yes, yes, Mr Impudence, I know that very well, and I was determined to find out where you had been to. I hope you like your house, Miss Marianne."

"My house? Oh, surely—"

"It is a very large one," the lady rattled on, "I know, and when I come to see you, I hope you will have new-furnished it, for it wanted it very much when I was there six years ago."

Marianne turned away in great confusion. Mrs Jennings laughed heartily, and Elinor found that in her resolution to know where they had been she had actually made her own woman enquire of Mr Willoughby's groom, and that she had by that method been informed that they had gone to Allenham and spent a considerable time there in walking about the garden and going all over the house.

Aghast, Elinor could hardly believe this to be true, as it seemed very unlikely that Willoughby should propose or Marianne consent to enter the house while Mrs Smith was in it, with whom Marianne had not the smallest acquaintance.

As soon as they left the dining room, Elinor took her sister to one side and enquired of her about it, and great was her surprise when she found that every circumstance related by Mrs Jennings was perfectly true. Marianne was quite angry with her for doubting it.

"Why should you imagine, Elinor, that we did not go there, or that we did not see the house? Is not it what you have often wished to do yourself?"

"Yes, Marianne, but I would not go while Mrs Smith was there, and with no other companion than Mr Willoughby."

"Mr Willoughby however is the only person who can have a right to show that house, and as he went in an open carriage, it was impossible to have any other companion. I never spent a pleasanter morning in my life."

"I am afraid," replied Elinor, "that the pleasantness of an employment does not always evince its propriety."

"On the contrary, nothing can be a stronger proof of it, Elinor. If there had been any real impropriety in what I did, I should have been sensible of it at the time, for we always know when we are acting wrong, and with such a conviction I could have had no pleasure."

"But my dear Marianne, as it has already exposed you to some very impertinent remarks, do you not now begin to doubt the discretion of your own conduct?"

"If the impertinent remarks of Mrs Jennings are to be the proof of impropriety in conduct, we are all offending every moment of our lives. I value not her censure any more than I should do her commendation. I am not sensible of having done anything wrong in walking over Mrs Smith's grounds, or in seeing her house. They will one day be Mr Willoughby's, and—"

"If they were one day to be your own, Marianne, you would not be justified in what you have done."

She blushed at this hint, but it was even visibly gratifying to her. After a ten minutes' interval of earnest thought, she came to her sister again and said with great good humour, "Perhaps, Elinor, it *was* rather ill-judged in me to go to Allenham. But Mr Willoughby wanted particularly to show me the place, and it is a charming house, I assure you. There is one remarkably pretty sitting room upstairs, of a nice comfortable size for constant use, and with modern furniture it would be delightful. It is a corner room and has windows on two sides. On one side you look across the bowling green behind the house to a beautiful hanging wood, and on the other you have a view of the church and village, and beyond them of those fine bold hills that we have so often admired. I did not see it to advantage, for nothing could be more forlorn than the furniture, but if it were newly fitted up—a couple of hundred pounds, Willoughby says, would make it one of the pleasantest summer rooms in England."

Could Elinor have listened to her without interruption from the others, she would have described every room in the house with equal delight.

Chapter Fourteen

The sudden termination of Colonel Brandon's visit at the park, with his steadiness in concealing its cause, filled the mind and raised the wonder of Mrs Jennings for two or three days. She was a great wonderer, as everyone must be who takes a very lively interest in all the comings and goings of all their acquaintance. She wondered with little intermission what could be the reason of it, was sure there must be some bad news and thought over every kind of distress that could have befallen him, with a fixed determination that he should not escape them all.

"Something very melancholy must be the matter, I am sure," said she. "I could see it in his face. Poor man! I am afraid his circumstances may be bad. The estate at Delaford was never reckoned more than two thousand a year, and his brother left everything sadly involved. I do think he must have been sent for about money matters, for what else can it be? I wonder whether it is so. I would give anything to know the truth of it. Perhaps it is about Miss Williams and by the bye, I dare say it is, because he looked so conscious when I mentioned her. Maybe she is ill in town. Nothing in the world more likely, for I have a notion she is always rather sickly. I would lay any wager it is about Miss Williams. It is not so very likely he should be distressed in his circumstances now, for he is a very prudent man, and to be sure must have cleared the estate by this time. I wonder what it can be! Maybe his sister is worse at Avignon and has sent for him over. His setting off in such a hurry seems very like it. Well, I wish him out of all his trouble with all my heart, and a good wife into the bargain."

So wondered, so talked Mrs Jennings. Her opinion varying with every fresh conjecture, and all seeming equally probable as they arose. Elinor, though she felt really interested in the welfare of Colonel Brandon, could not bestow all the wonder on his going so suddenly away which Mrs Jennings was desirous of her feeling. Besides that the circumstance did not in her opinion justify such lasting amazement or variety of speculation, her wonder was otherwise disposed of.

It was engrossed by the extraordinary silence of her sister and Willoughby on the subject which they must know to be peculiarly interesting to them all. As this silence continued, every day made it appear more strange and more incompatible with the disposition of both. Why they should not openly acknowledge to her mother and herself what their constant behaviour to each other declared to have taken place, Elinor could not imagine.

She could easily conceive that marriage might not be immediately in their power, for though Willoughby was independent, there was no reason to believe him rich. His estate had been rated by Sir John at about six or seven hundred a year, but he lived at an expense to which that income could hardly be equal and he had himself often complained of his poverty. But for this strange kind of secrecy maintained by them relative to their engagement, which in fact concealed nothing at all, she could not account, and it was so wholly contradictory to their general opinions and practice that a doubt sometimes entered her mind of their being really engaged, and this doubt was enough to prevent her making any enquiry of Marianne.

Nothing could be more expressive of attachment to them all than Willoughby's behaviour. To Marianne it had all the distinguishing tenderness which a lover's heart could give, and to the rest of the family it was the affectionate attention of a son and a brother. The cottage seemed to be considered and loved by him as his home. Many more of his hours were spent there than at Allenham, and if no general engagement collected them at the park, the exercise which called him out in the morning was almost certain of ending there, where the rest of the day was spent by himself at the side of Marianne and by his favourite pointer at her feet.

One evening in particular, about a week after Colonel Brandon left the country, his heart seemed more than usually open to every feeling of attachment to the objects around him. On Mrs Dashwood's happening to mention her design of improving the cottage in the spring, he warmly opposed every alteration of a place which affection had established as perfect with him.

"What!" he exclaimed. "Improve this dear cottage! No. That I will never consent to."

Elinor startled at his impertinence to imply he had a say in the appointments of their home. She glanced at Marianne, who merely nodded in agreement with him. *What* has *happened between them that he takes such ease remarking on this matter?*

Indeed, he went on and on. "Not a stone must be added to its walls, not an inch to its size, if my feelings are regarded."

"Do not be alarmed," said Miss Dashwood, "nothing of the kind will be done, for my mother will never have money enough to attempt it."

"I am heartily glad of it," he cried. "May she always be poor, if she can employ her riches no better."

"Thank you, Willoughby. But you may be assured that I would not sacrifice one sentiment of local attachment of yours or of anyone whom I loved for all the improvements in the world. Depend upon it that whatever unemployed sum may remain when I make up my accounts in the spring, I would even rather lay it uselessly by than dispose of it in a manner so painful to you. But are you really so attached to this place as to see no defect in it?"

"I am," said he. "To me it is faultless. Nay, more, I consider it as the only form of building in which happiness is attainable, and were I rich enough I would instantly pull Combe down and build it up again in the exact plan of this cottage."

"With dark narrow stairs and a kitchen that smokes, I suppose," said Elinor.

"Yes," cried he in the same eager tone, "with all and everything belonging to it. In no one convenience or inconvenience about it should the least variation be perceptible. Then and then only, under such a roof, I might perhaps be as happy at Combe as I have been at Barton."

"I flatter myself," replied Elinor, "that even under the disadvantage of better rooms and a broader staircase, you will hereafter find your own house as faultless as you now do this."

"There certainly are circumstances," said Willoughby, "which might greatly endear it to me, but this place will always have one claim of my affection which no other can possibly share."

Mrs Dashwood looked with pleasure at Marianne, whose fine eyes were fixed so expressively on Willoughby as plainly denoted how well she understood him.

"How often did I wish," added he, "when I was at Allenham this time twelvemonth, that Barton cottage were inhabited! I never passed within view of it without admiring its situation and grieving that no one should live in it. How little did I then think that the very first news I should hear from Mrs Smith when I next came into the country would be that Barton cottage was taken—and I felt an immediate satisfaction and interest in the event, which nothing but a kind of prescience of what happiness I should experience from it can account for. Must it not have been so, Marianne?" Speaking to her in a lowered voice.

Then continuing his former tone, he said, "And yet this house you would spoil, Mrs Dashwood? You would rob it of its simplicity by imaginary improvement! And this dear parlour in which our acquaintance first began, and in which so many happy hours have been since spent by us together, you would degrade to the condition of a common entrance. Everybody would be eager to pass through the room which has hitherto contained within itself more real accommodation and comfort than any other apartment of the handsomest dimensions in the world could possibly afford."

Mrs Dashwood again assured him that no alteration of the kind should be attempted.

"You are a good woman," he warmly replied. "Your promise makes me easy. Extend it a little farther, and it will make me happy. Tell me that not only your house will remain the same, but that I shall ever find you and yours as unchanged as your dwelling, and that you will always consider me with the kindness which has made everything belonging to you so dear to me."

The promise was readily given, and Willoughby's behaviour during the whole of the evening declared at once his affection and happiness.

"Shall we see you tomorrow to dinner?" said Mrs Dashwood when he was leaving them. "I do not ask you to come in the morning, for we must walk to the park to call on Lady Middleton."

He engaged to be with them by four o'clock.

Chapter Fifteen

Mrs Dashwood's visit to Lady Middleton took place the next day, and two of her daughters went with her. But Marianne excused herself from being of the party under some trifling pretext of employment, and her mother, who concluded that a promise had been made by Willoughby the night before of calling on her while they were absent, was perfectly satisfied with her remaining at home. Elinor, afraid of gossip, remarked to her mother that perhaps she not permit such freedom to Marianne, upon which Mrs Dashwood waved off her concerns. "We trust them both, do we not?"

Elinor understood that to respond in the negative was not her best answer.

On their return from the park they found Willoughby's curricle and servant in waiting at the cottage, and Mrs Dashwood was convinced that her conjecture had been just. So far it was all as she had foreseen, but on entering the house she beheld what no foresight had taught her to expect. They were no sooner in the passage than Marianne came hastily out of the parlour apparently in violent affliction, with her handkerchief at her eyes, and without noticing them ran upstairs. Surprised and alarmed they proceeded directly into the room she had just quitted, where they found only Willoughby, who was leaning against the mantelpiece with his back towards them. He turned round on their coming in, and his countenance showed that he strongly partook of the emotion which over-powered Marianne.

"Is anything the matter with her?" cried Mrs Dashwood as she entered. "Is she ill?"

"I hope not," he replied, trying to look cheerful, and with a forced smile presently added, "It is I who may rather expect to be ill—for I am now suffering under a very heavy disappointment!"

"Disappointment?"

"Yes, for I am unable to keep my engagement with you. Mrs Smith has this morning exercised the privilege of riches upon a poor dependent cousin by sending me on business to London. I have just received my dispatches and taken my farewell of Allenham, and by way of exhilaration I am now come to take my farewell of you."

"To London! And are you going this morning?"

"Almost this moment."

"This is very unfortunate. But Mrs Smith must be obliged, and her business will not detain you from us long I hope."

He coloured as he replied, "You are very kind, but I have no idea of returning into Devonshire immediately. My visits to Mrs Smith are never repeated within the twelvemonth."

"And is Mrs Smith your only friend? Is Allenham the only house in the neighbourhood to which you will be welcome? For shame, Willoughby, can you wait for an invitation here?"

His colour increased, and with his eyes fixed on the ground he only replied, "You are too good."

Mrs Dashwood looked at Elinor with surprise. Elinor felt equal amazement. For a few moments everyone was silent. Mrs Dashwood first spoke.

"I have only to add, my dear Willoughby, that at Barton cottage you will always be welcome. I will not press you to return here immediately, because you only can judge how far that might be pleasing to Mrs Smith, and on this head I shall be no more disposed to question your judgement than to doubt your inclination."

"My engagements at present," replied Willoughby confusedly, "are of such a nature—that—I dare not flatter myself—"

He stopped. Mrs Dashwood was too much astonished to speak, and another pause succeeded. This was broken by Willoughby, who said with a faint smile, "It is folly to linger in this manner. I will not torment myself any longer by remaining among friends whose society it is impossible for me now to enjoy."

He then hastily took leave of them all and left the room. They saw him step into his carriage, and in a minute it was out of sight.

Mrs Dashwood felt too much for speech, and instantly quitted the parlour to give way in solitude to the concern and alarm which this sudden departure occasioned.

Elinor's uneasiness was at least equal to her mother's. She thought of what had just passed with anxiety and distrust. Willoughby's behaviour in taking leave of them, his embarrassment and affectation of cheerfulness, and above all his unwillingness to accept her mother's invitation—a backwardness so unlike a lover, so unlike himself at his effusive best—greatly disturbed her. One moment she feared that no serious design had ever been formed on his side, and the next that some unfortunate quarrel had taken place between him and her sister. The distress in which Marianne had quitted the room was such as a serious quarrel could most reasonably account for, though when she considered what Marianne's love for him was, a quarrel seemed almost impossible.

But whatever might be the particulars of their separation, her sister's affliction was indubitable, and she thought with the tenderest compassion of that violent sorrow which Marianne was in all probability not merely giving way to as a relief but feeding and encouraging as a duty.

In about half an hour her mother returned, and though her eyes were red, her countenance was not uncheerful.

"Our dear Willoughby is now some miles from Barton, Elinor," said she as she sat down to work, "and with how heavy a heart does he travel?"

"It is all very strange. So suddenly to be gone! It seems but the work of a moment. And last night he was with us so happy, so cheerful, so affectionate? And now, after only ten minutes' notice— Gone too without intending to return! Something more than what he owned to us must have happened. He did not speak, he did not behave like himself. You must have seen the difference as well as I. What can it be? Can they have quarrelled? Why else should he have shown such unwillingness to accept your invitation here?"

"It was not inclination that he wanted, Elinor, I could plainly see that. He had not the power of accepting it. I have thought it all over, I assure you, and I can perfectly account for everything that at first seemed strange to me as well as to you."

"Can you, indeed!"

"Yes. I have explained it to myself in the most satisfactory way, but you, Elinor, who love to doubt where you can — it will not satisfy *you*, I know, but you shall not talk *me* out of my trust in it. I am persuaded that Mrs Smith suspects his regard for Marianne, disapproves of it — perhaps because she has other views for him — and on that account is eager to get him away, and that the business which she sends him off to transact is invented as an excuse to dismiss him. This is what I believe to have happened. He is, moreover, aware that she does disapprove the connection. He dares not therefore at present confess to her his engagement with Marianne, and he feels himself obliged from his dependent situation to give into her schemes and absent himself from Devonshire for a while. You will tell me, I know, that this may or may not have happened, but I will listen to no cavil unless you can point out any other method of understanding the affair as satisfactory at this. And now, Elinor, what have you to say?"

"Nothing, for you have anticipated my answer."

"Then you would have told me that it might or might not have happened. Oh, Elinor, how incomprehensible are your feelings! You had rather take evil upon credit than good. You had rather look out for misery for Marianne and guilt for poor Willoughby than an apology for the latter. You are resolved to think him blameable because he took leave of us with less affection than his usual behaviour has shown. And is no allowance to be made for inadvertence or for spirits depressed by recent disappointment? Are no probabilities to be accepted merely because they are not certainties? Is nothing due to the man whom we have all such reason to love, and no reason in the world to think ill of? To the possibility of motives unanswerable in themselves, though unavoidably secret for a while? And after all, what is it you suspect him of?"

That her mother had dressed her down so earnestly undid Elinor and she sought her words carefully. "I can hardly tell myself. But suspicion of something unpleasant is the inevitable consequence of such an alteration as we just witnessed in him. There is great truth, however, in what you have now urged of the allowances which ought to be made for him, and it is my wish to be candid in my judgement of everybody. Willoughby may undoubtedly have very sufficient reasons for his conduct, and I will hope that he has. But it would have been more like Willoughby to acknowledge them at once. Secrecy may be advisable, but still I cannot help wondering at its being practised by him."

"Do not blame him, however, for departing from his character where the deviation is necessary. But you really do admit the justice of what I have said in his defence? I am happy — and he is acquitted."

"Not entirely. It may be proper to conceal their engagement, if they *are* engaged, from Mrs Smith — and if that is the case, it must be highly expedient for Willoughby to be but little in Devonshire at present. But this is no excuse for their concealing it from us."

"Concealing it from us! My dear child, do you accuse Willoughby and Marianne of concealment?

This is strange indeed when your eyes have been reproaching them every day for incautiousness."

"I want no proof of their affection," said Elinor, for that was evident each time one of them gazed upon the other, "but of their engagement I do."

"I am perfectly satisfied of both."

"Yet not a syllable has been said to you on the subject by either of them."

"I have not wanted syllables where actions have spoken so plainly. Has not his behaviour to Marianne and to all of us for at least the last fortnight declared that he loved and considered her as his future wife, and that he felt for us the attachment of the nearest relation? Have we not perfectly understood each other? Has not my consent been daily asked by his looks, his manner, his attentive and affectionate respect? My Elinor, is it possible to doubt their engagement? How could such a thought occur to you? How is it to be supposed that Willoughby, persuaded as he must be of your sister's love, should leave her and leave her perhaps for months without telling her of his affection—that they should part without a mutual exchange of confidence?"

"I confess," replied Elinor, hoping against hope to convince her mother of her own view of the matter, "that every circumstance except one is in favour of their engagement, but that one is the total silence of both on the subject, and with me it almost outweighs every other."

"How strange this is! You must think wretchedly indeed of Willoughby if after all that has openly passed between them you can doubt the nature of the terms on which they are together. Has he been acting a part in his behaviour to your sister all this time? Do you suppose him really indifferent to her?"

"No, I cannot think that. He must and does love her, I am sure." *I have seen his passion with my own eyes. Heard it from their lips. Understood hers as love for him. But is his passion proof of his devotion? Or do I deceive myself?*

"But with a strange kind of tenderness, if he can leave her with such indifference, such carelessness of the future, as you attribute to him."

"You must remember, my dear mother, that I have never considered this matter as certain." *I wish I could, for my sister's sake as well as yours, Mother.* "I have had my doubts, I confess, but they are fainter than they were, and they may soon be entirely done away. If we find they correspond, every fear of mine will be removed."

"A mighty concession indeed! If you were to see them at the altar, you would suppose they were going to be married. Ungracious girl! But I require no such proof. Nothing in my opinion has ever passed to justify doubt, no secrecy has been attempted, all has been uniformly open and unreserved. You cannot doubt your sister's wishes. It must be Willoughby therefore whom you suspect. But why? Is he not a man of honour and feeling? Has there been any inconsistency on his side to create alarm? Can he be deceitful?"

"I hope not, I believe not," cried Elinor. "I love Willoughby, sincerely love him, and suspicion of his integrity cannot be more painful to yourself than to me. It has been involuntary, and I will not encourage it. I was startled, I confess, by the alteration in his manners this morning. He did not speak like himself and did not return your kindness with any cordiality. But all this may be explained by such a situation of his affairs as you have supposed.

"He had just parted from my sister, had seen her leave him in the greatest affliction, and if he felt obliged from a fear of offending Mrs Smith to resist the temptation of returning here soon, and yet aware that by declining your invitation—by saying that he was going away for some time—he should seem to act an ungenerous, a suspicious part by our family, he might well be embarrassed and disturbed. In such a case a plain and open avowal of his difficulties would have been more to his honour, I think, as well as more consistent with his general character, but I will not raise objections against anyone's conduct on so illiberal a foundation as a difference in judgement from myself or a deviation from what I may think right and consistent."

"You speak very properly. Willoughby certainly does not deserve to be suspected. Though we have not known him long, he is no stranger in this part of the world, and who has ever spoken to his disadvantage? Had he been in a situation to act independently and marry immediately, it might have been odd that he should leave us without acknowledging everything to me at once—but this is not the case. It is an engagement in some respects not prosperously begun, for their marriage must be at a very uncertain distance, and even secrecy, as far as it can be observed, may now be very advisable."

They were interrupted by the entrance of Margaret, and Elinor was then at liberty to think over the representations of her mother, to acknowledge the probability of many and hope for the justice of all.

They saw nothing of Marianne till dinner time, when she entered the room and took her place at the table without saying a word. Her eyes were red and swollen, and it seemed as if her tears were even then restrained with difficulty. She avoided the looks of them all, could neither eat nor speak and after some time, on her mother's silently pressing her hand with tender compassion, her small degree of fortitude was quite overcome. She burst into tears and left the room.

This violent oppression of spirits continued the whole evening. She was without any power, because she was without any desire of command over herself. The slightest mention of anything relative to Willoughby overpowered her in an instant, and though her family were most anxiously attentive to her comfort, it was impossible for them, if they spoke at all, to keep clear of every subject which her feelings connected with him.

Chapter Sixteen

Marianne would have thought herself very inexcusable had she been able to sleep at all the first night after parting from Willoughby. She would have been ashamed to look her family in the face the next morning had she not risen from her bed in more need of repose than when she lay down in it. But the feelings which made such composure a disgrace left her in no danger of incurring it. She was awake the whole night recalling every ecstatic minute she had spent in his company with his hands and lips and teeth upon her body, and she wept the greatest part of it. She got up with a headache, was unable to talk and unwilling to take any nourishment, giving pain every moment to her mother and sisters and forbidding all attempt at consolation from either. Her sensibility was potent enough!

When breakfast was over she walked out by herself and wandered about the village of Allenham, indulging the recollection of past enjoyment and crying over the present reverse for the chief of the morning. She noted every bend in the road where he had paused them and enveloped her in his strong arms. She smiled sadly at every tree where he had pressed her to the trunk, reached inside her bodice and rubbed her nipples and blessed them with his perfect mouth. She let her tears dribble down her cheeks when she saw each flower he might have picked for her, each bud of nature's glory to which he compared her plump petals and her sweet body's nectar.

The evening passed off in the equal indulgence of feeling. She played over every favourite song that she had been used to play to Willoughby, every air in which their voices had been oftenest joined, and sat at the instrument gazing on every line of music that he had written out for her till her heart was so heavy that no farther sadness could be gained. This nourishment of grief was every day applied. She spent whole hours at the pianoforte alternately singing and crying, her voice often totally suspended by her tears. In books too as well as in music she courted the misery which a contrast between the past and present was certain of giving. She read nothing but what they had been used to read together.

Such violence of affliction indeed could not be supported forever. It sank within a few days into a calmer melancholy, but these employments to which she daily recurred, her solitary walks and silent meditations, still produced occasional effusions of sorrow as lively as ever. She took to recreating Willoughby's caresses using her own hand to caress her breasts, bringing them to a high hard ache, then finally invaded her own cunny with her desperate fingertips. There she brought herself that self-same rapture which she had falsely concluded only he might offer her. The revelation that she might ease her want of him by her own hand startled her, confused her, but then delighted her. She created her own fantasies of him still with her, whispering his lewd love that so excited her. Soon, her hands were busy nigh unto each hour bringing herself the bliss that had so cruelly been torn from her.

No letter from Willoughby came and none seemed expected by Marianne. Her mother was surprised, and Elinor again became uneasy. But Mrs Dashwood could find explanations whenever she wanted them, which at least satisfied herself.

"Remember, Elinor," said she, "how very often Sir John fetches our letters himself from the post and carries them to it. We have already agreed that secrecy may be necessary, and we must acknowledge that it could not be maintained if their correspondence were to pass through Sir John's hands."

Elinor could not deny the truth of this, and she tried to find in it a motive sufficient for their silence. But there was one method so direct, so simple, and in her opinion so eligible of knowing the real state of the affair and of instantly removing all mystery that she could not help suggesting it to her mother.

"Why do you not ask Marianne at once," said she, nearly mad with the question of her sister's status so hanging over their heads, "whether she is or she is not engaged to Willoughby? From you, her mother, and so kind, so indulgent a mother, the question could not give offence. It would be the natural result of your affection for her. She used to be all unreserve, and to you more especially."

"I would not ask such a question for the world. Supposing it possible that they are not engaged, what distress would not such an enquiry inflict! At any rate it would be most ungenerous. I should never deserve her confidence again after forcing from her a confession of what is meant at present to be unacknowledged to anyone. I know Marianne's heart — I know that she dearly loves me, and that I shall not be the last to whom the affair is made known when circumstances make the revealment of it eligible. I would not attempt to force the confidence of anyone, of a child much less, because a sense of duty would prevent the denial which her wishes might direct."

Elinor thought this generosity overstrained considering her sister's youth, and urged the matter farther, but in vain. Common sense, common care, common prudence were all sunk in Mrs Dashwood's romantic delicacy. Elinor was left to wring her hands and gnash her teeth at the tensions of not knowing.

It was several days before Willoughby's name was mentioned before Marianne by any of her family. Sir John and Mrs Jennings indeed were not so nice. Their witticisms added pain to many a painful hour, but one evening Mrs Dashwood, accidentally taking up a volume of Shakespeare, exclaimed, "We have never finished *Hamlet*, Marianne. Our dear Willoughby went away before we could get through it. We will put it by that when he comes again... But it may be months perhaps before that happens."

"Months!" cried Marianne with strong surprise. "No — nor many weeks."

Mrs Dashwood was sorry for what she had said, but it gave Elinor pleasure, as it produced a reply from Marianne so expressive of confidence in Willoughby and knowledge of his intentions.

One morning, about a week after his leaving the country, Marianne was prevailed on to join her sisters in their usual walk instead of wandering away by herself. Hitherto she had carefully avoided every companion in her rambles. If her sisters intended to walk on the downs, she directly stole away towards the lanes. If they talked of the valley, she was as speedy in climbing the hills, and could never be found when the others set off. But at length she was secured by the exertions of Elinor, who greatly disapproved such continual seclusion.

They walked along the road through the valley, and chiefly in silence, for Marianne's mind could not be controlled and Elinor, satisfied with gaining one point, would not then attempt more. Beyond the entrance of the valley, where the country, though still rich, was less wild and more open, a long stretch of the road which they had travelled on first coming to Barton lay before them. On reaching that point they stopped to look around them and examine a prospect which formed the distance of their view from the cottage, from a spot which they had never happened to reach in any of their walks before.

Amongst the objects in the scene, they soon discovered an animated one. It was a man on horseback riding towards them. In a few minutes they could distinguish him to be a gentleman, and in a moment afterwards Marianne rapturously exclaimed, "It is he, it is indeed, I know it is!" and was hastening to meet him when Elinor cried out, "Indeed, Marianne, I think you are mistaken. It is not Willoughby. The person is not tall enough for him and has not his air."

"He has, he has," cried Marianne. "I am sure he has. His air, his coat, his horse. I knew how soon he would come."

She walked eagerly on as she spoke, and Elinor, to screen Marianne from particularity, as she felt almost certain of its not being Willoughby, quickened her pace and kept up with her. They were soon within thirty yards of the gentleman. Marianne looked again. Her heart sank within her, and abruptly turning round, she was hurrying back when the voices of both her sisters were raised to detain her. A third, almost as well-known as Willoughby's, joined them in begging her to stop, and she turned round with surprise to see and welcome Edward Ferrars.

He was the only person in the world who could at that moment be forgiven for not being Willoughby, the only one who could have gained a smile from her. But she dispersed her tears to smile on him, and in her sister's happiness forgot for a time her own disappointment.

He dismounted, and giving his horse to his servant, walked back with them to Barton, whither he was purposely coming to visit them.

He was welcomed by them all with great cordiality, but especially by Marianne, who showed more warmth of regard in her reception of him than even Elinor herself. To Marianne, indeed, the meeting between Edward and her sister was but a continuation of that unaccountable coldness which she had often observed at Norland in their mutual behaviour. On Edward's side more particularly there was a deficiency of all that a lover ought to look and say on such an occasion. He was confused, seemed scarcely sensible of pleasure in seeing them, looked neither rapturous nor gay, said little but what was forced from him by questions and distinguished Elinor by no mark of affection. He but removed his hat, bowed and offered his joy at seeing them, all of them.

Marianne saw and listened with increasing surprise. She began almost to feel a dislike of Edward, and it ended, as every feeling must end with her, by carrying back her thoughts to Willoughby, whose manners formed a contrast sufficiently striking to those of his brother elect.

After a short silence which succeeded the first surprise and enquiries of meeting, Marianne asked Edward if he came directly from London. No, he had been in Devonshire a fortnight.

"A fortnight!" she repeated, surprised at his being so long in the same county with Elinor without seeing her before.

He looked rather distressed as he added that he had been staying with some friends near Plymouth.

"Have you been lately in Sussex?" said Elinor.

"I was at Norland about a month ago."

"And how does dear, dear Norland look?" cried Marianne.

"Dear, dear Norland," said Elinor, "probably looks much as it always does at this time of the year. The woods and walks thickly covered with dead leaves."

"Oh," cried Marianne, "with what transporting sensation have I formerly seen them fall! How have I delighted as I walked to see them driven in showers about me by the wind! What feelings have they, the season, the air altogether inspired! Now there is no one to regard them. They are seen only as a nuisance, swept hastily off and driven as much as possible from the sight."

"It is not everyone," said Elinor, "who has your passion for dead leaves."

"No, my feelings are not often shared, not often understood. But sometimes they are." As she said this she sank into a reverie for a few moments, but rousing herself again, "Now, Edward," said she, calling his attention to the prospect, "here is Barton Valley. Look up to it, and be tranquil if you can. Look at those hills! Did you ever see their equals? To the left is Barton Park, amongst those woods and plantations. You may see the end of the house. And there, beneath that farthest hill which rises with such grandeur, is our cottage."

"It is a beautiful country," he replied, "but these bottoms must be dirty in winter."

"How can you think of dirt with such objects before you?"

"Because," replied he, smiling, "among the rest of the objects before me, I see a very dirty lane."

"How strange!" said Marianne to herself as she walked on.

"Have you an agreeable neighbourhood here? Are the Middletons pleasant people?"

"No, not all," answered Marianne uncharitably, "we could not be more unfortunately situated."

"Marianne," cried her sister, "how can you say so? How can you be so unjust? They are a very respectable family, Mr Ferrars, and towards us have behaved in the friendliest manner. Have you forgot, Marianne, how many pleasant days we have owed to them?"

"No," said Marianne, in a low voice, "nor how many painful moments."

Elinor took no notice of this, and directing her attention to their visitor endeavoured to support something like discourse with him by talking of their present residence, its conveniences, etc. extorting from him occasional questions and remarks. His coldness and reserve mortified her severely given the nature of their last encounter. She was vexed and half angry, but resolving to regulate her behaviour to him by the past rather than the present, she avoided every appearance of resentment or displeasure and treated him as she thought he ought to be treated from the family connection.

Chapter Seventeen

Mrs Dashwood was surprised only for a moment at seeing him, for his coming to Barton was in her opinion of all things the most natural. Her joy and expression of regard long outlived her wonder. He received the kindest welcome from her, and shyness, coldness, reserve could not stand against such a reception. They had begun to fail him before he entered the house, and they were quite overcome by the captivating manners of Mrs Dashwood. Indeed a man could not very well be in love with either of her daughters without extending the passion to her, and Elinor had the satisfaction of seeing him soon become more like himself. His affections seemed to reanimate towards them all, and his interest in their welfare again became perceptible. He was not in spirits, however—he praised their house, admired its prospect, was attentive and kind, but still he was not in spirits. The whole family perceived it, and Mrs Dashwood, attributing it to some want of liberality in his mother, sat down to table indignant against all selfish parents.

"What are Mrs Ferrars' views for you at present, Edward?" said she when dinner was over and they had drawn round the fire. "Are you still to be a great orator in spite of yourself?"

"No. I hope my mother is now convinced that I have no more talents than inclination for a public life!"

"But how is your fame to be established? For famous you must be to satisfy all your family, and with no inclination for expense, no affection for strangers, no profession and no assurance, you may find it a difficult matter."

"I shall not attempt it. I have no wish to be distinguished, and have every reason to hope I never shall. Thank Heaven! I cannot be forced into genius and eloquence."

"You have no ambition, I well know. Your wishes are all moderate."

"As moderate as those of the rest of the world, I believe. Happily middling in profession, income, taste and mate."

At the mention of a partner, and in such a manner, Elinor bristled. Of late she had much considered her own predilection for moderation in all things. On the one hand, she liked her own tendency towards it, yet she questioned what it had brought her. The moments with Edward at Norland had been ones of greatest bliss, yet they were fleeing, dimmed by time. She was yet young, she told herself, and could change her character if she wished. One fact which argued against acquiring a more emotional nature was the current state of inertia between the passionate and irrepressible Marianne and Willoughby.

Edward continued to answer her mother. "I wish as well as everybody else to be perfectly happy, but, like everybody else it must be in my own way. Greatness will not make me so."

"Strange that it would!" cried Marianne. "What have wealth or grandeur to do with happiness?"

"Grandeur has but little," said Elinor, "but wealth has much to do with it."

"Elinor, for shame!" said Marianne. "Money can only give happiness where there is nothing else to give it. Beyond a competence, it can afford no real satisfaction, as far as mere self is concerned."

"Perhaps," said Elinor, smiling, "we may come to the same point. Your competence and my wealth are very much alike, I dare say, and without them, as the world goes now, we shall both agree that every kind of external comfort must be wanting. Your ideas are only more noble than mine. Come, what is your competence?"

"About eighteen hundred or two thousand a year, not more than that."

Elinor laughed. "Two thousand a year! One is my wealth! I guessed how it would end."

"And yet two thousand a year is a very moderate income," said Marianne. "A family cannot well be maintained on a smaller. I am sure I am not extravagant in my demands. A proper establishment of servants, a carriage, perhaps two, and hunters cannot be supported on less."

Elinor smiled again, to hear her sister describing so accurately their future expenses at Combe Magna.

"Hunters!" repeated Edward. "But why must you have hunters? Everybody does not hunt."

Marianne coloured as she replied, "But most people do."

"I wish," said Margaret, striking out a novel thought, "that somebody would give us all a large fortune apiece!"

"Oh that they would!" cried Marianne, her eyes sparkling with animation and her cheeks glowing with the delight of such imaginary happiness.

"We are all unanimous in that wish, I suppose," said Elinor, "in spite of the insufficiency of wealth."

"Oh dear!" cried Margaret. "How happy I should be! I wonder what I should do with it!"

Marianne looked as if she had no doubt on that point.

"I should be puzzled to spend so large a fortune myself," said Mrs Dashwood, "if my children were all to be rich without my help."

"You must begin your improvements on this house," observed Elinor, "and your difficulties will soon vanish."

"What magnificent orders would travel from this family to London," said Edward, "in such an event! What a happy day for booksellers, music-sellers and print-shops! You, Miss Dashwood, would give a general commission for every new print of merit to be sent you—and as for Marianne, I know her greatness of soul, there would not be music enough in London to content her. And books! Thomson, Cowper, Scott— she would buy them all over and over again—she would buy up every copy, I believe, to prevent their falling into unworthy hands, and she would have every book that tells her how to admire an old twisted tree. Should not you, Marianne? Forgive me if I am very saucy. But I was willing to show you that I had not forgot our old disputes."

"I love to be reminded of the past, Edward— whether it be melancholy or gay, I love to recall it—

and you will never offend me by talking of former times. You are very right in supposing how my money would be spent—some of it, at least—my loose cash would certainly be employed in improving my collection of music and books."

"And the bulk of your fortune would be laid out in annuities on the authors or their heirs."

"No, Edward, I should have something else to do with it."

"Perhaps, then, you would bestow it as a reward on that person who wrote the ablest defence of your favourite maxim, that no one can ever be in love more than once in their life—your opinion on that point is unchanged, I presume?"

"Undoubtedly. At my time of life opinions are tolerably fixed. It is not likely that I should now see or hear anything to change them."

"Marianne is as steadfast as ever, you see," said Elinor, "she is not at all altered."

"She is only grown a little more grave than she was."

"Nay, Edward," said Marianne, "you need not reproach me. You are not very gay yourself."

"Why should you think so!" replied he with a sigh. "But gaiety never was a part of my character."

"Nor do I think it a part of Marianne's," said Elinor. "I should hardly call her a lively girl—she is very earnest, very eager in all she does—sometimes talks a great deal and always with animation—but she is not often really merry."

"I believe you are right," he replied, "and yet I have always set her down as a lively girl."

"I have frequently detected myself in such kind of mistakes," said Elinor, "in a total misapprehension of character in some point or other—fancying people so much more gay or grave, or ingenious or stupid than they really are, and I can hardly tell why or in what the deception originated. Sometimes one is guided by what they say of themselves, and very frequently by what other people say of them, without giving oneself time to deliberate and judge."

"But I thought it was right, Elinor," said Marianne, "to be guided wholly by the opinion of other people. I thought our judgements were given us merely to be subservient to those of neighbours. This has always been your doctrine, I am sure."

"No, Marianne, never. My doctrine has never aimed at the subjection of the understanding. All I have ever attempted to influence has been the behaviour. You must not confound my meaning. I am guilty, I confess, of having often wished you to treat our acquaintance in general with greater attention, but when have I advised you to adopt their sentiments or to conform to their judgement in serious matters?"

"You have not been able to bring your sister over to your plan of general civility," said Edward to Elinor. "Do you gain no ground?"

"Quite the contrary," replied Elinor, looking expressively at Marianne.

"My judgement," he returned, "is all on your side of the question, but I am afraid my practice is much more on your sister's. I never wish to offend, but I am so foolishly shy that I often seem negligent when I am only kept back by my natural awkwardness. I have frequently thought that I must have been intended by nature to be fond of low company. I am so little at my ease among strangers of gentility!"

"Marianne has not shyness to excuse any inattention of hers," said Elinor.

"She knows her own worth too well for false shame," replied Edward. "Shyness is only the effect of a sense of inferiority in some way or other. If I could persuade myself that my manners were perfectly easy and graceful, I should not be shy."

"But you would still be reserved," said Marianne, "and that is worse."

Edward started. "Reserved! Am I reserved, Marianne?"

"Yes, very."

"I do not understand you," replied he, colouring. "Reserved! How, in what manner? What am I to tell you? What can you suppose?"

Elinor looked surprised at his emotion, but trying to laugh off the subject, she said to him, "Do not you know my sister well enough to understand what she means? Do not you know she calls everyone reserved who does not talk as fast and admire what she admires as rapturously as herself?"

Edward made no answer. His gravity and thoughtfulness returned on him in their fullest extent — and he sat for some time silent and dull.

When the hour grew late and Marianne and her mother left Edward alone with Elinor, she hoped he might be more at ease. As she probed him on the subject of his family's health, he replied with no emotion at all.

Flummoxed, Elinor rose and told him she would retire.

Jumping up, he caught her hand and pressed it to his heart. "My Elinor, how I have wished for a moment alone with you. All these months — "

Searching his eyes for an indication of his intent, she waited.

But he stepped backward and she was left to wonder aloud why he had come here.

"To visit. To see you again. To enjoy your discourse."

So then, he had not come to do more than spend his days with her and her family. What a disappointment this was after those erotic minutes in his arms at Norland.

Collecting herself, she gave him a small smile. "And we welcome you, Edward. I am off to my bed. See you in the morning at breakfast, shall I?"

And she turned on her heel to leave him to his thoughts.

Chapter Eighteen

Elinor saw with great uneasiness the low spirits of her friend. His visit afforded her but a very partial satisfaction while his own enjoyment in it appeared so imperfect. It was evident that he was unhappy — she wished it were equally evident that he still distinguished her by the same affection which once she had felt no doubt of inspiring. But hitherto the continuance of his preference seemed very uncertain, and the reservedness of his manner towards her contradicted one moment what a more animated look had intimated the preceding one.

He joined her and Marianne in the breakfast room the next morning before the others were down, and Marianne, who was always eager to promote their happiness as far as she could, soon left them to themselves.

"I have forgotten my cloak and I do wish a walk before I take my breakfast," she told them as she rose, noting how stiff Edward seemed, not even venturing to sit close to Elinor as once he had always preferred.

Indeed she saw Elinor gaze at Edward longingly which hastened her own retreat. But before she was halfway upstairs she heard the parlour door open, and turning round, was astonished to see Edward himself come out.

"I am going into the village to see my horses," said he. "As you are not yet ready for breakfast, I shall be back again presently."

Edward returned to them with fresh admiration of the surrounding country. In his walk to the village he had seen many parts of the valley to advantage, and the village itself, in a much higher situation than the cottage, afforded a general view of the whole which had exceedingly pleased him. This was a subject which ensured Marianne's attention, and she was beginning to describe her own admiration of these scenes and to question him more minutely on the objects that had particularly struck him when Edward interrupted her by saying, "You must not enquire too far, Marianne — remember I have no knowledge in the picturesque, and I shall offend you by my ignorance and want of taste if we come to particulars. I shall call hills steep which ought to be bold, surfaces strange and uncouth which ought to be irregular and rugged, and distant objects out of sight which ought only to be indistinct through the soft medium of a hazy atmosphere.

"You must be satisfied with such admiration as I can honestly give. I call it a very fine country — the hills are steep, the woods seem full of fine timber and the valley looks comfortable and snug — with rich meadows and several neat farm houses scattered here and there. It exactly answers my idea of a fine country, because it unites beauty with utility — and I dare say it is a picturesque one too, because you admire it. I can easily believe it to be full of rocks and promontories, grey moss and brush wood, but these are all lost on me. I know nothing of the picturesque."

"I am afraid it is but too true," said Marianne, "but why should you boast of it?"

"I suspect," said Elinor, "that to avoid one kind of affectation, Edward here falls into another. Because he believes many people pretend to more admiration of the beauties of nature than they really feel, and is disgusted with such pretensions, he affects greater indifference and less discrimination in viewing them himself than he possesses. He is fastidious and will have an affectation of his own."

"It is very true," said Marianne, "that admiration of landscape scenery is become a mere jargon. Everybody pretends to feel and tries to describe with the taste and elegance of him who first defined what picturesque beauty was. I detest jargon of every kind, and sometimes I have kept my feelings to myself because I could find no language to describe them in but what was worn and hackneyed out of all sense and meaning."

"I am convinced," said Edward, "that you really feel all the delight in a fine prospect which you profess to feel. But in return, your sister must allow me to feel no more than I profess. I like a fine prospect, but not on picturesque principles. I do not like crooked, twisted, blasted trees. I admire them much more if they are tall, straight and flourishing. I do not like ruined, tattered cottages. I am not fond of nettles or thistles or heath blossoms. I have more pleasure in a snug farmhouse than a watchtower—and a troop of tidy, happy villages please me better than the finest banditti in the world."

Marianne looked with amazement at Edward, with compassion at her sister. Elinor only laughed.

The subject was continued no farther, and Marianne remained thoughtfully silent till a new object suddenly engaged her attention. She was sitting by Edward, and in taking his tea from Mrs Dashwood, his hand passed so directly before her as to make a ring with a plait of hair in the centre very conspicuous on one of his fingers.

"I never saw you wear a ring before, Edward," she cried. "Is that Fanny's hair? I remember her promising to give you some. But I should have thought her hair had been darker."

Marianne spoke inconsiderately what she really felt—but when she saw how much she had pained Edward, her own vexation at her want of thought could not be surpassed by his. He coloured very deeply, and giving a momentary glance at Elinor, replied, "Yes, it is my sister's hair. The setting always casts a different shade on it, you know."

Elinor had met his eye and looked conscious likewise. That the hair was her own she instantaneously felt as well satisfied as Marianne. The only difference in their conclusions was, that what Marianne considered as a free gift from her sister, Elinor was conscious must have been procured by some theft or contrivance unknown to herself. She was not in a humour, however, to regard it as an affront, and affecting to take no notice of what passed by instantly talking of something else, she internally resolved henceforward to catch every opportunity of eyeing the hair and of satisfying herself beyond all doubt that it was exactly the shade of her own.

Edward's embarrassment lasted some time, and it ended in an absence of mind still more settled. He was particularly grave the whole morning. Marianne severely censured herself for what she had said, but her own forgiveness might have been more speedy had she known how little offence it had given her sister.

Before the middle of the day, they were visited by Sir John and Mrs Jennings, who, having heard of the arrival of a gentleman at the cottage, came to take a survey of the guest. With the assistance of his mother-in-law, Sir John was not long in discovering that the name of Ferrars began with an F and this prepared a future mine of raillery against the devoted Elinor which nothing but the newness of their acquaintance with Edward could have prevented from being immediately sprung. But as it was, she only learned from some very significant looks how far their penetration, founded on Margaret's instructions, extended.

Sir John never came to the Dashwoods without either inviting them to dine at the park the next day or to drink tea with them that evening. On the present occasion, for the better entertainment of their visitor, towards whose amusement he felt himself bound to contribute, he wished to engage them for both.

"You must drink tea with us tonight," said he, "for we shall be quite alone—and tomorrow you must absolutely dine with us, for we shall be a large party."

Mrs Jennings enforced the necessity. "And who knows but you may raise a dance," said she. "And that will tempt you, Miss Marianne."

"A dance!" cried Marianne. "Impossible! Who is to dance?"

"Who! Why yourselves, and the Careys and Whitakers to be sure. What, you thought nobody could dance because a certain person that shall be nameless is gone!"

"I wish with all my soul," cried Sir John, "that Willoughby were among us again."

This and Marianne's blushing gave new suspicions to Edward. "And who is Willoughby?" said he in a low voice to Miss Dashwood, by whom he was sitting.

She gave him a brief reply. Marianne's countenance was more communicative. Edward saw enough to comprehend not only the meaning of others but such of Marianne's expressions as had puzzled him before. When their visitors left them he went immediately round her and said in a whisper, "I have been guessing. Shall I tell you my guess?"

"What do you mean?"

"Shall I tell you?"

"Certainly."

"Well then, I guess that Mr Willoughby hunts."

Marianne was surprised and confused, yet she could not help smiling at the quiet archness of his manner, and after a moment's silence, said, "Oh, Edward! How can you? But the time will come I hope... I am sure you will like him."

"I do not doubt it," replied he, rather astonished at her earnestness and warmth. Had he not imagined it to be a joke for the good of her acquaintance in general, founded only on a something or a nothing between Mr Willoughby and herself, he would not have ventured to mention it.

Chapter Nineteen

Edward remained a week at the cottage. He was earnestly pressed by Mrs Dashwood to stay longer, but, as if he were bent only on self-mortification, he seemed resolved to be gone when his enjoyment among his friends was at the height. His spirits during the last two or three days, though still very unequal, were greatly improved. He grew more and more partial to the house and environs—never spoke of going away without a sigh—declared his time to be wholly disengaged—even doubted to what place he should go when he left them—but still, go he must.

Never had any week passed so quickly—he could hardly believe it to be gone. He said so repeatedly. Other things he said too which marked the turn of his feelings and gave the lie to his actions. He had no pleasure at Norland, he detested being in town, but either to Norland or London he must go. He valued their kindness beyond anything, and his greatest happiness was in being with them. Yet he must leave them at the end of a week, in spite of their wishes and his own, and without any restraint on his time.

Elinor placed all that was astonishing in this way of acting to his mother's account. It was happy for her that he had a mother whose character was so imperfectly known to her as to be the general excuse for everything strange on the part of her son. Disappointed, however, and vexed as she was, and sometimes displeased with his uncertain behaviour to herself, she was very well disposed on the whole to regard his actions with all the candid allowances and generous qualifications which had been rather more painfully extorted from her for Willoughby's service by her mother. His want of spirits, of openness and of consistency were most usually attributed to his want of independence and his better knowledge of Mrs Ferrars' disposition and designs. The shortness of his visit, the steadiness of his purpose in leaving them originated in the same fettered inclination, the same inevitable necessity of temporising with his mother. The old well-established grievance of duty against will, parent against child, was the cause of all.

She would have been glad to know when these difficulties were to cease, this opposition was to yield, when Mrs Ferrars would be reformed and her son be at liberty to be happy. But from such vain wishes she was forced to turn for comfort to the renewal of her confidence in Edward's affection, to the remembrance of every mark of regard in look or word which fell from him while at Barton, and above all to that flattering proof of it which he constantly wore round his finger.

"I think, Edward," said Mrs Dashwood, as they were at breakfast the last morning, "you would be a happier man if you had any profession to engage your time and give an interest to your plans and actions. Some inconvenience to your friends, indeed, might result from it — you would not be able to give them so much of your time. But" — with a smile — "you would be materially benefited in one particular at least — you would know where to go when you left them."

"I do assure you," he replied, "that I have long thought on this point as you think now. It has been, and is, and probably will always be a heavy misfortune to me that I have had no necessary business to engage me, no profession to give me employment or afford me anything like independence. But unfortunately my own nicety, and the nicety of my friends, have made me what I am — an idle, helpless being.

"We never could agree in our choice of a profession. I always preferred the church, as I still do. But that was not smart enough for my family. They recommended the army. That was a great deal too smart for me. The law was allowed to be genteel enough. Many young men who had chambers in the Temple made a very good appearance in the first circles and drove about town in very knowing gigs. But I had no inclination for the law, even in this less abstruse study of it which my family approved. As for the navy, it had fashion on its side, but I was too old when the subject was first started to enter it. And at length, as there was no necessity for my having any profession at all, as I might be as dashing and expensive without a red coat on my back as with one, idleness was pronounced on the whole to be most advantageous and honourable, and a young man of eighteen is not in general so earnestly bent on being busy as to resist the solicitations of his friends to do nothing. I was therefore entered at Oxford and have been properly idle ever since."

"The consequence of which, I suppose, will be," said Mrs Dashwood, "since leisure has not promoted your own happiness, that your sons will be brought up to as many pursuits, employments, professions and trades as Columella's."

"They will be brought up," said he in a serious accent, "to be as unlike myself as is possible. In feeling, in action, in condition, in everything."

"Come, come, this is all an effusion of immediate want of spirits, Edward. You are in a melancholy humour, and fancy that anyone unlike yourself must be happy. But remember that the pain of parting from friends will be felt by everybody at times, whatever be their education or state. Know your own happiness. You want nothing but patience—or give it a more fascinating name, call it hope. Your mother will secure to you in time that independence you are so anxious for. It is her duty, and it will, it must ere long become her happiness to prevent your whole youth from being wasted in discontent. How much may not a few months do?"

"I think," replied Edward, "that I may defy many months to produce any good to me."

This desponding turn of mind, though it could not be communicated to Mrs Dashwood, gave additional pain to them all in the parting, which shortly took place in the same placid manner as his arrival and left an uncomfortable impression on Elinor's feelings especially, which required some trouble and time to subdue. But as it was her determination to subdue it, and to prevent herself from appearing to suffer more than what all her family suffered on his going away, she did not adopt the method so judiciously employed by Marianne on a similar occasion to augment and fix her sorrow by seeking silence, solitude and idleness. Their means were as different as their objects, and equally suited to the advancement of each.

Elinor sat down to her drawing table as soon as he was out of the house, busily employed herself the whole day, neither sought nor avoided the mention of his name, appeared to interest herself almost as much as ever in the general concerns of the family. And if by this conduct she did not lessen her own grief, it was at least prevented from unnecessary increase, and her mother and sisters were spared much solicitude on her account.

Such behaviour as this, so exactly the reverse of her own, appeared no more meritorious to Marianne than her own had seemed faulty to her. The business of self-command she settled very easily—with strong affections it was impossible, with calm ones it could have no merit. That her sister's affections were calm she dared not deny, though she blushed to acknowledge it, and of the strength of her own she gave a very striking proof by still loving and respecting that sister in spite of this mortifying conviction.

Without shutting herself up from her family, or leaving the house in determined solitude to avoid them, or lying awake the whole night to indulge meditation, Elinor found every day afforded her leisure enough to think of Edward and of Edward's behaviour in every possible variety which the different state of her spirits at different times could produce—with tenderness, pity, approbation, censure and doubt. There were moments in abundance when, if not by the absence of her mother and sisters, at least by the nature of their employments, conversation was forbidden among them and every effect of solitude was produced. Her mind was inevitably at liberty, her thoughts could not be chained elsewhere, and the past and the future on a subject so interesting must be before her, must force her attention and engross her memory, her reflection and her fancy.

From a reverie of this kind, as she sat at her drawing table, she was roused one morning soon after Edward's leaving them by the arrival of company. She happened to be quite alone. The closing of the little gate at the entrance of the green court in front of the house drew her eyes to the window, and she saw a large party walking up to the door. Amongst them were Sir John and Lady Middleton and Mrs Jennings, but there were two others, a gentleman and lady, who were quite unknown to her. She was sitting near the window, and as soon as Sir John perceived her he left the rest of the party to the ceremony of knocking at the door and, stepping across the turf, obliged her to open the casement to speak to him. Though the space was so short between the door and the window as to make it hardly possible to speak at one without being heard at the other.

"Well," said he, "we have brought you some strangers. How do you like them?"

"Hush! They will hear you."

"Never mind if they do. It is only the Palmers. Charlotte is very pretty, I can tell you. You may see her if you look this way."

As Elinor was certain of seeing her in a couple of minutes without taking that liberty, she begged to be excused.

"Where is Marianne? Has she run away because we are come? I see her instrument is open."

"She is walking, I believe."

They were now joined by Mrs Jennings, who had not patience enough to wait till the door was opened before she told her story. She came hallooing to the window. "How do you do, my dear? How does Mrs Dashwood do? And where are your sisters? What, all alone! you will be glad of a little company to sit with you. I have brought my other son and daughter to see you. Only think of their coming so suddenly! I thought I heard a carriage last night while we were drinking our tea, but it never entered my head that it could be them. I thought of nothing but whether it might not be Colonel Brandon come back again, so I said to Sir John, 'I do think I hear a carriage, perhaps it is Colonel Brandon come back again—'"

Elinor was obliged to turn from her in the middle of her story to receive the rest of the party. Lady Middleton introduced the two strangers. Mrs Dashwood and Margaret came downstairs at the same time, and they all sat down to look at one another while Mrs Jennings continued her story as she walked through the passage into the parlour, attended by Sir John.

Mrs Palmer was several years younger than Lady Middleton and totally unlike her in every respect. She was short and plump, had a very pretty face and the finest expression of good humour in it that could possibly be. Her manners were by no means so elegant as her sister's, but they were much more prepossessing. She came in with a smile, smiled all the time of her visit, except when she laughed, and smiled when she went away.

Her husband was a grave-looking young man of five or six and twenty, with an air of more fashion and sense than his wife, but of less willingness to please or be pleased. He entered the room with a look of self-consequence, slightly bowed to the ladies without speaking a word, and after briefly surveying them and their apartments took up a newspaper from the table and continued to read it as long as he stayed.

Mrs Palmer, on the contrary, who was strongly endowed by nature with a turn for being uniformly civil and happy, was hardly seated before her admiration of the parlour and everything in it burst forth.

"Well! What a delightful room this is! I never saw anything so charming! Only think, Mama, how it is improved since I was here last! I always thought it such a sweet place, ma'am" — turning to Mrs Dashwood — "but you have made it so charming! Only look, sister, how delightful everything is! How I should like such a house for myself! Should not you, Mr Palmer?"

Mr Palmer made her no answer, and did not even raise his eyes from the newspaper.

"Mr Palmer does not hear me," said she, laughing, "he never does sometimes. It is so ridiculous!"

This was quite a new idea to Mrs Dashwood. She had never been used to find wit in the inattention of anyone, and could not help looking with surprise at them both.

Mrs Jennings in the meantime talked on as loud as she could, and continued her account of their surprise the evening before on seeing their friends, without ceasing till everything was told. Mrs Palmer laughed heartily at the recollection of their astonishment, and everybody agreed two or three times over that it had been quite an agreeable surprise.

"You may believe how glad we all were to see them," added Mrs Jennings, leaning forward towards Elinor and speaking in a low voice as if she meant to be heard by no one else, though they were seated on different sides of the room, "but, however, I can't help wishing they had not travelled quite so fast, nor made such a long journey of it. They came all round by London upon account of some business. For you know" — nodding significantly and pointing to her daughter — "it was wrong in her situation. I wanted her to stay at home and rest this morning, but she would come with us, she longed so much to see you all!"

Mrs Palmer laughed and said it would not do her any harm.

"She expects to be confined in February," continued Mrs Jennings.

Lady Middleton could no longer endure such a conversation, and therefore exerted herself to ask Mr Palmer if there was any news in the paper.

"No, none at all," he replied, and read on.

"Here comes Marianne," cried Sir John. "Now, Palmer, you shall see a monstrous pretty girl."

He immediately went into the passage, opened the front door and ushered her in himself. Mrs Jennings asked her as soon as she appeared if she had not been to Allenham, and Mrs Palmer laughed so heartily at the question as to show she understood it. Mr Palmer looked up on her entering the room, stared at her some minutes then returned to his newspaper. Mrs Palmer's eye was now caught by the drawings which hung round the room. She got up to examine them.

"Oh, dear, how beautiful these are! Well, how delightful! Do but look, Mama, how sweet! I declare they are quite charming, I could look at them forever." And sitting down again, she very soon forgot that there were any such things in the room.

When Lady Middleton rose to go away, Mr Palmer rose also, laid down the newspaper, stretched himself and looked at them all around.

"My love, have you been asleep?" said his wife, laughing.

He made her no answer, and only observed after again examining the room that it was very low-pitched and that the ceiling was crooked. He then made his bow and departed with the rest.

Sir John had been very urgent with them all to spend the next day at the park. Mrs Dashwood, who did not choose to dine with them oftener than they dined at the cottage, absolutely refused on her own account. Her daughters might do as they pleased. But they had no curiosity to see how Mr and Mrs Palmer ate their dinner, and no expectation of pleasure from them in any other way. They attempted, therefore, likewise to excuse themselves. The weather was uncertain and not likely to be good. But Sir John would not be satisfied—the carriage should be sent for them and they must come. Lady Middleton too, though she did not press their mother, pressed them. Mrs Jennings and Mrs Palmer joined their entreaties. All seemed equally anxious to avoid a family party, and the young ladies were obliged to yield.

"Why should they ask us?" said Marianne as soon as they were gone. "The rent of this cottage is said to be low, but we have it on very hard terms if we are to dine at the park whenever anyone is staying either with them or with us."

"They mean no less to be civil and kind to us now," said Elinor, "by these frequent invitations than by those which we received from them a few weeks ago. The alteration is not in them, if their parties are grown tedious and dull. We must look for the change elsewhere."

Chapter Twenty

As the Miss Dashwoods entered the drawing room of the park the next day at one door, Mrs Palmer came running in at the other, looking as good-humoured and merry as before. She took them all most affectionately by the hand and expressed great delight in seeing them again.

"I am so glad to see you!" said she, seating herself between Elinor and Marianne. "It is so bad a day I was afraid you might not come, which would be a shocking thing, as we go away again tomorrow. We must go, for the Westons come to us next week, you know. It was quite a sudden thing our coming at all, and I knew nothing of it till the carriage was coming to the door, then Mr Palmer asked me if I would go with him to Barton. He is so droll! He never tells me anything! I am so sorry we cannot stay longer. However we shall meet again in town very soon, I hope."

They were obliged to put an end to such an expectation.

"Not go to town!" cried Mrs Palmer with a laugh. "I shall be quite disappointed if you do not. I could get the nicest house in world for you next door to ours in Hanover Square. You must come indeed. I am sure I shall be very happy to chaperon you at any time till I am confined, if Mrs Dashwood should not like to go into public."

They thanked her, but were obliged to resist all her entreaties.

"Oh, my love," cried Mrs Palmer to her husband, who just then entered the room, "you must help me to persuade the Miss Dashwoods to go to town this winter."

Her love made no answer, and after slightly bowing to the ladies, began complaining of the weather.

"How horrid all this is!" said he. "Such weather makes everything and everybody disgusting. Dullness is as much produced within doors as without by rain. It makes one detest all one's acquaintance. What the devil does Sir John mean by not having a billiard room in his house? How few people know what comfort is! Sir John is as stupid as the weather."

The rest of the company soon dropped in.

"I am afraid, Miss Marianne," said Sir John, "you have not been able to take your usual walk to Allenham today."

Marianne looked very grave and said nothing.

"Oh, don't be so sly before us," said Mrs Palmer, "for we know all about it, I assure you, and I admire your taste very much, for I think he is extremely handsome. We do not live a great way from him in the country, you know. Not above ten miles, I dare say."

"Much nearer thirty," said her husband.

"Ah, well, there is not much difference. I never was at his house, but they say it is a sweet pretty place."

"As vile a spot as I ever saw in my life," said Mr Palmer.

Marianne remained perfectly silent, though her countenance betrayed her interest in what was said.

"Is it very ugly?" continued Mrs Palmer. "Then it must be some other place that is so pretty I suppose."

When they were seated in the dining room, Sir John observed with regret that they were only eight all together.

"My dear," said he to his lady, "it is very provoking that we should be so few. Why did not you ask the Gilberts to come to us today?"

"Did not I tell you, Sir John, when you spoke to me about it before, that it could not be done? They dined with us last."

"You and I, Sir John," said Mrs Jennings, "should not stand upon such ceremony."

"Then you would be very ill-bred," cried Mr Palmer.

"My love, you contradict everybody," said his wife with her usual laugh. "Do you know that you are quite rude?"

"I did not know I contradicted anybody in calling your mother ill-bred."

"Ay, you may abuse me as you please," said the good-natured old lady, "you have taken Charlotte off my hands, and cannot give her back again. So there I have the whip hand of you."

Charlotte laughed heartily to think that her husband could not get rid of her, and exultingly said she did not care how cross he was to her, as they must live together. It was impossible for anyone to be more thoroughly good-natured or more determined to be happy than Mrs Palmer. The studied indifference, insolence and discontent of her husband gave her no pain, and when he scolded or abused her she was highly diverted.

"Mr Palmer is so droll!" said she in a whisper to Elinor. "He is always out of humour."

Elinor was not inclined, after a little observation, to give him credit for being so genuinely and unaffectedly ill-natured or ill-bred as he wished to appear. His temper might perhaps be a little soured by finding, like many others of his sex, that through some unaccountable bias in favour of beauty he was the husband of a very silly woman, but she knew that this kind of blunder was too common for any sensible man to be lastingly hurt by it. It was rather a wish of distinction, she believed, which produced his contemptuous treatment of everybody and his general abuse of everything before him. It was the desire of appearing superior to other people. The motive was too common to be wondered at, but the means, however they might succeed by establishing his superiority in ill-breeding, were not likely to attach anyone to him except his wife.

"Oh, my dear Miss Dashwood," said Mrs Palmer soon afterwards, "I have got such a favour to ask of you and your sister. Will you come and spend some time at Cleveland this Christmas? Now pray do, and come while the Westons are with us. You cannot think how happy I shall be! It will be quite delightful! My love," applying to her husband, "don't you long to have the Miss Dashwoods come to Cleveland?"

"Certainly," he replied, with a sneer. "I came into Devonshire with no other view."

"There now," said his lady, "you see Mr Palmer expects you, so you cannot refuse to come."

They both eagerly and resolutely declined her invitation.

"But indeed you must and shall come. I am sure you will like it of all things. The Westons will be with us, and it will be quite delightful. You cannot think what a sweet place Cleveland is, and we are so gay now, for Mr Palmer is always going about the country canvassing against the election, and so many people came to dine with us that I never saw before. It is quite charming! But poor fellow, it is very fatiguing to him, for he is forced to make everybody like him."

Elinor could hardly keep her countenance as she assented to the hardship of such an obligation.

"How charming it will be," said Charlotte, "when he is in Parliament! Won't it? How I shall laugh! It will be so ridiculous to see all his letters directed to him with an M.P. But do you know, he says, he will never frank for me? He declares he won't. Don't you, Mr Palmer?"

Mr Palmer took no notice of her.

"He cannot bear writing, you know," she continued, "he says it is quite shocking."

"No," said he, "I never said anything so irrational. Don't palm all your abuses of languages upon me."

"There now, you see how droll he is. This is always the way with him! Sometimes he won't speak to me for half a day together, then he comes out with something so droll—all about anything in the world."

She surprised Elinor very much as they returned into the drawing room by asking her whether she did not like Mr Palmer excessively.

"Certainly," said Elinor, "he seems very agreeable."

"Well—I am so glad you do. I thought you would, he is so pleasant, and Mr Palmer is excessively pleased with you and your sisters I can tell you, and you can't think how disappointed he will be if you don't come to Cleveland. I can't imagine why you should object to it."

Elinor was again obliged to decline her invitation, and by changing the subject, put a stop to her entreaties. She thought it probable that as they lived in the same county, Mrs Palmer might be able to give some more particular account of Willoughby's general character than could be gathered from the Middletons' partial acquaintance with him, and she was eager to gain from anyone such a confirmation of his merits as might remove the possibility of fear from Marianne. She began by enquiring if they saw much of Mr Willoughby at Cleveland and whether they were intimately acquainted with him.

"Oh dear, yes, I know him extremely well," replied Mrs Palmer. "Not that I ever spoke to him indeed, but I have seen him forever in town. Somehow or other I never happened to be staying at Barton while he was at Allenham. Mama saw him here once before, but I was with my uncle at Weymouth. However, I dare say we should have seen a great deal of him in Somersetshire, if it had not happened very unluckily that we should never have been in the country together. He is very little at Combe, I believe, but if he were ever so much there, I do not think Mr Palmer would visit him. He is in the opposition, you know, and besides it is such a way off. I know why you enquire about him very well. Your sister is to marry him. I am monstrous glad of it, for then I shall have her for a neighbour you know."

"Upon my word," replied Elinor, "you know much more of the matter than I do if you have any reason to expect such a match."

"Don't pretend to deny it, because you know it is what everybody talks of. I assure you I heard of it in my way through town."

"My dear Mrs Palmer!"

"Upon my honour I did. I met Colonel Brandon Monday morning in Bond Street, just before we left town, and he told me of it directly."

"You surprise me very much. Colonel Brandon tell you of it! Surely you must be mistaken. To give such intelligence to a person who could not be interested in it even if it were true is not what I should expect Colonel Brandon to do."

"But I do assure you it was so for all that, and I will tell you how it happened. When we met him he turned back and walked with us, and so we began talking of my brother and sister and one thing and another, and I said to him, 'So, Colonel, there is a new family come to Barton Cottage, I hear, and mama sends me word they are very pretty, and that one of them is going to be married to Mr Willoughby of Combe Magna. Is it true, pray? For of course you must know, as you have been in Devonshire so lately.'"

"And what did the Colonel say?"

"Oh—he did not say much, but he looked as if he knew it to be true, so from that moment I set it down as certain. It will be quite delightful, I declare! When is it to take place?"

"Mr Brandon was very well, I hope?"

"Oh yes, quite well, and so full of your praises, he did nothing but say fine things of you."

This was a pleasant surprise to have Brandon speak of her to others. "I am flattered by his commendation. He seems an excellent man, and I think him uncommonly pleasing."

"So do I. He is such a charming man that it is quite a pity he should be so grave and so dull. Mama says he was in love with your sister too. I assure you it was a great compliment if he was, for he hardly ever falls in love with anybody."

"Is Mr Willoughby much known in your part of Somersetshire?" said Elinor.

"Oh yes, extremely well. That is, I do not believe many people are acquainted with him, because Combe Magna is so far off, but they all think him extremely agreeable I assure you. Nobody is more liked than Mr Willoughby wherever he goes, and so you may tell your sister. She is a monstrous lucky girl to get him, upon my honour. Not but that he is much more lucky in getting her, because she is so very handsome and agreeable that nothing can be good enough for her. However, I don't think her hardly at all handsomer than you, I assure you, for I think you both excessively pretty, and so does Mr Palmer too I am sure, though we could not get him to own it last night."

Mrs Palmer's information respecting Willoughby was not very material, but any testimony in his favour, however small, was pleasing to her.

"I am so glad we are got acquainted at last," continued Charlotte. "And now I hope we shall always be great friends. You can't think how much I longed to see you! It is so delightful that you should live at the cottage! Nothing can be like it, to be sure! And I am so glad your sister is going to be well married! I hope you will be a great deal at Combe Magna. It is a sweet place, by all accounts."

"You have been long acquainted with Colonel Brandon, have not you?"

"Yes, a great while, ever since my sister married. He was a particular friend of Sir John's. I believe," she added in a low voice, "he would have been very glad to have had me if he could. Sir John and Lady Middleton wished it very much. But Mama did not think the match good enough for me, otherwise Sir

John would have mentioned it to the Colonel, and we should have been married immediately."

"Did not Colonel Brandon know of Sir John's proposal to your mother before it was made? Had he never owned his affection to yourself?"

"Oh, no, but if Mama had not objected to it, I dare say he would have liked it of all things. He had not seen me then above twice, for it was before I left school. However, I am much happier as I am. Mr Palmer is the kind of man I like."

Chapter Twenty-One

The Palmers returned to Cleveland the next day, and the two families at Barton were again left to entertain each other. But this did not last long. Elinor had hardly got their last visitors out of her head—had hardly done wondering at Charlotte's being so happy without a cause, at Mr Palmer's acting so simply with good abilities, and at the strange unsuitableness which often existed between husband and wife—before Sir John's and Mrs Jennings' active zeal in the cause of society procured her some other new acquaintance to see and observe.

In a morning's excursion to Exeter they had met with two young ladies whom Mrs Jennings had the satisfaction of discovering to be her relations, and this was enough for Sir John to invite them directly to the park as soon as their present engagements at Exeter were over. Their engagements at Exeter instantly gave way before such an invitation.

Lady Middleton was thrown into no little alarm on the return of Sir John by hearing that she was very soon to receive a visit from two girls whom she had never seen in her life, and of whose elegance, whose tolerable gentility even, she could have no proof. For the assurances of her husband and mother on that subject went for nothing at all. Their being her relations too made it so much the worse, and Mrs Jennings' attempts at consolation were therefore unfortunately founded when she advised her daughter not to care about their being so fashionable, because they were all cousins and must put up with one another.

As it was impossible, however, now to prevent their coming, Lady Middleton resigned herself to the idea of it with all the philosophy of a well-bred woman, contenting herself with merely giving her husband a gentle reprimand on the subject five or six times every day.

The young ladies arrived — their appearance was by no means ungenteel or unfashionable. Their dress was very smart, their manners very civil. They were delighted with the house, and in raptures with the furniture, and they happened to be so dotingly fond of children that Lady Middleton's good opinion was engaged in their favour before they had been an hour at the Park. She declared them to be very agreeable girls indeed, which for her ladyship was enthusiastic admiration.

Sir John's confidence in his own judgement rose with this animated praise, and he set off directly for the cottage to tell the Miss Dashwoods of the Miss Steeles' arrival and to assure them of their being the sweetest girls in the world. From such commendation as this, however, there was not much to be learned. Elinor well knew that the sweetest girls in the world were to be met with in every part of England under every possible variation of form, face, temper and understanding. Sir John wanted the whole family to walk to the Park directly and look at his guests. Benevolent, philanthropic man! It was painful to him even to keep a third cousin to himself.

"Do come now," said he, "pray come—you must come—I declare you shall come. You can't think how you will like them. Lucy is monstrous pretty, and so good-humoured and agreeable! The children are all hanging about her already as if she was an old acquaintance. And they both long to see you of all things, for they have heard at Exeter that you are the most beautiful creatures in the world, and I have told them it is all very true, and a great deal more. You will be delighted with them I am sure. They have brought the whole coach full of playthings for the children. How can you be so cross as not to come? Why they are your cousins, you know, after a fashion. You are my cousins, and they are my wife's, so you must be related."

But Sir John could not prevail. He could only obtain a promise of their calling at the Park within a day or two, then left them in amazement at their indifference to walk home and boast anew of their attractions to the Miss Steeles, as he had been already boasting of the Miss Steeles to them.

When their promised visit to the Park and consequent introduction to these young ladies took place, they found in the appearance of the eldest—who was nearly thirty, with a very plain and not a sensible face—nothing to admire. But in the other, who was not more than two or three and twenty, they acknowledged considerable beauty. Her features were pretty, and she had a sharp quick eye and a smartness of air which, though it did not give actual elegance or grace, gave distinction to her person.

Their manners were particularly civil, and Elinor soon allowed them credit for some kind of sense when she saw with what constant and judicious attention they were making themselves agreeable to Lady Middleton. With her children they were in continual raptures, extolling their beauty, courting their notice and humouring their whims. Such of their time as could be spared from the importunate demands which this politeness made on it was spent in admiration of whatever her ladyship was doing, if she happened to be doing anything, or in taking patterns of some elegant new dress in which her appearance the day before had thrown them into unceasing delight.

Fortunately for those who pay their court through such foibles, a fond mother, though in pursuit of praise for her children the most rapacious of human beings, is likewise the most credulous. Her demands are exorbitant, but she will swallow anything, and the excessive affection and endurance of the Miss Steeles towards her offspring were viewed therefore by Lady Middleton without the smallest surprise or distrust. She saw with maternal complacency all the impertinent encroachments and mischievous tricks to which her cousins submitted. She saw their sashes untied, their hair pulled about their ears, their work-bags searched and their knives and scissors stolen away, and felt no doubt of its being a reciprocal enjoyment. It suggested no other surprise than that Elinor and Marianne should sit so composedly by without claiming a share in what was passing.

"John is in such spirits today!" said she, on his taking Miss Steele's pocket handkerchief and throwing it out of the window. "He is full of monkey tricks."

And soon afterwards, on the second boy's violently pinching one of the same lady's fingers, she fondly observed, "How playful William is!"

"And here is my sweet little Annamaria," she added, tenderly caressing a little girl of three years old who had not made a noise for the last two minutes. "And she is always so gentle and quiet— Never was there such a quiet little thing!"

But unfortunately in bestowing these embraces, a pin in her ladyship's head dress slightly scratching the child's neck produced from this pattern of gentleness such violent screams as could hardly be outdone by any creature professedly noisy. The mother's consternation was excessive, but it could not surpass the alarm of the Miss Steeles, and everything was done by all three in so critical an emergency which affection could suggest as likely to assuage the agonies of the little sufferer. She was seated in her mother's lap, covered with kisses, her wound bathed with lavender water by one of the Miss Steeles, who was on her knees to attend her, and her mouth stuffed with sugar plums by the other.

With such a reward for her tears, the child was too wise to cease crying. She still screamed and sobbed lustily, kicked her two brothers for offering to touch her, and all their united soothings were ineffectual till Lady Middleton luckily remembering that in a scene of similar distress last week some apricot marmalade had been successfully applied for a bruised temple, the same remedy was eagerly proposed for this unfortunate scratch. A slight intermission of screams in the young lady on hearing it gave them reason to hope that it would not be rejected. She was carried out of the room therefore in her mother's arms in quest of this medicine, and as the two boys chose to follow, though earnestly entreated by their mother to stay behind, the four young ladies were left in a quietness which the room had not known for many hours.

"Poor little creatures!" said Miss Steele, as soon as they were gone. "It might have been a very sad accident."

"Yet I hardly know how," cried Marianne, "unless it had been under totally different circumstances. But this is the usual way of heightening alarm where there is nothing to be alarmed at in reality."

"What a sweet woman Lady Middleton is!" said Lucy Steele.

Marianne was silent. It was impossible for her to say what she did not feel, however trivial the occasion, and upon Elinor therefore the whole task of telling lies when politeness required it always fell. This role, in truth, Elinor was beginning to dislike intensely. She did her best when thus called on by speaking of Lady Middleton with more warmth than she felt, though with far less than Miss Lucy.

"And Sir John too," cried the elder sister, "what a charming man he is!"

Here too Miss Dashwood's commendation, being only simple and just, came in without any eclat. She merely observed that he was perfectly good-humoured and friendly.

"And what a charming little family they have! I never saw such fine children in my life. I declare I quite dote upon them already, and indeed I am always distractedly fond of children."

"I should guess so," said Elinor, with a smile, "from what I have witnessed this morning."

"I have a notion," said Lucy, "you think the little Middletons rather too much indulged. Perhaps they may be the outside of enough, but it is so natural in Lady Middleton, and for my part I love to see children full of life and spirits. I cannot bear them if they are tame and quiet."

"I confess," replied Elinor, "that while I am at Barton Park, I never think of tame and quiet children with any abhorrence."

A short pause succeeded this speech, which was first broken by Miss Steele, who seemed very much disposed for conversation, and who now said rather abruptly, "And how do you like Devonshire, Miss Dashwood? I suppose you were very sorry to leave Sussex."

In some surprise at the familiarity of this question, or at least of the manner in which it was spoken, Elinor replied that she was.

"Norland is a prodigious beautiful place, is not it?" added Miss Steele.

"We have heard Sir John admire it excessively," said Lucy, who seemed to think some apology necessary for the freedom of her sister.

"I think everyone must admire it," replied Elinor, "who ever saw the place, though it is not to be supposed that anyone can estimate its beauties as we do."

"And had you a great many smart beaux there? I suppose you have not so many in this part of the world. For my part, I think they are a vast addition always."

"But why should you think," said Lucy, looking ashamed of her sister, "that there are not as many genteel young men in Devonshire as Sussex?"

"Nay, my dear, I'm sure I don't pretend to say that there an't. I'm sure there's a vast many smart beaux in Exeter, but you know, how could I tell what smart beaux there might be about Norland? And I was only afraid the Miss Dashwoods might find it dull at Barton, if they had not so many as they used to have. But perhaps you young ladies may not care about the beaux and had as lief be without them as with them. For my part, I think they are vastly agreeable, provided they dress smart and behave civil. But I can't bear to see them dirty and nasty. Now there's Mr Rose at Exeter—a prodigious smart young man, quite a beau, clerk to Mr Simpson, you know—and yet if you do but meet him of a morning, he is not fit to be seen. I suppose your brother was quite a beau, Miss Dashwood, before he married, as he was so rich?"

"Upon my word," replied Elinor, "I cannot tell you, for I do not perfectly comprehend the meaning of the word. But this I can say, that if he ever was a beau before he married, he is one still. For there is not the smallest alteration in him."

"Oh, dear! One never thinks of married men's being beaux—they have something else to do."

"Lord! Anne," cried her sister, "you can talk of nothing but beaux. You will make Miss Dashwood believe you think of nothing else." And to turn the discourse, she began admiring the house and the furniture.

This specimen of the Miss Steeles was enough. The vulgar freedom and folly of the eldest left her no recommendation, and as Elinor was not blinded by the beauty or the shrewd look of the youngest to her want of real elegance and artlessness, she left the house without any wish of knowing them better.

Not so the Miss Steeles. They came from Exeter well provided with admiration for the use of Sir John Middleton, his family and all his relations. No niggardly proportion was now dealt out to his fair cousins, whom they declared to be the most beautiful, elegant, accomplished and agreeable girls they had ever beheld, and with whom they were particularly anxious to be better acquainted. And to be better acquainted therefore Elinor soon found was their inevitable lot. For as Sir John was entirely on the side of the Miss Steeles, their party would be too strong for opposition, and that kind of intimacy must be submitted to which consists of sitting an hour or two together in the same room almost every day. Sir John could do no more, but he did not know that any more was required—to be together was in his opinion to be intimate, and while his continual schemes for their meeting were effectual, he had not a doubt of their being established friends.

To do him justice, he did everything in his power to promote their unreserve by making the Miss Steeles acquainted with whatever he knew or supposed of his cousins' situations in the most delicate particulars. Elinor had not seen them more than twice before the eldest of them wished her joy on her sister's having been so lucky as to make a conquest of a very smart beau since she came to Barton.

"'Twill be a fine thing to have her married so young to be sure," said she, "and I hear he is quite a beau, and prodigious handsome. And I hope you may have as good luck yourself soon, but perhaps you may have a friend in the corner already."

Elinor could not suppose that Sir John would be more nice in proclaiming his suspicions of her regard for Edward than he had been with respect to Marianne. Indeed it was rather his favourite joke of the two, as being somewhat newer and more conjectural, and since Edward's visit, they had never dined together without his drinking to her best affections with so much significancy and so many nods and winks as to excite general attention. The letter F—had been likewise invariably brought forward and found productive of such countless jokes that its character as the wittiest letter in the alphabet had been long established with Elinor.

The Miss Steeles, as she expected, had now all the benefit of these jokes, and in the eldest of them they raised a curiosity to know the name of the gentleman alluded to, which though often impertinently expressed was perfectly of a piece with her general inquisitiveness into the concerns of their family. But Sir John did not sport long with the curiosity which he delighted to raise, for he had at least as much pleasure in telling the name as Miss Steele had in hearing it.

"His name is Ferrars," said he in a very audible whisper, "but pray do not tell it, for it's a great secret."

"Ferrars!" repeated Miss Steele. "Mr Ferrars is the happy man, is he? What, your sister-in-law's brother, Miss Dashwood? A very agreeable young man to be sure, I know him very well."

"How can you say so, Anne?" cried Lucy, who generally made an amendment to all her sister's assertions. "Though we have seen him once or twice at my uncle's, it is rather too much to pretend to know him very well."

Elinor heard all this with attention and surprise. "And who was this uncle? Where did he live? How came they acquainted?" She wished very much to have the subject continued, though she did not choose to join in it herself, but nothing more of it was said, and for the first time in her life she thought Mrs Jennings deficient either in curiosity after petty information or in a disposition to communicate it. The manner in which Miss Steele had spoken of Edward increased her curiosity, for it struck her as being rather ill-natured, and suggested the suspicion of that lady's knowing or fancying herself to know something to his disadvantage. But her curiosity was unavailing, for no farther notice was taken of Mr Ferrars' name by Miss Steele when alluded to or even openly mentioned by Sir John.

Chapter Twenty-Two

Marianne, who had never much toleration for anything like impertinence, vulgarity, inferiority of parts or even difference of taste from herself, was at this time particularly ill-disposed from the state of her spirits to be pleased with the Miss Steeles or to encourage their advances. To the invariable coldness of her behaviour towards them, which checked every endeavour at intimacy on their side, Elinor principally attributed that preference of herself which soon became evident in the manners of both, but especially of Lucy, who missed no opportunity of engaging her in conversation or of striving to improve their acquaintance by an easy and frank communication of her sentiments.

Lucy was naturally clever. Her remarks were often just and amusing, and as a companion for half an hour—no more, no less—Elinor frequently found her agreeable. But her powers had received no aid from education—she was ignorant and illiterate, and her deficiency of all mental improvement, her want of information in the most common particulars, could not be concealed from Miss Dashwood in spite of her constant endeavour to appear to advantage. Elinor saw and pitied her for the neglect of abilities which education might have rendered so respectable. But she saw with less tenderness of feeling the thorough want of delicacy, of rectitude and integrity of mind which her attentions, her assiduities, her flatteries at the Park betrayed. She could have no lasting satisfaction in the company of a person who joined insincerity with ignorance, whose want of instruction prevented their meeting in conversation on terms of equality and whose conduct towards others made every show of attention and deference towards herself perfectly valueless.

"You will think my question an odd one, I dare say," said Lucy to her one day as they were walking together from the park to the cottage, "but pray, are you personally acquainted with your sister-in-law's mother, Mrs Ferrars?"

Elinor did think the question a very odd one, and her countenance expressed it as she answered that she had never seen Mrs Ferrars.

"Indeed!" replied Lucy. "I wonder at that, for I thought you must have seen her at Norland sometimes. Then perhaps you cannot tell me what sort of a woman she is?"

"No," returned Elinor, cautious of giving her real opinion of Edward's mother and not very desirous of satisfying what seemed impertinent curiosity. "I know nothing of her."

"I am sure you think me very strange for enquiring about her in such a way," said Lucy, eyeing Elinor attentively as she spoke, "but perhaps there may be reasons—I wish I might venture, but however I hope you will do me the justice of believing that I do not mean to be impertinent."

On guard nonetheless, Elinor made her a civil reply, and they walked on for a few minutes in silence. It was broken by Lucy, who renewed the subject again by saying with some hesitation, "I cannot bear to have you think me impertinently curious. I am sure I would rather do anything in the world than be thought so by a person whose good opinion is so well worth having as yours. And I am sure I should not have the smallest fear of trusting you. Indeed, I should be very glad of your advice how to manage in such an uncomfortable situation as I am, but, however, there is no occasion to trouble you. I am sorry you do not happen to know Mrs Ferrars."

"I am sorry I do not," said Elinor in great astonishment, "if it could be of any use to you to know my opinion of her. But really I never understood that you were at all connected with that family, and therefore I am a little surprised, I confess, at so serious an enquiry into her character."

"I dare say you are, and I am sure I do not at all wonder at it. But if I dared tell you all, you would not be so much surprised. Mrs Ferrars is certainly nothing to me at present—but the time may come—how soon it will come must depend upon herself—when we may be very intimately connected."

She looked down as she said this, amiably bashful, with only one side glance at her companion to observe its effect on her.

"Good heavens!" cried Elinor. "What do you mean? Are you acquainted with Mr Robert Ferrars? Can you be?" And she did not feel much delighted with the idea of such a sister-in-law.

"No," replied Lucy, "not to Mr *Robert* Ferrars—I never saw him in my life, but"—fixing her eyes upon Elinor—"to his eldest brother."

What felt Elinor at that moment? Astonishment that would have been as painful as it was strong had not an immediate disbelief of the assertion attended it. She turned towards Lucy in silent amazement, unable to divine the reason or object of such a declaration, and though her complexion varied, she stood firm in incredulity and felt in no danger of an hysterical fit or a swoon.

"You may well be surprised," continued Lucy, "for to be sure you could have had no idea of it before. I dare say he never dropped the smallest hint of it to you or any of your family, because it was always meant to be a great secret, and I am sure has been faithfully kept so by me to this hour. Not a soul of all my relations know of it but Anne, and I never should have mentioned it to you if I had not felt the greatest dependence in the world upon your secrecy. I really thought my behaviour in asking so many questions about Mrs Ferrars must seem so odd that it ought to be explained. And I do not think Mr Ferrars can be displeased when he knows I have trusted you, because I know he has the highest opinion in the world of all your family, and looks upon yourself and the other Miss Dashwoods quite as his own sisters." She paused.

Elinor for a few moments remained silent. Her astonishment at what she heard was at first too great for words, but at length forcing herself to speak and to speak cautiously, she said with calmness of manner which tolerably well concealed her surprise and solicitude, "May I ask if your engagement is of long standing?"

"We have been engaged these four years."

"Four years!"

"Yes."

Elinor, though greatly shocked, still felt unable to believe it. "I did not know," said she, "that you were even acquainted till the other day."

"Our acquaintance, however, is of many years' date. He was under my uncle's care, you know, a considerable while."

"Your uncle!"

"Yes, Mr Pratt. Did you never hear him talk of Mr Pratt?"

"I think I have," replied Elinor, with an exertion of spirits which increased with her increase of emotion.

"He was four years with my uncle, who lives at Longstaple, near Plymouth. It was there our acquaintance began, for my sister and me was often staying with my uncle, and it was there our engagement was formed—though not till a year after he had quitted as a pupil, but he was almost always with us afterwards. I was very unwilling to enter into it, as you may imagine, without the knowledge and approbation of his mother, but I was too young and loved him too well to be so prudent as I ought to have been. Though you do not know him so well as me, Miss Dashwood, you must have seen enough of him to be sensible he is very capable of making a woman sincerely attached to him."

"Certainly," answered Elinor without knowing what she said, but after a moment's reflection she added, with revived security of Edward's honour and love and her companion's falsehood, "Engaged to Mr Edward Ferrars! I confess myself so totally surprised at what you tell me, that really—I beg your pardon, but surely there must be some mistake of person or name. We cannot mean the same Mr Ferrars."

"We can mean no other," cried Lucy, smiling. "Mr Edward Ferrars, the eldest son of Mrs Ferrars of Park Street and brother of your sister-in-law Mrs John Dashwood, is the person I mean. You must allow that I am not likely to be deceived as to the name of the man on who all my happiness depends."

"It is strange," replied Elinor in a most painful perplexity, "that I should never have heard him even mention your name."

"No, considering our situation, it was not strange. Our first care has been to keep the matter secret. You knew nothing of me or my family, and therefore there could be no occasion forever mentioning my name to you, and as he was always particularly afraid of his sister's suspecting anything, that was reason enough for his not mentioning it."

She was silent. Elinor's security sank, but her self-command did not sink with it.

"Four years you have been engaged," said she with a firm voice, her mind awhirl with the memories of Edward's caresses, his mindless declarations of passion. How would she go on knowing he had allowed himself such abandon and taken her with him to that wild barren point?

"Yes, and heaven knows how much longer we may have to wait. Poor Edward! It puts him quite out of heart. He has always been so ardent, so devoted in word and deed. Excuse me but you do know what I mean when I say he has exhibited his affections to me in the most bold and rapturous manner? He is quite a lover." Then taking a small miniature from her pocket, she added, "To prevent the possibility of mistake, be so good as to look at this face. It does not do him justice to be sure, but yet I think you cannot be deceived as to the person it was drew for. I have had it above these three years."

She put it into her hands as she spoke, and when Elinor saw the painting, whatever other doubts her fear of a too hasty decision or her wish of detecting falsehood might suffer to linger in her mind, she could have none of its being Edward's face. She returned it almost instantly, acknowledging the likeness.

"I have never been able," continued Lucy, "to give him my picture in return, which I am very much vexed at, for he has been always so anxious to get it! He claims I am the most beautiful girl he has ever seen. To keep me ever in his mind, I wanted to sit for a portrait. But I am determined to set for it the very first opportunity."

"You are quite in the right," replied Elinor calmly. They then proceeded a few paces in silence. Lucy spoke first.

"I am sure," said she, "I have no doubt in the world of your faithfully keeping this secret, because you must know of what importance it is to us not to have it reach his mother, for she would never approve of it, I dare say. I shall have no fortune, and I fancy she is an exceeding proud woman."

"I certainly did not seek your confidence," said Elinor, "but you do me no more than justice in imagining that I may be depended on. Your secret is safe with me, but pardon me if I express some surprise at so unnecessary a communication. You must at least have felt that my being acquainted with it could not add to its safety."

As she said this she looked earnestly at Lucy, hoping to discover something in her countenance, perhaps the falsehood of the greatest part of what she had been saying, but Lucy's countenance suffered no change.

"I was afraid you would think I was taking a great liberty with you," said she, "in telling you all this. I have not known you long to be sure, personally at least, but I have known you and all your family by description a great while, and as soon as I saw you I felt almost as if you was an old acquaintance. I knew quite a bit too about Marianne's attachment to Willoughby."

This alarmed Elinor but she bit her tongue. Whatever was being said abroad about her younger sister's relationship with Mr Willoughby always undid her composure. But Lucy took no notice of it.

"Besides in the present case, I really thought some explanation was due to you after my making such particular enquiries about Edward's mother, and I am so unfortunate that I have not a creature whose advice I can ask. Anne is the only person that knows of it, and she has no judgement at all. Indeed she does me a great deal more harm than good, for I am in constant fear of her betraying me. She does not know how to hold her tongue, as you must perceive, and I am sure I was in the greatest fright in the world t'other day when Edward's name was mentioned by Sir John lest she should out with it all. You can't think how much I go through in my mind from it altogether. I only wonder that I am alive after what I have suffered for Edward's sake these last four years. Everything in such suspense and uncertainty, and seeing him so seldom — we can hardly meet above twice a year. I am sure I wonder my heart is not quite broke."

Here she took out her handkerchief, but Elinor did not feel very compassionate.

"Sometimes." continued Lucy, after wiping her eyes, "I think whether it would not be better for us both to break off the matter entirely." As she said this, she looked directly at her companion and Elinor wondered if she were testing her to break her silence on her own relationship with Edward. "But then at other times I have not resolution enough for it. I cannot bear the thoughts of making him so miserable, as I know the very mention of such a thing would do. And on my own account too — so dear as he is to me — I don't think I could be equal to it. What would you advise me to do in such a case, Miss Dashwood? What would you do yourself?"

"Pardon me," replied Elinor, startled by the question, "but I can give you no advice under such circumstances. Your own judgement must direct you."

"To be sure," continued Lucy, after a few minutes' silence on both sides, "his mother must provide for him sometime or other, but poor Edward is so cast down by it! Did you not think him dreadful low-spirited when he was at Barton?"

Elinor froze to hear this woman's perspective of Edward's behaviour.

"He was so miserable when he left us at Longstaple to go to you that I was afraid you would think him quite ill."

"Did he come from your uncle's, then, when he visited us?"

"Oh, yes, he had been staying a fortnight with us. Did you think he came directly from town?"

"No," replied Elinor, most feelingly sensible of every fresh circumstance in favour of Lucy's veracity, "I remember he told us that he had been staying a fortnight with some friends near Plymouth." She remembered too her own surprise at the time at his mentioning nothing farther of those friends, at his total silence with respect even to their names. Now here at last was an explanation.

"Did not you think him sadly out of spirits?" repeated Lucy.

"We did indeed, particularly so when he first arrived."

"I begged him to exert himself for fear you should suspect what was the matter, but it made him so melancholy not being able to stay more than a fortnight with us and seeing me so much affected. Poor fellow! I am afraid it is just the same with him now, for he writes in wretched spirits. I heard from him just before I left Exeter." Taking a letter from her pocket and carelessly showing the direction to Elinor. "You know his hand, I dare say, a charming one it is, but that is not written so well as usual. He was tired, I dare say, for he had just filled the sheet to me as full as possible."

Wincing, Elinor saw that it was his hand, and she could doubt no longer. This picture, she had allowed herself to believe, might have been accidentally obtained, it might not have been Edward's gift, but a correspondence between them by letter could subsist only under a positive engagement, could be authorised by nothing else. For a few moments she was almost overcome — her heart sank within her, her grief at attempting to forget his passion towards her rising to a crescendo and she could hardly stand, but exertion was indispensably necessary and she struggled so resolutely against the oppression of her feelings that her success was speedy and for the time complete.

"Writing to each other," said Lucy, returning the letter into her pocket with a smile that Elinor would have sworn was more sneer than other, "is the only comfort we have in such long separations. Yes, I have one other comfort in his picture, but poor Edward has not even that. If he had but my picture, he says he should be easy. I gave him a lock of my hair set in a ring when he was at Longstaple last, and that was some comfort to him, he said, but not equal to a picture. Perhaps you might notice the ring when you saw him?"

"I did," said Elinor, with a composure of voice under which was concealed an emotion and distress beyond anything she had ever felt before. She was mortified, shocked, confounded. How could she have been so naïve to think it might be her hair in that ring? Is this what love's obsession did to one's reason? Oh, she should never have surrendered to it!

Fortunately for her, they had now reached the cottage, and the conversation could be continued no farther. After sitting with them a few minutes, the Miss Steeles returned to the Park, and Elinor was then at liberty to think and be wretched.

Chapter Twenty-Three

However small Elinor's general dependence on Lucy's veracity might be, it was impossible for her on serious reflection to suspect it in the present case, where no temptation could be answerable to the folly of inventing a falsehood of such a description. What Lucy had asserted to be true, therefore, Elinor could not—dared not—longer doubt, supported as it was too on every side by such probabilities and proofs and contradicted by nothing but her own wishes.

Their opportunity of acquaintance in the house of Mr Pratt was a foundation for the rest, at once indisputable and alarming. Edward's visit near Plymouth. His melancholy state of mind. His dissatisfaction at his own prospects. His uncertain behaviour towards herself. The intimate knowledge of the Miss Steeles as to Norland and their family connections which had often surprised her. The picture, the letter, the ring. It formed altogether such a body of evidence as overcame every fear of condemning him unfairly and established as a fact which no partiality could set aside his ill-treatment of herself.

Her resentment of such behaviour, her indignation at having been its dupe for a short time made her feel only for herself, but other ideas, other considerations soon arose. Had Edward been intentionally deceiving her? Had he feigned a regard for her which he did not feel? Was his engagement to Lucy an engagement of the heart? No, whatever it might once have been, she could not believe it such at present. His affection was all her own. She could not be deceived in that. Her mother, sisters, Fanny, all had been conscious of his regard for her at Norland. It was not an illusion of her own vanity. He certainly loved her. What a softener of the heart was this persuasion! His tender kisses, his sweet caresses of her all too eager body had been met not by refusal, but by joyous acceptance. How much could it not tempt her to forgive!

He had been blameable, highly blameable in remaining at Norland after he first felt her influence over him to be more than it ought to be. In that he could not be defended, but if he had injured her, how much more had he injured himself? If her case were pitiable, his was hopeless. His imprudence had made her miserable for a while, but it seemed to have deprived himself of all chance of ever being otherwise. She might in time regain tranquillity, but *he*, what had he to look forward to? Oh, poor man! Could he ever be tolerably happy with Lucy Steele? Could he stroke Lucy's tiny breasts or drive his fingers along her thin hips and find any equal to the fervour he had found with her? Could he, were his affection for herself out of the question, with his integrity, his delicacy and well-informed mind, be satisfied with a wife like her — illiterate, artful and selfish?

The youthful infatuation of nineteen would naturally blind him to everything but her beauty and good nature, but the four succeeding years—years which if rationally spent give such improvement to the understanding—must have opened his eyes to her defects of education. While the same period of time, spent on her side in inferior society and more frivolous pursuits, had perhaps robbed her of that simplicity which might once have given an interesting character to her beauty.

If in the supposition of his seeking to marry herself his difficulties from his mother had seemed great, how much greater were they now likely to be when the object of his engagement was undoubtedly inferior in connections and probably inferior in fortune to herself? These difficulties indeed, with a heart so alienated from Lucy, might not press very hard upon his patience, but melancholy was the state of the person by whom the expectation of family opposition and unkindness could be felt as a relief!

As these considerations occurred to her in painful succession, she wept for him more than for herself. Supported by the conviction of having done nothing to merit her present unhappiness, and consoled by the belief that Edward had done nothing to forfeit her esteem, she thought she could even now under the first smart of the heavy blow command herself enough to guard every suspicion of the truth from her mother and sisters. And so well was she able to answer her own expectations that when she joined them at dinner only two hours after she had first suffered the extinction of all her dearest hopes, no one would have supposed from the appearance of the sisters that Elinor was mourning in secret over obstacles which must divide her forever from the object of her love, and that Marianne was internally dwelling on the perfections of a man of whose whole heart she felt thoroughly possessed and whom she expected to see in every carriage which drove near their house.

The necessity of concealing from her mother and Marianne what had been entrusted in confidence to herself, though it obliged her to unceasing exertion, was no aggravation of Elinor's distress. On the contrary it was a relief to her to be spared the communication of what would give such affliction to them, and to be saved likewise from hearing that condemnation of Edward, which would probably flow from the excess of their partial affection for herself and which was more than she felt equal to support.

From their counsel or their conversation she knew she could receive no assistance. Their tenderness and sorrow must add to her distress, while her self-command would neither receive encouragement from their example nor from their praise. She was stronger alone, and her own good sense so well supported her that her firmness was as unshaken, her appearance of cheerfulness as invariable, as with regrets so poignant and so fresh it was possible for them to be.

Much as she had suffered from her first conversation with Lucy on the subject, she soon felt an earnest wish of renewing it, and this for more reasons than one. She wanted to hear many particulars of their engagement repeated again. She wanted more clearly to understand what Lucy really felt for Edward, whether there were any sincerity in her declaration of tender regard for him. And she particularly wanted to convince Lucy by her readiness to enter on the matter again and her calmness in conversing on it that she was no otherwise interested in it than as a friend, which she very much feared her involuntary agitation in their morning discourse must have left at least doubtful.

That Lucy was disposed to be jealous of her appeared very probable — it was plain that Edward had always spoken highly in her praise, not merely from Lucy's assertion, but from her venturing to trust her on so short a personal acquaintance with a secret so confessedly and evidently important. And even Sir John's joking intelligence must have had some weight. But indeed, while Elinor remained so well assured within herself of being really beloved by Edward, it required no other consideration of probabilities to make it natural that Lucy should be jealous — and that she was so her very confidence was a proof. What other reason for the disclosure of the affair could there be but that Elinor might be informed by it of Lucy's superior claims on Edward and be taught to avoid him in future? Offended, she would certainly do that, she vowed, if given the opportunity.

She had little difficulty in understanding thus much of her rival's intentions, and while she was firmly resolved to act by her as every principle of honour and honesty directed, to combat her own affection for Edward and to see him as little as possible, she could not deny herself the comfort of endeavouring to convince Lucy that her heart was unwounded. And as she could now have nothing more painful to hear on the subject than had already been told, she did not mistrust her own ability of going through a repetition of particulars with composure.

But it was not immediately that an opportunity of doing so could be commanded, though Lucy was as well disposed as herself to take advantage of any that occurred. The weather was not often fine enough to allow of their joining in a walk where they might most easily separate themselves from the others, and though they met at least every other evening either at the park or cottage, and chiefly at the former, they could not be supposed to meet for the sake of conversation. Such a thought would never enter either Sir John or Lady Middleton's head, and therefore very little leisure was ever given for a general chat, and none at all for particular discourse. They met for the sake of eating, drinking and laughing together, playing at cards or consequences or any other game that was sufficiently noisy.

One or two meetings of this kind had taken place without affording Elinor any chance of engaging Lucy in private when Sir John called at the cottage one morning to beg in the name of charity that they would all dine with Lady Middleton that day. He was obliged to attend the club at Exeter, and she would otherwise be quite alone except her mother and the two Miss Steeles. Elinor, who foresaw a fairer opening for the point she had in view – in such a party as this was likely to be, more at liberty among themselves under the tranquil and well-bred direction of Lady Middleton than when her husband united them together in one noisy purpose – immediately accepted the invitation. Margaret with her mother's permission was equally compliant, and Marianne, though always unwilling to join any of their parties, was persuaded by her mother, who could not bear to have her seclude herself from any chance of amusement, to go likewise.

The young ladies went, and Lady Middleton was happily preserved from the frightful solitude which had threatened her. The insipidity of the meeting was exactly such as Elinor had expected. It produced not one novelty of thought or expression, and nothing could be less interesting than the whole of their discourse both in the dining parlour and drawing room. To the latter, the children accompanied them, and while they remained there, she was too well convinced of the impossibility of engaging Lucy's attention to attempt it. They quitted it only with the removal of the tea things. The card table was then placed, and Elinor began to wonder at herself for having ever entertained a hope of finding time for conversation at the park. They all rose up in preparation for a round game.

"I am glad," said Lady Middleton to Lucy, "you are not going to finish poor little Annamaria's basket this evening, for I am sure it must hurt your eyes to work filigree by candlelight. And we will make the dear little love some amends for her disappointment tomorrow, and I hope she will not much mind it."

This hint was enough. Lucy recollected herself instantly and replied, "Indeed you are very much mistaken, Lady Middleton. I am only waiting to know whether you can make your party without me, or I should have been at my filigree already. I would not disappoint the little angel for all the world—and if you want me at the card table now, I am resolved to finish the basket after supper."

"You are very good. I hope it won't hurt your eyes. Will you ring the bell for some working candles? My poor little girl would be sadly disappointed, I know, if the basket was not finished tomorrow, for though I told her it certainly would not, I am sure she depends upon having it done."

Lucy directly drew her work table near her and reseated herself with an alacrity and cheerfulness which seemed to infer that she could taste no greater delight than in making a filigree basket for a spoilt child.

Lady Middleton proposed a rubber of Casino to the others. No one made any objection but Marianne, who with her usual inattention to the forms of general civility, exclaimed, "Your Ladyship will have the goodness to excuse me—you know I detest cards. I shall go to the pianoforte, I have not touched it since it was tuned." And without farther ceremony, she turned away and walked to the instrument.

Lady Middleton looked as if she thanked heaven that she had never made so rude a speech.

"Marianne can never keep long from that instrument you know, ma'am," said Elinor, endeavouring to smooth away the offence, "and I do not much wonder at it, for it is the very best toned pianoforte I ever heard."

The remaining five were now to draw their cards.

"Perhaps," continued Elinor, "if I should happen to cut out, I may be of some use to Miss Lucy Steele in rolling her papers for her. There is so much still to be done to the basket that it must be impossible I think for her labour singly to finish it this evening. I should like the work exceedingly, if she would allow me a share in it."

"Indeed I shall be very much obliged to you for your help," cried Lucy, "for I find there is more to be done to it than I thought there was, and it would be a shocking thing to disappoint dear Annamaria after all."

"Oh, that would be terrible, indeed," said Miss Steele. "Dear little soul, how I do love her!"

"You are very kind," said Lady Middleton to Elinor, "and as you really like the work, perhaps you will be as well pleased not to cut in till another rubber, or will you take your chance now?"

Elinor joyfully profited by the first of these proposals and thus, by a little of that address which Marianne could never condescend to practice, gained her own end and pleased Lady Middleton at the same time. Lucy made room for her with ready attention, and the two fair rivals were thus seated side by side at the same table and with the utmost harmony engaged in forwarding the same work. The pianoforte at which Marianne, wrapped up in her own music and her own thoughts, had by this time forgotten that anybody was in the room besides herself was luckily so near them that Miss Dashwood now judged she might safely under the shelter of its noise introduce the interesting subject without any risk of being heard at the card table.

Chapter Twenty-Four

In a firm though cautious tone, Elinor thus began.

"I should be undeserving of the confidence you have honoured me with if I felt no desire for its continuance or no farther curiosity on its subject. I will not apologise therefore for bringing it forward again."

"Thank you," cried Lucy warmly, "for breaking the ice. You have set my heart at ease by it, for I was somehow or other afraid I had offended you by what I told you that Monday."

"Offended me! How could you suppose so? Believe me," and Elinor spoke it with the truest sincerity, "nothing could be farther from my intention than to give you such an idea. Could you have a motive for the trust that was not honourable and flattering to me?"

"And yet I do assure you," replied Lucy, her little sharp eyes full of meaning, "there seemed to me to be a coldness and displeasure in your manner that made me quite uncomfortable. I felt sure that you was angry with me, and have been quarrelling with myself ever since for having took such a liberty as to trouble you with my affairs. But I am very glad to find it was only my own fancy and that you really do not blame me. If you knew what a consolation it was to me to relieve my heart speaking to you of what I am always thinking of every moment of my life, your compassion would make you overlook everything else I am sure."

"Indeed, I can easily believe that it was a very great relief to you to acknowledge your situation to me, and be assured that you shall never have reason to repent it. Your case is a very unfortunate one. You seem to me to be surrounded with difficulties, and you will have need of all your mutual affection to support you under them. Mr Ferrars, I believe, is entirely dependent on his mother."

"He has only two thousand pounds of his own. It would be madness to marry upon that, though for my own part, I could give up every prospect of more without a sigh. I have been always used to a very small income and could struggle with any poverty for him, but I love him too well to be the selfish means of robbing him perhaps of all that his mother might give him if he married to please her. We must wait, it may be for many years. With almost every other man in the world it would be an alarming prospect, but Edward's affection and constancy nothing can deprive me of, I know."

"That conviction must be everything to you, and he is undoubtedly supported by the same trust in yours. If the strength of your reciprocal attachment had failed, as between many people and under many circumstances it naturally would during a four years' engagement, your situation would have been pitiable indeed."

Lucy here looked up, but Elinor was careful in guarding her countenance from every expression that could give her words a suspicious tendency.

"Edward's love for me," said Lucy, "has been pretty well put to the test by our long, very long absence since we were first engaged, and it has stood the trial so well that I should be unpardonable to doubt it now. I can safely say that he has never gave me one moment's alarm on that account from the first."

Elinor hardly knew whether to smile or sigh at this assertion. Better yet, she could and should scream 'Traitor!' of this lady's hollow character!

Lucy went on. "I am rather of a jealous temper too by nature. Are you?" she challenged Elinor, who debated if she should respond as Marianne would with truth. "As for Edward and from our different situations in life, from his being so much more in the world than me, and our continual separation, I was enough inclined for suspicion to have found out the truth in an instant if there had been the slightest alteration in his behaviour to me when we met. Or any lowness of spirits that I could not account for, or if he had talked more of one lady than another, or seemed in any respect less happy at Longstaple than he used to be. I do not mean to say that I am particularly observant or quick-sighted in general, but in such a case I am sure I could not be deceived."

All this, thought Elinor, *is very pretty, but it can impose upon neither of us.*

"But what," said she after a short silence, "are your views? Or have you none but that of waiting for Mrs Ferrars' death, which is a melancholy and shocking extremity? Is her son determined to submit to this and to all the tediousness of the many years of suspense in which it may involve you rather than run the risk of her displeasure for a while by owning the truth?"

"If we could be certain that it would be only for a while! But Mrs Ferrars is a very headstrong proud woman, and in her first fit of anger upon hearing it would very likely secure everything to Robert, and the idea of that for Edward's sake frightens away all my inclination for hasty measures."

"And for your own sake too, or you are carrying your disinterestedness beyond reason."

Lucy looked at Elinor again, and was silent.

"Do you know Mr Robert Ferrars?" asked Elinor.

"Not at all — I never saw him, but I fancy he is very unlike his brother — silly and a great coxcomb."

"A great coxcomb!" repeated Miss Steele, whose ear had caught those words by a sudden pause in Marianne's music. "Oh, they are talking of their favourite beaux, I dare say."

"No, sister," cried Lucy, "you are mistaken there, our favourite beaux are *not* great coxcombs."

"I can answer for it that Miss Dashwood's is not," said Mrs Jennings, laughing heartily, "for he is one of the modestest, prettiest-behaved young men I ever saw, but as for Lucy, she is such a sly little creature, there is no finding out who *she* likes."

"Oh," cried Miss Steele, looking significantly round at them, "I dare say Lucy's beau is quite as modest and pretty-behaved as Miss Dashwood's."

Elinor blushed in spite of herself. Lucy bit her lip, and looked angrily at her sister. A mutual silence took place for some time. Lucy first put an end to it by saying in a lower tone, though Marianne was then giving them the powerful protection of a very magnificent concerto, "I will honestly tell you of one scheme which has lately come into my head for bringing matters to bear. Indeed I am bound to let you into the secret, for you are a party concerned.

"I dare say you have seen enough of Edward to know that he would prefer the church to every other profession. Now my plan is that he should take orders as soon as he can, then through your interest—which I am sure you would be kind enough to use out of friendship for him, and I hope out of some regard to me—your brother might be persuaded to give him Norland living, which I understand is a very good one and the present incumbent not likely to live a great while. That would be enough for us to marry upon, and we might trust to time and chance for the rest."

"I should always be happy," replied Elinor, "to show any mark of my esteem and friendship for Mr Ferrars, but do you not perceive that my interest on such an occasion would be perfectly unnecessary? He is brother to Mrs John Dashwood—that must be recommendation enough to her husband."

"But Mrs John Dashwood would not much approve of Edward's going into orders."

"Then I rather suspect that my interest would do very little."

They were again silent for many minutes. At length Lucy exclaimed with a deep sigh, "I believe it would be the wisest way to put an end to the business at once by dissolving the engagement. We seem so beset with difficulties on every side that though it would make us miserable for a time, we should be happier perhaps in the end. But you will not give me your advice, Miss Dashwood?"

"No," answered Elinor, with a smile which concealed very agitated feelings, "on such a subject I certainly will not. You know very well that my opinion would have no weight with you unless it were on the side of your wishes."

"Indeed you wrong me," replied Lucy with great solemnity. "I know nobody of whose judgement I think so highly as I do of yours, and I do really believe that if you was to say to me, 'I advise you by all means to put an end to your engagement with Edward Ferrars, it will be more for the happiness of both of you,' I should resolve upon doing it immediately."

Elinor blushed for the insincerity of Edward's future wife, and replied, "This compliment would effectually frighten me from giving any opinion on the subject had I formed one. It raises my influence much too high. The power of dividing two people so tenderly attached is too much for an indifferent person."

"'Tis because you are an *indifferent* person," said Lucy, with some pique and laying a particular stress on those words, "that your judgement might justly have such weight with me. If you could be supposed to be biased in any respect by your own feelings, your opinion would not be worth having."

Elinor thought it wisest to make no answer to this lest they might provoke each other to an unsuitable increase of ease and unreserve, and was even partly determined never to mention the subject again. Another pause therefore of many minutes' duration succeeded this speech, and Lucy was still the first to end it.

"Shall you be in town this winter, Miss Dashwood?" said she with all her customary complacency.

"Certainly not."

"I am sorry for that," returned the other, while her eyes brightened at the information. "It would have gave me such pleasure to meet you there! But I dare say you will go for all that. To be sure, your brother and sister will ask you to come to them."

"It will not be in my power to accept their invitation if they do."

"How unlucky that is! I had quite depended upon meeting you there. Anne and me are to go the latter end of January to some relations who have been wanting us to visit them these several years! But I only go for the sake of seeing Edward. He will be there in February, otherwise London would have no charms for me. I have not spirits for it."

Elinor was soon called to the card table by the conclusion of the first rubber. The confidential discourse of the two ladies was therefore at an end, to which both of them submitted without any reluctance, for nothing had been said on either side to make them dislike each other less than they had done before. Elinor sat down to the card table with the melancholy persuasion that Edward was not only without affection for the person who was to be his wife, but that he had not even the chance of being tolerably happy in marriage which sincere affection on her side would have given. For self-interest alone could induce a woman to keep a man to an engagement of which she seemed so thoroughly aware that he was weary.

From this time the subject was never revived by Elinor, and when entered on by Lucy, who seldom missed an opportunity of introducing it and was particularly careful to inform her confidante of her happiness whenever she received a letter from Edward, it was treated by the former with calmness and caution and dismissed as soon as civility would allow. She felt such conversations to be an indulgence which Lucy did not deserve and which were dangerous to herself. She suffered through conversations with Lucy regarding any matter, most of all those pertaining to Edward.

Then to Elinor's unspoken irritation, the visit of the Miss Steeles at Barton Park was lengthened far beyond what the first invitation implied. Their favour increased. They could not be spared. Sir John would not hear of their going, and in spite of their numerous and long-arranged engagements in Exeter, in spite of the absolute necessity of returning to fulfil them immediately which was in full force at the end of every week, they were prevailed on to stay nearly two months at the park and to assist in the due celebration of that festival which requires a more than ordinary share of private balls and large dinners to proclaim its importance.

Chapter Twenty-Five

Though Mrs Jennings was in the habit of spending a large portion of the year at the houses of her children and friends, she was not without a settled habitation of her own. Since the death of her husband, who had traded with success in a less elegant part of the town, she had resided every winter in a house in one of the streets near Portman Square. Towards this home she began on the approach of January to turn her thoughts, and thither she one day abruptly, and very unexpectedly by them, asked the elder Misses Dashwood to accompany her.

Elinor, without observing the varying complexion of her sister and the animated look which spoke no indifference to the plan, immediately gave a grateful but absolute denial for both in which she believed herself to be speaking their united inclinations. The reason alleged was their determined resolution of not leaving their mother at that time of the year. Mrs Jennings received the refusal with some surprise and repeated her invitation immediately.

"Oh, Lord! I am sure your mother can spare you very well, and I do beg you will favour me with your company, for I've quite set my heart upon it. Don't fancy that you will be any inconvenience to me, for I shan't put myself at all out of my way for you. It will only be sending Betty by the coach, and I hope I can afford *that*. We three shall be able to go very well in my chaise, and when we are in town, if you do not like to go wherever I do, well and good, you may always go with one of my daughters. I am sure your mother will not object to it, for I have had such good luck in getting my own children off my hands that she will think me a very fit person to have the charge of you, and if I don't get one of you at least well married before I have done with you it shall not be my fault. I shall speak a good word for you to all the young men, you may depend upon it."

"I have a notion," said Sir John, "that Miss Marianne would not object to such a scheme if her elder sister would come into it. It is very hard indeed that she should not have a little pleasure because Miss Dashwood does not wish it. So I would advise you two to set off for town when you are tired of Barton without saying a word to Miss Dashwood about it."

"Nay," cried Mrs Jennings, "I am sure I shall be monstrous glad of Miss Marianne's company whether Miss Dashwood will go or not. Only the more the merrier say I, and I thought it would be more comfortable for them to be together, because if they got tired of me they might talk to one another and laugh at my old ways behind my back. But one or the other, if not both of them, I must have. Lord bless me! How do you think I can live poking by myself, I who have been always used till this winter to have Charlotte with me. Come, Miss Marianne, let us strike hands upon the bargain, and if Miss Dashwood will change her mind by and bye, why so much the better."

"I thank you, ma'am, sincerely thank you," said Marianne with warmth. "Your invitation has insured my gratitude forever, and it would give me such happiness, yes, almost the greatest happiness I am capable of to be able to accept it. But my mother, my dearest, kindest mother — I feel the justice of what Elinor has urged, and if she were to be made less happy, less comfortable by our absence — Oh no, nothing should tempt me to leave her. It should not, must not be a struggle."

Mrs Jennings repeated her assurance that Mrs Dashwood could spare them perfectly well. Elinor, who now understood her sister and saw to what indifference to almost everything else she was carried by her eagerness to be with Willoughby again, made no farther direct opposition to the plan and merely referred it to her mother's decision. From whom, however, she scarcely expected to receive any support in her endeavour to prevent a visit which she could not approve of for Marianne and which on her own account she had particular reasons to avoid.

Whatever Marianne was desirous of, her mother would be eager to promote — she could not expect to influence the latter to cautiousness of conduct in an affair respecting which she had never been able to inspire her with distrust, and she dared not explain the motive of her own disinclination for going to London. That Marianne — fastidious as she was, thoroughly acquainted with Mrs Jennings' manners and invariably disgusted by them — should overlook every inconvenience of that kind, should disregard whatever must be most wounding to her irritable feelings in her pursuit of one object was such a proof so strong, so full, of the importance of that object to her as Elinor, in spite of all that had passed, was not prepared to witness.

On being informed of the invitation Mrs Dashwood, persuaded that such an excursion would be productive of much amusement to both her daughters and perceiving through all her affectionate attention to herself how much the heart of Marianne was in it, would not hear of their declining the offer upon her account. She insisted on their both accepting it directly then began to foresee, with her usual cheerfulness, a variety of advantages that would accrue to them all from this separation.

"I am delighted with the plan," she cried, "it is exactly what I could wish. Margaret and I shall be as much benefited by it as yourselves. When you and the Middletons are gone, we shall go on so quietly and happily together with our books and our music! You will find Margaret so improved when you come back again! I have a little plan of alteration for your bedrooms too, which may now be performed without any inconvenience to anyone. It is very right that you should go to town. I would have every young woman of your condition in life acquainted with the manners and amusements of London. You will be under the care of a motherly good sort of woman, of whose kindness to you I can have no doubt. And in all probability you will see your brother — and whatever may be his faults, or the faults of his wife, when I consider whose son he is I cannot bear to have you so wholly estranged from each other."

"Though with your usual anxiety for our happiness," said Elinor, "you have been obviating every impediment to the present scheme which occurred to you, there is still one objection which in my opinion cannot be so easily removed."

Marianne's countenance sank.

"And what," said Mrs Dashwood, "is my dear prudent Elinor going to suggest? What formidable obstacle is she now to bring forward? Do let me hear a word about the expense of it."

"My objection is this. Though I think very well of Mrs Jennings' heart, she is not a woman whose society can afford us pleasure or whose protection will give us consequence."

"That is very true," replied her mother, "but of her society separately from that of other people you will scarcely have anything at all, and you will almost always appear in public with Lady Middleton."

"If Elinor is frightened away by her dislike of Mrs Jennings," said Marianne, "at least it need not prevent *my* accepting her invitation. I have no such scruples, and I am sure I could put up with every unpleasantness of that kind with very little effort."

Elinor could not help smiling at this display of indifference towards the manners of a person to whom she had often had difficulty in persuading Marianne to behave with tolerable politeness, and resolved within herself that if her sister persisted in going, she would go likewise. She did not think it proper that Marianne should be left to the sole guidance of her own judgement, or that Mrs Jennings should be abandoned to the mercy of Marianne for all the comfort of her domestic hours. To this determination she was the more easily reconciled by recollecting that Edward Ferrars, by Lucy's account, was not to be in town before February, and that their visit without any unreasonable abridgement might be previously finished.

"I will have you both go," said Mrs Dashwood. "These objections are nonsensical. You will have much pleasure in being in London, and especially in being together, and if Elinor would ever condescend to anticipate enjoyment, she would foresee it there from a variety of sources. She would, perhaps, expect some from improving her acquaintance with her sister-in-law's family."

Elinor had often wished for an opportunity of attempting to weaken her mother's dependence on the attachment of Edward and herself, that the shock might be less when the whole truth were revealed. Now on this attack, though almost hopeless of success, she forced herself to begin her design by saying as calmly as she could, "I like Edward Ferrars very much and shall always be glad to see him, but as to the rest of the family, it is a matter of perfect indifference to me whether I am ever known to them or not."

Mrs Dashwood smiled and said nothing. Marianne lifted up her eyes in astonishment, and Elinor conjectured that she might as well have held her tongue.

After very little farther discourse it was finally settled that the invitation should be fully accepted. Mrs Jennings received the information with a great deal of joy and many assurances of kindness and care, nor was it a matter of pleasure merely to her. Sir John was delighted, for to a man whose prevailing anxiety was the dread of being alone, the acquisition of two to the number of inhabitants in London was something. Even Lady Middleton took the trouble of being delighted, which was putting herself rather out of her way, and as for the Miss Steeles, especially Lucy, they had never been so happy in their lives as this intelligence made them.

Elinor submitted to the arrangement which counteracted her wishes with less reluctance than she had expected to feel. With regard to herself, it was now a matter of unconcern whether she went to town or not. And when she saw her mother so thoroughly pleased with the plan and her sister exhilarated by it in look, voice and manner, restored to all her usual animation and elevated to more than her usual gaiety, she could not be dissatisfied with the cause and would hardly allow herself to distrust the consequence.

Marianne's joy was almost a degree beyond happiness, so great was the perturbation of her spirits and her impatience to be gone. Her unwillingness to quit her mother was her only restorative to calmness, and at the moment of parting her grief on that score was excessive. Her mother's affliction was hardly less, and Elinor was the only one of the three, who seemed to consider the separation as anything short of eternal.

Their departure took place in the first week in January. The Middletons were to follow in about a week. The Miss Steeles kept their station at the park, and were to quit it only with the rest of the family.

To this plan of travel Elinor rejoiced. Her days of tolerating the Miss Steeles had come to an end.

Chapter Twenty-Six

Elinor could not find herself in the carriage with Mrs Jennings, and beginning a journey to London under her protection and as her guest, without wondering at her own situation. So short had their acquaintance with that lady been, so wholly unsuited were they in age and disposition and so many had been her objections against such a measure only a few days before!

But these objections had all, with that happy ardour of youth which Marianne and her mother equally shared, been overcome or overlooked. Elinor, in spite of every occasional doubt of Willoughby's constancy, could not witness the rapture of delightful expectation which filled the whole soul and beamed in the eyes of Marianne without feeling how blank was her own prospect, how cheerless her own state of mind in the comparison and how gladly she would engage in the solicitude of Marianne's situation to have the same animating object in view, the same possibility of hope.

A short, a very short time however must now decide what Willoughby's intentions were. In all probability he was already in town. Marianne's eagerness to be gone declared her dependence on finding him there, and Elinor was resolved not only upon gaining every new light as to his character which her own observation or the intelligence of others could give her, but likewise upon watching his behaviour to her sister with such zealous attention as to ascertain what he was and what he meant before many meetings had taken place. Should the result of her observations be unfavourable, she was determined at all events to open the eyes of her sister. Should it be otherwise, her exertions would be of a different nature – she must then learn to avoid every selfish comparison and banish every regret which might lessen her satisfaction in the happiness of Marianne.

They were three days on their journey, and Marianne's behaviour as they travelled was a happy specimen of what future complaisance and companionableness to Mrs Jennings might be expected to be. She sat in silence almost all the way, wrapped in her own meditations and scarcely ever voluntarily speaking, except when any object of picturesque beauty within their view drew from her an exclamation of delight exclusively addressed to her sister.

To atone for this conduct therefore, Elinor took immediate possession of the post of civility which she had assigned herself, behaved with the greatest attention to Mrs Jennings, talked with her, laughed with her and listened to her whenever she could. Mrs Jennings on her side treated them both with all possible kindness, was solicitous on every occasion for their ease and enjoyment, and only disturbed that she could not make them choose their own dinners at the inn, nor extort a confession of their preferring salmon to cod or boiled fowls to veal cutlets. They reached town by three o'clock the third day, glad to be released after such a journey from the confinement of a carriage, and ready to enjoy all the luxury of a good fire.

The house was handsome and handsomely fitted up, and the young ladies were immediately put in possession of a very comfortable apartment. It had formerly been Charlotte's, and over the mantelpiece still hung a landscape in coloured silks of her performance, in proof of her having spent seven years at a great school in town to some effect.

As dinner was not to be ready in less than two hours from their arrival, Elinor determined to employ the interval in writing to her mother and sat down for that purpose. In a few moments Marianne did the same. "I am writing home, Marianne," said Elinor, "had not you better defer your letter for a day or two?"

"I am not going to write to my mother," replied Marianne hastily, and as if wishing to avoid any farther enquiry.

Elinor said no more. It immediately struck her that she must then be writing to Willoughby, and the conclusion which as instantly followed was that however mysteriously they might wish to conduct the affair, they must be engaged. This conviction, though not entirely satisfactory, gave her pleasure, and she continued her letter with greater alacrity.

Marianne's was finished in a very few minutes. In length it could be no more than a note. It was then folded up, sealed and directed with eager rapidity. Elinor thought she could distinguish a large W in the direction, and no sooner was it complete than

Marianne, ringing the bell, requested the footman who answered it to get that letter conveyed for her to the two-penny post. This decided the matter at once.

Her spirits still continued very high, but there was a flutter in them which prevented their giving much pleasure to her sister, and this agitation increased as the evening drew on. She could scarcely eat any dinner, and when they afterwards returned to the drawing room, seemed anxiously listening to the sound of every carriage.

It was a great satisfaction to Elinor that Mrs Jennings, by being much engaged in her own room, could see little of what was passing. The tea things were brought in, and already had Marianne been disappointed more than once by a rap at a neighbouring door when a loud one was suddenly heard which could not be mistaken for one at any other house. Elinor felt secure of its announcing Willoughby's approach, and Marianne, starting up, moved towards the door.

Everything was silent. This could not be borne many seconds. She opened the door, advanced a few steps towards the stairs and after listening half a minute returned into the room in all the agitation which a conviction of having heard him would naturally produce. In the ecstasy of her feelings at that instant she could not help exclaiming, "Oh, Elinor, it is Willoughby, indeed it is!" and seemed almost ready to throw herself into his arms when Colonel Brandon appeared.

It was too great a shock to be borne with calmness, and she immediately left the room. Elinor was disappointed for Marianne too, but at the same time her growing regard for Colonel Brandon ensured his welcome with her, and she felt particularly hurt that a man so partial to her sister should perceive that she experienced nothing but grief and disappointment in seeing him. She instantly saw that it was not unnoticed by him, that he even observed Marianne as she quitted the room with such astonishment and concern as hardly left him the recollection of what civility demanded towards herself.

"Is your sister ill?" said he.

Elinor answered in some distress that she was, then talked of headaches, low spirits and over-fatigues, and of everything to which she could decently attribute her sister's behaviour.

He heard her with the most earnest attention, but seeming to recollect himself said no more on the subject and began directly to speak of his pleasure at seeing them in London, making the usual enquiries about their journey and the friends they had left behind.

In this calm kind of way, with very little interest on either side, they continued to talk, both of them out of spirits and the thoughts of both engaged elsewhere. Elinor wished very much to ask whether Willoughby were then in town, but she was afraid of giving him pain by any enquiry after his rival, and at length, by way of saying something, she asked if he had been in London ever since she had seen him last.

"Yes," he replied with some embarrassment, "almost ever since. I have been once or twice at Delaford for a few days, but it has never been in my power to return to Barton."

This and the manner in which it was said immediately brought back to her remembrance all the circumstances of his quitting that place with the uneasiness and suspicions they had caused to Mrs Jennings, and she was fearful that her question had implied much more curiosity on the subject than she had ever felt.

Mrs Jennings soon came in. "Oh! Colonel," said she with her usual noisy cheerfulness, "I am monstrous glad to see you—sorry I could not come before—beg your pardon, but I have been forced to look about me a little and settle my matters. It is a long while since I have been at home, and you know one has always a world of little odd things to do after one has been away for any time, then I have had Cartwright to settle with—Lord, I have been as busy as a bee ever since dinner! But pray, Colonel, how came you to conjure out that I should be in town today?"

"I had the pleasure of hearing it at Mr Palmer's, where I have been dining."

"Oh, you did? Well, and how do they all do at their house? How does Charlotte do? I warrant you she is a fine size by this time."

"Mrs Palmer appeared quite well, and I am commissioned to tell you that you will certainly see her tomorrow."

"Ay, to be sure, I thought as much. Well, Colonel, I have brought two young ladies with me, you see— that is, you see but one of them now, but there is another somewhere. Your friend Miss Marianne too— which you will not be sorry to hear. I do not know what you and Mr Willoughby will do between you about her. Ay, it is a fine thing to be young and handsome. Well! I was young once, but I never was very handsome—worse luck for me. However, I got a very good husband, and I don't know what the greatest beauty can do more. Ah, poor man, he has been dead these eight years and better. But Colonel, where have you been to since we parted? And how does your business go on? Come, come, let's have no secrets among friends."

He replied with his customary mildness to all her enquiries, but without satisfying her in any. Elinor now began to make the tea, and Marianne was obliged to appear again.

After her entrance, Colonel Brandon became more thoughtful and silent than he had been before, and Mrs Jennings could not prevail on him to stay long. No other visitor appeared that evening, and the ladies were unanimous in agreeing to go early to bed.

Marianne rose the next morning with recovered spirits and happy looks. The disappointment of the evening before seemed forgotten in the expectation of what was to happen that day. They had not long finished their breakfast before Mrs Palmer's barouche stopped at the door, and in a few minutes she came laughing into the room—so delighted to see them all that it was hard to say whether she received most pleasure from meeting her mother or the Miss Dashwoods again. So surprised at their coming to town, though it was what she had rather expected all along, so angry at their accepting her mother's invitation after having declined her own, though at the same time she would never have forgiven them if they had not come!

"Mr Palmer will be so happy to see you," said she. "What do you think he said when he heard of your coming with Mama? I forget what it was now, but it was something so droll!"

After an hour or two spent in what her mother called comfortable chat, or in other words in every variety of enquiry concerning all their acquaintance on Mrs Jennings' side and in laughter without cause on Mrs Palmer's, it was proposed by the latter that they should all accompany her to some shops where she had business that morning. To which Mrs Jennings and Elinor readily consented as having likewise some purchases to make themselves, and Marianne, though declining it at first, was induced to go likewise.

Wherever they went, she was evidently always on the watch. In Bond Street especially, where much of their business lay, her eyes were in constant enquiry, and in whatever shop the party were engaged her mind was equally abstracted from everything actually before them, from all that interested and occupied the others. Restless and dissatisfied everywhere, her sister could never obtain her opinion of any article of purchase, however it might equally concern them both. She received no pleasure from anything, was only impatient to be at home again, and could with difficulty govern her vexation at the tediousness of Mrs Palmer, whose eye was caught by everything pretty, expensive or new, who was wild to buy all, could determine on none and dawdled away her time in rapture and indecision.

It was late in the morning before they returned home, and no sooner had they entered the house than Marianne flew eagerly upstairs, and when Elinor followed she found her turning from the table with a sorrowful countenance which declared that no Willoughby had been there.

"Has no letter been left here for me since we went out?" said she to the footman who then entered with the parcels. She was answered in the negative. "Are you quite sure of it?" she replied. "Are you certain that no servant, no porter has left any letter or note?"

The man replied that none had.

"How very odd!" said she in a low and disappointed voice as she turned away to the window.

How odd indeed! repeated Elinor within herself, regarding her sister with uneasiness. *If she had not known him to be in town she would not have written to him as she did, she would have written to Combe Magna, and if he is in town, how odd that he should neither come nor write! Oh, my dear mother, you must be wrong in permitting an engagement between a daughter so young, a man so little known, to be carried on in so doubtful, so mysterious a manner! I long to enquire, and how will* my *interference be borne?*

She determined after some consideration that if appearances continued many days longer as unpleasant as they now were, she would represent in the strongest manner to her mother the necessity of some serious enquiry into the affair.

Mrs Palmer and two elderly ladies of Mrs Jennings' intimate acquaintance, whom she had met and invited in the morning, dined with them. The former left them soon after tea to fulfil her evening engagements, and Elinor was obliged to assist in making a whist table for the others. Marianne was of no use on these occasions, as she would never learn the game, but though her time was therefore at her own disposal the evening was by no means more productive of pleasure to her than to Elinor, for it was spent in all the anxiety of expectation and the pain of disappointment. She sometimes endeavoured for a few minutes to read, but the book was soon thrown aside and she returned to the more interesting employment of walking backwards and forwards across the room, pausing for a moment whenever she came to the window in hopes of distinguishing the long-expected rap.

Chapter Twenty-Seven

"If this open weather holds much longer," said Mrs Jennings when they met at breakfast the following morning, "Sir John will not like leaving Barton next week. 'Tis a sad thing for sportsmen to lose a day's pleasure. Poor souls! I always pity them when they do, they seem to take it so much to heart."

"That is true," cried Marianne in a cheerful voice, and walking to the window as she spoke to examine the day. "I had not thought of that. This weather will keep many sportsmen in the country."

It was a lucky recollection. All her good spirits were restored by it. "It is charming weather for them indeed," she continued as she sat down to the breakfast table with a happy countenance. "How much they must enjoy it! But" — with a little return of anxiety — "it cannot be expected to last long. At this time of the year and after such a series of rain, we shall certainly have very little more of it. Frosts will soon set in, and in all probability with severity. In another day or two perhaps, this extreme mildness can hardly last longer—nay, perhaps it may freeze tonight!"

"At any rate," said Elinor, wishing to prevent Mrs Jennings from seeing her sister's thoughts as clearly as she did, "I dare say we shall have Sir John and Lady Middleton in town by the end of next week."

"Ay, my dear, I'll warrant you we do. Mary always has her own way."

And now, silently conjectured Elinor, *she will write to Combe by this day's post.*

But if she did, the letter was written and sent away with a privacy which eluded all her watchfulness to ascertain the fact. Whatever the truth of it might be, and far as Elinor was from feeling thorough contentment about it, yet while she saw Marianne in spirits she could not be very uncomfortable herself. And Marianne was in spirits, happy in the mildness of the weather and still happier in her expectation of a frost.

The morning was chiefly spent in leaving cards at the houses of Mrs Jennings' acquaintance to inform them of her being in town, and Marianne was all the time busy in observing the direction of the wind, watching the variations of the sky and imagining an alteration in the air.

"Don't you find it colder than it was in the morning, Elinor? There seems to me a very decided difference. I can hardly keep my hands warm even in my muff. It was not so yesterday, I think. The clouds seem parting too, the sun will be out in a moment and we shall have a clear afternoon."

Elinor was alternately diverted and pained, but Marianne persevered, and saw every night in the brightness of the fire and every morning in the appearance of the atmosphere the certain symptoms of approaching frost.

The Miss Dashwoods had no greater reason to be dissatisfied with Mrs Jennings' style of living and set of acquaintance than with her behaviour to themselves, which was invariably kind. Everything in her household arrangements was conducted on the most liberal plan, and excepting a few old city friends whom to Lady Middleton's regret she had never dropped, she visited no one to whom an introduction could at all discompose the feelings of her young companions. Pleased to find herself more comfortably situated in that particular than she had expected, Elinor was very willing to compound for the want of much real enjoyment from any of their evening parties, which whether at home or abroad formed only for cards, could have little to amuse her.

Colonel Brandon, who had a general invitation to the house, was with them almost every day. He came to look at Marianne, who said little to him, and talk to Elinor, who often derived more satisfaction from conversing with him than from any other daily occurrence, but who saw at the same time with much concern his continued regard for her sister. She feared it was a strengthening regard, especially because she herself began to enjoy his company more than she should.

One afternoon, he called with a book of poetry in hand. Marianne was indifferent to him and to his attempt to charm her with reading them. Elinor encouraged him. At first thought, she meant only to compensate for her sister's lack of interest. But the sound of his voice, the tempo, the tenor, the rhythm suddenly had its own melody. Her enchantment led her to rise and take a seat closer to him. He did not notice, so entranced was he by his own delight in the words he read. Elinor noticed – and so did her body. His voice was a baritone of rich timbre with a rough edge that pricked and prickled, soothed by his melodious delivery.

Elinor thought herself mad to enjoy his simple reading so much. Yet she found no explanation for her amusement other than her own need for male companionship. She tested her premise, brushing his sleeve as he read and tingling to her toes in rapt enjoyment. Putting a hand upon his sleeve, she shivered in new delights, her tremors fed by her loneliness – or so she had to convince herself. This infatuation with him was nothing more than a hopeless flight of fancy. And so she tamped down her own interest in him, deciding that her fantasies of him becoming as physically intimate with her as Edward were folly. Indeed, it grieved her for herself as well as him to see the earnestness with which he often watched Marianne, and his spirits were certainly worse than when at Barton.

About a week after their arrival, it became certain that Willoughby was also arrived. His card was on the table when they came in from the morning's drive.

"Good God!" cried Marianne. "He has been here while we were out."

Elinor, rejoiced to be assured of his being in London, now ventured to say, "Depend upon it, he will call again tomorrow." But Marianne seemed hardly to hear her, and on Mrs Jennings' entrance, escaped with the precious card.

This event, while it raised the spirits of Elinor, restored to those of her sister all and more than all their former agitation. From this moment her mind was never quiet. The expectation of seeing him every hour of the day made her unfit for anything. She insisted on being left behind the next morning when the others went out.

Elinor's thoughts were full of what might be passing in Berkeley Street during their absence, but a moment's glance at her sister when they returned was enough to inform her that Willoughby had paid no second visit there. A note was just then brought in and laid on the table.

"For me!" cried Marianne, stepping hastily forward.

"No, ma'am, for my mistress."

But Marianne, not convinced, took it instantly up. "It is indeed for Mrs Jennings. How provoking!"

"You are expecting a letter, then?" said Elinor, unable to be longer silent.

"Yes, a little—not much."

After a short pause. "You have no confidence in me, Marianne."

"Nay, Elinor, this reproach from you—you who have confidence in no one!"

"Me!" returned Elinor in some confusion. "Indeed, Marianne, I have nothing to tell."

"Nor I," answered Marianne with energy, "our situations then are alike. We have neither of us anything to tell, you because you do not communicate, and I because I conceal nothing."

Elinor, distressed by this charge of reserve in herself which she was not at liberty to do away, knew not how under such circumstances to press for greater openness in Marianne.

Mrs Jennings soon appeared, and the note being given her, she read it aloud. It was from Lady Middleton, announcing their arrival in Conduit Street the night before and requesting the company of her mother and cousins the following evening. Business on Sir John's part, and a violent cold on her own, prevented their calling in Berkeley Street. The invitation was accepted, but when the hour of appointment drew near, necessary as it was in common civility to Mrs Jennings that they should both attend her on such a visit, Elinor had some difficulty in persuading her sister to go. For still she had seen nothing of Willoughby, and therefore was not more indisposed for amusement abroad than unwilling to run the risk of his calling again in her absence.

Elinor found when the evening was over that disposition is not materially altered by a change of abode, for although scarcely settled in town, Sir John had contrived to collect around him nearly twenty young people and to amuse them with a ball. This was an affair, however, of which Lady Middleton did not approve. In the country an unpremeditated dance was very allowable, but in London, where the reputation of elegance was more important and less easily attained, it was risking too much for the gratification of a few girls to have it known that Lady Middleton had given a small dance of eight or nine couple of with two violins and a mere side-board collation.

Mr and Mrs Palmer were of the party. From the former, whom they had not seen before since their arrival in town, as he was careful to avoid the appearance of any attention to his mother-in-law and therefore never came near her, they received no mark of recognition on their entrance. He looked at them slightly without seeming to know who they were, and merely nodded to Mrs Jennings from the other side of the room. Marianne gave one glance round the apartment as she entered—it was enough, *he* was not there—and she sat down, equally ill-disposed to receive or communicate pleasure.

After they had been assembled about an hour, Mr Palmer sauntered towards the Miss Dashwoods to express his surprise on seeing them in town, though Colonel Brandon had been first informed of their arrival at his house and he had himself said something very droll on hearing that they were to come.

"I thought you were both in Devonshire," said he.

"Did you?" replied Elinor.

"When do you go back again?"

"I do not know." And thus ended their discourse.

Never had Marianne been so unwilling to dance in her life as she was that evening, and never so much fatigued by the exercise. She complained of it as they returned to Berkeley Street.

"Aye, aye," said Mrs Jennings, "we know the reason of all that very well. If a certain person who shall be nameless had been there, you would not have been a bit tired — and to say the truth it was not very pretty of him not to give you the meeting when he was invited."

"Invited!" cried Marianne.

"So my daughter Middleton told me, for it seems Sir John met him somewhere in the street this morning."

Marianne said no more, but looked exceedingly hurt. Impatient in this situation to be doing something that might lead to her sister's relief, Elinor resolved to write the next morning to her mother, and hoped by awakening her fears for the health of Marianne to procure those enquiries which had been so long delayed. She was still more eagerly bent on this measure by perceiving after breakfast on the morrow that Marianne was again writing to Willoughby, for she could not suppose it to be to any other person.

About the middle of the day Mrs Jennings went out by herself on business, and Elinor began her letter directly while Marianne, too restless for employment, too anxious for conversation, walked from one window to the other or sat down by the fire in melancholy meditation. Elinor was very earnest in her application to her mother, relating all that had passed, her suspicions of Willoughby's inconstancy, urging her by every plea of duty and affection to demand from Marianne an account of her real situation with respect to him.

Her letter was scarcely finished when a rap foretold a visitor and Colonel Brandon was announced. Marianne, who had seen him from the window and who hated company of any kind, left the room before he entered it.

He looked more than usually grave, and though expressing satisfaction at finding Miss Dashwood alone, as if he had somewhat in particular to tell her, sat for some time without saying a word. Elinor, persuaded that he had some communication to make in which her sister was concerned, impatiently expected its opening. It was not the first time of her feeling the same kind of conviction, for more than once before, beginning with the observation of "Your sister looks unwell today," or "Your sister seems out of spirits," he had appeared on the point either of disclosing or of enquiring something particular about her.

After a pause of several minutes their silence was broken by his asking her in a voice of some agitation when he was to congratulate her on the acquisition of a brother. Elinor was not prepared for such a question, and having no answer ready, was obliged to adopt the simple and common expedient of asking what he meant. He tried to smile as he replied, "Your sister's engagement to Mr Willoughby is very generally known."

"It cannot be generally known," returned Elinor, "for her own family do not know it."

He looked surprised and said, "I beg your pardon. I am afraid my enquiry has been impertinent, but I had not supposed any secrecy intended, as they openly correspond and their marriage is universally talked of."

"How can that be? By whom can you have heard it mentioned?"

"By many — by some of whom you know nothing, by others with whom you are most intimate. Mrs Jennings, Mrs Palmer and the Middletons. But still I might not have believed it — for where the mind is perhaps rather unwilling to be convinced, it will always find something to support its doubts — if I had not when the servant let me in today accidentally seen a letter in his hand directed to Mr Willoughby in your sister's writing. I came to enquire, but I was convinced before I could ask the question. Is everything finally settled? Is it impossible to — ? But I have no right, and I could have no chance of succeeding.

"Excuse me, Miss Dashwood. I believe I have been wrong in saying so much, but I hardly know what to do, and on your prudence I have the strongest dependence. Tell me that it is all absolutely resolved on, that any attempt — that in short concealment, if concealment be possible, is all that remains."

These words, which conveyed to Elinor a direct avowal of his love for her sister, affected her very much. Her disappointment that he cared for her sister equalled her jealousy. How could the man not see that his affection for Marianne was for naught? The girl loved another. His cause was lost. Yet Elinor was not immediately able to say anything, and even when her spirits were recovered she debated for a short time on the answer it would be most proper to give.

The real state of things between Willoughby and her sister was so little known to herself that in endeavouring to explain it, she might be as liable to say too much as too little. Yet as she was convinced that Marianne's affection for Willoughby could leave no hope of Colonel Brandon's success, whatever the event of that affection might be, and at the same time wished to shield her conduct from censure, she thought it most prudent and kind after some consideration to say more than she really knew or believed. She acknowledged therefore that though she had never been informed by themselves of the terms on which they stood with each other, of their mutual affection she had no doubt, and of their correspondence she was not astonished to hear.

He listened to her with silent attention, and on her ceasing to speak rose directly from his seat and after saying in a voice of emotion, "To your sister I wish all imaginable happiness, to Willoughby that he may endeavour to deserve her," took leave and went away.

Elinor derived no comfortable feelings from this conversation to lessen the uneasiness of her mind on other points. She was left on the contrary with a melancholy impression of Colonel Brandon's unhappiness, and was prevented even from wishing it removed by her anxiety for the very event that must confirm it.

Chapter Twenty-Eight

Nothing occurred during the next three or four days to make Elinor regret what she had done in applying to her mother, for Willoughby neither came nor wrote. They were engaged about the end of that time to attend Lady Middleton to a party, from which Mrs Jennings was kept away by the indisposition of her youngest daughter. For this party Marianne, wholly dispirited, careless of her appearance and seeming equally indifferent whether she went or stayed, prepared without one look of hope or one expression of pleasure. She sat by the drawing room fire after tea till the moment of Lady Middleton's arrival without once stirring from her seat or altering her attitude, lost in her own thoughts and insensible of her sister's presence, and when at last they were told that Lady Middleton waited for them at the door, she started as if she had forgotten that anyone was expected.

They arrived in due time at the place of destination, and as soon as the string of carriages before them would allow, alighted, ascended the stairs, heard their names announced from one landing-place to another in an audible voice and entered a room splendidly lit up, quite full of company and insufferably hot. When they had paid their tribute of politeness by curtsying to the lady of the house, they were permitted to mingle in the crowd and take their share of the heat and inconvenience to which their arrival must necessarily add. After some time spent in saying little or doing less, Lady Middleton sat down to Casino, and as Marianne was not in spirits for moving about, she and Elinor luckily succeeding to chairs, placed themselves at no great distance from the table.

They had not remained in this manner long before Elinor perceived Willoughby standing within a few yards of them in earnest conversation with a very fashionable-looking young woman. She soon caught his eye and he immediately bowed, but without attempting to speak to her or to approach Marianne, though he could not but see her, then continued his discourse with the same lady. Elinor turned involuntarily to Marianne to see whether it could be unobserved by her. At that moment she first perceived him, and her whole countenance glowing with sudden delight, she would have moved towards him instantly had not her sister caught hold of her.

"Good heavens!" she exclaimed. "He is there—he is there—Oh, why does he not look at me? Why cannot I speak to him?"

"Pray, pray be composed," cried Elinor, "and do not betray what you feel to everybody present. Perhaps he has not observed you yet."

This however was more than she could believe herself, and to be composed at such a moment was not only beyond the reach of Marianne, it was beyond her wish. She sat in an agony of impatience which affected every feature. She gazed at him, craning her neck, her mouth open, her hands kneaded together.

At last he turned round again and regarded them both. She started up, and pronouncing his name in a tone of affection, held out her hand to him. He approached, and addressing himself rather to Elinor than Marianne, as if wishing to avoid her eye and determined not to observe her attitude, enquired in a hurried manner after Mrs Dashwood and asked how long they had been in town.

Elinor was robbed of all presence of mind by such an address and was unable to say a word. But the feelings of her sister were instantly expressed. Her face was crimsoned over, and she exclaimed in a voice of the greatest emotion, "Good God! Willoughby, what is the meaning of this? Have you not received my letters? Will you not shake hands with me?"

He could not then avoid it, but her touch seemed painful to him, and he held her hand only for a moment. During all this time he was evidently struggling for composure. Elinor watched his countenance and saw its expression becoming more tranquil. After a moment's pause he spoke with calmness.

"I did myself the honour of calling in Berkeley Street last Tuesday, and very much regretted that I was not fortunate enough to find yourselves and Mrs Jennings at home. My card was not lost, I hope."

"But have you not received my notes?" cried Marianne in the wildest anxiety. "Here is some mistake I am sure—some dreadful mistake. What can be the meaning of it? Tell me, Willoughby, for heaven's sake tell me, what is the matter?"

He made no reply. His complexion changed and all his embarrassment returned. But as if, on catching the eye of the young lady with whom he had been previously talking, he felt the necessity of instant exertion, he recovered himself again, and after saying, "Yes, I had the pleasure of receiving the information of your arrival in town, which you were so good as to send me," turned hastily away with a slight bow and joined his friend.

Marianne, now looking dreadfully white and unable to stand, sank into her chair, and Elinor, expecting every moment to see her faint, tried to screen her from the observation of others while reviving her with lavender water.

"Go to him, Elinor," she cried as soon as she could speak, "and force him to come to me. Tell him I must see him again—must speak to him instantly. I cannot rest—I shall not have a moment's peace till this is explained—some dreadful misapprehension or other. Oh, go to him this moment."

"How can that be done? No, my dearest Marianne, you must wait. This is not the place for explanations. Wait only till tomorrow."

With difficulty however could she prevent her from following him herself, and to persuade her to check her agitation, to wait at least with the appearance of composure till she might speak to him with more privacy and more effect, was impossible. Marianne continued incessantly to give way in a low voice to the misery of her feelings by exclamations of wretchedness. Guests turned, others not, pretending they had not heard Marianne's agony. Marianne rose, only to be subdued by word and look of Elinor. She was making a spectacle of her despair.

In a short time Elinor saw Willoughby quit the room by the door towards the staircase, and telling Marianne that he was gone, urged the impossibility of speaking to him again that evening as a fresh argument for her to be calm. She instantly begged her sister would entreat Lady Middleton to take them home, as she was too miserable to stay a minute longer.

Lady Middleton, though in the middle of a rubber, on being informed that Marianne was unwell was too polite to object for a moment to her wish of going away, and making over her cards to a friend, they departed as soon the carriage could be found. Scarcely a word was spoken during their return to Berkeley Street. Marianne was in a silent agony, too much oppressed even for tears, but as Mrs Jennings was luckily not come home, they could go directly to their own room where hartshorn restored her a little to herself. She was soon undressed and in bed, and as she seemed desirous of being alone, her sister then left her, and while she waited the return of Mrs Jennings had leisure enough for thinking over the past.

That some kind of engagement had subsisted between Willoughby and Marianne she could not doubt, and that Willoughby was weary of it seemed equally clear. For however Marianne might still feed her own wishes, *she* could not attribute such behaviour to mistake or misapprehension of any kind. Nothing but a thorough change of sentiment could account for it. Her indignation would have been still stronger than it was had she not witnessed that embarrassment which seemed to speak a consciousness of his own misconduct, and prevented her from believing him so unprincipled as to have been sporting with the affections of her sister from the first, without any design that would bear investigation. Absence might have weakened his regard, and convenience might have determined him to overcome it, but that such a regard had formerly existed she could not bring herself to doubt.

As for Marianne, on the pangs which so unhappy a meeting must already have given her, and on those still more severe which might await her in its probable consequence, she could not reflect without the deepest concern. Her own situation gained in the comparison, for while she could *esteem* Edward as much as ever, however they might be divided in future, her mind might be always supported. But every circumstance that could embitter such an evil seemed uniting to heighten the misery of Marianne in a final separation from Willoughby—in an immediate and irreconcilable rupture with him.

Chapter Twenty-Nine

Before the housemaid had lit their fire the next day, or the sun gained any power over a cold, gloomy morning in January, Marianne, only half dressed, was kneeling against one of the window seats for the sake of all the little light she could command from it and writing as fast as a continual flow of tears would permit her. In this situation Elinor, roused from sleep by her agitation and sobs, first perceived her.

After observing her for a few moments with silent anxiety, she said in a tone of the most considerate gentleness, "Marianne, may I ask — ?"

"No, Elinor," she replied, "ask nothing, you will soon know all."

The sort of desperate calmness with which this was said lasted no longer than while she spoke, and was immediately followed by a return of the same excessive affliction. It was some minutes before she could go on with her letter, and the frequent bursts of grief which still obliged her at intervals to withhold her pen were proofs enough of her feeling how more than probable it was that she was writing for the last time to Willoughby.

Elinor paid her every quiet and unobtrusive attention in her power, and she would have tried to soothe and tranquilise her still more had not Marianne entreated her with all the eagerness of the most nervous irritability not to speak to her for the world. In such circumstances it was better for both that they should not be long together, and the restless state of Marianne's mind not only prevented her from remaining in the room a moment after she was dressed, but requiring at once solitude and continual change of place made her wander about the house till breakfast time, avoiding the sight of everybody.

At breakfast she neither ate nor attempted to eat anything, and Elinor's attention was then all employed not in urging her, not in pitying her, nor in appearing to regard her, but in endeavouring to engage Mrs Jennings' notice entirely to herself.

As this was a favourite meal with Mrs Jennings, it lasted a considerable time, and they were just setting themselves after it round the common working table when a letter was delivered to Marianne, which she eagerly caught from the servant and, turning of a death-like paleness, instantly ran out of the room. Elinor, who saw as plainly by this as if she had seen the direction that it must come from Willoughby, felt immediately such a sickness at heart as made her hardly able to hold up her head and sat in such a general tremor as made her fear it impossible to escape Mrs Jennings' notice.

That good lady, however, saw only that Marianne had received a letter from Willoughby, which appeared to her a very good joke, and which she treated accordingly by hoping with a laugh that she would find it to her liking. Of Elinor's distress she was too busily employed in measuring lengths of worsted for her rug to see anything at all, and calmly continuing her talk as soon as Marianne disappeared, she said, "Upon my word, I never saw a young woman so desperately in love in my life! My girls were nothing to her, and yet they used to be foolish enough, but as for Miss Marianne, she is quite an altered creature. I hope from the bottom of my heart he won't keep her waiting much longer, for it is quite grievous to see her look so ill and forlorn. Pray, when are they to be married?"

Elinor, though never less disposed to speak than at that moment, obliged herself to answer such an attack as this, and therefore trying to smile replied, "And have you really, ma'am, talked yourself into a persuasion of my sister's being engaged to Mr Willoughby? I thought it had been only a joke, but so serious a question seems to imply more, and I must beg therefore that you will not deceive yourself any longer. I do assure you that nothing would surprise me more than to hear of their being going to be married."

"For shame, for shame, Miss Dashwood! How can you talk so? Don't we all know that it must be a match, that they were over head and ears in love with each other from the first moment they met? Did not I see them together in Devonshire every day and all day long, and did not I know that your sister came to town with me on purpose to buy wedding clothes? Come, come, this won't do. Because you are so sly about it yourself, you think nobody else has any senses, but it is no such thing, I can tell you, for it has been known all over town this ever so long. I tell everybody of it and so does Charlotte."

"Indeed, ma'am," said Elinor very seriously, "you are mistaken. Indeed, you are doing a very unkind thing in spreading the report, and you will find that you have — though you will not believe me now."

Mrs Jennings laughed again, but Elinor had not spirits to say more, and eager at all events to know what Willoughby had written, hurried away to their room. On opening the door she saw Marianne stretched on the bed, almost choked by grief, one letter in her hand and two or three others laying by her. Elinor drew near, but without saying a word, and seating herself on the bed took her hand, kissed her affectionately several times then gave way to a burst of tears which at first was scarcely less violent than Marianne's.

The latter, though unable to speak, seemed to feel all the tenderness of this behaviour, and after some time thus spent in joint affliction she put all the letters into Elinor's hands then covering her face with her handkerchief almost screamed with agony. Elinor, who knew that such grief, shocking as it was to witness it, must have its course, watched by her till this excess of suffering had somewhat spent itself then turning eagerly to Willoughby's letter, read as follows —

Bond Street, January.
My dear madam,
I have just had the honour of receiving your letter, for which I beg to return my sincere acknowledgements. I am much concerned to find there was anything in my behaviour last night that did not meet your approbation, and though I am quite at a loss to discover in what point I could be so unfortunate as to offend you, I entreat your forgiveness of what I can assure you to have been perfectly unintentional.

I shall never reflect on my former acquaintance with your family in Devonshire without the most grateful pleasure, and flatter myself it will not be broken by any mistake or misapprehension of my actions. My esteem for your whole family is very sincere, but if I have been so unfortunate as to give rise to a belief of more than I felt or meant to express, I shall reproach myself for not having been more guarded in my professions of that esteem. That I should ever have meant more you will allow to be impossible when you understand that my affections have been long engaged elsewhere, and it will not be many weeks, I believe, before this engagement is fulfilled.

It is with great regret that I obey your commands in returning the letters with which I have been honoured from you, and the lock of hair which you so obligingly bestowed on me.

I am, dear madam, your most obedient humble servant,
John Willoughby

With what indignation such a letter as this must be read by Miss Dashwood may be imagined. Though aware before she began it that it must bring a confession of his inconstancy and confirm their separation forever, she was not aware that such language could be suffered to announce it. Nor could she have supposed Willoughby capable of departing so far from the appearance of every honourable and delicate feeling, so far from the common decorum of a gentleman, as to send a letter so impudently cruel. A letter which, instead of bringing with his desire of a release any professions of regret, acknowledged no breach of faith, denied all peculiar affection whatever. A letter of which every line was an insult and which proclaimed its writer to be deep in hardened villainy.

She paused over it for some time with indignant astonishment, then read it again and again, but every perusal only served to increase her abhorrence of the man. So bitter were her feelings against him that she dared not trust herself to speak lest she might wound Marianne still deeper by treating their disengagement not as a loss to her of any possible good but as an escape from the worst and most irremediable of all evils, a connection for life with an unprincipled man. A deliverance the most real, a blessing the most important.

In her earnest meditations on the contents of the letter, on the depravity of that mind which could dictate it, and probably on the very different mind of a very different person who had no other connection whatever with the affair than what her heart gave him with everything that passed, Elinor forgot the immediate distress of her sister. Forgot that she had three letters on her lap yet unread. And so entirely forgot how long she had been in the room that when on hearing a carriage drive up to the door she went to the window to see who could be coming so unreasonably early, she was all astonishment to perceive Mrs Jennings' chariot, which she knew had not been ordered till one.

Determined not to quit Marianne, though hopeless of contributing at present to her ease, she hurried away to excuse herself from attending Mrs Jennings on account of her sister being indisposed. Mrs Jennings, with a thoroughly good-humoured concern for its cause, admitted the excuse most readily. Elinor, after seeing her safe off, returned to Marianne, whom she found attempting to rise from the bed and whom she reached just in time to prevent her from falling on the floor, faint and giddy from a long want of proper rest and food. It was many days since she had any appetite, and many nights since she had really slept, and now when her mind was no longer supported by the fever of suspense the consequence of all this was felt in an aching head, a weakened stomach and a general nervous faintness.

A glass of wine, which Elinor procured for her directly, made her more comfortable, and she was at last able to express some sense of her kindness by saying, "Poor Elinor! How unhappy I make you!"

"I only wish," replied her sister, "there were anything I could do which might be of comfort to you."

This, as everything else would have been, was too much for Marianne, who could only exclaim in the anguish of her heart, "Oh! Elinor, I am miserable, indeed," before her voice was entirely lost in sobs.

Elinor could no longer witness this torrent of unresisted grief in silence. "Exert yourself, dear Marianne," she cried, "if you would not kill yourself and all who love you. Think of your mother, think of her misery while you suffer—for her sake you must exert yourself."

"I cannot, I cannot," cried Marianne. "Leave me, leave me, if I distress you, leave me, hate me, forget me! But do not torture me so. Oh, how easy for those who have no sorrow of their own to talk of exertion! Happy, happy Elinor, you cannot have an idea of what I suffer."

"Do you call me happy, Marianne? Ah, if you knew! And can you believe me to be so while I see you so wretched!"

"Forgive me, forgive me"—throwing her arms round her sister's neck—"I know you feel for me, I know what a heart you have, but yet you are—you must be happy. Edward loves you—what, oh what, can do away such happiness as that?"

"Many, many circumstances," said Elinor solemnly.

"No, no, no," cried Marianne wildly, "he loves you and only you. You can have no grief."

"I can have no pleasure while I see you in this state."

"And you will never see me otherwise. Mine is a misery which nothing can do away."

"You must not talk so, Marianne. Have you no comforts? No friends? Is your loss such as leaves no opening for consolation? Much as you suffer now, think of what you would have suffered if the discovery of his character had been delayed to a later period—if your engagement had been carried on for months and months, as it might have been, before he chose to put an end to it. Every additional day of unhappy confidence on your side would have made the blow more dreadful."

"Engagement!" cried Marianne. "There has been no engagement."

"No engagement!"

"No, he is not so unworthy as you believe him. He has broken no faith with me."

"But he told you that he loved you."

"Yes—no—never absolutely. It was every day implied, but never professedly declared. It was every day exemplified by deeds so sweet and intimate, but never consummated. Sometimes I thought it had been—but it never was."

Elinor felt staggered by this information. She waved a hand, wishing to ask about her sister's proper eligibility for a good and proper marriage. "Are you— still a maiden?"

Marianne frowned, then shrugged. "I am not certain. I have no proof that I am not. But we were...close...physically."

Elinor nodded. Yes, she had seen evidences of that. "Yet you wrote to him?"

"Yes—could that be wrong after all that had passed? But I cannot talk."

Elinor said no more, and turning again to the three letters which now raised a much stronger curiosity than before, directly ran over the contents of all. The first, which was what her sister had sent him on their arrival in town, was to this effect.

Berkeley Street, January.
How surprised you will be, Willoughby, on receiving this, and I think you will feel something more than surprise when you know that I am in town. An opportunity of coming hither, though with Mrs Jennings, was a temptation we could not resist. I wish you may receive this in time to come here tonight, but I will not depend on it. At any rate I shall expect you tomorrow. For the present, adieu.
M.D.

Her second note, which had been written on the morning after the dance at the Middletons', was in these words—

I cannot express my disappointment in having missed you the day before yesterday, nor my astonishment at not having received any answer to a note which I sent you above a week ago. I have been expecting to hear from you, and still more to see you, every hour of the day. Pray call again as soon as possible, and explain the reason of my having expected this in vain.

You had better come earlier another time, because we are generally out by one. We were last night at Lady Middleton's, where there was a dance. I have been told that you were asked to be of the party. But could it be so? You must be very much altered indeed since we parted, if that could be the case and you not there. But I will not suppose this possible, and I hope very soon to receive your personal assurance of its being otherwise.

M.D.

The contents of her last note to him were these—

What am I to imagine, Willoughby, by your behaviour last night? Again I demand an explanation of it. I was prepared to meet you with the pleasure which our separation naturally produced, with the familiarity which our intimacy at Barton appeared to me to justify. How could you delay your appearance by my side? After all we have enjoyed together, our bodies' intimacies welcomed by the other with such fervent glee, your reluctance to embrace me in public shocked me. I was repulsed indeed!

I have passed a wretched night in endeavouring to excuse a conduct which can scarcely be called less than insulting, but though I have not yet been able to form any reasonable apology for your behaviour, I am perfectly ready to hear your justification of it. You have perhaps been misinformed, or purposely deceived, in something concerning me, which may have lowered me in your opinion. Tell me what it is, explain the grounds on which you acted, and I shall be satisfied in being able to satisfy you.

It would grieve me indeed to be obliged to think ill of you, but if I am to do it – if I am to learn that you are not what we have hitherto believed you, that your regard for us all was insincere, that your behaviour to me was intended only to deceive – let it be told as soon as possible. My feelings are at present in a state of dreadful indecision. I wish to acquit you, but certainty on either side will be ease to what I now suffer. If your sentiments are no longer what they were, you will return my notes and the lock of my hair which is in your possession.

M.D.

That such letters, so full of affection and confidence, could have been so answered, Elinor, for Willoughby's sake, would have been unwilling to believe. But her condemnation of him did not blind her to the impropriety of their having been written at all, and she was silently grieving over the imprudence which had hazarded such unsolicited proofs of tenderness, not warranted by anything preceding and most severely condemned by the event, when Marianne, perceiving that she had finished the letters, observed to her that they contained nothing but what anyone would have written in the same situation.

"I felt myself," she added, "to be as solemnly engaged to him as if the strictest legal covenant had bound us to each other."

"I can believe it," said Elinor, "but unfortunately he did not feel the same."

"He did feel the same, Elinor — for weeks and weeks he felt it. I know he did."

"How can you believe that, Marianne?"

"I do. I must. Whatever may have changed him now — and nothing but the blackest art employed against me can have done it — I was once as dear to him as my own soul could wish. This lock of hair which now he can so readily give up was begged of me with the most earnest supplication. Had you seen his look, his manner, had you heard his voice at that moment! Have you forgot the last evening of our being together at Barton? The morning that we parted too! When he told me that it might be many weeks before we met again — his distress — can I ever forget his distress?"

For a moment or two she could say no more, but when this emotion had passed away, she added in a firmer tone, "Elinor, I have been cruelly used, but not by Willoughby."

"Dearest Marianne, who but himself? By whom can he have been instigated?"

"By all the world, rather than by his own heart."

Oh, could Elinor hear this? Did she not excuse her own lover his inconsistent behaviour? Did she not suffer for his weaknesses?

"I could rather believe every creature of my acquaintance leagued together to ruin me in his opinion than believe his nature capable of such cruelty. This woman of whom he writes — whoever she be — or anyone, in short, but your own dear self, Mama and Edward may have been so barbarous to bely me. Beyond you three, is there a creature in the world whom I would not rather suspect of evil than Willoughby, whose heart I know so well?"

Elinor would not contend, and only replied, "Whoever may have been so detestably your enemy, let them be cheated of their malignant triumph, my dear sister, by seeing how nobly the consciousness of your own innocence and good intentions supports your spirits. It is a reasonable and laudable pride which resists such malevolence."

"No, no," cried Marianne, "misery such as mine has no pride. I care not who knows that I am wretched. The triumph of seeing me so may be open to all the world. Elinor, Elinor, they who suffer little may be proud and independent as they like — may resist insult, or return mortification — but I cannot. I must feel — I must be wretched — and they are welcome to enjoy the consciousness of it that can."

"But for my mother's sake and mine —"

"I would do more than for my own. But to appear happy when I am so miserable—Oh! who can require it?"

Again they were both silent. Elinor was employed in walking thoughtfully from the fire to the window, from the window to the fire, without knowing that she received warmth from one or discerning objects through the other. Marianne, seated at the foot of the bed with her head leaning against one of its posts, again took up Willoughby's letter and after shuddering over every sentence exclaimed, "It is too much! Oh, Willoughby, Willoughby, could this be yours! Cruel, cruel—nothing can acquit you. Elinor, nothing can. Whatever he might have heard against me, ought he not to have suspended his belief? Ought he not to have told me of it, to have given me the power of clearing myself? 'The lock of hair'"— repeating it from the letter—"'which you so obligingly bestowed on me'. That is unpardonable. Willoughby, where was your heart when you wrote those words? Oh, barbarously insolent! Elinor, can he be justified?"

"No, Marianne, in no possible way."

"And yet this woman—who knows what her art may have been? How long it may have been premeditated, and how deeply contrived by her! Who is she? Who can she be? Whom did I ever hear him talk of as young and attractive among his female acquaintance? Oh, no one, no one—he talked to me only of myself."

Another pause ensued. Marianne was greatly agitated, and it ended thus. "Elinor, I must go home. I must go and comfort Mama. Cannot we be gone tomorrow?"

"Tomorrow, Marianne!"

"Yes, why should I stay here? I came only for Willoughby's sake—and now who cares for me? Who regards me?"

"It would be impossible to go tomorrow. We owe Mrs Jennings much more than civility, and civility of the commonest kind must prevent such a hasty removal as that."

"Well then, another day or two perhaps, but I cannot stay here long. I cannot stay to endure the questions and remarks of all these people. The Middletons and Palmers—how am I to bear their pity? The pity of such a woman as Lady Middleton! Oh, what would he say to that!"

Elinor advised her to lie down again, and for a moment she did so. But no attitude could give her ease, and in restless pain of mind and body she moved from one posture to another till growing more and more hysterical, her sister could with difficulty keep her on the bed at all, and for some time was fearful of being constrained to call for assistance. Some lavender drops however, which she was at length persuaded to take, were of use, and from that time till Mrs Jennings returned she continued on the bed quiet and motionless.

Chapter Thirty

Mrs Jennings came immediately to their room on her return, and without waiting to have her request of admittance answered, opened the door and walked in with a look of real concern.

"How do you do, my dear?" said she in a voice of great compassion to Marianne, who turned away her face without attempting to answer.

"How is she, Miss Dashwood? Poor thing! She looks very bad. No wonder. Ay, it is but too true. He is to be married very soon—a good-for-nothing fellow! I have no patience with him. Mrs Taylor told me of it half an hour ago, and she was told it by a particular friend of Miss Grey herself, else I am sure I should not have believed it, and I was almost ready to sink as it was. 'Well,' said I, 'all I can say is that if this be true he has used a young lady of my acquaintance abominably ill, and I wish with all my soul his wife may plague his heart out.' And so I shall always say, my dear, you may depend on it. I have no notion of men's going on in this way, and if ever I meet him again I will give him such a dressing as he has not had this many a day.

"But there is one comfort, my dear Miss Marianne. He is not the only young man in the world worth having, and with your pretty face you will never want admirers. Well, poor thing! I won't disturb her any longer, for she had better have her cry out at once and have done with. The Parrys and Sandersons luckily are coming tonight you know, and that will amuse her."

She then went away, walking on tiptoe out of the room as if she supposed her young friend's affliction could be increased by noise.

Marianne, to the surprise of her sister, determined on dining with them. Elinor even advised her against it. But no, she would go down, she could bear it very well and the bustle about her would be less. Elinor, pleased to have her governed for a moment by such a motive, though believing it hardly possible that she could sit out the dinner, said no more, and adjusting her dress for her as well as she could while Marianne still remained on the bed, was ready to assist her into the dining room as soon as they were summoned to it.

When there, though looking most wretchedly, she ate more and was calmer than her sister had expected. Had she tried to speak, or had she been conscious of half Mrs Jennings' well-meant but ill-judged attentions to her, this calmness could not have been maintained. But not a syllable escaped her lips, and the abstraction of her thoughts preserved her in ignorance of everything that was passing before her.

Elinor, who did justice to Mrs Jennings' kindness, though its effusions were often distressing and sometimes almost ridiculous, made her those acknowledgements and returned her those civilities which her sister could not make or return for herself. Their good friend saw that Marianne was unhappy, and felt that everything was due to her which might make her at all less so. She treated her therefore with all the indulgent fondness of a parent towards a favourite child on the last day of its holidays. Marianne was to have the best place by the fire, was to be tempted to eat by every delicacy in the house and to be amused by the relation of all the news of the day.

Had not Elinor in the sad countenance of her sister seen a check to all mirth, she could have been entertained by Mrs Jennings' endeavours to cure a disappointment in love by a variety of sweetmeats and olives and a good fire. As soon, however, as the consciousness of all this was forced by continual repetition on Marianne, she could stay no longer. With a hasty exclamation of misery, and a sign to her sister not to follow her, she directly got up and hurried out of the room.

"Poor soul!" cried Mrs Jennings as soon as she was gone. "How it grieves me to see her! And I declare if she is not gone away without finishing her wine! And the dried cherries too! Lord! Nothing seems to do her any good. I am sure if I knew of anything she would like, I would send all over the town for it. Well, it is the oddest thing to me that a man should use such a pretty girl so ill! But when there is plenty of money on one side and next to none on the other, Lord bless you, they care no more about such things!"

"The lady then — Miss Grey I think you called her — is very rich?"

"Fifty thousand pounds, my dear. Did you ever see her? A smart, stylish girl they say, but not handsome. No match for him, not like your dear sister is for him. Miss Grey is plain of face and unremarkable of form.

He will not revel in her bed, not with those thimble-sized tits, I tell you! I bet her quim is dry as dust. Ahem. Well. Yes, of course." She picked at her fichu, twitching her mouth, recovering from her breach of etiquette. "I remember her aunt very well, Biddy Henshawe, she married a very wealthy man. But the family are all rich together. Fifty thousand pounds! And by all accounts, it won't come before it's wanted, for they say he is all to pieces. No wonder! Dashing about with his curricle and hunters! Well, it don't signify talking, but when a young man, be who he will, comes and makes love to a pretty girl and promises marriage, he has no business to fly off from his word only because he grows poor and a richer girl is ready to have him. Why don't he in such a case sell his horses, let his house, turn off his servants and make a thorough reform at once? I warrant you Miss Marianne would have been ready to wait till matters came round. But that won't do nowadays. Nothing in the way of pleasure can ever be given up by the young men of this age."

"Do you know what kind of a girl Miss Grey is? Is she said to be amiable?"

"I never heard any harm of her. Indeed I hardly ever heard her mentioned except that Mrs Taylor did say this morning that one day Miss Walker hinted to her that she believed Mr and Mrs Ellison would not be sorry to have Miss Grey married, for she and Mrs Ellison could never agree."

"And who are the Ellisons?"

"Her guardians, my dear. But now she is of age and may choose for herself, and a pretty choice she has made! What now" —after pausing a moment—"your poor sister is gone to her own room, I suppose, to moan by herself. Is there nothing one can get to comfort her? Poor dear, it seems quite cruel to let her be alone. Well, by-and-by we shall have a few friends, and that will amuse her a little. What shall we play at? She hates whist I know, but is there no round game she cares for?"

"Dear ma'am, this kindness is quite unnecessary. Marianne, I dare say, will not leave her room again this evening. I shall persuade her if I can to go early to bed, for I am sure she wants rest."

"Aye, I believe that will be best for her. Let her name her own supper and go to bed. Lord! No wonder she has been looking so bad and so cast down this last week or two, for this matter I suppose has been hanging over her head as long as that. And so the letter that came today finished it! Poor soul! I am sure if I had had a notion of it, I would not have joked her about it for all my money. But then you know, how should I guess such a thing? I made sure of its being nothing but a common love letter, and you know young people like to be laughed at about them. Lord, how concerned Sir John and my daughters will be when they hear it! If I had my senses about me I might have called in Conduit Street in my way home, and told them of it. But I shall see them tomorrow."

"It would be unnecessary, I am sure, for you to caution Mrs Palmer and Sir John against ever naming Mr Willoughby or making the slightest allusion to what has passed before my sister. Their own good nature must point out to them the real cruelty of appearing to know anything about it when she is present, and the less that may ever be said to myself on the subject the more my feelings will be spared, as you my dear madam will easily believe."

"Oh! Lord! Yes, that I do indeed. It must be terrible for you to hear it talked of, and as for your sister, I am sure I would not mention a word about it to her for the world. You saw I did not all dinner time. No more would Sir John, nor my daughters, for they are all very thoughtful and considerate, especially if I give them a hint, as I certainly will. For my part, I think the less that is said about such things the better, the sooner 'tis blown over and forgot. And what does talking ever do you know?"

"In this affair it can only do harm, more so perhaps than in many cases of a similar kind, for it has been attended by circumstances which for the sake of everyone concerned in it make it unfit to become the public conversation. I must do this justice to Mr Willoughby — he has broken no positive engagement with my sister."

"Law, my dear! Don't pretend to defend him. No positive engagement indeed! After taking her all over Allenham House, up to the sitting room for hours and fixing on the very rooms they were to live in hereafter!"

Aghast at what Mrs Jennings knew of the couple of's activities that day at Allenham, Elinor for her sister's sake could not press the subject farther. She hoped it was not required of her for Willoughby's, fearing too that Mrs Jennings would let slip all she knew of that day in her haphazard way of chattering, since though Marianne might lose much, he could gain very little by the enforcement of the real truth.

After a short silence on both sides, Mrs Jennings with all her natural hilarity burst forth again. "Well, my dear, 'tis a true saying about an ill-wind, for it will be all the better for Colonel Brandon. He will have her at last, aye, if he's a mind to take Willoughby's leavings he can take her, that he will. Mind me now if they an't married by midsummer. Lord, how he'll chuckle over this news! I hope he will come tonight. It will be all to one a better match for your sister. Two thousand a year without debt or drawback—except the little love-child indeed, aye, I had forgot her, but she may be 'prenticed out at a small cost, then what does it signify?

"Delaford is a nice place, I can tell you, exactly what I call a nice old-fashioned place. Full of comforts and conveniences, quite shut in with great garden walls that are covered with the best fruit trees in the country, and such a mulberry tree in one corner! Lord, how Charlotte and I did stuff the only time we were there! Then there is a dived-cote, some delightful stew-ponds and a very pretty canal, and everything in short that one could wish for. And moreover, it is close to the church, and only a quarter of a mile from the turnpike-road, so 'tis never dull, for if you only go and sit up in an old yew arbour behind the house, you may see all the carriages that pass along.

"Oh, 'tis a nice place! A butcher hard by in the village, and the parsonage house within a stone's throw. To my fancy, a thousand times prettier than Barton Park, where they are forced to send three miles for their meat? and have not a neighbour nearer than your mother. Well, I shall spirit up the Colonel as soon as I can. One shoulder of mutton, you know, drives another down. If we can but put Willoughby out of her head!"

"Ay, if we can do *that*, ma'am," said Elinor, "we shall do very well with or without Colonel Brandon."

And rising, she went away to join Marianne, whom she found as she expected in her own room, leaning in silent misery over the small remains of a fire, which till Elinor's entrance had been her only light.

"You had better leave me," was all the notice that her sister received from her.

"I will leave you," said Elinor, "if you will go to bed." But this, from the momentary perverseness of impatient suffering, she at first refused to do. Her sister's earnest though gentle persuasion, however, soon softened her to compliance, and Elinor saw her lay her aching head on the pillow, and as she hoped, in a way to get some quiet rest before she left her.

In the drawing room whither she then repaired, she was soon joined by Mrs Jennings with a wine glass full of something in her hand.

"My dear," said she, entering, "I have just recollected that I have some of the finest old Constantia wine in the house that ever was tasted, so I have brought a glass of it for your sister. My poor husband! How fond he was of it! Whenever he had a touch of his old colicky gout, he said it did him more good than anything else in the world. Do take it to your sister."

"Dear ma'am," replied Elinor, smiling at the difference of the complaints for which it was recommended, "how good you are! But I have just left Marianne in bed, and I hope almost asleep, and as I think nothing will be of so much service to her as rest, if you will give me leave, I will drink the wine myself."

Mrs Jennings, though regretting that she had not been five minutes earlier, was satisfied with the compromise. Elinor, as she swallowed the chief of it, reflected that though its effects on a colicky gout were at present of little importance to her, its healing powers on a disappointed heart might be as reasonably tried on herself as on her sister.

Colonel Brandon came in while the party were at tea, and by his manner of looking round the room for Marianne, Elinor immediately fancied that he neither expected nor wished to see her there, and in short that he was already aware of what occasioned her absence. Mrs Jennings was not struck by the same thought, for soon after his entrance she walked across the room to the tea table where Elinor presided and whispered, "The Colonel looks as grave as ever you see. He knows nothing of it. Do tell him, my dear."

He shortly afterwards drew a chair close to hers, and with a look which perfectly assured her of his good information, enquired after her sister.

"Marianne is not well," said she. "She has been indisposed all day, and we have persuaded her to go to bed."

"Perhaps then," he hesitatingly replied, "what I heard this morning may be—there may be more truth in it than I could believe possible at first."

"What did you hear?"

"That a gentleman whom I had reason to think—in short, that a man whom I knew to be engaged—but how shall I tell you? If you know it already, as surely you must, I may be spared."

"You mean," answered Elinor, with forced calmness, "Mr Willoughby's marriage with Miss Grey. Yes, we do know it all. This seems to have been a day of general elucidation, for this very morning first unfolded it to us. Mr Willoughby is unfathomable! Where did you hear it?"

"In a stationer's shop in Pall Mall, where I had business. Two ladies were waiting for their carriage, and one of them was giving the other an account of the intended match in a voice so little attempting concealment that it was impossible for me not to hear all. The name of Willoughby, John Willoughby, frequently repeated first caught my attention, and what followed was a positive assertion that everything was now finally settled respecting his marriage with Miss Grey. It was no longer to be a secret—it would take place even within a few weeks, with many particulars of preparations and other matters. One thing especially I remember, because it served to identify the man still more—as soon as the ceremony was over they were to go to Combe Magna, his seat in Somersetshire. My astonishment! But it would be impossible to describe what I felt. The communicative lady I learnt on enquiry, for I stayed in the shop till they were gone, was a Mrs Ellison, and that, as I have been since informed, is the name of Miss Grey's guardian."

"It is. But have you likewise heard that Miss Grey has fifty thousand pounds? In that, if in anything, we may find an explanation."

"It may be so, but Willoughby is capable—at least I think—" He stopped a moment, then added in a voice which seemed to distrust itself, "And your sister—how did she—"

"Her sufferings have been very severe. I have only to hope that they may be proportionately short. It has been, it is a most cruel affliction. Till yesterday, I believe, she never doubted his regard, and even now perhaps—but I am almost convinced that he never was really attached to her. He has been very deceitful! And in some points there seems a hardness of heart about him."

"Ah!" said Colonel Brandon. "There is, indeed! But your sister does not—I think you said so—she does not consider quite as you do?"

"You know her disposition, and may believe how eagerly she would still justify him if she could."

He made no answer and soon afterwards, by the removal of the tea things and the arrangement of the card parties, the subject was necessarily dropped. Mrs Jennings, who had watched them with pleasure while they were talking and who expected to see the effect of Miss Dashwood's communication in such an instantaneous gaiety on Colonel Brandon's side as might have become a man in the bloom of youth, of hope and happiness, saw him with amazement remain the whole evening more serious and thoughtful than usual.

Chapter Thirty-One

From a night of more sleep than she had expected, Marianne awoke the next morning to the same consciousness of misery in which she had closed her eyes.

Elinor encouraged her as much as possible to talk of what she felt, and before breakfast was ready they had gone through the subject again and again, and with the same steady conviction and affectionate counsel on Elinor's side, the same impetuous feelings and varying opinions on Marianne's as before. Sometimes she could believe Willoughby to be as unfortunate and as innocent as herself, and at others lost every consolation in the impossibility of acquitting him. At one moment she was absolutely indifferent to the observation of all the world, at another she would seclude herself from it forever, and at a third could resist it with energy. In one thing, however, she was uniform when it came to the point in avoiding where it was possible the presence of Mrs Jennings, and in a determined silence when obliged to endure it. Her heart was hardened against the belief of Mrs Jennings' entering into her sorrows with any compassion.

"No, no, no, it cannot be," she cried, "she cannot feel. Her kindness is not sympathy, her good nature is not tenderness. All that she wants is gossip, and she only likes me now because I supply it."

Elinor flinched at Marianne's obstinacy. Could not her sister see how her own rigidity had contributed to this sorry state of affairs? Elinor had not needed this to be assured of the injustice to which her sister was often led in her opinion of others by the irritable refinement of her own mind and the too great importance placed by her on the delicacies of a strong sensibility and the graces of a polished manner. Like half the rest of the world, if more than half there be that are clever and good, Marianne, with excellent abilities and an excellent disposition, was neither reasonable nor candid. She expected from other people the same opinions and feelings as her own, and she judged of their motives by the immediate effect of their actions on herself.

Thus a circumstance occurred while the sisters were together in their own room after breakfast which sunk the heart of Mrs Jennings still lower in her estimation, because through her own weakness it chanced to prove a source of fresh pain to herself, though Mrs Jennings was governed in it by an impulse of the utmost goodwill.

With a letter in her outstretched hand and countenance gaily smiling from the persuasion of bringing comfort, she entered their room saying, "Now, my dear, I bring you something that I am sure will do you good."

Marianne heard enough. In one moment her imagination placed before her a letter from

Willoughby, full of tenderness and contrition, explanatory of all that had passed, satisfactory, convincing and instantly followed by Willoughby himself, rushing eagerly into the room to enforce at her feet by the eloquence of his eyes the assurances of his letter. He would want her, sweep her into her arms and both of them would forget the past in favour of a joyous future.

The work of one moment was destroyed by the next. The handwriting of her mother, never till then unwelcome, was before her, and in the acuteness of the disappointment which followed such an ecstasy of more than hope, she felt as if till that instant she had never suffered.

The cruelty of Mrs Jennings no language within her reach in her moments of happiest eloquence could have expressed. Now she could reproach her only by the tears which streamed from her eyes with passionate violence — a reproach however so entirely lost on its object that after many expressions of pity she withdrew, still referring her to the letter of comfort. But the letter, when she was calm enough to read it, brought little comfort. Willoughby filled every page. Her mother, still confident of their engagement and relying as warmly as ever on his constancy, had only been roused by Elinor's application to entreat from Marianne greater openness towards them both. This with such tenderness towards her, such affection for Willoughby and such a conviction of their future happiness in each other that she wept with agony through the whole of it.

All her impatience to be at home again now returned. Her mother was dearer to her than ever, dearer through the very excess of her mistaken confidence in Willoughby, and she was wildly urgent to be gone. Elinor, unable herself to determine whether it were better for Marianne to be in London or at Barton, offered no counsel of her own except of patience till their mother's wishes could be known, and at length she obtained her sister's consent to wait for that knowledge.

Mrs Jennings left them earlier than usual, for she could not be easy till the Middletons and Palmers were able to grieve as much as herself, and positively refusing Elinor's offered attendance, went out alone for the rest of the morning. Elinor with a very heavy heart, aware of the pain she was going to communicate and perceiving by Marianne's letter how ill she had succeeded in laying any foundation for it, then sat down to write her mother an account of what had passed and entreat her directions for the future. While Marianne, who came into the drawing room on Mrs Jennings' going away, remained fixed at the table where Elinor wrote, watching the advancement of her pen, grieving over her for the hardship of such a task and grieving still more fondly over its effect on her mother.

In this manner they had continued about a quarter of an hour when Marianne, whose nerves could not then bear any sudden noise, was startled by a rap at the door.

"Who can this be?" cried Elinor. "So early too! I thought we had been safe."

Marianne moved to the window. "It is Colonel Brandon!" said she with vexation. "We are never safe from him."

"He will not come in, as Mrs Jennings is from home."

"I will not trust to *that*." Retreating to her own room. "A man who has nothing to do with his own time has no conscience in his intrusion on that of others."

The event proved her conjecture right, though it was founded on injustice and error. For Colonel Brandon did come in, and Elinor, who was convinced that solicitude for Marianne brought him thither and who saw that solicitude in his disturbed and melancholy look and in his anxious though brief enquiry after her, could not forgive her sister for esteeming him so lightly.

"I met Mrs Jennings in Bond Street," said he after the first salutation, "and she encouraged me to come on. I was the more easily encouraged because I thought it probable that I might find you alone, which I was very desirous of doing. My object—my wish—my sole wish in desiring it—I hope, I believe it is—is to be a means of giving comfort, no, I must not say comfort—not present comfort—but conviction, lasting conviction to your sister's mind. My regard for her, for yourself, for your mother—will you allow me to prove it, by relating some circumstances which nothing but a very sincere regard—nothing but an earnest desire of being useful—I think I am justified—though where so many hours have been spent in convincing myself that I am right, is there not some reason to fear I may be wrong?" He stopped.

"I understand you," said Elinor. "You have something to tell me of Mr Willoughby that will open his character farther. Your telling it will be the greatest act of friendship that can be shown Marianne. My gratitude will be ensured immediately by any information tending to that end, and hers must be gained by it in time. Pray, pray let me hear it."

"You shall, and to be brief, when I quitted Barton last October—but this will give you no idea—I must go farther back. You will find me a very awkward narrator, Miss Dashwood. I hardly know where to begin. A short account of myself, I believe, will be necessary, and it shall be a short one. On such a subject"—sighing heavily—"can I have little temptation to be diffuse."

He stopped a moment for recollection, then, with another sigh, went on.

"You have probably entirely forgotten a conversation—it is not to be supposed that it could make any impression on you—a conversation between us one evening at Barton Park. It was the evening of a dance in which I alluded to a lady I had once known as resembling in some measure your sister Marianne."

"Indeed," answered Elinor, "I have not forgotten it."

He looked pleased by this remembrance and added, "If I am not deceived by the uncertainty, the partiality of tender recollection, there is a very strong resemblance between them as well in mind as person. The same warmth of heart, the same eagerness of fancy and spirits. This lady was one of my nearest relations, an orphan from her infancy, and under the guardianship of my father. Our ages were nearly the same, and from our earliest years we were playfellows and friends.

"I cannot remember the time when I did not love Eliza, and my affection for her as we grew up was such as perhaps, judging from my present forlorn and cheerless gravity, you might think me incapable of having ever felt. Hers for me was, I believe, fervent as the attachment of your sister to Mr Willoughby and it was, though from a different cause, no less unfortunate. At seventeen she was lost to me forever.

She was married—married against her inclination to my brother. Her fortune was large, and our family estate much encumbered. And this, I fear, is all that can be said for the conduct of one who was at once her uncle and guardian.

"My brother did not deserve her. He did not even love her. I had hoped that her regard for me would support her under any difficulty, and for some time it did, but at last the misery of her situation, for she experienced great unkindness, overcame all her resolution, and though she had promised me that nothing—but how blindly I relate! I have never told you how this was brought on.

"We were within a few hours of eloping together for Scotland. The treachery or the folly of my cousin's maid betrayed us. I was banished to the house of a relation far distant, and she was allowed no liberty, no society, no amusement till my father's point was gained. I had depended on her fortitude too far, and the blow was a severe one—but had her marriage been happy, so young as I then was, a few months must have reconciled me to it, or at least I should not have now to lament it.

"This however was not the case. My brother had no regard for her. His pleasures were not what they ought to have been, and from the first he treated her unkindly. The consequence of this upon a mind so young, so lively, so inexperienced as Mrs Brandon's was but too natural. She resigned herself at first to all the misery of her situation, and happy had it been if she had not lived to overcome those regrets which the remembrance of me occasioned. But can we wonder that with such a husband to provoke inconstancy, and without a friend to advise or restrain her—for my father lived only a few months after their marriage and I was with my regiment in the East Indies—she should fall? Had I remained in England, perhaps—but I meant to promote the happiness of both by removing from her for years, and for that purpose had procured my exchange.

"The shock which her marriage had given me," he continued in a voice of great agitation, "was of trifling weight—was nothing to what I felt when I heard about two years afterwards of her divorce. It was that which threw this gloom. Even now the recollection of what I suffered—"

He could say no more, and rising hastily walked for a few minutes about the room. Elinor had misjudged him entirely. Thinking him rational, reasoned, she had assumed he had always been that way. Once, however, he had welcomed a grand passion. So had the woman whom he had loved. Was he capable of such wild emotion again? Elinor, affected by his relation and still more by his distress, could not speak. He saw her concern, and coming to her, took her hand, pressed it and kissed it with grateful respect. A few minutes more of silent exertion enabled him to proceed with composure.

"It was nearly three years after this unhappy period before I returned to England. My first care when I did arrive was of course to seek for her, but the search was as fruitless as it was melancholy. I could not trace her beyond her first seducer, and there was every reason to fear that she had removed from him only to sink deeper in a life of sin. Her legal allowance was not adequate to her fortune, nor sufficient for her comfortable maintenance, and I learnt from my brother that the power of receiving it had been made over some months before to another person. He imagined, and calmly could he imagine it, that her extravagance and consequent distress had obliged her to dispose of it for some immediate relief.

"At last however, and after I had been six months in England, I did find her. Regard for a former servant of my own who had since fallen into misfortune carried me to visit him in a sponging house where he was confined for debt, and there in the same house under a similar confinement was my unfortunate sister. So altered—so faded—worn down by acute suffering of every kind! Hardly could I believe the melancholy and sickly figure before me to be the remains of the lovely, blooming, healthful girl on whom I had once doted.

"What I endured in so beholding her—but I have no right to wound your feelings by attempting to describe it—I have pained you too much already. That she was to all appearance in the last stage of a consumption was—yes, in such a situation it was my greatest comfort. Life could do nothing for her beyond giving time for a better preparation for death, and that was given. I saw her placed in comfortable lodgings, and under proper attendants, I visited her every day during the rest of her short life—I was with her in her last moments."

Again he stopped to recover himself, and Elinor spoke her feelings in an exclamation of tender concern at the fate of his unfortunate friend.

"Your sister, I hope, cannot be offended," said he, "by the resemblance I have fancied between her and my poor disgraced relation. Their fates, their fortunes cannot be the same, and had the natural sweet disposition of the one been guarded by a firmer mind or a happier marriage, she might have been all that you will live to see the other be.

"But to what does all this lead? I seem to have been distressing you for nothing. Ah! Miss Dashwood—a subject such as this—untouched for fourteen years—it is dangerous to handle it at all! I will be more collected—more concise.

"She left to my care her only child, a little girl, the offspring of her first guilty connection, who was then about three years old. She loved the child and had always kept it with her. It was a valued, a precious trust to me, and gladly would I have discharged it in the strictest sense by watching over her education myself had the nature of our situations allowed it. But I had no family, no home, and my little Eliza was therefore placed at school. I saw her there whenever I could, and after the death of my brother—which happened about five years ago and which left to me the possession of the family property—she visited me at Delaford. I called her a distant relation, but I am well aware that I have in general been suspected of a much nearer connection with her.

"It is now three years ago—she had just reached her fourteenth year—that I removed her from school to place her under the care of a very respectable woman residing in Dorsetshire, who had the charge of four or five other girls of about the same time of life. And for two years I had every reason to be pleased with her situation. But last February, almost a twelvemonth back, she suddenly disappeared.

"I had allowed her—imprudently, as it has since turned out—at her earnest desire to go to Bath with one of her young friends, who was attending her father there for his health. I knew him to be a very good sort of man, and I thought well of his daughter. Better than she deserved, for with a most obstinate and ill-judged secrecy she would tell nothing, would give no clue, though she certainly knew all. He—her father, a well-meaning but not a quick-sighted man—

could really I believe give no information, for he had been generally confined to the house while the girls were ranging over the town and making what acquaintance they chose. He tried to convince me as thoroughly as he was convinced himself of his daughter's being entirely unconcerned in the business. In short, I could learn nothing but that she was gone. All the rest for eight long months was left to conjecture. What I thought, what I feared may be imagined, and what I suffered too."

"Good heavens!" cried Elinor. "Could it be—could Willoughby!"

"The first news that reached me of her," he continued, "came in a letter from herself last October. It was forwarded to me from Delaford. I received it on the very morning of our intended party to Whitwell, and this was the reason of my leaving Barton so suddenly, which I am sure must at the time have appeared strange to everybody and which I believe gave offence to some.

"Little did Mr Willoughby imagine, I suppose, when his looks censured me for incivility in breaking up the party, that I was called away to the relief of one whom he had made poor and miserable. But had he known it, what would it have availed? Would he have been less gay or less happy in the smiles of your sister? No, he had already done that which no man who can feel for another would do. He had left the girl whose youth and innocence he had seduced in a situation of the utmost distress, with no creditable home, no help, no friends, ignorant of his address! He had left her promising to return. He neither returned nor wrote nor relieved her."

"This is beyond everything!" exclaimed Elinor, unable to fathom such perversion by a man she had known and whose company she had enjoyed.

"His character is now before you, expensive, dissipated and worse than both. Knowing all this as I have now known it many weeks, guess what I must have felt on seeing your sister as fond of him as ever, and on being assured that she was to marry him— guess what I must have felt for all your sakes. When I came to you last week and found you alone I came determined to know the truth, though irresolute what to do when it was known. My behaviour must have seemed strange to you then, but now you will comprehend it. To suffer you all to be so deceived, to see your sister—but what could I do? I had no hope of interfering with success, and sometimes I thought your sister's influence might yet reclaim him. But now, after such dishonourable usage, who can tell what were his designs on her.

"Whatever they may have been however, she may now and hereafter doubtless *will* turn with gratitude towards her own condition when she compares it with that of my poor Eliza. When she considers the wretched and hopeless situation of this poor girl and pictures her to herself with an affection for him so strong, still as strong as her own, and with a mind tormented by self-reproach which must attend her through life.

"Surely this comparison must have its use with her. She will feel her own sufferings to be nothing. They proceed from no misconduct and can bring no disgrace. On the contrary, every friend must be made still more her friend by them. Concern for her unhappiness and respect for her fortitude under it must strengthen every attachment. Use your own discretion, however, in communicating to her what I have told you. You must know best what will be its effect, but had I not seriously and from my heart believed it might be of service, might lessen her regrets, I would not have suffered myself to trouble you with this account of my family afflictions, with a recital which may seem to have been intended to raise myself at the expense of others."

Elinor's thanks followed this speech with grateful earnestness, attended too with the assurance of her expecting material advantage to Marianne from the communication of what had passed.

"I have been more pained," said she, "by her endeavours to acquit him than by all the rest, for it irritates her mind more than the most perfect conviction of his unworthiness can do. Now, though at first she will suffer much, I am sure she will soon become easier. Have you," she continued after a short silence, "ever seen Mr Willoughby since you left him at Barton?"

"Yes," he replied gravely, "once I have. One meeting was unavoidable."

Elinor, startled by his manner, looked at him anxiously, saying, "What? Have you met him to—?"

"I could meet him no other way. Eliza had confessed to me, though most reluctantly, the name of her lover, and when he returned to town, which was within a fortnight after myself, we met by appointment—he to defend, I to punish his conduct. We returned unwounded, and the meeting therefore never got abroad."

Elinor sighed over the fancied necessity of this, but to a man and a soldier she presumed not to censure it.

"Such," said Colonel Brandon after a pause, "has been the unhappy resemblance between the fate of mother and daughter! And so imperfectly have I discharged my trust!"

"Is she still in town?"

"No—as soon as she recovered from her lying-in, for I found her near her delivery, I removed her and her child into the country, and there she remains."

Her hand covering her mouth, Elinor caught her breath. This woman's plight could have been Marianne's! Indeed, it could have been her own! Circumstances had saved Marianne from ruin and public disgrace at Willoughby's hands. Determination would save Elinor from the same. All depended upon her strength to stay far from Edward.

Recollecting soon afterwards that he was probably dividing Elinor from her sister, he put an end to his visit, receiving from her again the same grateful acknowledgements and leaving her full of compassion and esteem for him.

Chapter Thirty-Two

When the particulars of this conversation were repeated by Miss Dashwood to her sister, as they very soon were, the effect on her was not entirely such as the former had hoped to see. Not that Marianne appeared to distrust the truth of any part of it, for she listened to it all with the most steady and submissive attention, made neither objection nor remark, attempted no vindication of Willoughby and seemed to show by her tears that she felt it to be impossible. But though this behaviour assured Elinor that the conviction of this guilt was carried home to her mind, though she saw with satisfaction the effect of it in her no longer avoiding Colonel Brandon when he called — in her speaking to him, even voluntarily speaking, with a kind of compassionate respect — and though she saw her spirits less violently irritated than before, she did not see her less wretched.

Her mind did become settled, but it was settled in a gloomy dejection. She felt the loss of Willoughby's character yet more heavily than she had felt the loss of his heart. His seduction and desertion of Miss Williams, the misery of that poor girl and the doubt of what his designs might once have been on herself preyed altogether so much on her spirits that she could not bring herself to speak of what she felt even to Elinor. Brooding over her sorrows in silence gave more pain to her sister than could have been communicated by the most open and most frequent confession of them.

To give the feelings or the language of Mrs Dashwood on receiving and answering Elinor's letter would be only to give a repetition of what her daughters had already felt and said, of a disappointment hardly less painful than Marianne's and an indignation even greater than Elinor's. Long letters from her quickly succeeding each other arrived to tell all that she suffered and thought, to express her anxious solicitude for Marianne and entreat she would bear up with fortitude under this misfortune. Bad indeed must the nature of Marianne's affliction be when her mother could talk of fortitude! Mortifying and humiliating must be the origin of those regrets which *she* could wish her not to indulge!

Against the interest of her own individual comfort, Mrs Dashwood had determined that it would be better for Marianne to be anywhere at that time than at Barton, where everything within her view would be bringing back the past in the strongest and most afflicting manner by constantly placing Willoughby before her such as she had always seen him there. She recommended it to her daughters therefore by all means not to shorten their visit to Mrs Jennings, the length of which, though never exactly fixed, had been expected by all to comprise at least five or six weeks. A variety of occupations, of objects and of company which could not be procured at Barton would be inevitable there, and might yet, she hoped, cheat Marianne at times into some interest beyond herself, and even into some amusement, much as the ideas of both might now be spurned by her.

From all danger of seeing Willoughby again her mother considered her to be at least equally safe in town as in the country, since his acquaintance must now be dropped by all who called themselves her friends. Design could never bring them in each other's way. Negligence could never leave them exposed to a surprise, and chance had less in its favour in the crowd of London than even in the retirement of Barton, where it might force him before her while paying that visit at Allenham on his marriage which Mrs Dashwood, from foreseeing at first as a probable event, had brought herself to expect as a certain one.

She had yet another reason for wishing her children to remain where they were. A letter from her son-in-law had told her that he and his wife were to be in town before the middle of February, and she judged it right that they should sometimes see their brother.

Marianne had promised to be guided by her mother's opinion, and she submitted to it therefore without opposition. Though it proved perfectly different from what she wished and expected. Though she felt it to be entirely wrong, formed on mistaken grounds. And that by requiring her longer continuance in London it deprived her of the only possible alleviation of her wretchedness, the personal sympathy of her mother, and doomed her to such society and such scenes as must prevent her ever knowing a moment's rest.

But it was a matter of great consolation to her that what brought evil to herself would bring good to her sister, and Elinor on the other hand, suspecting that it would not be in her power to avoid Edward entirely, comforted herself by thinking that though their longer stay would therefore militate against her own happiness, it would be better for Marianne than an immediate return into Devonshire.

Her carefulness in guarding her sister from ever hearing Willoughby's name mentioned was not thrown away. Marianne, though without knowing it herself, reaped all its advantage, for neither Mrs Jennings nor Sir John nor even Mrs Palmer herself ever spoke of him before her. Elinor wished that the same forbearance could have extended towards herself, but that was impossible, and she was obliged to listen day after day to the indignation of them all.

Sir John could not have thought it possible. A man of whom he had always had such reason to think well! Such a good-natured fellow! He did not believe there was a bolder rider in England! It was an unaccountable business. He wished him at the devil with all his heart. He would not speak another word to him, meet him where he might, for all the world! No, not if it were to be by the side of Barton covert, and they were kept watching for two hours together. Such a scoundrel of a fellow! Such a deceitful dog! It was only the last time they met that he had offered him one of Folly's puppies! And this was the end of it!

Mrs Palmer, in her way, was equally angry. She was determined to drop his acquaintance immediately, and she was very thankful that she had never been acquainted with him at all. She wished with all her heart Combe Magna was not so near Cleveland, but it did not signify, for it was a great deal too far off to visit. She hated him so much that she was resolved never to mention his name again, and she should tell everybody she saw how good-for-nothing he was.

The rest of Mrs Palmer's sympathy was shown in procuring all the particulars in her power of the approaching marriage and communicating them to Elinor. She could soon tell at what coachmaker's the new carriage was building, by what painter Mr Willoughby's portrait was drawn and at what warehouse Miss Grey's clothes might be seen.

The calm and polite unconcern of Lady Middleton on the occasion was a happy relief to Elinor's spirits, oppressed as they often were by the clamorous kindness of the others. It was a great comfort to her to be sure of exciting no interest in one person at least among their circle of friends — a great comfort to know that there was one who would meet her without feeling any curiosity after particulars or any anxiety for her sister's health.

Every qualification is raised at times by the circumstances of the moment to more than its real value, and she was sometimes worried down by officious condolence to rate good-breeding as more indispensable to comfort than good-nature.

Lady Middleton expressed her sense of the affair about once every day, or twice if the subject occurred very often, by saying, "It is very shocking indeed!" By the means of this continual though gentle vent she was able not only to see the Miss Dashwoods from the first without the smallest emotion, but very soon to see them without recollecting a word of the matter. Having thus supported the dignity of her own sex and spoken her decided censure of what was wrong in the other, she thought herself at liberty to attend to the interest of her own assemblies and therefore determined — though rather against the opinion of Sir

John—that as Mrs Willoughby would at once be a woman of elegance and fortune, to leave her card with her as soon as she married.

Colonel Brandon's delicate, unobtrusive enquiries were never unwelcome to Miss Dashwood. He had abundantly earned the privilege of intimate discussion of her sister's disappointment by the friendly zeal with which he had endeavoured to soften it, and they always conversed with confidence. Elinor admonished herself to think of his confidences as nothing more than friendship for her person and concern for Marianne. Her own tendencies to imagine him as her lover were foolish, especially so after one fine afternoon's conversation.

Brandon had bid adieu to her, ready to leave, when at the door he turned back to her with tears in his eyes. "I wonder that I continue to come here. My hope for a happy outcome seems greater than my reason."

Elinor knew he spoke of Marianne, not of her. After that, she dashed her own fantasies about Brandon and she. They were, she concluded, groundless and merely an outgrowth of her own disappointment in love with Edward.

Brandon's chief reward for the painful exertion of disclosing past sorrows and present humiliations was given in the pitying eye with which Marianne sometimes observed him, and the gentleness of her voice whenever—though it did not often happen—she was obliged or could oblige herself to speak to him. These assured him that his exertion had produced an increase of goodwill towards himself, and these gave Elinor hopes of its being farther augmented hereafter. But Mrs Jennings, who knew nothing of all this—who knew only that the Colonel continued as grave as ever and that she could neither prevail on him to make the offer himself, nor commission her to make it for him — began at the end of two days to think that instead of Midsummer they would not be married till Michaelmas, and by the end of a week that it would not be a match at all. The good understanding between the Colonel and Miss Dashwood seemed rather to declare that the honours of the mulberry tree, the canal and the yew arbour would all be made over to her, and Mrs Jennings had for some time ceased to think at all of Mrs Ferrars.

Early in February, within a fortnight from the receipt of Willoughby's letter, Elinor had the painful office of informing her sister that he was married. She had taken care to have the intelligence conveyed to herself as soon as it was known that the ceremony was over, as she was desirous that Marianne should not receive the first notice of it from the public papers, which she saw her eagerly examining every morning.

She received the news with resolute composure, made no observation on it and at first shed no tears, but after a short time they would burst out, and for the rest of the day she was in a state hardly less pitiable than when she first learnt to expect the event.

The Willoughbys left town as soon as they were married, and Elinor now hoped, as there could be no danger of her seeing either of them, to prevail on her sister, who had never yet left the house since the blow first fell, to go out again by degrees as she had done before.

About this time the two Miss Steeles, lately arrived at their cousin's house in Bartlett's Buildings, Holborn, presented themselves again before their more grand relations in Conduit and Berkeley Streets and were welcomed by them all with great cordiality.

Elinor only was sorry to see them. Their presence always gave her pain, and she hardly knew how to make a very gracious return to the overpowering delight of Lucy in finding her still in town.

"I should have been quite disappointed if I had not found you here *still*," said she repeatedly, with a strong emphasis on the word. "But I always thought I should. I was almost sure you would not leave London yet a while, though you told me, you know, at Barton, that you should not stay above a month. But I thought at the time that you would most likely change your mind when it came to the point. It would have been such a great pity to have went away before your brother and sister came. And now to be sure you will be in no hurry to be gone. I am amazingly glad you did not keep to *your word*."

Elinor perfectly understood her, and was forced to use all her self-command to make it appear that she did not.

"Well, my dear," said Mrs Jennings, "and how did you travel?"

"Not in the stage, I assure you," replied Miss Steele with quick exultation. "We came post all the way, and had a very smart beau to attend us. Dr Davies was coming to town, and so we thought we'd join him in a post-chaise, and he behaved very genteelly and paid ten or twelve shillings more than we did."

"Oh, oh!" cried Mrs Jennings. "Very pretty, indeed! And the Doctor is a single man, I warrant you."

"There now," said Miss Steele, affectedly simpering and making Elinor grind her teeth at her false exuberance, "everybody laughs at me so about the Doctor, and I cannot think why. My cousins say they are sure I have made a conquest, but for my part I declare I never think about him from one hour's end to another. 'Lord! Here comes your beau, Nancy,' my cousin said t'other day when she saw him crossing the street to the house. 'My beau indeed!' said I. 'I cannot think who you mean. The Doctor is no beau of mine.'"

"Aye, aye, that is very pretty talking — but it won't do — the Doctor is the man, I see."

"No indeed!" replied her cousin with affected earnestness. "And I beg you will contradict it if you ever hear it talked of."

Mrs Jennings directly gave her the gratifying assurance that she certainly would not, and Miss Steele was made completely happy.

"I suppose you will go and stay with your brother and sister, Miss Dashwood, when they come to town," said Lucy, returning after a cessation of hostile hints to the charge.

"No, I do not think we shall."

"Oh, yes, I dare say you will."

Elinor would not humour her by farther opposition.

"What a charming thing it is that Mrs Dashwood can spare you both for so long a time together!"

"Long a time indeed!" interposed Mrs Jennings. "Why, their visit is but just begun!"

Lucy was silenced.

"I am sorry we cannot see your sister, Miss Dashwood," said Miss Steele. "I am sorry she is not well—" For Marianne had left the room on their arrival.

"You are very good. My sister will be equally sorry to miss the pleasure of seeing you, but she has been very much plagued lately with nervous headaches which make her unfit for company or conversation."

"Oh, dear, that is a great pity! But such old friends as Lucy and me! I think she might see *us*, and I am sure we would not speak a word."

Elinor, with great civility, declined the proposal. Her sister was perhaps laid down upon the bed or in her dressing gown, and therefore not able to come to them.

"Oh, if that's all," cried Miss Steele, "we can just as well go and see *her*."

Elinor began to find this impertinence too much for her temper, but she was saved the trouble of checking it by Lucy's sharp reprimand, which now as on many occasions, though it did not give much sweetness to the manners of one sister, was of advantage in governing those of the other.

Chapter Thirty-Three

After some opposition, Marianne yielded to her sister's entreaties and consented to go out with her and Mrs Jennings one morning for half an hour. She expressly conditioned however for paying no visits, and would do no more than accompany them to Grey's in Sackville Street, where Elinor was carrying on a negotiation for the exchange of a few old-fashioned jewels of her mother.

When they stopped at the door Mrs Jennings recollected that there was a lady at the other end of the street on whom she ought to call, and as she had no business at Grey's, it was resolved that while her young friends transacted theirs she should pay her visit and return for them.

On ascending the stairs the Miss Dashwoods found so many people before them in the room that there was not a person at liberty to tend to their orders, and they were obliged to wait. All that could be done was to sit down at that end of the counter which seemed to promise the quickest succession.

One gentleman only was standing there, and it is probable that Elinor was not without hope of exciting his politeness to a quicker despatch. But the correctness of his eye and the delicacy of his taste proved to be beyond his politeness. He was giving orders for a toothpick case for himself, and till its size, shape and ornaments were determined, all of which after examining and debating for a quarter of an hour over every toothpick case in the shop were finally arranged by his own inventive fancy, he had no leisure to bestow any other attention on the two ladies than what was comprised in three or four very broad stares. A kind of notice which served to imprint on Elinor the remembrance of a person and face of strong, natural, sterling insignificance, though adorned in the first style of fashion.

Marianne was spared from the troublesome feelings of contempt and resentment on this impertinent examination of their features, and on the puppyism of his manner in deciding on all the different horrors of the different toothpick cases presented to his inspection, by remaining unconscious of it all. She was as well able to collect her thoughts within herself and be as ignorant of what was passing around her in Mr Grey's shop as in her own bedroom.

At last the affair was decided. The ivory, the gold and the pearls all received their appointment, and the gentleman named the last day on which his existence could be continued without the possession of the toothpick case. He drew on his gloves with leisurely care and bestowing another glance on the Miss Dashwoods, but such a one as seemed rather to demand than express admiration, walked off with a happy air of real conceit and affected indifference.

Elinor lost no time in bringing her business forward, was on the point of concluding it when another gentleman presented himself at her side. She turned her eyes towards his face and found him with some surprise to be her brother.

Their affection and pleasure in meeting was just enough to make a very creditable appearance in Mr Grey's shop. John Dashwood was really far from being sorry to see his sisters again, it rather gave them satisfaction, and his enquiries after their mother were respectful and attentive.

Elinor found that he and Fanny had been in town two days. *Two days,* she thought to herself, *and you had not a moment to call upon your own sisters?* That was not like him to be so discourteous. At the very least, he kept up appearances.

"I wished very much to call upon you yesterday," said he, "but it was impossible, for we were obliged to take Harry to see the wild beasts at Exeter Exchange and we spent the rest of the day with Mrs Ferrars. Harry was vastly pleased. This morning I had fully intended to call on you if I could possibly find a spare half hour, but one has always so much to do on first coming to town. I am come here to bespeak Fanny a seal. But tomorrow I think I shall certainly be able to call in Berkeley Street and be introduced to your friend Mrs Jennings. I understand she is a woman of very good fortune. And the Middletons too, you must introduce me to them. As my mother-in-law's relations, I shall be happy to show them every respect. They are excellent neighbours to you in the country, I understand."

"Excellent indeed. Their attention to our comfort, their friendliness in every particular is more than I can express."

"I am extremely glad to hear it, upon my word, extremely glad indeed. But so it ought to be. They are people of large fortune, they are related to you and every civility and accommodation that can serve to make your situation pleasant might be reasonably expected. And so you are most comfortably settled in your little cottage and want for nothing! Edward brought us a most charming account of the place — the most complete thing of its kind, he said, that ever was, and you all seemed to enjoy it beyond anything. It was a great satisfaction to us to hear it, I assure you."

Elinor did feel a little ashamed of her brother, and was not sorry to be spared the necessity of answering him by the arrival of Mrs Jennings' servant, who came to tell her that his mistress waited for them at the door.

Mr Dashwood attended them downstairs, was introduced to Mrs Jennings at the door of her carriage and repeating his hope of being able to call on them the next day, took leave.

His visit was duly paid. He came with a pretence at an apology from their sister-in-law for not coming too, but she was so much engaged with her mother that really she had no leisure for going anywhere. Mrs Jennings, however, assured him directly that she should not stand upon ceremony, for they were all cousins, or something like it, and she should certainly wait on Mrs John Dashwood very soon and bring her sisters to see her. His manners to them, though calm, were perfectly kind, to Mrs Jennings most attentively civil, and on Colonel Brandon's coming in soon after himself, he eyed him with a curiosity which seemed to say that he only wanted to know him to be rich to be equally civil to him.

After staying with them half an hour, he asked Elinor to walk with him to Conduit Street and introduce him to Sir John and Lady Middleton. The weather was remarkably fine, and she readily consented. As soon as they were out of the house, his enquiries began.

"Who is Colonel Brandon? Is he a man of fortune?"

"Yes, he has very good property in Dorsetshire."

"I am glad of it. He seems a most gentlemanlike man, and I think, Elinor, I may congratulate you on the prospect of a very respectable establishment in life."

"Me, brother! What do you mean?"

"He likes you. I observed him narrowly, and am convinced of it. What is the amount of his fortune?"

"I believe about two thousand a year."

"Two thousand a year," and working himself up to a pitch of enthusiastic generosity, he added, "Elinor, I wish with all my heart it were *twice* as much for your sake."

"Indeed I believe you," replied Elinor, "but I am very sure that Colonel Brandon has not the smallest wish of marrying *me*."

"You are mistaken, Elinor, you are very much mistaken. A very little trouble on your side secures him."

Was that so? Could she bat her eyelashes, caress his arm, put her palm to his chest and induce him, or seduce him, into such a permanent end to their friendship? Oh, no! What was she thinking? That would be catastrophic. Brandon cared for Marianne and it was in her sister's best interests to marry the man. Elinor should not intervene in any way.

"Perhaps just at present he may be undecided. The smallness of your fortune may make him hang back, his friends may all advise him against it. But some of those little attentions and encouragements which ladies can so easily give will fix him in spite of himself. And there can be no reason why you should not try for him. It is not to be supposed that any prior attachment on your side—in short, you know, as to an attachment of that kind it is quite out of the question, the objections are insurmountable—you have too much sense not to see all that. Colonel Brandon must be the man, and no civility shall be wanting on my part to make him pleased with you and your family. It is a match that must give universal satisfaction. In short, it is a kind of thing that"—lowering his voice to an important whisper—"will be exceedingly welcome to *all parties.*"

Recollecting himself however, he added, "That is, I mean to say—your friends are all truly anxious to see you well settled. Fanny particularly, for she has your interest very much at heart, I assure you. And her mother too, Mrs Ferrars, a very good-natured woman, I am sure it would give her great pleasure. She said as much the other day."

Elinor would not vouchsafe any answer.

"It would be something remarkable now," he continued, "something droll, if Fanny should have a brother and I a sister settling at the same time. And yet it is not very unlikely."

"Is Mr Edward Ferrars," said Elinor with resolution to remain calm, "going to be married?"

"It is not actually settled, but there is such a thing in agitation. He has a most excellent mother. Mrs Ferrars with the utmost liberality will come forward and settle on him a thousand a year if the match takes place. The lady is the Honourable Miss Morton, only daughter of the late Lord Morton, with thirty thousand pounds. A very desirable connection on both sides, and I have not a doubt of its taking place in time. A thousand a year is a great deal for a mother to give away, to make over forever, but Mrs Ferrars has a noble spirit. To give you another instance of her liberality—the other day as soon as we came to town, aware that money could not be very plenty with us just now, she put banknotes into Fanny's hands to the amount of two hundred pounds. And extremely acceptable it is, for we must live at a great expense while we are here."

He paused for her assent and compassion, and she forced herself to say, "Your expenses both in town and country must certainly be considerable, but your income is a large one."

"Not so large, I dare say, as many people suppose. I do not mean to complain, however. It is undoubtedly a comfortable one, and I hope will in time be better. The enclosure of Norland Common, now carrying on, is a most serious drain. And I have made a little purchase within this half year—East Kingham Farm, you must remember the place, where old Gibson used to live. The land was so very desirable for me in every respect, so immediately adjoining my own property, that I felt it my duty to buy it. I could not have answered it to my conscience to let it fall into any other hands. A man must pay for his convenience, and it has cost me a vast deal of money."

"More than you think it really and intrinsically worth."

"Why, I hope not that. I might have sold it again the next day for more than I gave—but with regard to the purchase money I might have been very unfortunate indeed, for the stocks were at that time so low that if I had not happened to have the necessary sum in my banker's hands, I must have sold out to very great loss."

Elinor could only smile.

"Other great and inevitable expenses too we have had on first coming to Norland. Our respected father, as you well know, bequeathed all the Stanhill effects that remained at Norland—and very valuable they were—to your mother. Far be it from me to repine at his doing so, he had an undoubted right to dispose of his own property as he chose, but in consequence of it we have been obliged to make large purchases of linen, china, etc. to supply the place of what was taken away. You may guess after all these expenses how very far we must be from being rich, and how acceptable Mrs Ferrars' kindness is."

"Certainly," said Elinor, "and assisted by her liberality, I hope you may yet live to be in easy circumstances."

"Another year or two may do much towards it," he gravely replied, "but however there is still a great deal to be done. There is not a stone laid of Fanny's greenhouse, and nothing but the plan of the flower garden marked out."

"Where is the greenhouse to be?"

"Upon the knoll behind the house. The old walnut trees are all come down to make room for it. It will be a very fine object from many parts of the park, and the flower garden will slope down just before it and be exceedingly pretty. We have cleared away all the old thorns that grew in patches over the brow."

Elinor kept her concern and her censure to herself, and was very thankful that Marianne was not present to share the provocation.

Having now said enough to make his poverty clear and to do away the necessity of buying a pair of earrings for each of his sisters, in his next visit at Grey's his thoughts took a cheerfuller turn and he began to congratulate Elinor on having such a friend as Mrs Jennings.

"She seems a most valuable woman indeed. Her house, her style of living all bespeak an exceeding good income, and it is an acquaintance that has not only been of great use to you hitherto, but in the end may prove materially advantageous. Her inviting you to town is certainly a vast thing in your favour, and indeed it speaks altogether so great a regard for you that in all probability when she dies you will not be forgotten. She must have a great deal to leave."

"Nothing at all, I should rather suppose, for she has only her jointure, which will descend to her children."

"But it is not to be imagined that she lives up to her income. Few people of common prudence will do *that*, and whatever she saves, she will be able to dispose of."

"And do you not think it more likely that she should leave it to her daughters than to us?"

"Her daughters are both exceedingly well married, and therefore I cannot perceive the necessity of her remembering them farther. Whereas in my opinion, by her taking so much notice of you and treating you in this kind of way, she has given you a sort of claim on her future consideration which a conscientious woman would not disregard. Nothing can be kinder than her behaviour, and she can hardly do all this without being aware of the expectation it raises."

"But she raises none in those most concerned. Indeed, brother, your anxiety for our welfare and prosperity carries you too far."

"Why, to be sure," said he, seeming to recollect himself, "people have little, have very little in their power. But my dear Elinor, what is the matter with Marianne? She looks very unwell, has lost her colour and is grown quite thin. Is she ill?"

"She is not well. She has had a nervous complaint on her for several weeks."

"I am sorry for that. At her time of life, anything of an illness destroys the bloom forever! Hers has been a very short one! She was as handsome a girl last September as I ever saw and as likely to attract the man. There was something in her style of beauty to please them particularly. I remember Fanny used to say that she would marry sooner and better than you did, not but what she is exceedingly fond of you, but so it happened to strike her. She will be mistaken, however. I question whether Marianne now will marry a man worth more than five or six hundred a year at the utmost, and I am very much deceived if you do not do better. Dorsetshire! I know very little of Dorsetshire, but my dear Elinor, I shall be exceedingly glad to know more of it, and I think I can answer for your having Fanny and myself among the earliest and best pleased of your visitors."

Elinor tried very seriously to convince him that there was no likelihood of her marrying Colonel Brandon, but it was an expectation of too much pleasure to himself to be relinquished. He was really resolved on seeking an intimacy with that gentleman and promoting the marriage by every possible attention. He had just compunction enough for having done nothing for his sisters himself to be exceedingly anxious that everybody else should do a great deal, and an offer from Colonel Brandon or a legacy from Mrs Jennings was the easiest means of atoning for his own neglect.

They were lucky enough to find Lady Middleton at home, and Sir John came in before their visit ended. Abundance of civilities passed on all sides. Sir John was ready to like anybody, and though Mr Dashwood did not seem to know much about horses, he soon set him down as a very good-natured fellow, while Lady Middleton saw enough of fashion in his appearance to think his acquaintance worth having. Mr Dashwood went away delighted with both.

"I shall have a charming account to carry to Fanny," said he as he walked back with his sister. "Lady Middleton is really a most elegant woman! Such a woman as I am sure Fanny will be glad to know. And Mrs Jennings too, an exceedingly well-behaved woman, though not so elegant as her daughter. Your sister need not have any scruple even of visiting her, which to say the truth has been a little the case, and very naturally. For we only knew that Mrs Jennings was the widow of a man who had got all his money in a low way, and Fanny and Mrs Ferrars were both strongly prepossessed that neither she nor her daughters were such kind of women as Fanny would like to associate with. But now I can carry her a most satisfactory account of both."

Chapter Thirty-Four

Mrs John Dashwood had so much confidence in her husband's judgement that she waited the very next day both on Mrs Jennings and her daughter, and her confidence was rewarded by finding even the former, even the woman with whom her sisters were staying, by no means unworthy of her notice. And as for Lady Middleton, she found her one of the most charming women in the world!

Lady Middleton was equally pleased with Mrs Dashwood. There was a kind of cold-hearted selfishness on both sides which mutually attracted them, and they sympathised with each other in an insipid propriety of demeanour and a general want of understanding.

The same manners, however, which recommended Mrs John Dashwood to the good opinion of Lady Middleton did not suit the fancy of Mrs Jennings. To her she appeared nothing more than a little proud-looking woman of uncordial address who met her husband's sisters without any affection, and almost without having anything to say to them, for of the quarter of an hour bestowed on Berkeley Street she sat at least seven minutes and a half in silence.

Elinor wanted very much to know, though she did not choose to ask, whether Edward was then in town, but nothing would have induced Fanny voluntarily to mention his name before her till able to tell her that his marriage with Miss Morton was resolved on or till her husband's expectations on Colonel Brandon were answered. She believed them still so very much attached to each other that they could not be too sedulously divided in word and deed on every occasion. The intelligence, however, which she would not give soon flowed from another quarter. Lucy came very shortly to claim Elinor's compassion on being unable to see Edward, though he had arrived in town with Mr and Mrs Dashwood. He dared not come to Bartlett's Buildings for fear of detection, and though their mutual impatience to meet was not to be told, they could do nothing at present but write.

Edward assured them himself of his being in town within a very short time by twice calling in Berkeley Street. Twice was his card found on the table when they returned from their morning's engagements. Elinor was pleased that he had called, and still more pleased that she had missed him. Her feelings regarding him all a jumble, she did not have any idea how to receive him or to converse once met. Her heart beat too rapidly. Her skin flushed. Her breasts tingled. Such reactions confused her, muddled her mind and transformed her into a flighty bird of paradise.

The Dashwoods were so prodigiously delighted with the Middletons that, though not much in the habit of giving anything, they determined to give them a dinner. Soon after their acquaintance began they invited them to dine in Harley Street, where they had taken a very good house for three months.

Their sisters and Mrs Jennings were invited likewise, and John Dashwood was careful to secure Colonel Brandon who, always glad to be where the Miss Dashwoods were, received his eager civilities with some surprise but much more pleasure. They were to meet Mrs Ferrars, but Elinor could not learn whether her sons were to be of the party. The expectation of seeing *her*, however, was enough to make her interested in the engagement. For though she could now meet Edward's mother without that strong anxiety which had once promised to attend such an introduction, though she could now see her with perfect indifference as to her opinion of herself, her desire of being in company with Mrs Ferrars, her curiosity to know what she was like, was as lively as ever.

The interest with which she thus anticipated the party was soon afterwards increased, more powerfully than pleasantly, by her hearing that the Miss Steeles were also to be at it.

So well had they recommended themselves to Lady Middleton, so agreeable had their assiduities made them to her that though Lucy was certainly not so elegant, and her sister not even genteel, she was as ready as Sir John to ask them to spend a week or two in Conduit Street. It happened to be particularly convenient to the Miss Steeles as soon as the Dashwoods' invitation was known that their visit should begin a few days before the party took place.

Their claims to the notice of Mrs John Dashwood as the nieces of the gentleman who for many years had had the care of her brother might not have done much, however, towards procuring them seats at her table.

But as Lady Middleton's guests they must be welcome, and Lucy, who had long wanted to be personally known to the family, to have a nearer view of their characters and her own difficulties and to have an opportunity of endeavouring to please them, had seldom been happier in her life than she was on receiving Mrs John Dashwood's card.

On Elinor its effect was very different. She began immediately to determine that Edward, who lived with his mother, must be asked as his mother was to a party given by his sister. And to see him for the first time after all that passed in the company of Lucy! She hardly knew how she could bear it!

These apprehensions perhaps were not founded entirely on reason, and certainly not at all on truth. They were relieved however, not by her own recollection, but by the good will of Lucy, who believed herself to be inflicting a severe disappointment when she told her that Edward certainly would not be in Harley Street on Tuesday, and even hoped to be carrying the pain still farther by persuading her that he was kept away by the extreme affection for herself which he could not conceal when they were together.

The important Tuesday came that was to introduce the two young ladies to this formidable mother-in-law.

"Pity me, dear Miss Dashwood!" said Lucy, as much to Elinor's chagrin they walked up the stairs together—for the Middletons arrived so directly after Mrs Jennings that they all followed the servant at the same time. "There is nobody here but you that can feel for me. I declare I can hardly stand. Good gracious! In a moment I shall see the person that all my happiness depends on—that is to be my mother!"

Elinor could have given her immediate relief by suggesting the possibility of its being Miss Morton's mother rather than her own whom they were about to behold, but instead of doing that she assured her, and with great sincerity, that she did pity her. To the utter amazement of Lucy, who though really uncomfortable herself hoped at least to be an object of irrepressible envy to Elinor.

Mrs Ferrars was a little, thin woman, upright even to formality in her figure, and serious even to sourness in her aspect. Her complexion was sallow and her features small, without beauty and naturally without expression. But a lucky contraction of the brow had rescued her countenance from the disgrace of insipidity by giving it the strong characters of pride and ill nature. She was not a woman of many words, for unlike people in general she proportioned them to the number of her ideas, and of the few syllables that did escape her not one fell to the share of Miss Dashwood, whom she eyed with the spirited determination of disliking her at all events.

Elinor could not now be made unhappy by this behaviour. A few months ago it would have hurt her exceedingly, but it was not in Mrs Ferrars' power to distress her by it now, and the difference of her manners to the Miss Steeles, a difference which seemed purposely made to humble her more, only amused her. She could not but smile to see the graciousness of both mother and daughter towards the very person — for Lucy was particularly distinguished — whom of all others, had they known as much as she did, they would have been most anxious to mortify. While she herself, who had comparatively no power to wound them, sat pointedly slighted by both. But while she smiled at a graciousness so misapplied, she could not reflect on the mean-spirited folly from which it sprang, nor observe the studied attentions with which the Miss Steeles courted its continuance, without thoroughly despising them all four.

Lucy was all exultation on being so honourably distinguished, and Miss Steele wanted only to be teased about Dr Davies to be perfectly happy.

The dinner was a grand one, the servants were numerous and everything bespoke the mistress's inclination for show and the master's ability to support it. In spite of the improvements and additions which were making to the Norland estate, and in spite of its owner having once been within some thousand pounds of being obliged to sell out at a loss, nothing gave any symptom of that indigence which he had tried to infer from it. No poverty of any kind, except of conversation, appeared — but there the deficiency was considerable. John Dashwood had not much to say for himself that was worth hearing and his wife had still less. But there was no peculiar disgrace in this, for it was very much the case with the chief of their visitors, who almost all laboured under one or other of these disqualifications for being agreeable. Want of sense, either natural or improved — want of elegance — want of spirits — or want of temper.

When the ladies withdrew to the drawing room after dinner this poverty was particularly evident, for the gentlemen had supplied the discourse with some variety — the variety of politics, inclosing land and breaking horses. But then it was all over, and one subject only engaged the ladies till coffee came in, which was the comparative heights of Harry Dashwood and Lady Middleton's second son William, who were nearly of the same age.

Had both the children been there the affair might have been determined too easily by measuring them at once, but as Harry only was present, it was all conjectural assertion on both sides, and everybody had a right to be equally positive in their opinion and to repeat it over and over again as often as they liked.

The parties stood thus. The two mothers, though each really convinced that her own son was the tallest, politely decided in favour of the other. The two grandmothers, with not less partiality but more sincerity, were equally earnest in support of their own descendant. Lucy, who was hardly less anxious to please one parent than the other, thought the boys were both remarkably tall for their age and could not conceive that there could be the smallest difference in the world between them, and Miss Steele with yet greater address gave it as fast as she could in favour of each.

Elinor, having once delivered her opinion on William's side, by which she offended Mrs Ferrars and Fanny still more, did not see the necessity of enforcing it by any farther assertion. And Marianne, when called on for hers, offended them all by declaring that she had no opinion to give, as she had never thought about it.

Before her removing from Norland Elinor had painted a very pretty pair of screens for her sister-in-law, which being now just mounted and brought home ornamented her present drawing room. These screens, catching the eye of John Dashwood on his following the other gentlemen into the room, were officiously handed by him to Colonel Brandon for his admiration.

"These are done by my eldest sister," said he, "and you as a man of taste will, I dare say, be pleased with them. I do not know whether you have ever happened to see any of her performances before, but she is in general reckoned to draw extremely well."

The Colonel, though disclaiming all pretensions to connoisseurship, warmly admired the screens as he would have done anything painted by Miss Dashwood, and on the curiosity of the others being of course excited they were handed round for general inspection. Mrs Ferrars, not aware of their being Elinor's work, particularly requested to look at them, and after they had received gratifying testimony of Lady Middleton's approbation, Fanny presented them to her mother, considerately informing her at the same time that they were done by Miss Dashwood.

"Hum," said Mrs Ferrars, "very pretty," and without regarding them at all returned them to her daughter.

Perhaps Fanny thought for a moment that her mother had been quite rude enough—for, colouring a little, she immediately said, "They are very pretty, ma'am—an't they?" But then again the dread of having been too civil, too encouraging herself probably came over her, for she presently added, "Do you not think they are something in Miss Morton's style of painting, Ma'am? She does paint most delightfully! How beautifully her last landscape is done!"

"Beautifully indeed! But *she* does everything well."

Marianne could not bear this. She was already greatly displeased with Mrs Ferrars, and such ill-timed praise of another at Elinor's expense, though she had not any notion of what was principally meant by it, provoked her immediately to say with warmth, "This is admiration of a very particular kind! What is Miss Morton to us? Who knows, or who cares, for her? It is Elinor of whom we think and speak."

And so saying, she took the screens out of her sister-in-law's hands to admire them herself as they ought to be admired.

Mrs Ferrars looked exceedingly angry, and drawing herself up more stiffly than ever, pronounced in retort this bitter philippic. "Miss Morton is Lord Morton's daughter."

Fanny looked very angry too, and her husband was all in a fright at his sister's audacity. Elinor was much more hurt by Marianne's warmth than she had been by what produced it, but Colonel Brandon's eyes, as they were fixed on Marianne, declared that he noticed only what was amiable in it, the affectionate heart which could not bear to see a sister slighted in the smallest point.

Marianne's feelings did not stop here. The cold insolence of Mrs Ferrars' general behaviour to her sister seemed to her to foretell such difficulties and distresses to Elinor as her own wounded heart taught her to think of with horror. Urged by a strong impulse of affectionate sensibility, she moved after a moment to her sister's chair, and putting one arm round her neck and one cheek close to hers, said in a low but eager voice, "Dear, dear Elinor, don't mind them. Don't let them make *you* unhappy."

She could say no more. Her spirits were quite overcome, and hiding her face on Elinor's shoulder, she burst into tears.

Everybody's attention was called, and almost everybody was concerned. Colonel Brandon rose up and went to them without knowing what he did. Mrs Jennings, with a very intelligent, "Ah! Poor dear," immediately gave her her salts, and Sir John felt so desperately enraged against the author of this nervous distress that he instantly changed his seat to one close by Lucy Steele and gave her in a whisper a brief account of the whole shocking affair.

In a few minutes, however, Marianne was recovered enough to put an end to the bustle and sit down among the rest, though her spirits retained the impression of what had passed the whole evening.

"Poor Marianne!" said her brother to Colonel Brandon in a low voice as soon as he could secure his attention. "She has not such good health as her sister. She is very nervous, she has not Elinor's constitution, and one must allow that there is something very trying to a young woman who *has been* a beauty in the loss of her personal attractions. You would not think it perhaps, but Marianne was remarkably handsome a few months ago, quite as handsome as Elinor. Now you see it is all gone."

Chapter Thirty-Five

Elinor's curiosity to see Mrs Ferrars was satisfied. She had found in her everything that could tend to make a farther connection between the families undesirable. She had seen enough of her pride, her meanness and her determined prejudice against herself to comprehend all the difficulties that must have perplexed the engagement and retarded the marriage of Edward and herself had he been otherwise free. She had seen almost enough to be thankful for her own sake that one greater obstacle preserved her from suffering under any other of Mrs Ferrars' creation, preserved her from all dependence upon her caprice or any solicitude for her good opinion. Or at least, if she did not bring herself quite to rejoice in Edward's being fettered to Lucy, she determined that had Lucy been more amiable, she *ought* to have rejoiced.

She wondered that Lucy's spirits could be so very much elevated by the civility of Mrs Ferrars, that her interest and her vanity should so very much blind her as to make the attention which seemed only paid her because she was not Elinor appear a compliment to herself — or to allow her to derive encouragement from a preference only given her because her real situation was unknown. But that it was so had not only been declared by Lucy's eyes at the time, but was declared over again the next morning more openly, for at her particular desire Lady Middleton set her down in Berkeley Street on the chance of seeing Elinor alone to tell her how happy she was.

The chance proved a lucky one, for a message from Mrs Palmer soon after she arrived carried Mrs Jennings away.

"My dear friend," cried Lucy as soon as they were by themselves, "I come to talk to you of my happiness. Could anything be so flattering as Mrs Ferrars' way of treating me yesterday? So exceeding affable as she was! You know how I dreaded the thoughts of seeing her, but the very moment I was introduced there was such an affability in her behaviour as really should seem to say she had quite took a fancy to me. Now was not it so? You saw it all, and was not you quite struck with it?"

"She was certainly very civil to you."

"Civil! Did you see nothing but only civility? I saw a vast deal more. Such kindness as fell to the share of nobody but me! No pride, no hauteur, and your sister just the same — all sweetness and affability!"

Elinor suppressed a laugh and wished to talk of something else, but Lucy still pressed her to own that she had reason for her happiness, and Elinor was obliged to go on.

"Undoubtedly, if they had known your engagement," said she, "nothing could be more flattering than their treatment of you, but as that was not the case — "

"I guessed you would say so," replied Lucy quickly, "but there was no reason in the world why Mrs Ferrars should seem to like me if she did not, and her liking me is everything. You shan't talk me out of my satisfaction. I am sure it will all end well, and there will be no difficulties at all to what I used to think. Mrs Ferrars is a charming woman, and so is your sister. They are both delightful women indeed! I wonder I should never hear you say how agreeable Mrs Dashwood was!"

To this Elinor had no answer to make, and did not attempt any.

"Are you ill, Miss Dashwood? You seem low — you don't speak, sure you ain't well."

"I never was in better health."

"I am glad of it with all my heart, but really you did not look it. I should be sorry to have you ill, you that have been the greatest comfort to me in the world! Heaven knows what I should have done without your friendship."

Elinor tried to make a civil answer, though doubting her own success. But it seemed to satisfy Lucy, for she directly replied, "Indeed I am perfectly convinced of your regard for me, and next to Edward's love it is the greatest comfort I have. Poor Edward! But now there is one good thing. We shall be able to meet, and meet pretty often. Lady Middleton's delighted with Mrs Dashwood, so we shall be a good deal in Harley Street, I dare say, and Edward spends half his time with his sister — besides, Lady Middleton and Mrs Ferrars will visit now, and Mrs Ferrars and your sister were both so good to say more than once they should always be glad to see me. They are such charming women! I am sure if ever you tell your sister what I think of her, you cannot speak too high."

But Elinor would not give her any encouragement to hope that she should tell her sister. Lucy continued.

"I am sure I should have seen it in a moment if Mrs Ferrars had took a dislike to me. If she had only made me a formal courtesy for instance, without saying a word, and never after had took any notice of me and never looked at me in a pleasant way—you know what I mean. If I had been treated in that forbidding sort of way, I should have gave it all up in despair. I could not have stood it. For where she does dislike, I know it is most violent."

Elinor was prevented from making any reply to this civil triumph by the door's being thrown open, the servant's announcing Mr Ferrars and Edward's immediately walking in.

He appeared agitated, pale. Had he not slept well since last she saw him? Had he been ill? Dare Elinor think he had declined in health because he and she had not been near each other? Oh, folly, to dare to think that!

It was a very awkward moment, and the countenance of each showed that it was so. They all looked exceedingly foolish, and Edward seemed to have as great an inclination to walk out of the room again as to advance farther into it. The very circumstance in its unpleasantest form which they would each have been most anxious to avoid had fallen on them. They were not only all three together, but were together without the relief of any other person.

The ladies recovered themselves first. It was not Lucy's business to put herself forward, and the appearance of secrecy must still be kept up. She could therefore only look her tenderness, and after slightly addressing him said no more.

But Elinor had more to do, and so anxious was she for his sake and her own to do it well that she forced herself after a moment's recollection to welcome him with a look and manner that were almost easy and almost open, and another struggle, another effort still improved them. She would not allow the presence of Lucy nor the consciousness of some injustice towards herself to deter her from saying that she was happy to see him, and that she had very much regretted being from home when he called before in Berkeley Street. She would not be frightened from paying him those attentions which as a friend and almost a relation were his due by the observant eyes of Lucy, though she soon perceived them to be narrowly watching her.

Her manners gave some reassurance to Edward, and he had courage enough to sit down, but his embarrassment still exceeded that of the ladies in a proportion which the case rendered reasonable, though his sex might make it rare. For his heart had not the indifference of Lucy's, nor could his conscience have quite the ease of Elinor's.

Lucy, with a demure and settled air, seemed determined to make no contribution to the comfort of the others and would not say a word, and almost everything that was said proceeded from Elinor, who was obliged to volunteer all the information about her mother's health, their coming to town, etc. which Edward ought to have enquired about but never did.

Her exertions did not stop here, for she soon afterwards felt herself so heroically disposed as to determine under pretence of fetching Marianne to leave the others by themselves. And she really did it, and that in the handsomest manner, for she loitered away several minutes on the landing place with the most high-minded fortitude before she went to her sister. When that was once done, however, it was time for the raptures of Edward to cease, for Marianne's joy hurried her into the drawing room immediately. Her pleasure in seeing him was like every other of her feelings, strong in itself and strongly spoken. She met him with a hand that would be taken and a voice that expressed the affection of a sister.

"Dear Edward!" she cried. "This is a moment of great happiness! This would almost make amends for everything."

Edward tried to return her kindness as it deserved, but before such witnesses he dared not say half what he really felt. Again they all sat down, and for a moment or two all were silent while Marianne was looking with the most speaking tenderness sometimes at Edward and sometimes at Elinor, regretting only that their delight in each other should be checked by Lucy's unwelcome presence. Edward was the first to speak, and it was to notice Marianne's altered looks and express his fear of her not finding London agree with her.

"Oh, don't think of me!" she replied with spirited earnestness, though her eyes were filled with tears as she spoke. "Don't think of my health. Elinor is well, you see. That must be enough for us both."

This remark was not calculated to make Edward or Elinor more easy, nor to conciliate the good will of Lucy, who looked up at Marianne with no very benignant expression.

"Do you like London?" said Edward, willing to say anything that might introduce another subject.

"Not at all. I expected much pleasure in it, but I have found none. The sight of you, Edward, is the only comfort it has afforded, and thank Heaven, you are what you always were!"

She paused—no one spoke.

"I think, Elinor," she presently added, "we must employ Edward to take care of us in our return to Barton. In a week or two, I suppose we shall be going, and I trust Edward will not be very unwilling to accept the charge."

Poor Edward muttered something, but what it was nobody knew, not even himself. But Marianne, who saw his agitation and could easily trace it to whatever cause best pleased herself, was perfectly satisfied and soon talked of something else.

"We spent such a day, Edward, in Harley Street yesterday! So dull, so wretchedly dull! But I have much to say to you on that head which cannot be said now."

And with this admirable discretion did she defer the assurance of her finding their mutual relatives more disagreeable than ever, and of her being particularly disgusted with his mother, till they were more in private.

"But why were you not there, Edward? Why did you not come?"

"I was engaged elsewhere."

"Engaged! But what was that, when such friends were to be met?"

"Perhaps, Miss Marianne," cried Lucy, eager to take some revenge on her, "you think young men never stand upon engagements if they have no mind to keep them, little as well as great."

Elinor was very angry, but Marianne seemed entirely insensible of the sting, for she calmly replied, "Not so indeed. For seriously speaking, I am very sure that conscience only kept Edward from Harley Street.

And I really believe he has the most delicate conscience in the world, the most scrupulous in performing every engagement, however minute, and however it may make against his interest or pleasure. He is the most fearful of giving pain, of wounding expectation, and the most incapable of being selfish of anybody I ever saw. Edward, it is so, and I will say it. What, are you never to hear yourself praised! Then you must be no friend of mine, for those who will accept of my love and esteem must submit to my open commendation."

The nature of her commendation in the present case however happened to be particularly ill-suited to the feelings of two thirds of her auditors, and was so very unexhilarating to Edward that he very soon got up to go away.

"Going so soon!" said Marianne. "My dear Edward, this must not be."

And drawing him a little aside, she whispered her persuasion that Lucy could not stay much longer. But even this encouragement failed, for he would go, and Lucy, who would have outstayed him had his visit lasted two hours, soon afterwards went away.

"What can bring her here so often?" said Marianne, on her leaving them. "Could not she see that we wanted her gone! How teasing to Edward!"

"Why so? We were all his friends, and Lucy has been the longest known to him of any. It is but natural that he should like to see her as well as ourselves."

Marianne looked at her steadily and said, "You know, Elinor, that this is a kind of talking which I cannot bear. If you only hope to have your assertion contradicted, as I must suppose to be the case, you ought to recollect that I am the last person in the world to do it. I cannot descend to be tricked out of assurances that are not really wanted."

She then left the room, and Elinor dared not follow her to say more. For bound as she was by her promise of secrecy to Lucy, she could give no information that would convince Marianne, and painful as the consequences of her still continuing in an error might be, she was obliged to submit to it. All that she could hope was that Edward would not often expose her or himself to the distress of hearing Marianne's mistaken warmth, nor to the repetition of any other part of the pain that had attended their recent meeting — and this she had every reason to expect.

Chapter Thirty-Six

Within a few days after this meeting the newspapers announced to the world that the lady of Thomas Palmer, Esquire was safely delivered of a son and heir, a very interesting and satisfactory paragraph, at least to all those intimate connections who knew it before.

This event, highly important to Mrs Jennings' happiness, produced a temporary alteration in the disposal of her time and influenced in a like degree the engagements of her young friends. For as she wished to be as much as possible with Charlotte, she went thither every morning as soon as she was dressed and did not return till late in the evening, and the Miss Dashwoods, at the particular request of the Middletons, spent the whole of every day in Conduit Street.

For their own comfort they would much rather have remained at least all the morning in Mrs Jennings' house, but it was not a thing to be urged against the wishes of everybody. Their hours were therefore made over to Lady Middleton and the two Miss

Steeles, by whom their company in fact was as little valued as it was professedly sought.

They had too much sense to be desirable companions to the former, and by the latter they were considered with a jealous eye as intruding on their ground and sharing the kindness which they wanted to monopolise. Though nothing could be more polite than Lady Middleton's behaviour to Elinor and Marianne, she did not really like them at all. Because they neither flattered herself nor her children, she could not believe them good-natured, and because they were fond of reading, she fancied them satirical — perhaps without exactly knowing what it was to be satirical, but that did not signify. It was censure in common use, and easily given.

Their presence was a restraint both on her and on Lucy. It checked the idleness of one and the business of the other. Lady Middleton was ashamed of doing nothing before them, and the flattery which Lucy was proud to think of and administer at other times she feared they would despise her for offering. Miss Steele was the least discomposed of the three by their presence, and it was in their power to reconcile her to it entirely. Would either of them only have given her a full and minute account of the whole affair between Marianne and Mr Willoughby, she would have thought herself amply rewarded for the sacrifice of the best place by the fire after dinner which their arrival occasioned.

But this conciliation was not granted. For though she often threw out expressions of pity for her sister to Elinor, and more than once dropped a reflection on the inconstancy of beaux before Marianne, no effect was produced but a look of indifference from the former or of disgust in the latter. An effort even yet lighter might have made her their friend. Would they only have laughed at her about the Doctor! But so little were they any more than the others inclined to oblige her that if Sir John dined from home, she might spend a whole day without hearing any other raillery on the subject than what she was kind enough to bestow on herself.

All these jealousies and discontents, however, were so totally unsuspected by Mrs Jennings that she thought it a delightful thing for the girls to be together, and generally congratulated her young friends every night on having escaped the company of a stupid old woman so long. She joined them sometimes at Sir John's, sometimes at her own house, but wherever it was she always came in excellent spirits—full of delight and importance, attributing Charlotte's well doing to her own care and ready to give so exact, so minute a detail of her situation as only Miss Steele had curiosity enough to desire.

One thing did disturb her, and of that she made her daily complaint. Mr Palmer maintained the common but unfatherly opinion among his sex of all infants being alike, and though she could plainly perceive at different times the most striking resemblance between this baby and every one of his relations on both sides, there was no convincing his father of it, no persuading him to believe that it was not exactly like every other baby of the same age. Nor could he even be brought to acknowledge the simple proposition of its being the finest child in the world.

I come now to the relation of a misfortune which about this time befell Mrs John Dashwood. It so happened that while her two sisters with Mrs Jennings were first calling on her in Harley Street, another of her acquaintance had dropped in—a circumstance in itself not apparently likely to produce evil to her. But while the imaginations of other people will carry them away to form wrong judgements of our conduct, and to decide on it by slight appearances, one's happiness must in some measure be always at the mercy of chance. In the present instance, this last-arrived lady allowed her fancy to so far outrun truth and probability that on merely hearing the name of the Miss Dashwoods and understanding them to be Mr Dashwood's sisters, she immediately concluded them to be staying in Harley Street. This misconstruction produced within a day or two afterwards cards of invitation for them as well as for their brother and sister to a small musical party at her house.

The consequence of which was that Mrs John Dashwood was obliged to submit not only to the exceedingly great inconvenience of sending her carriage for the Miss Dashwoods, but what was still worse, must be subject to all the unpleasantness of appearing to treat them with attention—and who could tell that they might not expect to go out with her a second time? The power of disappointing them, it was true, must always be hers. But that was not enough, for when people are determined on a mode of conduct which they know to be wrong, they feel injured by the expectation of anything better from them.

Marianne had now been brought by degrees so much into the habit of going out every day that it was become a matter of indifference to her whether she went or not. She prepared quietly and mechanically for every evening's engagement, though without expecting the smallest amusement from any, and very often without knowing till the last moment where it was to take her.

To her dress and appearance, she was grown so perfectly indifferent as not to bestow half the consideration on it during the whole of her toilet which it received from Miss Steele in the first five minutes of their being together when it was finished. Nothing escaped *her* minute observation and general curiosity. She saw everything and asked everything, was never easy till she knew the price of every part of Marianne's dress, could have guessed the number of her gowns altogether with better judgement than Marianne herself and was not without hopes of finding out before they parted how much her washing cost per week and how much she had every year to spend upon herself.

The impertinence of these kind of scrutinies, moreover, was generally concluded with a compliment, which though meant as its douceur was considered by Marianne as the greatest impertinence of all. For after undergoing an examination into the value and make of her gown, the colour of her shoes and the arrangement of her hair, she was almost sure of being told that upon her word she looked vastly smart, and she dared to say she would make a great many conquests.

With such encouragement as this was she dismissed on the present occasion to her brother's carriage, which they were ready to enter five minutes after it stopped at the door. A punctuality not very agreeable to their sister-in-law, who had preceded them to the house of her acquaintance and was there hoping for some delay on their part that might inconvenience either herself or her coachman.

The events of this evening were not very remarkable. The party, like other musical parties, comprehended a great many people who had real taste for the performance and a great many more who had none at all, and the performers themselves were as usual in their own estimation and that of their immediate friends the first private performers in England.

As Elinor was neither musical nor affecting to be so, she made no scruple of turning her eyes from the grand pianoforte whenever it suited her, and unrestrained even by the presence of a harp and violoncello, would fix them at pleasure on any other object in the room. In one of these excursive glances she perceived among a group of young men the very he who had given them a lecture on toothpick cases at Grey's. She perceived him soon afterwards looking at herself and speaking familiarly to her brother, and had just determined to find out his name from the latter when they both came towards her, and Mr Dashwood introduced him to her as Mr Robert Ferrars.

He addressed her with easy civility and twisted his head into a bow which assured her as plainly as words could have done that he was exactly the coxcomb she had heard him described to be by Lucy. Happy had it been for her, if her regard for Edward had depended less on his own merit than on the merit of his nearest relations! For then his brother's bow must have given the finishing stroke to what the ill-humour of his mother and sister would have begun.

But while she wondered at the difference of the two young men, she did not find that the emptiness of conceit of the one put her out of all charity with the modesty and worth of the other. Why they were different Robert exclaimed to her himself in the course of a quarter of an hour's conversation, for talking of his brother and lamenting the extreme gaucherie which he really believed kept him from mixing in proper society, he candidly and generously attributed it much less to any natural deficiency than to the misfortune of a private education. While he himself, though probably without any particular, any material superiority by nature, merely from the advantage of a public school was as well fitted to mix in the world as any other man.

"Upon my soul," he added, "I believe it is nothing more, and so I often tell my mother when she is grieving about it. 'My dear madam,' I always say to her, 'you must make yourself easy. The evil is now irremediable, and it has been entirely your own doing. Why would you be persuaded by my uncle, Sir Robert, against your own judgement to place Edward under private tuition at the most critical time of his life? If you had only sent him to Westminster as well as myself instead of sending him to Mr Pratt's, all this would have been prevented.' This is the way in which I always consider the matter, and my mother is perfectly convinced of her error."

Elinor would not oppose his opinion because, whatever might be her general estimation of the advantage of a public school, she could not think of Edward's abode in Mr Pratt's family with any satisfaction.

"You reside in Devonshire, I think," was his next observation, "in a cottage near Dawlish."

Elinor set him right as to its situation, and it seemed rather surprising to him that anybody could live in Devonshire, without living near Dawlish. He bestowed his hearty approbation however on their species of house.

"For my own part," said he, "I am excessively fond of a cottage. There is always so much comfort, so much elegance about them. And I protest, if I had any money to spare, I should buy a little land and build one myself within a short distance of London, where I might drive myself down at any time and collect a few friends about me and be happy. I advise everybody who is going to build to build a cottage. My friend Lord Courtland came to me the other day on purpose to ask my advice, and laid before me three different plans of Bonomi's. I was to decide on the best of them. 'My dear Courtland,' said I, immediately throwing them all into the fire, 'do not adopt either of them, but by all means build a cottage.' And that I fancy will be the end of it.

"Some people imagine that there can be no accommodations, no space in a cottage, but this is all a mistake. I was last month at my friend Elliott's near Dartford. Lady Elliott wished to give a dance. 'But how can it be done?' said she. 'My dear Ferrars, do tell me how it is to be managed. There is not a room in this cottage that will hold ten couple of, and where can the supper be?' I immediately saw that there could be no difficulty in it, so I said, 'My dear Lady Elliott, do not be uneasy. The dining parlour will admit eighteen couple of with ease, card tables may be placed in the drawing room, the library may be open for tea and other refreshments and let the supper be set out in the saloon.'

"Lady Elliott was delighted with the thought. We measured the dining room and found it would hold exactly eighteen couple of, and the affair was arranged precisely after my plan. So that in fact, you see, if people do but know how to set about it, every comfort may be as well enjoyed in a cottage as in the most spacious dwelling."

Elinor agreed to it all, for she did not think he deserved the compliment of rational opposition.

As John Dashwood had no more pleasure in music than his eldest sister, his mind was equally at liberty to fix on anything else, and a thought struck him during the evening which he communicated to his wife for her approbation when they got home. The consideration of Mrs Dennison's mistake in supposing his sisters their guests had suggested the propriety of their being really invited to become such while Mrs Jennings' engagements kept her from home. The expense would be nothing, the inconvenience not more, and it was altogether an attention which the delicacy of his conscience pointed out to be requisite to its complete enfranchisement from his promise to his father. Fanny was startled at the proposal.

"I do not see how it can be done," said she, with a pretty pout, to her husband, "without affronting Lady Middleton, for they spend every day with her, otherwise I should be exceedingly glad to do it. You know I am always ready to pay them any attention in my power, as my taking them out this evening shows. But they are Lady Middleton's visitors. How can I ask them away from her?"

Her husband, but with great humility, did not see the force of her objection. They had already spent a week in this manner in Conduit Street, and Lady Middleton could not be displeased at their giving the same number of days to such near relations.

Fanny paused a moment, then with fresh vigour strolled towards him to sit in his lap and stroke his lower lip with her fingertip, and said, "My love, I would ask them with all my heart, if it was in my power. But I had just settled within myself to ask the Miss Steeles to spend a few days with us. They are very well behaved, good kind of girls, and I think the attention is due to them, as their uncle did so very well by Edward. We can ask your sisters some other year, you know, but the Miss Steeles may not be in town any more. I am sure you will like them — indeed, you *do* like them, you know, very much already, and so does my mother, and they are such favourites with Harry!"

Mr Dashwood was convinced. He saw the necessity of inviting the Miss Steeles immediately, and his conscience was pacified by the resolution of inviting his sisters another year, at the same time however slyly suspecting that another year would make the invitation needless by bringing Elinor to town as Colonel Brandon's wife and Marianne as their visitor.

Fanny, rejoicing in her escape and proud of the ready wit that had procured it, wrote the next morning to Lucy to request her company and her sister's for some days in Harley Street as soon as Lady Middleton could spare them. This was enough to make Lucy really and reasonably happy. Mrs Dashwood seemed actually working for her herself, cherishing all her hopes and promoting all her views! Such an opportunity of being with Edward and his family was above all things the most material to her interest and such an invitation the most gratifying to her feelings! It was an advantage that could not be too gratefully acknowledged, nor too speedily made use of, and the visit to Lady Middleton, which had not before had any precise limits, was instantly discovered to have been always meant to end in two days' time.

When the note was shown to Elinor, as it was within ten minutes after its arrival, it gave her for the first time some share in the expectations of Lucy. Such a mark of uncommon kindness vouchsafed on so short an acquaintance seemed to declare that the goodwill towards her arose from something more than merely malice against herself, and might be brought by time and address to do everything that Lucy wished. Her flattery had already subdued the pride of Lady Middleton and made an entry into the close heart of Mrs John Dashwood, and these were effects that laid open the probability of greater.

The Miss Steeles removed to Harley Street, and all that reached Elinor of their influence there strengthened her expectation of the event. Sir John, who called on them more than once, brought home such accounts of the favour they were in as must be universally striking. Mrs Dashwood had never been so much pleased with any young women in her life as she was with them, had given each of them a needle book made by some emigrant, called Lucy by her Christian name and did not know whether she should ever be able to part with them.

Chapter Thirty-Seven

Mrs Palmer was so well at the end of a fortnight that her mother felt it no longer necessary to give up the whole of her time to her. Contenting herself with visiting her once or twice a day, she returned from that period to her own home and her own habits, in which she found the Miss Dashwoods very ready to resume their former share.

About the third or fourth morning after their being thus resettled in Berkeley Street, Mrs Jennings on returning from her ordinary visit to Mrs Palmer entered the drawing room where Elinor was sitting by herself with an air of such hurrying importance as prepared her to hear something wonderful. Giving her time only to form that idea, she began directly to justify it by saying, "Lord, my dear Miss Dashwood! Have you heard the news?"

"No, ma'am. What is it?"

"Something so strange! But you shall hear it all. When I got to Mr Palmer's I found Charlotte quite in a fuss about the child. She was sure it was very ill—it cried and fretted and was all over pimples. So I looked at it directly and, 'Lord, my dear,' says I, 'it is nothing in the world but the red gum—' And nurse said just the same. But Charlotte, she would not be satisfied, so Mr Donavan was sent for, and luckily he happened to just come in from Harley Street so he stepped over directly. And as soon as ever he saw the child, he said just as we did, that it was nothing in the world but the red gum, then Charlotte was easy.

"And so just as he was going away again it came into my head—I am sure I do not know how I happened to think of it—but it came into my head to ask him if there was any news. So upon that he smirked and simpered and looked grave, and seemed to know something or other, and at last he said in a whisper, 'For fear any unpleasant report should reach the young ladies under your care as to their sister's indisposition, I think it advisable to say that I believe there is no great reason for alarm. I hope Mrs Dashwood will do very well.'"

"What! Is Fanny ill?"

"That is exactly what I said, my dear. 'Lord!' says I. 'Is Mrs Dashwood ill?' So then it all came out, and the long and the short of the matter by all I can learn seems to be this. Mr Edward Ferrars, the very young man I used to joke with you about—but however, as it turns out, I am monstrous glad there was never anything in it—Mr Edward Ferrars it seems has been engaged above this twelvemonth to my cousin Lucy! There's for you, my dear! And not a creature knowing a syllable of the matter except Nancy! Could you have believed such a thing possible? There is no great wonder in their liking one another, but that matters should be brought so forward between them and nobody suspect it! That is strange! I never happened to see them together, or I am sure I should have found it out directly.

"Well, and so this was kept a great secret for fear of Mrs Ferrars, and neither she nor your brother or sister suspected a word of the matter till this very morning. Poor Nancy, who you know is a well-meaning creature but no conjurer, popped it all out. 'Lord!' thinks she to herself. 'They are all so fond of Lucy, to be sure they will make no difficulty about it.' And so away she went to your sister, who was sitting all alone at her carpetwork little suspecting what was to come—for she had just been saying to your brother only five minutes before that she thought to make a match between Edward and some Lord's daughter or other, I forget who. So you may think what a blow it was to all her vanity and pride.

"She fell into violent hysterics immediately, with such screams as reached your brother's ears as he was sitting in his own dressing room downstairs, thinking about writing a letter to his steward in the country. So up he flew directly, and a terrible scene took place, for Lucy was come to them by that time, little dreaming what was going on. Poor soul! I pity her. And I must say I think she was used very hardly, for your sister scolded like any fury, and soon drove her into a fainting fit. Nancy, she fell upon her knees and cried bitterly, and your brother, he walked about the room and said he did not know what to do.

"Mrs Dashwood declared they should not stay a minute longer in the house, and your brother was forced to go down upon his knees too to persuade her to let them stay till they had packed up their clothes. Then she fell into hysterics again, and he was so frightened that he would send for Mr Donavan, and Mr Donavan found the house in all this uproar.

"The carriage was at the door ready to take my poor cousins away, and they were just stepping in as he came off — poor Lucy in such a condition, he says, she could hardly walk. And Nancy, she was almost as bad. I declare I have no patience with your sister, and I hope with all my heart it will be a match in spite of her.

"Lord! What a taking poor Mr Edward will be in when he hears of it! To have his love used so scornfully! For they say he is monstrous fond of her, as well he may. I should not wonder if he was to be in the greatest passion! And Mr Donavan thinks just the same. He and I had a great deal of talk about it, and the best of all is that he is gone back again to Harley Street that he may be within call when Mrs Ferrars is told of it, for she was sent for as soon as ever my cousins left the house. For your sister was sure she would be in hysterics too, and so she may, for what I care.

"I have no pity for either of them. I have no notion of people's making such a to-do about money and greatness. There is no reason on earth why Mr Edward and Lucy should not marry, for I am sure Mrs Ferrars may afford to do very well by her son, and though Lucy has next to nothing herself, she knows better than anybody how to make the most of everything. I dare say if Mrs Ferrars would only allow him five hundred a year, she would make as good an appearance with it as anybody else would with eight. Lord! How snug they might live in such another cottage as yours — or a little bigger — with two maids and two men, and I believe I could help them to a housemaid, for my Betty has a sister out of place that would fit them exactly."

Here Mrs Jennings ceased, and as Elinor had had time enough to collect her thoughts she was able to give such an answer and make such observations as the subject might naturally be supposed to produce. Happy to find that she was not suspected of any extraordinary interest in it, that Mrs Jennings — as she had of late often hoped might be the case — had ceased to imagine her at all attached to Edward, and happy above all the rest in the absence of Marianne, she felt very well able to speak of the affair without embarrassment, and to give her judgement as she believed with impartiality on the conduct of everyone concerned in it.

She could hardly determine what her own expectation of its event really was, though she earnestly tried to drive away the notion of its being possible to end otherwise at last than in the marriage of Edward and Lucy. What Mrs Ferrars would say and do, though there could not be a doubt of its nature, she was anxious to hear, and still more anxious to know how Edward would conduct himself. For him she felt much compassion, for Lucy very little — and it cost her some pains to procure that little — for the rest of the party none at all.

As Mrs Jennings could talk on no other subject, Elinor soon saw the necessity of preparing Marianne for its discussion. No time was to be lost in undeceiving her, in making her acquainted with the real truth and in endeavouring to bring her to hear it talked of by others without betraying that she felt any uneasiness for her sister or any resentment against Edward.

Elinor's office was a painful one. She was going to remove what she really believed to be her sister's chief consolation, to give such particulars of Edward as she feared would ruin him forever in her good opinion—and to make Marianne, by a resemblance in their situations which to her fancy would seem strong, feel all her own disappointment over again. But unwelcome as such a task must be, it was necessary to be done and Elinor therefore hastened to perform it.

She was very far from wishing to dwell on her own feelings or to represent herself as suffering much any otherwise than as the self-command she had practiced since her first knowledge of Edward's engagement might suggest a hint of what was practicable to Marianne. Her narration was clear and simple, and though it could not be given without emotion, it was not accompanied by violent agitation nor impetuous grief. That belonged rather to the hearer, for Marianne listened with horror and cried excessively. Elinor was to be the comforter of others in her own distresses no less than in theirs, and all the comfort that could be given by assurances of her own composure of mind and a very earnest vindication of Edward from every charge but of imprudence was readily offered.

But Marianne for some time would give credit to neither. Edward seemed a second Willoughby, and acknowledging as Elinor did that she had loved him most sincerely, could she feel less than herself! As for Lucy Steele, she considered her so totally unamiable, so absolutely incapable of attaching a sensible man that she could not be persuaded at first to believe and afterwards to pardon any former affection of Edward for her. She would not even admit it to have been natural, and Elinor left her to be convinced that it was so, by that which only could convince her—a better knowledge of mankind.

Her first communication had reached no farther than to state the fact of the engagement and the length of time it had existed. Marianne's feelings had then broken in and put an end to all regularity of detail, and for some time all that could be done was to soothe her distress, lessen her alarms and combat her resentment. The first question on her side which led to farther particulars was, "How long has this been known to you, Elinor? Has he written to you?"

"I have known it these four months. When Lucy first came to Barton Park last November, she told me in confidence of her engagement."

At these words, Marianne's eyes expressed the astonishment which her lips could not utter. After a pause of wonder, she exclaimed, "Four months! Have you known of this four months?"

Elinor confirmed it.

"What! While attending me in all my misery, has this been on your heart? And I have reproached you for being happy!"

"It was not fit that you should then know how much I was the reverse!"

"Four months!" cried Marianne again. "So calm! So cheerful! How have you been supported?"

"By feeling that I was doing my duty. My promise to Lucy obliged me to be secret. I owed it to her therefore to avoid giving any hint of the truth, and I owed it to my family and friends not to create in them a solicitude about me which it could not be in my power to satisfy."

Marianne seemed much struck.

"I have very often wished to undeceive yourself and my mother," added Elinor, "and once or twice I have attempted it, but without betraying my trust I never could have convinced you."

"Four months! And yet you loved him!"

"Yes. But I did not love only him, you see, but others, yes, others as well. And while the comfort of others was dear to me, I was glad to spare them from knowing how much I felt. Now I can think and speak of it with little emotion. I would not have you suffer on my account, for I assure you I no longer suffer materially myself. I have many things to support me. I am not conscious of having provoked the disappointment by any imprudence of my own, I have borne it as much as possible without spreading it farther.

"I acquit Edward of essential misconduct. I wish him very happy, and I am so sure of his always doing his duty that though now he may harbour some regret, in the end he must become so. Lucy does not want sense, I can vouch for that after all my encounters with her, and that is the foundation on which everything good may be built. And after all, Marianne, after all that is bewitching in the idea of a single and constant attachment, and all that can be said of one's happiness depending entirely on any particular person, it is not meant — it is not fit — it is not possible that it should be so. Edward will marry Lucy. He will marry a woman superior in person and understanding to half her sex, though in those arts many of us rue. And time and habit will teach him to forget that he ever thought another superior to her."

"If such is your way of thinking," said Marianne, "if the loss of what is most valued is so easily to be made up by something else, your resolution, your self-command are perhaps a little less to be wondered at. They are brought more within my comprehension."

"I understand you. You do not suppose that I have ever felt much. For four months, Marianne, I have had all this hanging on my mind without being at liberty to speak of it to a single creature, knowing that it would make you and my mother most unhappy whenever it were explained to you yet unable to prepare you for it in the least. It was told me, it was in a manner forced on me by the very person herself whose prior engagement ruined all my prospects, and told me, as I thought, with triumph. This person's suspicions, therefore, I have had to oppose by endeavouring to appear indifferent where I have been most deeply interested. And it has not been only once—I have had her hopes and exultation to listen to again and again.

"I have known myself to be divided from Edward forever without hearing one circumstance that could make me less desire the connection. Nothing has proved him unworthy, nor has anything declared him indifferent to me. I have had to contend against the unkindness of his sister and the insolence of his mother, and have suffered the punishment of an attachment without enjoying its advantages. And all this has been going on at a time when, as you know too well, it has not been my only unhappiness. If you can think me capable of ever feeling—surely you may suppose that I have suffered now.

"The composure of mind with which I have brought myself at present to consider the matter, the consolation that I have been willing to admit, have been the effect of constant and painful exertion. They did not spring up of themselves, they did not occur to relieve my spirits at first. No, Marianne. Then, if I had not been bound to silence, perhaps nothing could have kept me entirely—not even what I owed to my dearest friends—from openly showing that I was very unhappy."

Marianne was quite subdued.

"Oh! Elinor," she cried, "you have made me hate myself forever. How barbarous have I been to you! You who have been my only comfort, who have borne with me in all my misery, who have seemed to be only suffering for me! Is this my gratitude? Is this the only return I can make you? Because your merit cries out upon myself, I have been trying to do it away."

The tenderest caresses followed this confession. In such a frame of mind as she was now in, Elinor had no difficulty in obtaining from her whatever promise she required. At her request Marianne engaged never to speak of the affair to anyone with the least appearance of bitterness, to meet Lucy without betraying the smallest increase of dislike to her, and even to see Edward himself if chance should bring them together without any diminution of her usual cordiality. These were great concessions, but where Marianne felt that she had injured, no reparation could be too much for her to make.

She performed her promise of being discreet to admiration. She attended to all that Mrs Jennings had to say upon the subject with an unchanging complexion, dissented from her in nothing and was heard three times to say, "Yes, ma'am." She listened to her praise of Lucy with only moving from one chair to another, and when Mrs Jennings talked of Edward's affection it cost her only a spasm in her throat. Such advances towards heroism in her sister made Elinor feel equal to anything herself.

The next morning brought a farther trial of it in a visit from their brother, who came with a most serious aspect to talk over the dreadful affair and bring them news of his wife.

"You have heard, I suppose," said he with great solemnity as soon as he was seated, "of the very shocking discovery that took place under our roof yesterday."

They all looked their assent. It seemed too awful a moment for speech.

"Your sister," he continued, "has suffered dreadfully. Mrs Ferrars too—in short it has been a scene of such complicated distress—but I will hope that the storm may be weathered without our being any of us quite overcome. Poor Fanny! She was in hysterics all yesterday. But I would not alarm you too much. Donavan says there is nothing materially to be apprehended. Her constitution is a good one and her resolution equal to anything. She has borne it all, with the fortitude of an angel! She says she never shall think well of anybody again, and one cannot wonder at it after being so deceived! Meeting with such ingratitude where so much kindness had been shown, so much confidence had been placed!

"It was quite out of the benevolence of her heart that she had asked these young women to her house, merely because she thought they deserved some attention, were harmless, well-behaved girls and would be pleasant companions, for otherwise we both wished very much to have invited you and Marianne to be with us while your kind friend there was attending her daughter. And now to be so rewarded! 'I wish with all my heart,' says poor Fanny in her affectionate way, 'that we had asked your sisters instead of them.'"

Here he stopped to be thanked, though with a polite simplicity on the part of each of his sisters, which being done he went on.

"What poor Mrs Ferrars suffered when first Fanny broke it to her is not to be described. While she with the truest affection had been planning a most eligible connection for him, was it to be supposed that he could be all the time secretly engaged to another person! Such a suspicion could never have entered her head! If she suspected any prepossession elsewhere, it could not be in that quarter. 'There, to be sure,' said she, 'I might have thought myself safe.' She was quite in an agony.

"We consulted together, however, as to what should be done, and at last she determined to send for Edward. He came. But I am sorry to relate what ensued. All that Mrs Ferrars could say to make him put an end to the engagement, assisted too as you may well suppose by my arguments and Fanny's entreaties, was of no avail. Duty, affection, everything was disregarded. I never thought Edward so stubborn, so unfeeling before. His mother explained to him her liberal designs in case of his marrying Miss Morton, told him she would settle on him the Norfolk estate, which clear of land tax brings in a good thousand a year, offered even when matters grew desperate to make it twelve hundred, and in opposition to this, if he still persisted in this low connection, represented to him the certain penury that must attend the match. His own two thousand pounds she protested should be his all. She would never see him again, and so far would she be from affording him the smallest assistance that if he were to enter into any profession with a view of better support, she would do all in her power to prevent him advancing in it."

Here Marianne, in an ecstasy of indignation, clapped her hands together and cried, "Gracious God! Can this be possible!"

"Well may you wonder, Marianne," replied her brother, "at the obstinacy which could resist such arguments as these. Your exclamation is very natural."

Marianne was going to retort, but she remembered her promises and forbore.

"All this, however," he continued, "was urged in vain. Edward said very little, but what he did say was in the most determined manner. Nothing should prevail on him to give up his engagement. He would stand to it, cost him what it might."

"Then," cried Mrs Jennings with blunt sincerity, no longer able to be silent, "he has acted like an honest man! I beg your pardon, Mr Dashwood, but if he had done otherwise, I should have thought him a rascal. I have some little concern in the business, as well as yourself, for Lucy Steele is my cousin, and I believe there is not a better kind of girl in the world, nor one who more deserves a good husband."

John Dashwood was greatly astonished, but his nature was calm, not open to provocation, and he never wished to offend anybody, especially anybody of good fortune. He therefore replied without any resentment, "I would by no means speak disrespectfully of any relation of yours, madam. Miss Lucy Steele is, I dare say, a very deserving young woman, but in the present case you know, the connection must be impossible. And to have entered into a secret engagement with a young man under her uncle's care, the son of a woman especially of such very large fortune as Mrs Ferrars, is perhaps altogether a little extraordinary. In short, I do not mean to reflect upon the behaviour of any person whom you have a regard for, Mrs Jennings. We all wish her extremely happy, and Mrs Ferrars' conduct throughout the whole has been such as every conscientious good mother in like circumstances would adopt. It has been dignified and liberal.

Edward has drawn his own lot, and I fear it will be a bad one."

Marianne sighed out her similar apprehension, and Elinor's heart wrung for the feelings of Edward, while braving his mother's threats for a woman who could not reward him.

"Well, sir," said Mrs Jennings, "and how did it end?"

"I am sorry to say, ma'am, in a most unhappy rupture—Edward is dismissed forever from his mother's notice. He left her house yesterday, but where he is gone or whether he is still in town I do not know, for we of course can make no enquiry."

"Poor young man! And what is to become of him?"

"What indeed, ma'am! It is a melancholy consideration. Born to the prospect of such affluence! I cannot conceive a situation more deplorable. The interest of two thousand pounds—how can a man live on it? And when to that is added the recollection that he might but for his own folly within three months have been in the receipt of two thousand five hundred a year—for Miss Morton has thirty thousand pounds—I cannot picture to myself a more wretched condition. We must all feel for him, and the more so because it is totally out of our power to assist him."

"Poor young man!" cried Mrs Jennings. "I am sure he should be very welcome to bed and board at my house, and so I would tell him if I could see him. It is not fit that he should be living about at his own charge now at lodgings and taverns."

Elinor's heart thanked her for such kindness towards Edward, though she could not forbear smiling at the form of it.

"If he would only have done as well by himself," said John Dashwood, "as all his friends were disposed to do by him, he might now have been in his proper situation and would have wanted for nothing. But as it is, it must be out of anybody's power to assist him. And there is one thing more preparing against him which must be worse than all—his mother has determined, with a very natural kind of spirit, to settle that estate upon Robert immediately which might have been Edward's on proper conditions. I left her this morning with her lawyer, talking over the business."

"Well!" said Mrs Jennings. "That is her revenge. Everybody has a way of their own. But I don't think mine would be to make one son independent because another had plagued me."

Marianne got up and walked about the room.

Elinor's despair for Edward's situation doubled. Fretting for his future on such poor means, she wrung her hands and imagined his utter sadness.

"Can anything be more galling to the spirit of a man," continued John, "than to see his younger brother in possession of an estate which might have been his own? Poor Edward! I feel for him sincerely."

A few minutes more spent in the same kind of effusion concluded his visit, and with repeated assurances to his sisters that he really believed there was no material danger in Fanny's indisposition and that they need not therefore be very uneasy about it, he went away, leaving the three ladies unanimous in their sentiments on the present occasion, as far at least as it regarded Mrs Ferrars' conduct, the Dashwoods' and Edward's.

Marianne's indignation burst forth as soon as he quitted the room, and as her vehemence made reserve impossible in Elinor and unnecessary in Mrs Jennings, they all joined in a very spirited critique upon the party.

Chapter Thirty-Eight

Mrs Jennings was very warm in her praise of Edward's conduct, but only Elinor and Marianne understood its true merit. They only knew how little he had had to tempt him to be disobedient, and how small was the consolation, beyond the consciousness of doing right, that could remain to him in the loss of friends and fortune. Elinor gloried in his integrity, and Marianne forgave all his offences in compassion for his punishment. But though confidence between them was by this public discovery restored to its proper state, it was not a subject on which either of them were fond of dwelling when alone.

Elinor avoided it upon principle as tending to fix still more upon her thoughts by the too warm, too positive assurances of Marianne that belief of Edward's continued affection for herself which she rather wished to do away. And Marianne's courage soon failed her in trying to converse upon a topic which always left her more dissatisfied with herself than ever by the comparison it necessarily produced between Elinor's conduct and her own.

She felt all the force of that comparison, but not as her sister had hoped, to urge her to exertion now. She felt it with all the pain of continual self-reproach, regretted most bitterly that she had never exerted herself before, but it brought only the torture of penitence without the hope of amendment. Her mind was so much weakened that she still fancied present exertion impossible, and therefore it only dispirited her more.

Nothing new was heard by them for a day or two afterwards of affairs in Harley Street or Bartlett's Buildings. But though so much of the matter was known to them already that Mrs Jennings might have had enough to do in spreading that knowledge farther without seeking after more, she had resolved from the first to pay a visit of comfort and enquiry to her cousins as soon as she could, and nothing but the hindrance of more visitors than usual had prevented her going to them within that time.

The third day succeeding their knowledge of the particulars was so fine, so beautiful a Sunday as to draw many to Kensington Gardens, though it was only the second week in March. Mrs Jennings and Elinor were of the number, but Marianne, who knew that the Willoughbys were again in town and had a constant dread of meeting them, chose rather to stay at home than venture into so public a place.

An intimate acquaintance of Mrs Jennings joined them soon after they entered the Gardens, and Elinor was not sorry that by her continuing with them and engaging all Mrs Jennings' conversation she was herself left to quiet reflection. She saw nothing of the Willoughbys, nothing of Edward, and for some time nothing of anybody who could by any chance whether grave or gay be interesting to her. But at last she found herself with some surprise accosted by Miss Steele, who, though looking rather shy, expressed great satisfaction in meeting them, and on receiving encouragement from the particular kindness of Mrs Jennings, left her own party for a short time to join theirs.

Mrs Jennings immediately whispered to Elinor, "Get it all out of her, my dear. She will tell you anything if you ask. You see I cannot leave Mrs Clarke."

It was lucky, however, for Mrs Jennings' curiosity and Elinor's too, that she would tell anything without being asked, for nothing would otherwise have been learnt.

"I am so glad to meet you," said Miss Steele, taking her familiarly by the arm. "For I wanted to see you of all things in the world." And lowering her voice, "I suppose Mrs Jennings has heard all about it. Is she angry?"

"Not at all, I believe, with you."

"That is a good thing. And Lady Middleton, is *she* angry?"

"I cannot suppose it possible that she should."

"I am monstrous glad of it. Good gracious! I have had such a time of it! I never saw Lucy in such a rage in my life. She vowed at first she would never trim me up a new bonnet nor do anything else for me again so long as she lived, but now she is quite come to and we are as good friends as ever. Look, she made me this bow to my hat and put in the feather last night. There now, you are going to laugh at me too. But why should not I wear pink ribbons? I do not care if it is the Doctor's favourite colour. I am sure for my part I should never have known he did like it better than any other colour if he had not happened to say so. My cousins have been so plaguing me! I declare sometimes I do not know which way to look before them."

She had wandered away to a subject on which Elinor had nothing to say, and therefore soon judged it expedient to find her way back again to the first.

"Well, but Miss Dashwood" — speaking triumphantly — "people may say what they choose about Mr Ferrars' declaring he would not have Lucy, for it is no such thing I can tell you, and it is quite a shame for such ill-natured reports to be spread abroad. Whatever Lucy might think about it herself, you know, it was no business of other people to set it down for certain."

"I never heard anything of the kind hinted at before, I assure you," said Elinor.

"Oh, did not you? But it was said, I know, very well, and by more than one. For Miss Godby told Miss Sparks that nobody in their senses could expect Mr Ferrars to give up a woman like Miss Morton, with thirty thousand pounds to her fortune, for Lucy Steele that had nothing at all. And I had it from Miss Sparks myself. And besides that, my cousin Richard said himself that when it came to the point he was afraid Mr Ferrars would be off, and when Edward did not come near us for three days I could not tell what to think myself.

"I believe in my heart Lucy gave it up all for lost, for we came away from your brother's Wednesday, and we saw nothing of him not all Thursday, Friday and Saturday, and did not know what was become of him. Once Lucy thought to write to him, but then her spirits rose against that. However this morning he came just as we came home from church, then it all

came out—how he had been sent for Wednesday to
Harley Street and been talked to by his mother and all
of them, and how he had declared before them all that
he loved nobody but Lucy, and nobody but Lucy
would he have. And how he had been so worried by
what passed that as soon as he had went away from
his mother's house he had got upon his horse and
ridden into the country somewhere or other, and how
he had stayed about at an inn all Thursday and Friday
on purpose to get the better of it.

"And after thinking it all over and over again, he
said it seemed to him as if now he had no fortune and
no nothing at all, it would be quite unkind to keep her
on to the engagement, because it must be for her loss.
For he had nothing but two thousand pounds, and no
hope of anything else, and if he was to go into orders,
as he had some thoughts, he could get nothing but a
curacy, and how was they to live upon that? He could
not bear to think of her doing no better, and so he
begged, if she had the least mind for it, to put an end
to the matter directly and leave him shift for himself.

"I heard him say all this as plain as could possibly
be. And it was entirely for her sake, and upon her
account, that he said a word about being off, and not
upon his own. I will take my oath he never dropped a
syllable of being tired of her or of wishing to marry
Miss Morton or anything like it. But to be sure, Lucy
would not give ear to such kind of talking, so she told
him directly—with a great deal about sweet and love,
you know, and all that—Oh, la, one can't repeat such
kind of things you know—she told him directly she
had not the least mind in the world to be off, for she
could live with him upon a trifle. And how little so
ever he might have, she should be very glad to have it
all, you know, or something of the kind.

"So then he was monstrous happy and talked on some time about what they should do, and they agreed he should take orders directly, and they must wait to be married till he got a living. And just then I could not hear any more, for my cousin called from below to tell me Mrs Richardson was come in her coach and would take one of us to Kensington Gardens. So I was forced to go into the room and interrupt them to ask Lucy if she would like to go, but she did not care to leave Edward, so I just ran upstairs and put on a pair of silk stockings and came off with the Richardsons."

"I do not understand what you mean by interrupting them," said Elinor, "you were all in the same room together, were not you?"

"No indeed, not us. La! Miss Dashwood, do you think people make love when anybody else is by? Oh, for shame! To be sure you must know better than that"—laughing affectedly—"no, no, they were shut up in the drawing room together, and all I heard was only by listening at the door."

"How!" cried Elinor. "Have you been repeating to me what you only learnt yourself by listening at the door? I am sorry I did not know it before, for I certainly would not have suffered you to give me particulars of a conversation which you ought not to have known yourself. How could you behave so unfairly by your sister?"

"Oh, la, there is nothing in that. I only stood at the door and heard what I could. And I am sure Lucy would have done just the same by me, for a year or two back, when Martha Sharpe and I had so many secrets together, she never made any bones of hiding in a closet or behind a chimney board on purpose to hear what we said."

Elinor tried to talk of something else, but Miss Steele could not be kept beyond a couple of of minutes from what was uppermost in her mind.

"Edward talks of going to Oxford soon," said she, "but now he is lodging at No. — Pall Mall. What an ill-natured woman his mother is, an't she? And your brother and sister were not very kind! However, I shan't say anything against them to you, and to be sure they did send us home in their own chariot, which was more than I looked for. And for my part, I was all in a fright for fear your sister should ask us for the huswifes she had gave us a day or two before, but however nothing was said about them and I took care to keep mine out of sight.

"Edward have got some business at Oxford, he says, so he must go there for a time, and after that as soon as he can light upon a bishop he will be ordained. I wonder what curacy he will get! Good gracious!" Giggling as she spoke. "I'd lay my life I know what my cousins will say when they hear of it. They will tell me I should write to the Doctor to get Edward the curacy of his new living. I know they will, but I am sure I would not do such a thing for all the world. 'La!' I shall say directly. 'I wonder how you could think of such a thing? I write to the Doctor, indeed!'"

"Well," said Elinor, "it is a comfort to be prepared against the worst. You have got your answer ready."

Miss Steele was going to reply on the same subject, but the approach of her own party made another more necessary.

"Oh, la, here come the Richardsons. I had a vast deal more to say to you, but I must not stay away from them not any longer. I assure you they are very genteel people. He makes a monstrous deal of money, and they keep their own coach. I have not time to speak to Mrs Jennings about it myself, but pray tell her I am quite happy to hear she is not in anger against us, and Lady Middleton the same, and if anything should happen to take you and your sister away and Mrs Jennings should want company, I am sure we should be very glad to come and stay with her for as long a time as she likes. I suppose Lady Middleton won't ask us any more this bout. Goodbye, I am sorry Miss Marianne was not here. Remember me kindly to her. La, if you have not got your spotted muslin on! I wonder you was not afraid of its being torn."

Such was her parting concern, for after this she had time only to pay her farewell compliments to Mrs Jennings before her company was claimed by Mrs Richardson, and Elinor was left in possession of knowledge which might feed her powers of reflection some time. Though she had learnt very little more than what had been already foreseen and foreplanned in her own mind. Edward's marriage with Lucy was as firmly determined on, and the time of its taking place remained as absolutely uncertain, as she had concluded it would be. Everything depended exactly after her expectation on his getting that preferment, of which at present there seemed not the smallest chance.

As soon as they returned to the carriage Mrs Jennings was eager for information, but as Elinor wished to spread as little as possible intelligence that had in the first place been so unfairly obtained, she confined herself to the brief repetition of such simple particulars as she felt assured that Lucy, for the sake of her own consequence, would choose to have known. The continuance of their engagement and the means that were able to be taken for promoting its end was all her communication, and this produced from Mrs Jennings the following natural remark.

"Wait for his having a living! Ay, we all know how that will end—they will wait a twelvemonth, and finding no good comes of it, will set down upon a curacy of fifty pounds a year with the interest of his two thousand pounds and what little matter Mr Steele and Mr Pratt can give her. Then they will have a child every year! And Lord help 'em, how poor they will be! I must see what I can give them towards furnishing their house. Two maids and two men, indeed, as I talked of t'other day. No, no, they must get a stout girl of all works. Betty's sister would never do for them now."

The next morning brought Elinor a letter by the two-penny post from Lucy herself. It was as follows.

Bartlett's Building, March.

I hope my dear Miss Dashwood will excuse the liberty I take of writing to her, but I know your friendship for me will make you pleased to hear such a good account of myself and my dear Edward after all the troubles we have went through lately. Therefore will make no more apologies, but proceed to say that thank God, though we have suffered dreadfully, we are both quite well now and as happy as we must always be in one another's love. We have had great trials and great persecutions, but, however, at the same time gratefully acknowledge many friends, yourself not the least among them, whose great kindness I shall always thankfully remember. As will Edward too, who I have told of it.

I am sure you will be glad to hear, as likewise dear Mrs Jennings, I spent two happy hours with him yesterday afternoon. He would not hear of our parting—though earnestly did I, as I thought my duty required, urge him to it for prudence sake, and would have parted forever on the spot would he consent to it. But he said it should never be.

He did not regard his mother's anger while he could have my affections.

Our prospects are not very bright to be sure, but we must wait and hope for the best. He will be ordained shortly, and should it ever be in your power to recommend him to anybody that has a living to bestow, am very sure you will not forget us. And dear Mrs Jennings too, trust she will speak a good word for us to Sir John or Mr Palmer or any friend that may be able to assist us. Poor Anne was much to blame for what she did, but she did it for the best, so I say nothing.

Hope Mrs Jennings won't think it too much trouble to give us a call should she come this way any morning. 'Twould be a great kindness, and my cousins would be proud to know her. My paper reminds me to conclude, and begging to be most gratefully and respectfully remembered to her, and to Sir John and Lady Middleton and the dear children when you chance to see them, and love to Miss Marianne.

I am, etc.

As soon as Elinor had finished it, she performed what she concluded to be its writer's real design by placing it in the hands of Mrs Jennings, who read it aloud with many comments of satisfaction and praise.

"Very well indeed! How prettily she writes! Aye, that was quite proper to let him be off if he would. That was just like Lucy. Poor soul! I wish I could get him a living with all my heart. She calls me dear Mrs Jennings, you see. She is a good-hearted girl as ever lived. Very well upon my word. That sentence is very prettily turned. Yes, yes, I will go and see her, sure enough. How attentive she is to think of everybody! Thank you, my dear, for showing it me. It is as pretty a letter as ever I saw, and does Lucy's head and heart great credit."

Chapter Thirty-Nine

The Miss Dashwoods had now been rather more than two months in town, and Marianne's impatience to be gone increased every day. She sighed for the air, the liberty, the quiet of the country, and fancied that if any place could give her ease, Barton must do it. Elinor was hardly less anxious than herself for their removal, and only so much less bent on its being effected immediately as that she was conscious of the difficulties of so long a journey, which Marianne could not be brought to acknowledge. She began, however, seriously to turn her thoughts towards its accomplishment. She had already mentioned their wishes to their kind hostess, who resisted them with all the eloquence of her goodwill, when a plan was suggested which, though detaining them from home yet a few weeks longer, appeared to Elinor altogether much more eligible than any other.

The Palmers were to remove to Cleveland about the end of March for the Easter holidays, and Mrs Jennings, with both her friends, received a very warm invitation from Charlotte to go with them. This would not in itself have been sufficient for the delicacy of Miss Dashwood, but it was enforced with so much real politeness by Mr Palmer himself as, joined to the very great amendment of his manners towards them since her sister had been known to be unhappy, induced her to accept it with pleasure.

When she told Marianne what she had done, however, her first reply was not very auspicious.

"Cleveland!" she cried with great agitation. "No, I cannot go to Cleveland."

"You forget," said Elinor gently, "that its situation is not…that it is not in the neighbourhood of…"

"But it is in Somersetshire. I cannot go into Somersetshire. There, where I looked forward to going… No, Elinor, you cannot expect me to go there."

Elinor would not argue upon the propriety of overcoming such feelings. She only endeavoured to counteract them by working on others, and represented it therefore as a measure which would fix the time of her returning to that dear mother whom she so much wished to see in a more eligible, more comfortable manner than any other plan could do, and perhaps without any greater delay. From Cleveland, which was within a few miles of Bristol, the distance to Barton was not beyond one day, though a long day's journey, and their mother's servant might easily come there to attend them down. And as there could be no occasion of their staying above a week at Cleveland, they might now be at home in little more than three weeks' time. As Marianne's affection for her mother was sincere, it must triumph with little difficulty over the imaginary evils she had started.

Mrs Jennings was so far from being weary of her guests that she pressed them very earnestly to return with her again from Cleveland. Elinor was grateful for the attention, but it could not alter her design, and their mother's concurrence being readily gained, everything relative to their return was arranged as far as it could be, and Marianne found some relief in drawing up a statement of the hours that were yet to divide her from Barton.

"Ah! Colonel, I do not know what you and I shall do without the Miss Dashwoods," was Mrs Jennings' address to him when he first called on her after their leaving her was settled. "For they are quite resolved upon going home from the Palmers, and how forlorn we shall be when I come back! Lord! We shall sit and gape at one another as dull as two cats."

Perhaps Mrs Jennings was in hopes by this vigorous sketch of their future ennui to provoke him to make that offer which might give himself an escape from it. And if so, she had soon afterwards good reason to think her object gained, for on Elinor's moving to the window to take more expeditiously the dimensions of a print which she was going to copy for her friend, he followed her to it with a look of particular meaning and conversed with her there for several minutes.

The effect of his discourse on the lady too could not escape her observation. For though she was too honourable to listen, and had even changed her seat on purpose that she might not hear to one close by the piano forte on which Marianne was playing, she could not keep herself from seeing that Elinor changed colour, attended with agitation and was too intent on what he said to pursue her employment. Still farther in confirmation of her hopes, in the interval of Marianne's turning from one lesson to another, some words of the Colonel's inevitably reached her ear in which he seemed to be apologising for the badness of his house.

This set the matter beyond a doubt. She wondered indeed at his thinking it necessary to do so, but supposed it to be the proper etiquette. What Elinor said in reply she could not distinguish, but judged from the motion of her lips, that she did not think that any material objection, and Mrs Jennings commended her in her heart for being so honest. They then talked on for a few minutes longer without her catching a syllable, when another lucky stop in Marianne's performance brought her these words in the Colonel's calm voice. "I am afraid it cannot take place very soon."

Astonished and shocked at so unlover-like a speech, she was almost ready to cry out, "Lord! What should hinder it?" but checking her desire, confined herself to this silent ejaculation. *This is very strange! Sure he need not wait to be older.*

This delay on the Colonel's side, however, did not seem to offend or mortify his fair companion in the least. For on their breaking up the conference soon afterwards and moving different ways, Mrs Jennings very plainly heard Elinor say, and with a voice which showed her to feel what she said, "I shall always think myself very much obliged to you."

Mrs Jennings was delighted with her gratitude, and only wondered that after hearing such a sentence, the Colonel should be able to take leave of them as he immediately did with the utmost sangfroid and go away without making her any reply! She had not thought her old friend could have made so indifferent a suitor.

What had really passed between them was to this effect.

"I have heard," said he with great compassion, "of the injustice your friend Mr Ferrars has suffered from his family, for if I understand the matter right, he has been entirely cast off by them for persevering in his engagement with a very deserving young woman. Have I been rightly informed? Is it so?"

Elinor told him that it was.

"The cruelty, the impolitic cruelty," he replied with great feeling, "of dividing, or attempting to divide, two young people long attached to each other, is terrible. Mrs Ferrars does not know what she may be doing—what she may drive her son to. I have seen Mr Ferrars two or three times in Harley Street, and am much pleased with him. He is not a young man with whom one can be intimately acquainted in a short time, but I have seen enough of him to wish him well for his own sake, and as a friend of yours I wish it still more.

"I understand that he intends to take orders. Will you be so good as to tell him that the living of Delaford, now just vacant, as I am informed by this day's post, is his, if he think it worth his acceptance—but that perhaps, so unfortunately circumstanced as he is now, it may be nonsense to appear to doubt. I only wish it were more valuable. It is a rectory, but a small one. The late incumbent I believe did not make more than two hundred pounds per annum, and though it is certainly capable of improvement, I fear not to such an amount as to afford him a very comfortable income. Such as it is, however, my pleasure in presenting him to it will be very great. Pray assure him of it."

Elinor's astonishment at this commission could hardly have been greater had the Colonel been really making her an offer of his hand. The preferment which only two days before she had considered as hopeless for Edward was already provided to enable him to marry, and she, of all people in the world, was fixed on to bestow it!

Her emotion was such as Mrs Jennings had attributed to a very different cause, but whatever minor feelings less pure, less pleasing, might have a share in that emotion, her esteem for the general benevolence and her gratitude for the particular friendship which together prompted Colonel Brandon to this act were strongly felt and warmly expressed. She thanked him for it with all her heart, spoke of Edward's principles and disposition with that praise which she knew them to deserve, and promised to undertake the commission with pleasure, if it were really his wish to put off so agreeable an office to another. But at the same time, she could not help thinking that no one could so well perform it as himself.

It was an office in short from which, unwilling to give Edward the pain of receiving an obligation from her, she would have been very glad to be spared herself, but Colonel Brandon on motives of equal delicacy declining it likewise, still seemed so desirous of its being given through her means that she would not on any account make farther opposition. Edward, she believed, was still in town, and fortunately she had heard his address from Miss Steele. She could undertake therefore to inform him of it in the course of the day.

After this had been settled Colonel Brandon began to talk of his own advantage in securing so respectable and agreeable a neighbour, and then it was that he mentioned with regret that the house was small and indifferent, an evil which Elinor, as Mrs Jennings had supposed her to do, made very light of, at least as far as regarded its size.

"The smallness of the house," said she, "I cannot imagine any inconvenience to them, for it will be in proportion to their family and income."

By which the Colonel was surprised to find that she was considering Mr Ferrars' marriage as the certain consequence of the presentation, for he did not suppose it possible that Delaford living could supply such an income as anybody in his style of life would venture to settle on—and he said so.

"This little rectory can do no more than make Mr Ferrars comfortable as a bachelor, it cannot enable him to marry. I am sorry to say that my patronage ends with this, and my interest is hardly more extensive. If, however, by an unforeseen chance it should be in my power to serve him farther, I must think very differently of him from what I now do if I am not as ready to be useful to him then as I sincerely wish I could be at present. What I am now doing indeed, seems nothing at all, since it can advance him so little towards what must be his principal, his only object of happiness. His marriage must still be a distant good. At least, I am afraid it cannot take place very soon."

Such was the sentence which, when misunderstood, so justly offended the delicate feelings of Mrs Jennings. But after this narration of what really passed between Colonel Brandon and Elinor while they stood at the window, the gratitude expressed by the latter on their parting may perhaps appear in general not less reasonably excited, nor less properly worded than if it had arisen from an offer of marriage.

Chapter Forty

"Well, Miss Dashwood," said Mrs Jennings, sagaciously smiling as soon as the gentleman had withdrawn, "I do not ask you what the Colonel has been saying to you, for though upon my honour I *tried* to keep out of hearing, I could not help catching enough to understand his business. And I assure you I never was better pleased in my life and I wish you joy of it with all my heart."

"Thank you, ma'am," said Elinor. "It is a matter of great joy to me, and I feel the goodness of Colonel Brandon most sensibly. There are not many men who would act as he has done. Few people who have so compassionate a heart! I never was more astonished in my life."

"Lord, my dear, you are very modest. I an't the least astonished at it in the world, for I have often thought of late there was nothing more likely to happen."

"You judged from your knowledge of the Colonel's general benevolence, but at least you could not foresee that the opportunity would so very soon occur."

"Opportunity!" repeated Mrs Jennings. "Oh, as to that, when a man has once made up his mind to such a thing, somehow or other he will soon find an opportunity. Well, my dear, I wish you joy of it again and again, and if ever there was a happy couple of in the world I think I shall soon know where to look for them."

"You mean to go to Delaford after them I suppose," said Elinor, with a faint smile.

"Aye, my dear, that I do indeed. And as to the house being a bad one, I do not know what the Colonel would be at, for it is as good a one as ever I saw."

"He spoke of its being out of repair."

"Well, and whose fault is that? Why don't he repair it? Who should do it but himself?"

They were interrupted by the servant's coming in to announce the carriage being at the door, and Mrs Jennings immediately preparing to go said, "Well, my dear, I must be gone before I have had half my talk out. But, however, we may have it all over in the evening, for we shall be quite alone. I do not ask you to go with me, for I dare say your mind is too full of the matter to care for company, and besides you must long to tell your sister all about it."

Marianne had left the room before the conversation began.

"Certainly, ma'am, I shall tell Marianne of it, but I shall not mention it at present to anybody else."

"Oh, very well," said Mrs Jennings rather disappointed. "Then you would not have me tell it to Lucy, for I think of going as far as Holborn today."

"No, ma'am, not even Lucy if you please. One day's delay will not be very material, and till I have written to Mr Ferrars I think it ought not to be mentioned to anybody else. I shall do that directly. It is of importance that no time should be lost with him, for he will of course have much to do relative to his ordination."

This speech at first puzzled Mrs Jennings exceedingly. Why Mr Ferrars was to have been written to about it in such a hurry, she could not immediately comprehend. A few moments' reflection, however, produced a very happy idea, and she exclaimed, "Oh ho! I understand you. Mr Ferrars is to be the man. Well, so much the better for him. Ay, to be sure he must be ordained in readiness, and I am very glad to find things are so forward between you. But my dear, is not this rather out of character? Should not the Colonel write himself? Sure he is the proper person."

Elinor did not quite understand the beginning of Mrs Jennings' speech, neither did she think it worth enquiring into, and therefore only replied to its conclusion.

"Colonel Brandon is so delicate a man that he rather wished anyone to announce his intentions to Mr Ferrars than himself."

"And so you are forced to do it. Well, that is an odd kind of delicacy! However, I will not disturb you" — seeing her preparing to write—"you know your own concerns best. So goodbye, my dear. I have not heard of anything to please me so well since Charlotte was brought to bed."

And away she went, but returning again in a moment.

"I have just been thinking of Betty's sister, my dear. I should be very glad to get her so good a mistress. But whether she would do for a lady's maid I am sure I can't tell. She is an excellent housemaid and works very well at her needle. However, you will think of all that at your leisure."

"Certainly, ma'am," replied Elinor, not hearing much of what she said and more anxious to be alone than to be mistress of the subject.

How she should begin—how she should express herself in her note to Edward—was now all her concern. The particular circumstances between them made a difficulty of that which to any other person would have been the easiest thing in the world, but she equally feared to say too much or too little, and sat deliberating over her paper with the pen in her hand till broken in on by the entrance of Edward himself.

He had met Mrs Jennings at the door in her way to the carriage as he came to leave his farewell card, and she, after apologising for not returning herself, had obliged him to enter by saying that Miss Dashwood was above and wanted to speak with him on very particular business.

Elinor had just been congratulating herself in the midst of her perplexity that however difficult it might be to express herself properly by letter, it was at least preferable to giving the information by word of mouth, when her visitor entered to force her upon this greatest exertion of all. Her astonishment and confusion were very great on his so sudden appearance. She had not seen him before since his engagement became public, and therefore not since his knowing her to be acquainted with it, which, with the consciousness of what she had been thinking of and what she had to tell him, made her feel particularly uncomfortable for some minutes. He too was much distressed, and they sat down together in a most promising state of embarrassment. Whether he had asked her pardon for his intrusion on first coming into the room he could not recollect, but determining to be on the safe side, he made his apology in form as soon as he could say anything after taking a chair.

"Mrs Jennings told me," said he, "that you wished to speak with me, at least I understood her so—or I certainly should not have intruded on you in such a manner. Though at the same time, I should have been extremely sorry to leave London without seeing you and your sister, especially as it will most likely be some time—it is not probable that I should soon have the pleasure of meeting you again. I go to Oxford tomorrow."

"You would not have gone, however," said Elinor, recovering herself and determined to get over what she so much dreaded as soon as possible, "without receiving our good wishes, even if we had not been able to give them in person. Mrs Jennings was quite right in what she said. I have something of consequence to inform you of, which I was on the point of communicating by paper. I am charged with a most agreeable office"—breathing rather faster than usual as she spoke—"Colonel Brandon, who was here only ten minutes ago, has desired me to say that understanding you mean to take orders, he has great pleasure in offering you the living of Delaford now just vacant, and only wishes it were more valuable. Allow me to congratulate you on having so respectable and well-judging a friend, and to join in his wish that the living—it is about two hundred a-year—were much more considerable, and such as might better enable you to—as might be more than a temporary accommodation to yourself—such, in short, as might establish all your views of happiness."

What Edward felt, as he could not say it himself, it cannot be expected that anyone else should say for him. He looked all the astonishment which such unexpected, such unthought-of information could not fail of exciting, but he said only these two words. "Colonel Brandon!"

"Yes," continued Elinor, gathering more resolution, as some of the worst was over. "Colonel Brandon means it as a testimony of his concern for what has lately passed—for the cruel situation in which the unjustifiable conduct of your family has placed you— a concern which I am sure Marianne, myself and all your friends must share. And likewise as a proof of his high esteem for your general character and his particular approbation of your behaviour on the present occasion."

"Colonel Brandon give *me* a living! Can it be possible?"

"The unkindness of your own relations has made you astonished to find friendship anywhere."

"No," replied he with sudden consciousness, "not to find it in *you*, for I cannot be ignorant that to you, to your goodness, I owe it all. I feel it—I would express it if I could—but as you well know, I am no orator."

"You are very much mistaken. I do assure you that you owe it entirely, at least almost entirely, to your own merit and Colonel Brandon's discernment of it. I have had no hand in it. I did not even know till I understood his design that the living was vacant, nor had it ever occurred to me that he might have had such a living in his gift. As a friend of mine, of my family, he may perhaps—indeed I know he has still greater pleasure in bestowing it, but upon my word you owe nothing to my solicitation."

Truth obliged her to acknowledge some small share in the action, but she was at the same time so unwilling to appear as the benefactress of Edward that she acknowledged it with hesitation, which probably contributed to fix that suspicion in his mind which had recently entered it. For a short time he sat deep in thought after Elinor had ceased to speak. At last, and as if it were rather an effort, he said, "Colonel Brandon seems a man of great worth and respectability. I have always heard him spoken of as such, and your brother I know esteems him highly. He is undoubtedly a sensible man, and in his manners perfectly the gentleman."

"Indeed," replied Elinor. "I believe that you will find him on farther acquaintance all that you have heard him to be, and as you will be such very near neighbours — for I understand the parsonage is almost close to the mansion house — it is particularly important that he should be all this."

Edward made no answer, but when she had turned away her head, gave her a look so serious, so earnest, so uncheerful as seemed to say that he might hereafter wish the distance between the parsonage and the mansion house much greater.

"Colonel Brandon, I think, lodges in St James Street," said he soon afterwards, rising from his chair.

Elinor told him the number of the house.

"I must hurry away then to give him those thanks which you will not allow me to give *you*, to assure him that he has made me a very — an exceedingly happy man."

Staring at Elinor until she glanced away blushing, Edward caught one of her hands and drew her up. "Dear Elinor —"

She stepped backward. "Please, come no closer."

"I wish to show you the gratitude my heart demands I give." He pulled her towards him and enfolded her in his arms. His lips to her forehead, he murmured, "Would that I might do more than this meagre showing."

"We must not." She pushed at his chest, her yearning to continue with him in this vein shimmering through her body like a shower of fireworks.

But he would not let her go and pressed nearer. He kneaded her derrière with one hand, entrancing her. He let his other roam to her mound where he found her seam and her wet heat. "How I long to possess you totally. Yet not in this lifetime! Not in this universe!"

He steadied her on her feet, groaning as he removed his person from her own. Then, turning on his heel, he made his excuses and headed for the door.

Elinor did not offer to detain him, and they parted with a very earnest assurance on her side of her unceasing good wishes for his happiness in every change of situation that might befall him, on his with rather an attempt to return the same good will than the power of expressing it.

"When I see him again," said Elinor to herself, as the door shut him out, "I shall see him the husband of Lucy."

And with this pleasing anticipation she sat down to reconsider the past, recall the words and endeavour to comprehend all the feelings of Edward, and of course to reflect on her own with discontent. How she had wanted him to continue with his outrageously decadent advances! How ashamed she had been to want his hand between her thighs, his fingers inside her quim and his cock there too. He had educated her as to the ecstasies which now by circumstances she was denied. She had even gone so far in her desires as to cast Colonel Brandon in the light of a potential suitor, or to be more accurate, a potential lover. As if the taste of sensual delights created an eternal hunger for more, Elinor knew now she was ensnared by an addiction to which she wished no end!

When Mrs Jennings came home, though she returned from seeing people whom she had never seen before and of whom therefore she must have a great deal to say, her mind was so much more occupied by the important secret in her possession than by anything else that she reverted to it again as soon as Elinor appeared.

"Well, my dear," she cried, "I sent you up the young man. Did not I do right? And I suppose you had no great difficulty — You did not find him very unwilling to accept your proposal?"

"No, ma'am, that was not very likely."

"Well, and how soon will he be ready? For it seems all to depend upon that."

"Really," said Elinor, "I know so little of these kind of forms that I can hardly even conjecture as to the time or the preparation necessary, but I suppose two or three months will complete his ordination."

"Two or three months!" cried Mrs Jennings. "Lord! My dear, how calmly you talk of it, and can the Colonel wait two or three months! Lord bless me! I am sure it would put me quite out of patience! And though one would be very glad to do a kindness by poor Mr Ferrars, I do think it is not worthwhile to wait two or three months for him. Sure somebody else might be found that would do as well, somebody that is in orders already."

"My dear ma'am," said Elinor, "what can you be thinking of? Why, Colonel Brandon's only object is to be of use to Mr Ferrars."

"Lord bless you, my dear! Sure you do not mean to persuade me that the Colonel only marries you for the sake of giving ten guineas to Mr Ferrars!"

The deception could not continue after this, and an explanation immediately took place by which both gained considerable amusement for the moment without any material loss of happiness to either. For Mrs Jennings only exchanged one form of delight for another, and still without forfeiting her expectation of the first.

"Aye, aye, the parsonage is but a small one," said she after the first ebullition of surprise and satisfaction was over, "and very likely may be out of repair, but to hear a man apologising as I thought for a house that to my knowledge has five sitting rooms on the ground floor, and I think the housekeeper told me could make up fifteen beds! And to you too, that had been used to live in Barton cottage! It seems quite ridiculous. But my dear, we must touch up the Colonel to do something to the parsonage and make it comfortable for them before Lucy goes to it."

"But Colonel Brandon does not seem to have any idea of the living's being enough to allow them to marry."

"The Colonel is a ninny, my dear. Because he has two thousand a year himself, he thinks that nobody else can marry on less. Take my word for it that if I am alive I shall be paying a visit at Delaford Parsonage before Michaelmas, and I am sure I shan't go if Lucy an't there."

Elinor was quite of her opinion as to the probability of their not waiting for anything more.

Chapter Forty-One

Edward, having carried his thanks to Colonel Brandon, proceeded with his happiness of place and position to Lucy. Such was the excess of it by the time he reached Bartlett's Buildings that she was able to assure Mrs Jennings, who called on her again the next day with her congratulations, that she had never seen him in such spirits before in her life.

Her own happiness and her own spirits were at least very certain, and she joined Mrs Jennings most heartily in her expectation of their being all comfortably together in Delaford Parsonage before Michaelmas. So far was she at the same time from any backwardness to give Elinor that credit which Edward would give her that she spoke of her friendship for them both with the most grateful warmth, was ready to own all their obligation to her and openly declared that no exertion for their good on Miss Dashwood's part, either present or future, would ever surprise her. For she believed her capable of doing anything in the world for those she really valued. As for Colonel

Brandon, she was not only ready to worship him as a saint, but was moreover truly anxious that he should be treated as one in all worldly concerns, anxious that his tithes should be raised to the utmost and scarcely resolved to avail herself at Delaford as far as she possibly could of his servants, his carriage, his cows and his poultry.

It was now above a week since John Dashwood had called in Berkeley Street, and as since that time no notice had been taken by them of his wife's indisposition beyond one verbal enquiry, Elinor began to feel it necessary to pay her a visit. This was an obligation however which not only opposed her own inclination, but which had not the assistance of any encouragement from her companions. Marianne, not contented with absolutely refusing to go herself, was very urgent to prevent her sister's going at all. Mrs Jennings, though her carriage was always at Elinor's service, so very much disliked Mrs John Dashwood that not even her curiosity to see how she looked after the late discovery nor her strong desire to affront her by taking Edward's part could overcome her unwillingness to be in her company again. The consequence was that Elinor set out by herself to pay a visit for which no one could really have less inclination and to run the risk of a tête-à-tête with a woman whom neither of the others had so much reason to dislike.

Mrs Dashwood was denied, but before the carriage could turn from the house, her husband accidentally came out. He expressed great pleasure in meeting Elinor, told her that he had been just going to call in Berkeley Street and, assuring her that Fanny would be very glad to see her, invited her to come in.

They walked upstairs in to the drawing room. Nobody was there.

"Fanny is in her own room, I suppose," said he. "I will go to her presently, for I am sure she will not have the least objection in the world to seeing you. Very far from it, indeed. Now especially there cannot be — but however, you and Marianne were always great favourites. Why would not Marianne come?"

Elinor made what excuse she could for her.

"I am not sorry to see you alone," he replied, "for I have a good deal to say to you. This living of Colonel Brandon's — can it be true? Has he really given it to Edward? I heard it yesterday by chance, and was coming to you on purpose to enquire farther about it."

"It is perfectly true. Colonel Brandon has given the living of Delaford to Edward."

"Really! Well, this is very astonishing! No relationship! No connection between them! And now that livings fetch such a price! What was the value of this?"

"About two hundred a year."

"Very well — and for the next presentation to a living of that value — supposing the late incumbent to have been old and sickly, and likely to vacate it soon — he might have got I dare say fourteen hundred pounds. And how came he not to have settled that matter before this person's death? Now indeed it would be too late to sell it, but a man of Colonel Brandon's sense! I wonder he should be so improvident in a point of such common, such natural concern! Well, I am convinced that there is a vast deal of inconsistency in almost every human character. I suppose, however — on recollection — that the case may probably be this. Edward is only to hold the living till the person to whom the Colonel has really sold the presentation is old enough to take it. Aye, aye, that is the fact, depend upon it."

Elinor contradicted it, however, very positively, and by relating that she had herself been employed in conveying the offer from Colonel Brandon to Edward and therefore must understand the terms on which it was given, obliged him to submit to her authority.

"It is truly astonishing!" he cried after hearing what she said. "What could be the Colonel's motive?"

"A very simple one — to be of use to Mr Ferrars."

"Well, well, whatever Colonel Brandon may be, Edward is a very lucky man. You will not mention the matter to Fanny, however, for though I have broke it to her and she bears it vastly well, she will not like to hear it much talked of."

Elinor had some difficulty here to refrain from observing that she thought Fanny might have borne with composure an acquisition of wealth to her brother by which neither she nor her child could be possibly impoverished. This certainly should please the woman who had done so much to deny others in the family of their proper due.

"Mrs Ferrars," added he, lowering his voice to the tone becoming so important a subject, "knows nothing about it at present, and I believe it will be best to keep it entirely concealed from her as long as may be. When the marriage takes place, I fear she must hear of it all."

"But why should such precaution be used? Though it is not to be supposed that Mrs Ferrars can have the smallest satisfaction in knowing that her son has money enough to live upon, for that must be quite out of the question, yet why upon her late behaviour is she supposed to feel at all? She has done with her son, she cast him off forever and has made all those over whom she had any influence cast him off likewise.

Surely after doing so she cannot be imagined liable to any impression of sorrow or of joy on his account—she cannot be interested in anything that befalls him. She would not be so weak as to throw away the comfort of a child and yet retain the anxiety of a parent!"

"Ah! Elinor," said John, "your reasoning is very good, but it is founded on ignorance of human nature. When Edward's unhappy match takes place, depend upon it his mother will feel as much as if she had never discarded him, and therefore every circumstance that may accelerate that dreadful event must be concealed from her as much as possible. Mrs Ferrars can never forget that Edward is her son."

"You surprise me, I should think it must nearly have escaped her memory by this time."

"You wrong her exceedingly. Mrs Ferrars is one of the most affectionate mothers in the world."

And one of the most unnatural, as well. Yet Elinor was silent.

"We think now," said Mr Dashwood after a short pause, "of *Robert's* marrying Miss Morton."

Elinor, smiling at the grave and decisive importance of her brother's tone, calmly replied, "The lady, I suppose, has no choice in the affair."

"Choice! How do you mean?"

"I only mean that I suppose from your manner of speaking it must be the same to Miss Morton whether she marry Edward or Robert."

"Certainly there can be no difference, for Robert will now to all intents and purposes be considered as the eldest son, and as to anything else they are both very agreeable young men—I do not know that one is superior to the other."

Elinor said no more, and John was also for a short time silent. His reflections ended thus.

"Of one thing, my dear sister" — kindly taking her hand and speaking in an awful whisper — "I may assure you, and I *will* do it, because I know it must gratify you. I have good reason to think — indeed I have it from the best authority, or I should not repeat it, for otherwise it would be very wrong to say anything about it. But I have it from the very best authority — not that I ever precisely heard Mrs Ferrars say it herself, but her daughter did and I have it from her. That in short whatever objections there might be against a certain — a certain connection — you understand me — it would have been far preferable to her, it would not have given her half the vexation that *this* does. I was exceedingly pleased to hear that Mrs Ferrars considered it in that light — a very gratifying circumstance you know to us all. 'It would have been beyond comparison,' she said, 'the least evil of the two.' And she would be glad to compound now for nothing worse.

"But however, all that is quite out of the question — not to be thought of or mentioned — as to any attachment you know — it never could be — all that is gone by. But I thought I would just tell you of this because I knew how much it must please you. Not that you have any reason to regret, my dear Elinor. There is no doubt of your doing exceedingly well — quite as well, or better perhaps, all things considered. Has Colonel Brandon been with you lately?"

Elinor had heard enough, if not to gratify her vanity and raise her self-importance, to agitate her nerves and fill her mind. She was therefore glad to be spared from the necessity of saying much in reply herself, and from the danger of hearing anything more from her brother, by the entrance of Mr Robert Ferrars. After a few moments' chat John Dashwood, recollecting that Fanny was yet uninformed of her sister's being there, quitted the room in quest of her, and Elinor was left to improve her acquaintance with Robert. By the gay unconcern, the happy self-complacency of his manner while enjoying so unfair a division of his mother's love and liberality to the prejudice of his banished brother, earned only by his own dissipated course of life and that brother's integrity, he was confirming her most unfavourable opinion of his head and heart.

They had scarcely been two minutes by themselves before he began to speak of Edward, for he too had heard of the living and was very inquisitive on the subject. Elinor repeated the particulars of it as she had given them to John, and their effect on Robert, though very different, was not less striking than it had been on him. He laughed most immoderately. The idea of Edward's being a clergyman and living in a small parsonage house diverted him beyond measure, and when to that was added the fanciful imagery of Edward reading prayers in a white surplice and publishing the banns of marriage between John Smith and Mary Brown, he could conceive nothing more ridiculous.

Elinor, while she waited in silence and immovable gravity the conclusion of such folly, could not restrain her eyes from being fixed on him with a look that spoke all the contempt it excited. She should have liked to beat him about the head, he was so childish, so self-centred, so inconsiderate and disloyal to his brother. She glared at him. It was a look however very well bestowed, for it relieved her own feelings and gave no intelligence to him. He was recalled from wit to wisdom not by any reproof of hers but by his own sensibility.

"We may treat it as a joke," said he at last, recovering from the affected laugh which had considerably lengthened out the genuine gaiety of the moment, "but upon my soul, it is a most serious business. Poor Edward! He is ruined forever. I am extremely sorry for it—for I know him to be a very good-hearted creature, as well-meaning a fellow perhaps as any in the world. You must not judge of him, Miss Dashwood, from your slight acquaintance. Poor Edward! His manners are certainly not the happiest in nature. But we are not all born, you know, with the same powers, the same address. Poor fellow! To see him in a circle of strangers! To be sure it was pitiable enough! But upon my soul, I believe he has as good a heart as any in the kingdom, and I declare and protest to you I never was so shocked in my life as when it all burst forth.

"I could not believe it. My mother was the first person who told me of it, and I, feeling myself called on to act with resolution, immediately said to her, 'My dear madam, I do not know what you may intend to do on the occasion, but as for myself I must say that if Edward does marry this young woman, I never will see him again.' That was what I said immediately. I was most uncommonly shocked indeed! Poor Edward! He has done for himself completely—shut himself out forever from all decent society! But as I directly said to my mother, I am not in the least surprised at it. From his style of education it was always to be expected. My poor mother was half frantic."

"Have you ever seen the lady?"

"Yes, once while she was staying in this house I happened to drop in for ten minutes, and I saw quite enough of her. The merest awkward country girl, without style or elegance and almost without beauty. I remember her perfectly. Just the kind of girl I should suppose likely to captivate poor Edward."

At this, Elinor flinched. Was she herself also, by definition, an awkward country girl, sans style and grace and looks? Ye gods! Although she had never approved of Lucy, to take her poor character and use it to ridicule Edward was beyond tolerating. "Sir, really! We must not discuss Edward and Lucy's relationship."

"Whyever not? I offered immediately, as soon as my mother related the affair to me, to talk to him myself and dissuade him from the match, but it was too late then, I found, to do anything. Unluckily I was not in the way at first and knew nothing of it till after the breach had taken place, when it was not for me, you know, to interfere. But had I been informed of it a few hours earlier — I think it is most probable that something might have been hit on. I certainly should have represented it to Edward in a very strong light. 'My dear fellow,' I should have said, 'consider what you are doing. You are making a most disgraceful connection, and such a one as your family are unanimous in disapproving.' I cannot help thinking, in short, that means might have been found. But now it is all too late. He must be starved, you know, that is certain, absolutely starved."

He had just settled this point with great composure when the entrance of Mrs John Dashwood put an end to the subject. But though she never spoke of it out of her own family, Elinor could see its influence on her mind in the something like confusion of countenance with which she entered and an attempt at cordiality in her behaviour to herself. She even proceeded so far as to be concerned to find that Elinor and her sister were so soon to leave town, as she had hoped to see more of them—an exertion in which her husband, who attended her into the room and hung enamoured over her accents, seemed to distinguish everything that was most affectionate and graceful.

Chapter Forty-Two

One other short call in Harley Street, in which Elinor received her brother's congratulations on their travelling so far towards Barton without any expense and on Colonel Brandon's being to follow them to Cleveland in a day or two, completed the intercourse of the brother and sisters in town. A faint invitation from Fanny to come to Norland whenever it should happen to be in their way, which of all things was the most unlikely to occur, with a more warm though less public assurance from John to Elinor of the promptitude with which he should come to see her at Delaford, was all that foretold any meeting in the country.

It amused her sorely to observe that all her friends seemed determined to send her to Delaford, a place in which of all others she would now least choose to visit or wish to reside—for not only was it considered as her future home by her brother and Mrs Jennings, but even Lucy when they parted gave her a pressing invitation to visit her there.

Very early in April, and tolerably early in the day, the two parties from Hanover Square and Berkeley Street set out from their respective homes to meet by appointment on the road. For the convenience of Charlotte and her child, they were to be more than two days on their journey, and Mr Palmer, travelling more expeditiously with Colonel Brandon, was to join them at Cleveland soon after their arrival.

Marianne, few as had been her hours of comfort in London and eager as she had long been to quit it, could not when it came to the point bid adieu to the house in which she had for the last time enjoyed those hopes and that confidence in Willoughby which were now extinguished forever without great pain. Nor could she leave the place in which Willoughby remained, busy in new engagements and new schemes in which she could have no share, without shedding many tears.

Elinor's satisfaction at the moment of removal was more positive. She had no such object for her lingering thoughts to fix on. She left no creature behind from whom it would give her a moment's regret to be divided forever. She was pleased to be free herself from the persecution of Lucy's friendship. She was grateful for bringing her sister away unseen by Willoughby since his marriage. And she looked forward with hope to what a few months of tranquillity at Barton might do towards restoring Marianne's peace of mind and confirming her own.

Their journey was safely performed. The second day brought them into the cherished, or the prohibited, county of Somerset—for as such was it dwelt on by turns in Marianne's imagination—and in the forenoon of the third they drove up to Cleveland.

Cleveland was a spacious, modern-built house situated on a sloping lawn. It had no park, but the pleasure grounds were tolerably extensive, and like every other place of the same degree of importance it had its open shrubbery and closer wood walk. A road of smooth gravel winding round a plantation led to the front. The lawn was dotted over with timber. The house itself was under the guardianship of the fir, the mountain ash and the acacia, and a thick screen of them altogether interspersed with tall Lombardy poplars shut out the offices.

Marianne entered the house with a heart swelling with emotion from the consciousness of being only eighty miles from Barton and not thirty from Combe Magna. Before she had been five minutes within its walls, while the others were busily helping Charlotte to show her child to the housekeeper, she quitted it again. Stealing away through the winding shrubberies, now just beginning to be in beauty, to gain a distant eminence where from its Grecian temple her eye, wandering over a wide tract of country to the southeast, could fondly rest on the farthest ridge of hills in the horizon and fancy that from their summits Combe Magna might be seen.

In such moments of precious, invaluable misery, she rejoiced in tears of agony to be at Cleveland, and as she returned by a different circuit to the house, feeling all the happy privilege of country liberty of wandering from place to place in free and luxurious solitude, she resolved to spend almost every hour of every day while she remained with the Palmers in the indulgence of such solitary rambles.

She returned just in time to join the others as they quitted the house on an excursion through its more immediate premises, and the rest of the morning was easily whiled away in lounging round the kitchen garden, examining the bloom upon its walls and listening to the gardener's lamentations upon blights. In dawdling through the greenhouse, where the loss of her favourite plants unwarily exposed and nipped by the lingering frost raised the laughter of Charlotte. And in visiting her poultry yard where—in the disappointed hopes of her dairy-maid, by hens forsaking their nests or being stolen by a fox, or in the rapid decrease of a promising young brood—she found fresh sources of merriment.

The morning was fine and dry, and Marianne in her plan of employment abroad had not calculated for any change of weather during their stay at Cleveland. With great surprise therefore did she find herself prevented by a settled rain from going out again after dinner. She had depended on a twilight walk to the Grecian temple, and perhaps all over the grounds, and an evening merely cold or damp would not have deterred her from it, but a heavy and settled rain even she could not fancy dry or pleasant weather for walking.

Their party was small, and the hours passed quietly away. Mrs Palmer had her child, and Mrs Jennings her carpetwork. They talked of the friends they had left behind, arranged Lady Middleton's engagements and wondered whether Mr Palmer and Colonel Brandon would get farther than Reading that night. Elinor, however little concerned in it, joined in their discourse, and Marianne, who had the knack of finding her way in every house to the library however it might be avoided by the family in general, soon procured herself a book.

Nothing was wanting on Mrs Palmer's side that constant and friendly good humour could do to make them feel themselves welcome. The openness and heartiness of her manner more than atoned for that want of recollection and elegance which made her often deficient in the forms of politeness. Her kindness, recommended by so pretty a face, was engaging. Her folly, though evident, was not disgusting because it was not conceited, and Elinor could have forgiven everything but her laugh.

The two gentlemen arrived the next day to a very late dinner, affording a pleasant enlargement of the party and a very welcome variety to their conversation, which a long morning of the same continued rain had reduced very low.

Elinor had seen so little of Mr Palmer, and in that little had seen so much variety in his address to her sister and herself that she knew not what to expect to find him in his own family. She found him, however, perfectly the gentleman in his behaviour to all his visitors, and only occasionally rude to his wife and her mother. She found him very capable of being a pleasant companion, and only prevented from being so always by too great an aptitude to fancy himself as much superior to people in general as he must feel himself to be to Mrs Jennings and Charlotte.

For the rest of his character and habits, they were marked, as far as Elinor could perceive, with no traits at all unusual in his sex and time of life. He was nice in his eating, uncertain in his hours, fond of his child though affecting to slight it, and idled away the mornings at billiards which ought to have been devoted to business. She liked him, however, upon the whole much better than she had expected, and in her heart was not sorry that she could like him no more — not sorry to be driven by the observation of his Epicurism, his selfishness and his conceit to rest with complacency on the remembrance of Edward's generous temper, simple taste and diffident feelings.

Of Edward, or at least of some of his concerns, she now received intelligence from Colonel Brandon, who had been into Dorsetshire lately and who, treating her at once as the disinterested friend of Mr Ferrars and the kind of confidant of himself, talked to her a great deal of the parsonage at Delaford, described its deficiencies and told her what he meant to do himself towards removing them. His behaviour to her in this as well as in every other particular, his open pleasure in meeting her after an absence of only ten days, his readiness to converse with her and his deference for her opinion, might very well justify Mrs Jennings' persuasion of his attachment. And it would have been enough perhaps had not Elinor still, as from the first, believed Marianne his real favourite to make her suspect it herself.

But as it was, such a notion had scarcely ever entered her head except by Mrs Jennings' suggestion, and she could not help believing herself the nicest observer of the two. She watched his eyes while Mrs Jennings thought only of his behaviour, and while his looks of anxious solicitude on Marianne's feeling in her head and throat the beginning of a heavy cold, because unexpressed by words, entirely escaped the latter lady's observation, she could discover in them the quick feelings and needless alarm of a lover.

Two delightful twilight walks on the third and fourth evenings of her being there, not merely on the dry gravel of the shrubbery but all over the grounds and especially in the most distant parts of them, where there was something more of wildness than in the rest, where the trees were the oldest and the grass was the longest and wettest, had—assisted by the still greater imprudence of sitting in her wet shoes and stockings—given Marianne a cold so violent as, though for a day or two trifled with or denied, would force itself by increasing ailments on the concern of everybody and the notice of herself. Prescriptions poured in from all quarters, and as usual were all declined. Though heavy and feverish, with a pain in her limbs and a cough and a sore throat, a good night's rest was to cure her entirely, and it was with difficulty that Elinor prevailed on her when she went to bed to try one or two of the simplest of the remedies.

Chapter Forty-Three

Marianne got up the next morning at her usual time, to every enquiry replied that she was better, and tried to prove herself so by engaging in her customary employments. But a day spent in sitting shivering over the fire with a book in her hand which she was unable to read, or in lying weary and languid on a sofa, did not speak much in favour of her amendment. When at last she went early to bed, more and more indisposed, Colonel Brandon was only astonished at her sister's composure, who, though attending and nursing her the whole day against Marianne's inclination and forcing proper medicines on her at night, trusted like Marianne to the certainty and efficacy of sleep and felt no real alarm.

A very restless and feverish night, however, disappointed the expectation of both, and when Marianne after persisting in rising confessed herself unable to sit up and returned voluntarily to her bed, Elinor was very ready to adopt Mrs Jennings' advice of sending for the Palmers' apothecary.

He came, examined his patient, and though encouraging Miss Dashwood to expect that a very few days would restore her sister to health, yet by pronouncing her disorder to have a putrid tendency and allowing the word "infection" to pass his lips gave instant alarm to Mrs Palmer on her baby's account. Mrs Jennings, who had been inclined from the first to think Marianne's complaint more serious than Elinor, now looked very grave on Mr Harris' report and confirming Charlotte's fears and caution urged the necessity of her immediate removal with her infant. Mr Palmer, though treating their apprehensions as idle, found the anxiety and importunity of his wife too great to be withstood.

Her departure therefore was fixed on, and within an hour after Mr Harris' arrival she set off with her little boy and his nurse for the house of a near relation of Mr Palmer's who lived a few miles on the other side of Bath. Whither her husband promised at her earnest entreaty to join her in a day or two, and whither she was almost equally urgent with her mother to accompany her.

Mrs Jennings, however, with a kindness of heart which made Elinor really love her, declared her resolution of not stirring from Cleveland as long as Marianne remained ill, and of endeavouring by her own attentive care to supply to her the place of the mother she had taken her from. Elinor found her on every occasion a most willing and active helpmate, desirous to share in all her fatigues, and often by her better experience in nursing of material use.

Poor Marianne, languid and low from the nature of her malady and feeling herself universally ill, could no longer hope that tomorrow would find her recovered, and the idea of what tomorrow would have produced but for this unlucky illness made every ailment severe. For on that day they were to have begun their journey home, and attended the whole way by a servant of Mrs Jennings, were to have taken their mother by surprise on the following forenoon. The little she said was all in lamentation of this inevitable delay, though Elinor tried to raise her spirits and make her believe, as she then really believed herself, that it would be a very short one.

The next day produced little or no alteration in the state of the patient. She certainly was not better, and except that there was no amendment did not appear worse. Their party was now farther reduced, for Mr Palmer, though very unwilling to go as well from real humanity and good nature as from a dislike of appearing to be frightened away by his wife, was persuaded at last by Colonel Brandon to perform his promise of following her. While he was preparing to go, Colonel Brandon himself with a much greater exertion began to talk of going likewise.

Here however the kindness of Mrs Jennings interposed most acceptably, for to send the Colonel away while his love was in so much uneasiness on her sister's account would be to deprive them both, she thought, of every comfort. Therefore telling him at once that his stay at Cleveland was necessary to herself, that she should want him to play at piquet of an evening while Miss Dashwood was above with her sister, &c. she urged him so strongly to remain that he, who was gratifying the first wish of his own heart by a compliance, could not long even affect to demur. Especially as Mrs Jennings' entreaty was warmly seconded by Mr Palmer, who seemed to feel a relief to himself in leaving behind him a person so well able to assist or advise Miss Dashwood in any emergence.

Marianne was of course kept in ignorance of all these arrangements. She knew not that she had been the means of sending the owners of Cleveland away in about seven days from the time of their arrival. It gave her no surprise that she saw nothing of Mrs Palmer, and as it gave her likewise no concern, she never mentioned her name.

Two days passed away from the time of Mr Palmer's departure, and her situation continued with little variation the same. Mr Harris, who attended her every day, still talked boldly of a speedy recovery, and Miss Dashwood was equally sanguine, but the expectation of the others was by no means so cheerful. Mrs Jennings had determined very early in the seizure that Marianne would never get over it, and Colonel Brandon, who was chiefly of use in listening to Mrs Jennings' forebodings, was not in a state of mind to resist their influence. He tried to reason himself out of fears which the different judgement of the apothecary seemed to render absurd, but the many hours of each day in which he was left entirely alone were but too favourable for the admission of every melancholy idea, and he could not expel from his mind the persuasion that he should see Marianne no more.

On the morning of the third day however, the gloomy anticipations of both were almost done away, for when Mr Harris arrived he declared his patient materially better. Her pulse was much stronger and every symptom more favourable than on the preceding visit. Elinor, confirmed in every pleasant hope, was all cheerfulness, rejoicing that in her letters to her mother she had pursued her own judgement rather than her friend's in making very light of the indisposition which delayed them at Cleveland and almost fixing on the time when Marianne would be able to travel.

But the day did not close so auspiciously as it began. Towards the evening Marianne became ill again, growing more heavy, restless and uncomfortable than before. Her sister however, still sanguine, was willing to attribute the change to nothing more than the fatigue of having sat up to have her bed made, and carefully administering the cordials prescribed saw her with satisfaction sink at last into a slumber from which she expected the most beneficial effects. Her sleep, though not so quiet as Elinor wished to see it, lasted a considerable time, and anxious to observe the result of it herself she resolved to sit with her during the whole of it. Mrs Jennings, knowing nothing of any change in the patient, went unusually early to bed. Her maid, who was one of the principal nurses, was recreating herself in the housekeeper's room, and Elinor remained alone with Marianne.

The repose of the latter became more and more disturbed, and her sister, who watched with unremitting attention her continual change of posture and heard the frequent but inarticulate sounds of complaint which passed her lips, was almost wishing to rouse her from so painful a slumber when Marianne, suddenly awakened by some accidental noise in the house, started hastily up and with feverish wildness cried out, "Is Mama coming?"

"Not yet," cried the other, concealing her terror and assisting Marianne to lie down again, "but she will be here, I hope, before it is long. It is a great way, you know, from hence to Barton."

"But she must not go round by London," cried Marianne in the same hurried manner. "I shall never see her if she goes by London."

Elinor perceived with alarm that she was not quite herself, and while attempting to soothe her eagerly felt her pulse. It was lower and quicker than ever! And Marianne still talking wildly of Mama, her alarm increased so rapidly as to determine her on sending instantly for Mr Harris and despatching a messenger to Barton for her mother. To consult with Colonel Brandon on the best means of effecting the latter was a thought which immediately followed the resolution of its performance, and as soon she had rung up the maid to take her place by her sister, she hastened down to the drawing room where she knew he was generally to be found at a much later hour than the present.

It was no time for hesitation. Her fears and her difficulties were immediately before him. Her fears he had no courage, no confidence to attempt the removal of — he listened to them in silent despondence. But her difficulties were instantly obviated, for with a readiness that seemed to speak the occasion and the service pre-arranged in his mind, he offered himself as the messenger who should fetch Mrs Dashwood. Elinor made no resistance that was not easily overcome. She thanked him with brief though fervent gratitude, and while he went to hurry off his servant with a message to Mr Harris and an order for post-horses directly, she wrote a few lines to her mother.

The comfort of such a friend at that moment as Colonel Brandon — or such a companion for her mother — how gratefully was it felt! A companion whose judgement would guide, whose attendance must relieve and whose friendship might soothe her! As far as the shock of such a summons could be lessened to her, his presence, his manners, his assistance would lessen it.

He, meanwhile, whatever he might feel, acted with all the firmness of a collected mind, made every necessary arrangement with the utmost despatch and calculated with exactness the time in which she might look for his return. Not a moment was lost in delay of any kind. The horses arrived even before they were expected, and Colonel Brandon only pressing her hand with a look of solemnity and a few words spoken too low to reach her ear, hurried into the carriage.

It was then about twelve o'clock, and she returned to her sister's apartment to wait for the arrival of the apothecary and to watch by her the rest of the night. It was a night of almost equal suffering to both. Hour after hour passed away in sleepless pain and delirium on Marianne's side, and in the most cruel anxiety on Elinor's, before Mr Harris appeared. Her apprehensions once raised paid by their excess for all her former security, and the servant who sat up with her, for she would not allow Mrs Jennings to be called, only tortured her more by hints of what her mistress had always thought.

Marianne's ideas were still at intervals fixed incoherently on her mother. Whenever she mentioned her name it gave a pang to the heart of poor Elinor, who, reproaching herself for having trifled with so many days of illness and wretched for some immediate relief, fancied that all relief might soon be in vain, that everything had been delayed too long. She pictured to herself her suffering mother arriving too late to see this darling child, or to see her rational.

She was on the point of sending again for Mr Harris, or if he could not come for some other advice, when the former – but not till after five o'clock – arrived. His opinion, however, made some little amends for his delay, for though acknowledging a very unexpected and unpleasant alteration in his patient, he would not allow the danger to be material and talked of the relief which a fresh mode of treatment must procure with a confidence which in a lesser degree was communicated to Elinor. He promised to call again in the course of three or four hours, and left both the patient and her anxious attendant more composed than he had found them.

With strong concern and with many reproaches for not being called to their aid did Mrs Jennings hear in the morning of what had passed. Her former apprehensions, now with greater reason restored, left her no doubt of the event, and though trying to speak comfort to Elinor, her conviction of her sister's danger would not allow her to offer the comfort of hope.

Her heart was really grieved. The rapid decay, the early death of a girl so young, so lovely as Marianne must have struck a less interested person with concern. On Mrs Jennings' compassion she had other claims. She had been for three months her companion, was still under her care, and she was known to have been greatly injured and long unhappy. The distress of her sister too, particularly a favourite, was before her, and as for their mother, when Mrs Jennings considered that Marianne might probably be to her what Charlotte was to herself, her sympathy in her sufferings was very sincere.

Mr Harris was punctual in his second visit, but he came to be disappointed in his hopes of what the last would produce. His medicines had failed, the fever was unabated and Marianne only more quiet—not more herself—remained in a heavy stupor. Elinor, catching all and more than all his fears in a moment, proposed to call in further advice. But he judged it unnecessary—he had still something more to try, some more fresh application of whose success he was as confident as the last, and his visit concluded with encouraging assurances which reached the ear but could not enter the heart of Miss Dashwood.

She was calm, except when she thought of her mother, but she was almost hopeless. In this state she continued till noon, scarcely stirring from her sister's bed, her thoughts wandering from one image of grief, one suffering friend to another, and her spirits oppressed to the utmost by the conversation of Mrs Jennings, who scrupled not to attribute the severity and danger of this attack to the many weeks of previous indisposition which Marianne's disappointment had brought on. Elinor felt all the reasonableness of the idea, and it gave fresh misery to her reflections.

About noon, however, she began—but with a caution—a dread of disappointment which for some time kept her silent even to her friend—to fancy, to hope she could perceive a slight amendment in her sister's pulse. She waited, watched and examined it again and again, and at last with an agitation more difficult to bury under exterior calmness than all her foregoing distress, ventured to communicate her hopes.

Mrs Jennings, though forced on examination to acknowledge a temporary revival, tried to keep her young friend from indulging a thought of its continuance, and Elinor, conning over every injunction of distrust, told herself likewise not to hope. But it was too late. Hope had already entered, and feeling all its anxious flutter, she bent over her sister to watch—she hardly knew for what.

Half an hour passed away, and the favourable symptom yet blessed her. Others even arose to confirm it. Her breath, her skin, her lips all flattered Elinor with signs of amendment, and Marianne fixed her eyes on her with a rational, though languid, gaze. Anxiety and hope now oppressed her in equal degrees and left her no moment of tranquillity till the arrival of Mr Harris at four o'clock, when his assurances, his felicitations on a recovery in her sister even surpassing his expectation, gave her confidence, comfort and tears of joy.

Marianne was in every respect materially better, and he declared her entirely out of danger. Mrs Jennings, perhaps satisfied with the partial justification of her forebodings which had been found in their late alarm, allowed herself to trust in his judgement, and admitted with unfeigned joy and soon with unequivocal cheerfulness the probability of an entire recovery.

Elinor could not be cheerful. Her joy was of a different kind, and led to anything rather than to gaiety. Marianne restored to life, health, friends and to her doting mother was an idea to fill her heart with sensations of exquisite comfort and expand it in fervent gratitude, but it led to no outward demonstrations of joy, no words, no smiles. All within Elinor's breast was satisfaction, silent and strong.

She continued by the side of her sister with little intermission the whole afternoon, calming every fear, satisfying every enquiry of her enfeebled spirits, supplying every succour and watching almost every look and every breath. The possibility of a relapse would of course in some moments occur to remind her of what anxiety was — but when she saw on her frequent and minute examination that every symptom of recovery continued, and saw Marianne at six o'clock sink into a quiet, steady and to all appearance comfortable sleep, she silenced every doubt.

The time was now drawing on when Colonel Brandon might be expected back. At ten o'clock, she trusted, or at least not much later her mother would be relieved from the dreadful suspense in which she must now be travelling towards them. The Colonel too, perhaps scarcely less an object of pity! Oh, how slow was the progress of time which yet kept them in ignorance!

At seven o'clock, leaving Marianne still sweetly asleep, she joined Mrs Jennings in the drawing room to tea. Of breakfast she had been kept by her fears, and of dinner by their sudden reverse, from eating much, and the present refreshment therefore with such feelings of content as she brought to it was particularly welcome. Mrs Jennings would have persuaded her at its conclusion to take some rest before her mother's arrival and allow her to take her place by Marianne, but Elinor had no sense of fatigue, no capability of sleep at that moment about her, and she was not to be kept away from her sister an unnecessary instant. Mrs Jennings therefore attending her upstairs into the sick chamber to satisfy herself that all continued right, left her there again to her charge and her thoughts, and retired to her own room to write letters and sleep.

The night was cold and stormy. The wind roared round the house and the rain beat against the windows, but Elinor, all happiness within, regarded it not. Marianne slept through every blast, and the travellers—they had a rich reward in store for every present inconvenience.

The clock struck eight. Had it been ten, Elinor would have been convinced that at that moment she heard a carriage driving up to the house. So strong was the persuasion that she did, in spite of the almost impossibility of their being already come, that she moved into the adjoining dressing-closet and opened a window shutter to be satisfied of the truth. She instantly saw that her ears had not deceived her. The flaring lamps of a carriage were immediately in view. By their uncertain light she thought she could discern it to be drawn by four horses, and this, while it told the excess of her poor mother's alarm, gave some explanation to such unexpected rapidity.

Never in her life had Elinor found it so difficult to be calm as at that moment. The knowledge of what her mother must be feeling as the carriage stopped at the door—of her doubt—her dread—perhaps her despair! And of what she had to tell! With such knowledge it was impossible to be calm. All that remained to be done was to be speedy, and therefore staying only till she could leave Mrs Jennings' maid with her sister, she hurried downstairs.

The bustle in the vestibule as she passed along an inner lobby assured her that they were already in the house. She rushed to the drawing room, she entered it, and saw only Willoughby.

Chapter Forty-Four

Elinor, starting back with a look of horror at the sight of him, obeyed the first impulse of her heart in turning instantly to quit the room. Her hand was already on the lock when its action was suspended by his hastily advancing and saying in a voice rather of command than supplication, "Miss Dashwood, for half an hour — for ten minutes — I entreat you to stay."

"No, sir," she replied with firmness, "I shall not stay. Your business cannot be with *me*. The servants, I suppose, forgot to tell you that Mr Palmer was not in the house."

"Had they told me," he cried with vehemence, "that Mr Palmer and all his relations were at the devil, it would not have turned me from the door. My business is with you and only you."

"With me!" In the utmost amazement. "Well, sir, be quick — and if you can — less violent."

"Sit down, and I will be both."

She hesitated. She knew not what to do. The possibility of Colonel Brandon's arriving and finding her there came across her. But she had promised to hear him, and her curiosity no less than her honour was engaged. After a moment's recollection therefore, concluding that prudence required dispatch and that her acquiescence would best promote it, she walked silently towards the table and sat down. He took the opposite chair, and for half a minute not a word was said by either.

"Pray be quick, sir," said Elinor impatiently. "I have no time to spare."

He was sitting in an attitude of deep meditation, and seemed not to hear her.

"Your sister," said he with abruptness a moment afterwards, "is out of danger. I heard it from the servant. God be praised! But is it true? Is it really true?"

Elinor would not speak. He repeated the enquiry with yet greater eagerness.

"For God's sake tell me, is she out of danger or is she not?"

"We hope she is."

He rose up and walked across the room.

"Had I known as much half an hour ago — But since I *am* here" — speaking with a forced vivacity as he returned to his seat—"what does it signify? For once, Miss Dashwood — it will be the last time, perhaps — let us be cheerful together. I am in a fine mood for gaiety. Tell me honestly" — a deeper glow overspreading his cheeks — "do you think me most a knave or a fool?"

Elinor looked at him with greater astonishment than ever. She began to think that he must be in liquor. The strangeness of such a visit and of such manners seemed no otherwise intelligible. And with this impression she immediately rose, saying, "Mr Willoughby, I advise you at present to return to

Combe—I am not at leisure to remain with you longer. Whatever your business may be with me, will it be better recollected and explained tomorrow."

"I understand you," he replied with an expressive smile and a voice perfectly calm. "Yes, I am very drunk. A pint of porter with my cold beef at Marlborough was enough to over-set me."

"At Marlborough!" cried Elinor, more and more at a loss to understand what he would be at.

"Yes, I left London this morning at eight o'clock, and the only ten minutes I have spent out of my chaise since that time procured me a nuncheon at Marlborough."

The steadiness of his manner and the intelligence of his eye as he spoke convincing Elinor that whatever other unpardonable folly might bring him to Cleveland, he was not brought there by intoxication, she said after a moment's recollection, "Mr Willoughby, you *ought* to feel, and I certainly do, that after what has passed your coming here in this manner and forcing yourself upon my notice requires a very particular excuse. What is it that you mean by it?"

"I mean," said he with serious energy, "if I can, to make you hate me one degree less than you do now. I mean to offer some kind of explanation, some kind of apology for the past, to open my whole heart to you, and by convincing you that though I have been always a blockhead I have not been always a rascal, to obtain something like forgiveness from Ma—from your sister."

"Is this the real reason of your coming?"

"Upon my soul it is," was his answer, with a warmth which brought all the former Willoughby to her remembrance, and in spite of herself made her think him sincere.

"If that is all, you may be satisfied already, for Marianne does — she has long forgiven you."

"Has she?" he cried in the same eager tone. "Then she has forgiven me before she ought to have done it. But she shall forgive me again, and on more reasonable grounds. Now will you listen to me?"

Elinor bowed her assent.

"I do not know," said he after a pause of expectation on her side and thoughtfulness on his own, "how you may have accounted for my behaviour to your sister, or what diabolical motive you may have imputed to me. Perhaps you will hardly think the better of me. It is worth the trial however, and you shall hear everything.

"When I first became intimate in your family, I had no other intention, no other view in the acquaintance than to pass my time pleasantly while I was obliged to remain in Devonshire more pleasantly than I had ever done before. Your sister's lovely person and interesting manners could not but please me, and her behaviour to me almost from the first was of a kind — It is astonishing, when I reflect on what it was and what *she* was, that my heart should have been so insensible!

"But at first I must confess, my vanity only was elevated by it. Careless of her happiness, thinking only of my own amusement, giving way to feelings which I had always been too much in the habit of indulging, I endeavoured by every means in my power to make myself pleasing to her without any design of returning her affection."

Miss Dashwood at this point, turning her eyes on him with the most angry contempt, stopped him by saying, "It is hardly worthwhile, Mr Willoughby, for you to relate or for me to listen any longer. Such a beginning as this cannot be followed by anything. Do not let me be pained by hearing anything more on the subject."

"I insist on you hearing the whole of it," he replied. "My fortune was never large, and I had always been expensive, always in the habit of associating with people of better income than myself. Every year since my coming of age, or even before, I believe, had added to my debts. And though the death of my old cousin, Mrs Smith, was to set me free, yet that event being uncertain and possibly far distant, it had been for some time my intention to re-establish my circumstances by marrying a woman of fortune. To attach myself to your sister, therefore, was not a thing to be thought of, and with a meanness, selfishness, cruelty — which no indignant, no contemptuous look even of yours, Miss Dashwood, can ever reprobate too much — I was acting in this manner, trying to engage her regard without a thought of returning it.

"But one thing may be said for me. Even in that horrid state of selfish vanity, I did not know the extent of the injury I meditated, because I did not then know what it was to love. But have I ever known it? Well may it be doubted, for had I really loved, could I have sacrificed my feelings to vanity, to avarice? Or what is more, could I have sacrificed hers? But I have done it. To avoid a comparative poverty which her affection and her society would have deprived of all its horrors, I have by raising myself to affluence lost everything that could make it a blessing."

"You did then," said Elinor, a little softened, "believe yourself at one time attached to her?"

"To have resisted such attractions, to have withstood such tenderness! Is there a man on earth who could have done it? Yes, I found myself by insensible degrees sincerely fond of her, and the happiest hours of my life were what I spent with her when I felt my intentions were strictly honourable and my feelings blameless. Even then, however, when fully determined on paying my addresses to her, I allowed myself most improperly to put off from day to day the moment of doing it, from an unwillingness to enter into an engagement while my circumstances were so greatly embarrassed.

"I will not reason here—nor will I stop for you to expatiate on the absurdity and the worse than absurdity of scrupling to engage my faith where my honour was already bound. The event has proved that I was a cunning fool, providing with great circumspection for a possible opportunity of making myself contemptible and wretched forever. At last, however, my resolution was taken, and I had determined as soon as I could engage her alone to justify the attentions I had so invariably paid her and openly assure her of an affection which I had already taken such pains to display. But in the interim—in the interim of the very few hours that were to pass before I could have an opportunity of speaking with her in private—a circumstance occurred—an unlucky circumstance, to ruin all my resolution, and with it all my comfort.

"A discovery took place..." Here he hesitated and looked down. "Mrs Smith had somehow or other been informed, I imagine by some distant relation whose interest it was to deprive me of her favour, of an affair, a connection—but I need not explain myself farther," he added, looking at her with an heightened colour and an enquiring eye. "Your particular intimacy—you have probably heard the whole storey long ago."

"I have," returned Elinor, colouring likewise and hardening her heart anew against any compassion for him. "I have heard it all. And how you will explain away any part of your guilt in that dreadful business I confess is beyond my comprehension."

"Remember," cried Willoughby, "from whom you received the account. Could it be an impartial one? I acknowledge that her situation and her character ought to have been respected by me. I do not mean to justify myself, but at the same time cannot leave you to suppose that I have nothing to urge—that because she was injured she was irreproachable, and because I was a libertine, she must be a saint. If the violence of her passions, the weakness of her understanding—I do not mean, however, to defend myself. Her affection for me deserved better treatment, and I often with great self-reproach recall the tenderness which for a very short time had the power of creating any return. I wish—I heartily wish it had never been. But I have injured more than herself, and I have injured one whose affection for me—may I say it?—was scarcely less warm than hers, and whose mind—Oh! How infinitely superior!"

"Your indifference, however, towards that unfortunate girl—I must say it, unpleasant to me as the discussion of such a subject may well be—your indifference is no apology for your cruel neglect of her. Do not think yourself excused by any weakness, any natural defect of understanding on her side, in the wanton cruelty so evident on yours. You must have known that while you were enjoying yourself in Devonshire pursuing fresh schemes, always gay, always happy, she was reduced to the extremest indigence."

"But upon my soul, I did *not* know it," he warmly replied. "I did not recollect that I had omitted to give her my direction, and common sense might have told her how to find it out."

"Well, sir, and what said Mrs Smith?"

"She taxed me with the offence at once, and my confusion may be guessed. The purity of her life, the formality of her notions, her ignorance of the world — everything was against me. The matter itself I could not deny, and vain was every endeavour to soften it. She was previously disposed, I believe, to doubt the morality of my conduct in general, and was moreover discontented with the very little attention, the very little portion of my time that I had bestowed on her in my present visit. In short, it ended in a total breach.

"By one measure I might have saved myself. In the height of her morality, good woman, she offered to forgive the past if I would marry Eliza. That could not be — and I was formally dismissed from her favour and her house.

"The night following this affair — I was to go the next morning — was spent by me in deliberating on what my future conduct should be. The struggle was great — but it ended too soon. My affection for Marianne, my thorough conviction of her attachment to me — it was all insufficient to outweigh that dread of poverty, or get the better of those false ideas of the necessity of riches, which I was naturally inclined to feel and expensive society had increased. I had reason to believe myself secure of my present wife, if I chose to address her, and I persuaded myself to think that nothing else in common prudence remained for me to do.

"A heavy scene however awaited me before I could leave Devonshire. I was engaged to dine with you on that very day. Some apology was therefore necessary for my breaking this engagement. But whether I should write this apology or deliver it in person was a point of long debate. To see Marianne I felt would be dreadful, and I even doubted whether I could see her again and keep to my resolution. In that point, however, I undervalued my own magnanimity, as the event declared. For I went, I saw her, and saw her miserable, and left her miserable—and left her hoping never to see her again."

"Why did you call, Mr Willoughby?" said Elinor reproachfully. "A note would have answered every purpose. Why was it necessary to call?"

"It was necessary to my own pride. I could not bear to leave the country in a manner that might lead you or the rest of the neighbourhood to suspect any part of what had really passed between Mrs Smith and myself—and I resolved therefore on calling at the cottage in my way to Honiton. The sight of your dear sister, however, was really dreadful, and to heighten the matter, I found her alone.

"You were all gone I do not know where. I had left her only the evening before, so fully, so firmly resolved within myself on doing right! A few hours were to have engaged her to me forever, and I remember how happy, how gay were my spirits as I walked from the cottage to Allenham, satisfied with myself, delighted with everybody!

"But in this our last interview of friendship, I approached her with a sense of guilt that almost took from me the power of dissembling. Her sorrow, her disappointment, her deep regret when I told her that I was obliged to leave Devonshire so immediately—I never shall forget it—united too with such reliance, such confidence in me! Oh, God! What a hard-hearted rascal I was!"

They were both silent for a few moments. Elinor first spoke. "Did you tell her that you should soon return?"

"I do not know what I told her," he replied impatiently. "Less than was due to the past beyond a doubt, and in all likelihood much more than was justified by the future. I cannot think of it. It won't do. Then came your dear mother to torture me farther, with all her kindness and confidence. Thank Heaven! It did torture me. I was miserable. Miss Dashwood, you cannot have an idea of the comfort it gives me to look back on my own misery. I owe such a grudge to myself for the stupid, rascally folly of my own heart that all my past sufferings under it are only triumph and exultation to me now.

"Well, I went, left all that I loved, and went to those to whom at best I was only indifferent. My journey to town—travelling with my own horses, and therefore so tediously—no creature to speak to—my own reflections so cheerful—when I looked forward everything so inviting! When I looked back at Barton, the picture so soothing! Oh, it was a blessed journey!"

He stopped.

"Well, sir," said Elinor, who though pitying him grew impatient for his departure, "and this is all?"

"Ah! No, have you forgot what passed in town? That infamous letter—Did she show it you?"

"Yes, I saw every note that passed."

"When the first of hers reached me—as it immediately did, for I was in town the whole time—what I felt is, in the common phrase, not to be expressed in a more simple one—perhaps too simple to raise any emotion—my feelings were very, very painful. Every line, every word was—in the hackneyed metaphor which their dear writer, were she here, would forbid—a dagger to my heart. To know that Marianne was in town was—in the same language—a thunderbolt. Thunderbolts and daggers! What a reproof would she have given me! Her taste, her opinions—I believe they are better known to me than my own, and I am sure they are dearer."

Elinor's heart, which had undergone many changes in the course of this extraordinary conversation, was now softened again, yet she felt it her duty to check such ideas in her companion as the last.

"This is not right, Mr Willoughby. Remember that you are married. Relate only what in your conscience you think necessary for me to hear."

"Marianne's note, by assuring me that I was still as dear to her as in former days, that in spite of the many, many weeks we had been separated she was as constant in her own feelings and as full of faith in the constancy of mine as ever, awakened all my remorse. I say awakened because time and London, business and dissipation had in some measure quieted it, and I had been growing a fine hardened villain, fancying myself indifferent to her and choosing to fancy that she too must have become indifferent to me. Talking to myself of our past attachment as a mere idle, trifling business. Shrugging up my shoulders in proof of its being so. Silencing every reproach, overcoming every scruple by secretly saying now and then, 'I shall be heartily glad to hear she is well married.'

"But this note made me know myself better. I felt that she was infinitely dearer to me than any other woman in the world, and that I was using her infamously. But everything was then just settled between Miss Grey and me. To retreat was impossible.

All that I had to do was to avoid you both. I sent no answer to Marianne, intending by that to preserve myself from her farther notice, and for some time I was even determined not to call in Berkeley Street. But at last, judging it wiser to affect the air of a cool, common acquaintance than anything else, I watched you all safely out of the house one morning and left my name."

"Watched us out of the house!"

"Even so. You would be surprised to hear how often I watched you, how often I was on the point of falling in with you on the street or the park. I have entered many a shop to avoid your sight as the carriage drove by. Lodging as I did in Bond Street, there was hardly a day in which I did not catch a glimpse of one or other of you, the sunlight on Marianne's face, the breeze ruffling her hair, and nothing but the most constant watchfulness on my side, a most invariably prevailing desire to keep out of your sight, could have separated us so long.

"I avoided the Middletons as much as possible, as well as everybody else who was likely to prove an acquaintance in common. Not aware of their being in town, however, I blundered on Sir John I believe the first day of his coming, and the day after I had called at Mrs Jennings'. He asked me to a party, a dance at his house in the evening. Had he not told me as an inducement that you and your sister were to be there, I should have felt it too certain a thing to trust myself near him.

"The next morning brought another short note from Marianne—still affectionate, open, artless, confiding—everything that could make my conduct most hateful. I could not answer it. I tried—but could not frame a sentence. But I thought of her, I believe, every moment of the day. If you can pity me, Miss Dashwood, pity my situation as it was then. With my head and heart full of your sister, I was forced to play the happy lover to another woman! Those three or four weeks were worse than all.

"Well, at last, as I need not tell you, you were forced on me, and what a sweet figure I cut! What an evening of agony it was! Marianne, beautiful as an angel on one side, calling me Willoughby in such a tone! Oh, God! Holding out her hand to me, asking me for an explanation, with those bewitching eyes fixed in such speaking solicitude on my face! and Sophia, jealous as the devil on the other hand, looking all that was — Well, it does not signify, it is over now. Such an evening!

"I ran away from you all as soon as I could, but not before I had seen Marianne's sweet face as white as death. That was the last, last look I ever had of her, the last manner in which she appeared to me. It was a horrid sight! Yet when I thought of her today as really dying, it was a kind of comfort to me to imagine that I knew exactly how she would appear to those who saw her last in this world. She was before me, constantly before me as I travelled in the same look and hue."

A short pause of mutual thoughtfulness succeeded. Willoughby first rousing himself broke it thus. "Well, let me make haste and be gone. Your sister is certainly better, certainly out of danger?"

"We are assured of it."

"Your poor mother, too! Doting on Marianne."

"But the letter, Mr Willoughby, your own letter, have you anything to say about that?"

"Yes, yes, that in particular. Your sister wrote to me again, you know, the very next morning. You saw what she said. I was breakfasting at the Ellisons, and her letter with some others was brought to me there from my lodgings. It happened to catch Sophia's eye before it caught mine—and its size, the elegance of the paper, the handwriting altogether immediately gave her a suspicion. Some vague report had reached her before of my attachment to some young lady in Devonshire, and what had passed within her observation the preceding evening had marked who the young lady was, and made her more jealous than ever. Affecting that air of playfulness therefore which is delightful in a woman one loves, she opened the letter directly and read its contents.

"She was well paid for her impudence. She read what made her wretched. Her wretchedness I could have borne, but her passion—her malice—At all events it must be appeased. And in short—what do you think of my wife's style of letter-writing? Delicate—tender—truly feminine—was it not?"

"Your wife! The letter was in your own handwriting."

"Yes, but I had only the credit of servilely copying such sentences as I was ashamed to put my name to. The original was all her own—her own happy thoughts and gentle diction. But what could I do! We were engaged, everything in preparation, the day almost fixed—But I am talking like a fool. Preparation! Day! In honest words, her money was necessary to me, and in a situation like mine anything was to be done to prevent a rupture. And after all, what did it signify to my character in the opinion of Marianne and her friends in what language my answer was couched? It must have been only to one end. My business was to declare myself a scoundrel, and whether I did it with a bow or a bluster was of little importance.

"'I am ruined forever in their opinion,' said I to myself. 'I am shut out forever from their society. They already think me an unprincipled fellow, this letter will only make them think me a blackguard one.' Such were my reasonings as in a sort of desperate carelessness I copied my wife's words and parted with the last relics of Marianne. Her three notes—unluckily they were all in my pocketbook, or I should have denied their existence and hoarded them forever—I was forced to put them up, and could not even kiss them. And the lock of hair—that too I had always carried about me in the same pocketbook which was now searched by Madam with the most ingratiating virulence, the dear lock—all, every memento was torn from me."

"You are very wrong, Mr Willoughby, very blameable," said Elinor, while her voice in spite of herself betrayed her compassionate emotion. "You ought not to speak in this way either of Mrs Willoughby or my sister. You had made your own choice. It was not forced on you. Your wife has a claim to your politeness, to your respect, at least. She must be attached to you or she would not have married you. To treat her with unkindness, to speak of her slightingly is no atonement to Marianne—nor can I suppose it a relief to your own conscience."

"Do not talk to me of my wife," said he with a heavy sigh. "She does not deserve your compassion. She knew I had no regard for her when we married. Well, married we were, and came down to Combe Magna to be happy, and afterwards returned to town to be gay. And now do you pity me, Miss Dashwood? Or have I said all this to no purpose? Am I—be it only one degree—am I less guilty in your opinion than I was before? My intentions were not always wrong. Have I explained away any part of my guilt?"

"Yes, you have certainly removed something — a little. You have proved yourself on the whole less faulty than I had believed you. You have proved your heart less wicked, much less wicked. But I hardly know — the misery that you have inflicted — I hardly know what could have made it worse."

"Will you repeat to your sister when she is recovered, what I have been telling you? Let me be a little lightened too in her opinion as well as in yours. You tell me that she has forgiven me already. Let me be able to fancy that a better knowledge of my heart and of my present feelings will draw from her a more spontaneous, more natural, more gentle, less dignified forgiveness. Tell her of my misery and my penitence — tell her that my heart was never inconstant to her, and if you will, that at this moment she is dearer to me than ever."

"I will tell her all that is necessary to what may comparatively be called your justification. But you have not explained to me the particular reason of your coming now, nor how you heard of her illness."

"Last night in Drury Lane lobby I ran against Sir John Middleton, and when he saw who I was — for the first time these two months — he spoke to me. That he had cut me ever since my marriage I had seen without surprise or resentment. Now, however, his good-natured, honest, stupid soul, full of indignation against me and concern for your sister, could not resist the temptation of telling me what he knew ought to — though probably he did not think it *would* — vex me horridly.

"As bluntly as he could speak it therefore, he told me that Marianne Dashwood was dying of a putrid fever at Cleveland. A letter that morning received from Mrs Jennings declared her danger most imminent—the Palmers are all gone off in a fright, etc. I was too much shocked to be able to pass myself off as insensible even to the undiscerning Sir John. His heart was softened in seeing mine suffer, and so much of his ill-will was done away that when we parted he almost shook me by the hand while he reminded me of an old promise about a pointer puppy.

"What I felt on hearing that your sister was dying— and dying too believing me the greatest villain upon earth, scorning, hating me in her latest moments—for how could I tell what horrid projects might not have been imputed? One person I was sure would represent me as capable of anything—What I felt was dreadful! My resolution was soon made, and at eight o'clock this morning I was in my carriage. Now you know all."

Elinor made no answer. Her thoughts were silently fixed on the irreparable injury which too early an independence and its consequent habits of idleness, dissipation and luxury had made in the mind, the character, the happiness of a man who to every advantage of person and talents united a disposition naturally open and honest and a feeling, affectionate temper.

The world had made him extravagant and vain. Extravagance and vanity had made him cold-hearted and selfish. Vanity, while seeking its own guilty triumph at the expense of another, had involved him in a real attachment which extravagance, or at least its offspring necessity, had required to be sacrificed. Each faulty propensity in leading him to evil had led him likewise to punishment. The attachment from which against honour, against feeling, against every better interest he had outwardly torn himself, now when no longer allowable governed every thought. And the connection for the sake of which he had with little scruple left her sister to misery was likely to prove a source of unhappiness to himself of a far more incurable nature.

From a reverie of this kind she was recalled at the end of some minutes by Willoughby, who, rousing himself from a reverie at least equally painful, started up in preparation for going and said, "There is no use in staying here. I must be off."

"Are you going back to town?"

"No—to Combe Magna. I have business there, from thence to town in a day or two. Goodbye."

He held out his hand. She could not refuse to give him hers. He pressed it with affection.

"And you do think something better of me than you did?" said he, letting it fall and leaning against the mantelpiece as if forgetting he was to go.

Elinor assured him that she did, that she forgave, pitied, wished him well—was even interested in his happiness—and added some gentle counsel as to the behaviour most likely to promote it. His answer was not very encouraging.

"As to that," said he, "I must rub through the world as well as I can. Domestic happiness is out of the question. If, however, I am allowed to think that you and yours feel an interest in my fate and actions, it may be the means—it may put me on my guard—at least it may be something to live for. Marianne to be sure is lost to me forever. Were I even by any blessed chance at liberty again—"

Elinor stopped him with a reproof.

"Well," he replied, "once more goodbye. I shall now go away and live in dread of one event."

"What do you mean?"

"Your sister's marriage."

"You are very wrong. She can never be more lost to you than she is now."

"But she will be gained by someone else. And if that someone should be the very he whom of all others I could least bear—but I will not stay to rob myself of all your compassionate goodwill by showing that where I have most injured I can least forgive. Goodbye, God bless you!"

And with these words, he almost ran out of the room.

Chapter Forty-Five

Elinor, for some time after he left her, for some time even after the sound of his carriage had died away, remained too much oppressed by a crowd of ideas, widely differing in themselves but of which sadness was the general result, to think even of her sister.

Willoughby, he whom only half an hour ago she had abhorred as the most worthless of men, Willoughby in spite of all his faults excited a degree of commiseration for the sufferings produced by them which made her think of him as now separated forever from her family with a tenderness, a regret rather in proportion — as she soon acknowledged within herself — to his wishes than to his merits. She felt that his influence over her mind was heightened by circumstances which ought not in reason to have weight, by that person of uncommon attraction, by that open, affectionate and lively manner which it was no merit to possess and by that still ardent love for Marianne which it was not even innocent to indulge. But she felt that it was so, long, long before she could feel his influence less.

When at last she returned to the unconscious Marianne she found her just awaking, refreshed by so long and sweet a sleep to the extent of her hopes. Elinor's heart was full. The past, the present, the future, Willoughby's visit, Marianne's safety and her mother's expected arrival threw her altogether into an agitation of spirits which kept off every indication of fatigue and made her only fearful of betraying herself to her sister. Short was the time however in which that fear could affect her, for within half an hour after Willoughby's leaving the house she was again called downstairs by the sound of another carriage. Eager to save her mother from every unnecessary moment's horrible suspense, she ran immediately into the hall and reached the outward door just in time to receive and support her as she entered it.

Mrs Dashwood, whose terror as they drew near the house had produced almost the conviction of Marianne's being no more, had no voice to enquire after her, no voice even for Elinor. But she, waiting neither for salutation nor enquiry, instantly gave the joyful relief, and her mother, catching it with all her usual warmth, was in a moment as much overcome by her happiness as she had been before by her fears. She was supported into the drawing room between her daughter and her friend and there, shedding tears of joy though still unable to speak, embraced Elinor again and again, turning from her at intervals to press Colonel Brandon's hand with a look which spoke at once her gratitude and her conviction of his sharing with herself in the bliss of the moment. He shared it, however, in a silence even greater than her own.

As soon as Mrs Dashwood had recovered herself, to see Marianne was her first desire, and in two minutes she was with her beloved child, rendered dearer to her than ever by absence, unhappiness and danger. Elinor's delight as she saw what each felt in the meeting was only checked by an apprehension of its robbing Marianne of farther sleep, but Mrs Dashwood could be calm, could be even prudent, when the life of a child was at stake. And Marianne, satisfied in knowing her mother was near her and conscious of being too weak for conversation, submitted readily to the silence and quiet prescribed by every nurse around her.

Mrs Dashwood *would* sit up with her all night, and Elinor, in compliance with her mother's entreaty, went to bed. But the rest which one night entirely sleepless and many hours of the most wearing anxiety seemed to make requisite was kept off by irritation of spirits. Willoughby, 'poor Willoughby', as she now allowed herself to call him, was constantly in her thoughts. She would not but have heard his vindication for the world, and now blamed, now acquitted herself for having judged him so harshly before. But her promise of relating it to her sister was invariably painful.

She dreaded the performance of it. Dreaded what its effect on Marianne might be. Doubted whether after such an explanation she could ever be happy with another. And for a moment wished Willoughby a widower. Then remembering Colonel Brandon, reproved herself, felt that to *his* sufferings and his constancy far more than to his rival's the reward of her sister was due, and wished anything rather than Mrs Willoughby's death.

The shock of Colonel Brandon's errand at Barton had been much softened to Mrs Dashwood by her own previous alarm. For so great was her uneasiness about Marianne that she had already determined to set out for Cleveland on that very day without waiting for any further intelligence, and had so far settled her journey before his arrival that the Careys were then expected every moment to fetch Margaret away, as her mother was unwilling to take her where there might be infection.

Marianne continued to mend every day, and the brilliant cheerfulness of Mrs Dashwood's looks and spirits proved her to be, as she repeatedly declared herself, one of the happiest women in the world. Elinor could not hear the declaration nor witness its proofs without sometimes wondering whether her mother ever recollected Edward. But Mrs Dashwood, trusting to the temperate account of her own disappointment which Elinor had sent her, was led away by the exuberance of her joy to think only of what would increase it. Marianne was restored to her from a danger in which, as she now began to feel, her own mistaken judgement in encouraging the unfortunate attachment to Willoughby had contributed to place her, and in her recovery she had yet another source of joy unthought of by Elinor. It was thus imparted to her as soon as any opportunity of private conference between them occurred.

"At last we are alone. My Elinor, you do not yet know all my happiness. Colonel Brandon loves Marianne. He has told me so himself."

Her daughter, feeling by turns both pleased and pained, surprised and not surprised, was all silent attention.

"You are never like me, dear Elinor, or I should wonder at your composure now. Had I sat down to wish for any possible good to my family, I should have fixed on Colonel Brandon's marrying one of you as the object most desirable. And I believe Marianne will be the most happy with him of the two."

Elinor was half inclined to ask her reason for thinking so, because satisfied that none founded on an impartial consideration of their age, characters or feelings could be given, but her mother must always be carried away by her imagination on any interesting subject, and therefore instead of an enquiry she passed it off with a smile.

"He opened his whole heart to me yesterday as we travelled. It came out quite unawares, quite undesignedly. I, you may well believe, could talk of nothing but my child. He could not conceal his distress. I saw that it equalled my own, and he perhaps thinking that mere friendship, as the world now goes, would not justify so warm a sympathy—or rather not thinking at all, I suppose—giving way to irresistible feelings, made me acquainted with his earnest, tender, constant affection for Marianne. He has loved her, my Elinor, ever since the first moment of seeing her."

Here however Elinor perceived not the language, not the professions of Colonel Brandon, but the natural embellishments of her mother's active fancy, which fashioned everything delightful to her as it chose.

"His regard for her, infinitely surpassing anything that Willoughby ever felt or feigned, as much more warm, as more sincere or constant—whichever we are to call it—has subsisted through all the knowledge of dear Marianne's unhappy prepossession for that worthless young man! And without selfishness—without encouraging a hope! Could he have seen her happy with another—Such a noble mind! Such openness, such sincerity! No one can be deceived in *him*."

"Colonel Brandon's character," said Elinor, "as an excellent man is well established."

"I know it is," replied her mother seriously, "or after such a warning I should be the last to encourage such affection, or even to be pleased by it. But his coming for me as he did, with such active, such ready friendship, is enough to prove him one of the worthiest of men."

"His character, however," answered Elinor, "does not rest on *one* act of kindness to which his affection for Marianne, were humanity out of the case, would have prompted him. To Mrs Jennings, to the Middletons, he has been long and intimately known. They equally love and respect him, and even my own knowledge of him, though lately acquired, is very considerable. And so highly do I value and esteem him that if Marianne can be happy with him, I shall be as ready as yourself to think our connection the greatest blessing to us in the world. What answer did you give him? Did you allow him to hope?"

"Oh! My love, I could not then talk of hope to him or to myself. Marianne might at that moment be dying. But he did not ask for hope or encouragement. His was an involuntary confidence, an irrepressible effusion to a soothing friend — not an application to a parent. Yet after a time I *did* say, for at first I was quite overcome, that if she lived, as I trusted she might, my greatest happiness would lie in promoting their marriage. And since our arrival, since our delightful security, I have repeated it to him more fully, have given him every encouragement in my power. Time, a very little time, I tell him, will do everything. Marianne's heart is not to be wasted forever on such a man as Willoughby. His own merits must soon secure it."

"To judge from the Colonel's spirits, however, you have not yet made him equally sanguine."

"No. He thinks Marianne's affection too deeply rooted for any change in it under a great length of time, and even supposing her heart again free, is too diffident of himself to believe that with such a difference of age and disposition he could ever attach her. There however he is quite mistaken. His age is only so much beyond hers as to be an advantage, as to make his character and principles fixed, and his disposition I am well convinced is exactly the very one to make your sister happy. And his person, his manners too are all in his favour. My partiality does not blind me, he certainly is not so handsome as Willoughby—but at the same time, there is something much more pleasing in his countenance. There was always a something, if you remember, in Willoughby's eyes at times which I did not like."

Elinor could not remember it, but her mother without waiting for her assent continued. "And his manners, the Colonel's manners are not only more pleasing to me than Willoughby's ever were, but they are of a kind I well know to be more solidly attaching to Marianne. Their gentleness, their genuine attention to other people and their manly unstudied simplicity is much more accordant with her real disposition than the liveliness—often artificial and often ill-timed—of the other. I am very sure myself that had Willoughby turned out as really amiable as he has proved himself the contrary, Marianne would yet never have been so happy with *him* as she will be with Colonel Brandon."

She paused. Her daughter could not quite agree with her, but her dissent was not heard and therefore gave no offence.

"At Delaford she will be within an easy distance of me," added Mrs Dashwood, "even if I remain at Barton. And in all probability, for I hear it is a large village, indeed there certainly *must* be some small house or cottage close by that would suit us quite as well as our present situation."

Poor Elinor! Here was a new scheme for getting her to Delaford! But her spirit was stubborn.

"His fortune too! For at my time of life you know, everybody cares about *that*, and though I neither know nor desire to know what it really is, I am sure it must be a good one."

Here they were interrupted by the entrance of a third person, and Elinor withdrew to think it all over in private, to wish success to her friend, and yet in wishing it to feel a pang for Willoughby.

Chapter Forty-Six

Marianne's illness, though weakening in its kind, had not been long enough to make her recovery slow. With youth, natural strength and her mother's presence in aid, it proceeded so smoothly as to enable her to remove within four days after the arrival of the latter into Mrs Palmer's dressing room. When there, at her own particular request—for she was impatient to pour forth her thanks to him for fetching her mother—Colonel Brandon was invited to visit her.

His emotion on entering the room, in seeing her altered looks and in receiving the pale hand which she immediately held out to him, was such as in Elinor's conjecture must arise from something more than his affection for Marianne or the consciousness of its being known to others. She soon discovered in his melancholy eye and varying complexion as he looked at her sister the probable recurrence of many past scenes of misery to his mind, brought back by that resemblance between Marianne and Eliza already acknowledged and now strengthened by the hollow eye, the sickly skin, the posture of reclining weakness and the warm acknowledgement of peculiar obligation.

Mrs Dashwood, not less watchful of what passed than her daughter but with a mind very differently influenced and therefore watching to very different effect, saw nothing in the Colonel's behaviour but what arose from the most simple and self-evident sensations. While in the actions and words of Marianne she persuaded herself to think that something more than gratitude already dawned. Were her daughter's affections for Colonel Brandon blossoming amid their conversations of books and music? Or was Marianne realising that a man might be appealing in quiet, unassuming ways? That a caller need not regale a young lady to show her the joy of living seemed to be the message of Colonel Brandon's pursuit of her daughter, if indeed one could call his calm presence so forceful an act as pursuit.

At the end of another day or two, Marianne growing visibly stronger every twelve hours, Mrs Dashwood, urged equally by her own and her daughter's wishes, began to talk of removing to Barton. On her measures depended those of her two friends. Mrs Jennings could not quit Cleveland during the Dashwoods' stay, and Colonel Brandon was soon brought by their united request to consider his own abode there as equally determinate, if not equally indispensable. At his and Mrs Jennings' united request in return, Mrs Dashwood was prevailed on to accept the use of his carriage on her journey back for the better accommodation of her sick child, and the Colonel at the joint invitation of Mrs Dashwood and Mrs Jennings, whose active good nature made her friendly and hospitable for other people as well as herself, engaged with pleasure to redeem it by a visit at the cottage in the course of a few weeks.

The day of separation and departure arrived, and Marianne — after taking so particular and lengthened a leave of Mrs Jennings, one so earnestly grateful, so full of respect and kind wishes as seemed due to her own heart from a secret acknowledgement of past inattention, and bidding Colonel Brandon farewell with a cordiality of a friend — was carefully assisted by him into the carriage, of which he seemed anxious that she should engross at least half. Indeed, he fussed over her like a dotty nursemaid, securing a blanket for her lap and a warm brick for her feet. Satisfied at long last that Marianne would find some comfort in the travel, he shut the door and spoke to his driver with such specific directions that the rest of the travelling party grew weary of the road before they set upon it. Mrs Dashwood and Elinor then followed, and the others were left by themselves to talk of the travellers and feel their own dullness till Mrs Jennings was summoned to her chaise to take comfort in the gossip of her maid for the loss of her two young companions, and Colonel Brandon immediately afterwards took his solitary way to Delaford.

The Dashwoods were two days on the road, and Marianne bore her journey on both without essential fatigue. Everything that the most zealous affection, the most solicitous care could do to render her comfortable was the office of each watchful companion, and each found their reward in her bodily ease and her calmness of spirits. To Elinor the observation of the latter was particularly grateful. She who had seen her week after week so constantly suffering, oppressed by anguish of heart which she had neither courage to speak of nor fortitude to conceal, now saw with a joy which no other could equally share an apparent composure of mind which, in being the result as she trusted of serious reflection, must eventually lead her to contentment and cheerfulness.

As they approached Barton indeed, and entered on scenes of which every field and every tree brought some peculiar, some painful recollection, she grew silent and thoughtful, and turning away her face from their notice sat earnestly gazing through the window. But here Elinor could neither wonder nor blame, and when she saw as she assisted Marianne from the carriage that she had been crying, she saw only an emotion too natural in itself to raise anything less tender than pity and in its unobtrusiveness entitled to praise.

In the whole of her subsequent manner she traced the direction of a mind awakened to reasonable exertion. For no sooner had they entered their common sitting room than Marianne turned her eyes around it with a look of resolute firmness, as if determined at once to accustom herself to the sight of every object with which the remembrance of Willoughby could be connected. She said little, but every sentence aimed at cheerfulness, and though a sigh sometimes escaped her, it never passed away without the atonement of a smile.

After dinner she would try her pianoforte. She went to it, but the music on which her eye first rested was an opera procured for her by Willoughby, containing some of their favourite duets and bearing on its outward leaf her own name in his handwriting. That would not do. She shook her head, put the music aside and after running over the keys for a minute complained of feebleness in her fingers and closed the instrument again, declaring however with firmness as she did so that she should in future practice much.

The next morning produced no abatement in these happy symptoms. On the contrary, with a mind and body alike strengthened by rest she looked and spoke with more genuine spirit, anticipating the pleasure of Margaret's return and talking of the dear family party which would then be restored, of their mutual pursuits and cheerful society as the only happiness worth a wish.

"When the weather is settled and I have recovered my strength," said she, "we will take long walks together every day. We will walk to the farm at the edge of the down and see how the children go on. We will walk to Sir John's new plantations at Barton Cross, and the Abbeyland, and we will often go the old ruins of the Priory and try to trace its foundations as far as we are told they once reached. I know we shall be happy. I know the summer will pass happily away. I mean never to be later in rising than six, and from that time till dinner I shall divide every moment between music and reading.

"I have formed my plan, and am determined to enter on a course of serious study. Our own library is too well known to me to be resorted to for anything beyond mere amusement. But there are many works well worth reading at the Park, and there are others of more modern production which I know I can borrow of Colonel Brandon. He encouraged me to and I shall avail myself of the pleasure. By reading only six hours a day, I shall gain in the course of a twelvemonth a great deal of instruction which I now feel myself to want."

Elinor honoured her for a plan which originated so nobly as this, though smiling to see the same eager fancy which had been leading her to the extreme of languid indolence and selfish repining now at work in introducing excess into a scheme of such rational employment and virtuous self-control. Her smile however changed to a sigh when she remembered that promise to Willoughby was yet unfulfilled, and feared she had that to communicate which might again unsettle the mind of Marianne and ruin at least for a time this fair prospect of busy tranquillity. Willing therefore to delay the evil hour, she resolved to wait till her sister's health were more secure before she appointed it. But the resolution was made only to be broken.

Marianne had been two or three days at home before the weather was fine enough for an invalid like herself to venture out. But at last a soft, genial morning appeared such as might tempt the daughter's wishes and the mother's confidence, and Marianne, leaning on Elinor's arm, was authorised to walk as long as she could without fatigue in the lane before the house.

The sisters set out at a pace slow as the feebleness of Marianne in an exercise hitherto untried since her illness required. They had advanced only so far beyond the house as to admit a full view of the hill, the important hill behind, when pausing with her eyes turned towards it Marianne calmly said, "There, exactly there" — pointing with one hand — "on that projecting mound, there I fell and there I first saw Willoughby."

Her voice sank with the word, but presently reviving she added, "I am thankful to find that I can look with so little pain on the spot! Shall we ever talk on that subject, Elinor?" Hesitatingly it was said. "Or will it be wrong? I can talk of it now, I hope, as I ought to do."

Elinor tenderly invited her to be open.

"As for regret," said Marianne, "I have done with that as far as he is concerned. I do not mean to talk to you of what my feelings have been for him, but what they are now. At present if I could be satisfied on one point, if I could be allowed to think that he was not always acting a part, not always deceiving me, but above all if I could be assured that he never was so very wicked as my fears have sometimes fancied him since the storey of that unfortunate girl — "

She stopped. Elinor joyfully treasured her words as she answered, "If you could be assured of that, you think you should be easy."

"Yes. My peace of mind is doubly involved in it, for not only is it horrible to suspect a person who has been what he has been to me of such designs, but what must it make me appear to myself? What in a situation like mine but a most shamefully unguarded affection could expose me to?"

"How then," asked her sister, "would you account for his behaviour?"

"I would suppose him — oh, how gladly would I suppose him — only fickle, very, very fickle."

Elinor said no more. She was debating within herself on the eligibility of beginning her storey directly or postponing it till Marianne were in stronger health, and they crept on for a few minutes in silence.

"I am not wishing him too much good," said Marianne at last with a sigh, "when I wish his secret reflections may be no more unpleasant than my own. He will suffer enough in them."

"Do you compare your conduct with his?"

"No. I compare it with what it ought to have been. I compare it with yours."

"Our situations have borne little resemblance."

"They have borne more than our conduct. Do not, my dearest Elinor, let your kindness defend what I know your judgement must censure. My illness has made me think—It has given me leisure and calmness for serious recollection. Long before I was enough recovered to talk, I was perfectly able to reflect. I considered the past—I saw in my own behaviour since the beginning of our acquaintance with him last autumn nothing but a series of imprudence towards myself and want of kindness to others. I saw that my own feelings had prepared my sufferings, that my own scandalous actions with him had created a madness in me that encouraged excess, and that my want of fortitude under them had almost led me to the grave.

"My illness I well knew had been entirely brought on by myself by such negligence of my own health as I had felt even at the time to be wrong. Had I died, it would have been self-destruction. I did not know my danger till the danger was removed, but with such feelings as these reflections gave me, I wonder at my recovery, wonder that the very eagerness of my desire to live, to have time for atonement to my God and to you all did not kill me at once. Had I died, in what peculiar misery should I have left you, my nurse, my friend, my sister! You who had seen all the fretful selfishness of my latter days, who had known all the murmurings of my heart! How should I have lived in your remembrance! My mother too! How could you have consoled her!

"I cannot express my own abhorrence of myself. Whenever I looked towards the past, I saw some duty neglected or some failing indulged. Everybody seemed injured by me. The kindness, the unceasing kindness of Mrs Jennings I had repaid with ungrateful contempt. To the Middletons, to the Palmers, the Steeles, to every common acquaintance even I had been insolent and unjust, with a heart hardened against their merits and a temper irritated by their very attention. To John, to Fanny, yes, even to them, little as they deserve, I had given less than their due.

"But you, you above all, above my mother, had been wronged by me. I and only I knew your heart and its sorrows, yet to what did it influence me? Not to any compassion that could benefit you or myself. Your example was before me, but to what avail? Was I more considerate of you and your comfort? Did I imitate your forbearance or lessen your restraints by taking any part in those offices of general complaisance or particular gratitude which you had hitherto been left to discharge alone? No, not less when I knew you to be unhappy than when I had believed you at ease did I turn away from every exertion of duty or friendship, scarcely allowing sorrow to exist but with me, regretting only *that* heart which had deserted and wronged me, and leaving you for whom I professed an unbounded affection to be miserable for my sake."

Here ceased the rapid flow of her self-reproving spirit, and Elinor, impatient to soothe though too honest to flatter, gave her instantly that praise and support which her frankness and her contrition so well deserved. Marianne pressed her hand and replied, "You are very good. The future must be my proof. I have laid down my plan, and if I am capable of adhering to it—my feelings shall be governed and my temper improved. They shall no longer worry others nor torture myself.

"I shall now live solely for my family. You, my mother and Margaret must henceforth be all the world to me. You will share my affections entirely between you. From you, from my home, I shall never again have the smallest incitement to move, and if I do mix in other society it will be only to show that my spirit is humbled, my heart amended and that I can practice the civilities, the lesser duties of life with gentleness and forbearance. As for Willoughby—to say that I shall soon or that I shall ever forget him would be idle. His remembrance can be overcome by no change of circumstances or opinions. But it shall be regulated, it shall be checked by religion, by reason, by constant employment."

She paused—and added in a low voice, "If I could but know his heart, everything would become easy."

Elinor, who had now been for some time reflecting on the propriety or impropriety of speedily hazarding her narration without feeling at all nearer decision than at first, heard this, and perceiving that as reflection did nothing resolution must do all, soon found herself leading to the fact.

She managed the recital, as she hoped, with address, prepared her anxious listener with caution, related simply and honestly the chief points on which Willoughby grounded his apology, did justice to his repentance and softened only his protestations of present regard. Marianne said not a word. She trembled, her eyes were fixed on the ground and her lips became whiter than even sickness had left them. A thousand enquiries sprang up from her heart, but she dared not urge one. She caught every syllable with panting eagerness. Her hand, unknowingly to herself, closely pressed her sister's, and tears covered her cheeks.

Elinor, dreading her being tired, led her towards home. Till they reached the door of the cottage, easily conjecturing what her curiosity must be though no question was suffered to speak it, she talked of nothing but Willoughby and their conversation together, and was carefully minute in every particular of speech and look where minuteness could be safely indulged.

As soon as they entered the house, Marianne with a kiss of gratitude and these two words just articulate through her tears, "Tell Mama," withdrew from her sister and walked slowly upstairs. Elinor would not attempt to disturb a solitude so reasonable as what she now sought, and with a mind anxiously prearranging its result and a resolution of reviving the subject again should Marianne fail to do it, she turned into the parlour to fulfil her parting injunction.

Chapter Forty-Seven

Mrs Dashwood did not hear unmoved the vindication of her former favourite. She rejoiced in his being cleared from some part of his imputed guilt, she was sorry for him, she wished him happy. But the feelings of the past could not be recalled. Nothing could restore him with a faith unbroken — a character unblemished — to Marianne. Nothing could do away the knowledge of what the latter had suffered through his means, nor remove the guilt of his conduct towards Eliza. Nothing could replace him therefore in her former esteem, nor injure the interests of Colonel Brandon.

Had Mrs Dashwood like her daughter heard Willoughby's storey from himself — had she witnessed his distress and been under the influence of his countenance and his manner — it is probable that her compassion would have been greater. But it was neither in Elinor's power nor in her wish to rouse such feelings in another by her retailed explanation as had at first been called forth in herself. Reflection had given calmness to her judgement and sobered her own opinion of Willoughby's deserts. She wished therefore to declare only the simple truth and lay open such facts as were really due to his character, without any embellishment of tenderness to lead the fancy astray.

In the evening when they were all three together Marianne began voluntarily to speak of him again, but that it was not without an effort, the restless, unquiet thoughtfulness in which she had been for some time previously sitting, her rising colour as she spoke and her unsteady voice plainly showed.

"I wish to assure you both," said she, "that I see everything—as you can desire me to do."

Mrs Dashwood would have interrupted her instantly with soothing tenderness had not Elinor, who really wished to hear her sister's unbiased opinion, by an eager sign engaged her silence. Marianne slowly continued, "It is a great relief to me—what Elinor told me this morning—I have now heard exactly what I wished to hear." For some moments her voice was lost, but recovering herself she added and with greater calmness than before, "I am now perfectly satisfied, I wish for no change. I never could have been happy with him after knowing, as sooner or later I must have known, all this. I should have had no confidence, no esteem. Nothing could have done it away to my feelings."

"I know it—I know it," cried her mother. "Happy with a man of libertine practices! With one who so injured the peace of the dearest of our friends and the best of men! No—my Marianne has not a heart to be made happy with such a man! Her conscience, her sensitive conscience, would have felt all that the conscience of her husband ought to have felt."

Marianne sighed and repeated, "I wish for no change."

"You consider the matter," said Elinor, "exactly as a good mind and a sound understanding must consider it. I dare say you perceive as well as myself, not only in this but in many other circumstances, reason enough to be convinced that your marriage must have involved you in many certain troubles and disappointments in which you would have been poorly supported by an affection on his side much less certain.

"Had you married, you must have been always poor. His expensiveness is acknowledged even by himself, and his whole conduct declares that self-denial is a word hardly understood by him. His demands and your inexperience together on a small, very small income must have brought on distresses which would not be the less grievous to you from having been entirely unknown and unthought of before.

"Your sense of honour and honesty would have led you, I know, when aware of your situation, to attempt all the economy that would appear to you possible. And perhaps as long as your frugality retrenched only on your own comfort, you might have been suffered to practice it, but beyond that—and how little could the utmost of your single management do to stop the ruin which had begun before your marriage? Beyond that had you endeavoured, however reasonably, to abridge his enjoyments, is it not to be feared that instead of prevailing on feelings so selfish to consent to it, you would have lessened your own influence on his heart and made him regret the connection which had involved him in such difficulties?"

Marianne's lips quivered and she repeated the word "Selfish?" in a tone that implied, *Do you really think him selfish?*

"The whole of his behaviour," replied Elinor, "from the beginning to the end of the affair has been grounded on selfishness. It was selfishness which first made him sport with your affections, which afterwards when his own were engaged made him delay the confession of it, and which finally carried him from Barton. His own enjoyment, or his own ease, was in every particular his ruling principle."

"It is very true. My happiness never was his object."

"At present," continued Elinor, "he regrets what he has done. And why does he regret it? Because he finds it has not answered towards himself. It has not made him happy. His circumstances are now unembarrassed—he suffers from no evil of that kind, and he thinks only that he has married a woman of a less amiable temper than yourself. But does it follow that had he married you, he would have been happy? The inconveniences would have been different. He would then have suffered under the pecuniary distresses which, because they are removed, he now reckons as nothing. He would have had a wife of whose temper he could make no complaint, but he would have been always necessitous—always poor. And probably would soon have learned to rank the innumerable comforts of a clear estate and good income as of far more importance, even to domestic happiness, than the mere temper of a wife."

"I have not a doubt of it," said Marianne, "and I have nothing to regret—nothing but my own folly."

"Rather say your mother's imprudence, my child," said Mrs Dashwood. "*She* must be answerable."

Marianne would not let her proceed, and Elinor, satisfied that each felt their own error, wished to avoid any survey of the past that might weaken her sister's spirits. She therefore pursuing the first subject immediately continued, "One observation may, I think, be fairly drawn from the whole of the storey — that all Willoughby's difficulties have arisen from the first offence against virtue in his behaviour to Eliza Williams. That crime has been the origin of every lesser one and of all his present discontents."

Marianne assented most feelingly to the remark, and her mother was led by it to an enumeration of Colonel Brandon's injuries and merits, warm as friendship and design could unitedly dictate. Her daughter did not look, however, as if much of it were heard by her.

Elinor, according to her expectation, saw on the two or three following days that Marianne did not continue to gain strength as she had done, but while her resolution was unsubdued and she still tried to appear cheerful and easy, her sister could safely trust to the effect of time upon her health.

Margaret returned and the family were again all restored to each other, again quietly settled at the cottage, and if not pursuing their usual studies with quite so much vigour as when they first came to Barton, at least planning a vigorous prosecution of them in future.

Elinor grew impatient for some tidings of Edward. She had heard nothing of him since her leaving London, nothing new of his plans, nothing certain even of his present abode. Some letters had passed between her and her brother in consequence of Marianne's illness, and in the first of John's there had been this sentence. *We know nothing of our unfortunate Edward, and can make no enquiries on so prohibited a subject, but conclude him to be still at Oxford.* Which was all the intelligence of Edward afforded her by the correspondence, for his name was not even mentioned in any of the succeeding letters. She was not doomed, however, to be long in ignorance of his measures.

Their man-servant had been sent one morning to Exeter on business, and when as he waited at table he had satisfied the enquiries of his mistress as to the event of his errand, this was his voluntary communication.

"I suppose you know, ma'am, that Mr Ferrars is married."

Marianne gave a violent start, fixed her eyes upon Elinor, saw her turning pale and fell back in her chair in hysterics. Mrs Dashwood, whose eyes as she answered the servant's enquiry had intuitively taken the same direction, was shocked to perceive by Elinor's countenance how much she really suffered, and a moment afterwards, alike distressed by Marianne's situation, knew not on which child to bestow her principal attention.

The servant, who saw only that Miss Marianne was taken ill, had sense enough to call one of the maids, who with Mrs Dashwood's assistance supported her into the other room. By that time Marianne was rather better, and her mother leaving her to the care of Margaret and the maid returned to Elinor, who though still much disordered had so far recovered the use of her reason and voice as to be just beginning an enquiry of Thomas as to the source of his intelligence. Mrs Dashwood immediately took all that trouble on herself, and Elinor had the benefit of the information without the exertion of seeking it.

"Who told you that Mr Ferrars was married, Thomas?"

"I see Mr Ferrars myself, ma'am, this morning in Exeter, and his lady too, Miss Steele as was. They was stopping in a chaise at the door of the New London Inn as I went there with a message from Sally at the Park to her brother, who is one of the post-boys. I happened to look up as I went by the chaise, and so I see directly it was the youngest Miss Steele. So I took off my hat, and she knew me and called to me and enquired after you, ma'am, and the young ladies, especially Miss Marianne, and bid me I should give her compliments and Mr Ferrars', their best compliments and service, and how sorry they was they had not time to come on and see you, but they was in a great hurry to go forwards, for they was going further down for a little while, but however when they come back they'd make sure to come and see you."

"But did she tell you she was married, Thomas?"

"Yes, ma'am. She smiled and said how she had changed her name since she was in these parts. She was always a very affable and free-spoken young lady, and very civil behaved. So, I made free to wish her joy."

"Was Mr Ferrars in the carriage with her?"

"Yes, ma'am, I just see him leaning back in it, but he did not look up, he never was a gentleman much for talking."

Elinor's heart could easily account for his not putting himself forward, and Mrs Dashwood probably found the same explanation.

"Was there no one else in the carriage?"

"No, ma'am, only they two."

"Do you know where they came from?"

"They come straight from town, as Miss Lucy—Mrs Ferrars told me."

"And are they going farther westward?"

"Yes, ma'am—but not to bide long. They will soon be back again, and they'd be sure and call here."

Mrs Dashwood now looked at her daughter, but Elinor knew better than to expect them. She recognised the whole of Lucy in the message, and was very confident that Edward would never come near them. She observed in a low voice to her mother that they were probably going down to Mr Pratt's near Plymouth.

Thomas' intelligence seemed over. Elinor looked as if she wished to hear more.

"Did you see them off before you came away?"

"No, ma'am—the horses were just coming out, but I could not bide any longer, I was afraid of being late."

"Did Mrs Ferrars look well?"

"Yes, ma'am, she said how she was very well, and to my mind she was always a very handsome young lady—and she seemed vastly contented."

Mrs Dashwood could think of no other question, and Thomas and the tablecloth, now alike needless, were soon afterwards dismissed. Marianne had already sent to say that she should eat nothing more. Mrs Dashwood's and Elinor's appetites were equally lost, and Margaret might think herself very well off that with so much uneasiness as both her sisters had lately experienced, so much reason as they had often had to be careless of their meals, she had never been obliged to go without her dinner before.

When the dessert and the wine were arranged and Mrs Dashwood and Elinor were left by themselves, they remained long together in a similarity of thoughtfulness and silence. Mrs Dashwood feared to hazard any remark and ventured not to offer consolation. She now found that she had erred in relying on Elinor's representation of herself, and justly concluded that everything had been expressly softened at the time to spare her from an increase of unhappiness, suffering as she then had suffered for Marianne. She found that she had been misled by the careful, the considerate attention of her daughter to think the attachment which once she had so well understood much slighter in reality than she had been wont to believe or than it was now proved to be. She feared that under this persuasion she had been unjust, inattentive, nay, almost unkind to her Elinor. That Marianne's affliction because more acknowledged, more immediately before her, had too much engrossed her tenderness and led her away to forget that in Elinor she might have a daughter suffering almost as much, certainly with less self-provocation and greater fortitude.

Chapter Forty-Eight

Elinor now found the difference between the expectation of an unpleasant event, however certain the mind may be told to consider it, and certainty itself. She now found that in spite of herself she had always admitted a hope while Edward remained single that something would occur to prevent his marrying Lucy, that some resolution of his own, some mediation of friends or some more eligible opportunity of establishment for the lady would arise to assist the happiness of all. But he was now married, and she condemned her heart for the lurking flattery which so much heightened the pain of the intelligence.

That he should be married soon, before—as she imagined—he could be in orders, and consequently before he could be in possession of the living, surprised her a little at first. But she soon saw how likely it was that Lucy, in her self-provident care, in her haste to secure him, should overlook everything but the risk of delay. They were married, married in town, and now hastening down to her uncle's. What had Edward felt on being within four miles from Barton, on seeing her mother's servant, on hearing Lucy's message! Had he thought of her? Had he remembered his amorous seductions of her? Her enjoyment of his advances? If he did, would he compare them to his wife's? And in that comparison, which woman was wanting?

The very idea of being a foil for Lucy agitated Elinor. The uncommon emotion was so virulent, so vile, she hated to admit its existence. Yet she could not rid herself of its overpowering might. She pictured Lucy in the same amorous situations with Edward as she herself had been and she blushed. She burned, excited as she had been in his embrace. She fumed, angry with herself for regretting what she had given freely and without promise of wedded bliss or even enduring romantic rapture.

She chided herself for wasting time, indulging in memories that gave her no joy and in self-recriminations that gave her no shelter. Her despair doubled, too, when she found herself at all hours of day or night speculating how the newly married couple of got on in bed and out.

They would soon, she supposed, be settled at Delaford. Delaford, that place in which so much conspired to give her an interest, which she wished to be acquainted with and yet desired to avoid. She saw them in an instant in their parsonage house, saw in Lucy the active, contriving manager, uniting at once a desire of smart appearance with the utmost frugality, and ashamed to be suspected of half her economical practices, pursuing her own interest in every thought, courting the favour of Colonel Brandon, of Mrs Jennings and of every wealthy friend. In Edward—she knew not what she saw, nor what she wished to see.

Happy or unhappy, nothing pleased her. She turned away her head from every sketch of him.

Elinor flattered herself that someone of their connections in London would write to them to announce the event and give farther particulars, but day after day passed off and brought no letter, no tidings. Were they purposely hiding facts from her? Did all conspire to deprive her of those titbits that would feed her outrage and her anguish? Or were they merely protecting her feelings? Though uncertain that anyone were to blame, she found fault with every absent friend. They were all thoughtless or indolent.

"When do you write to Colonel Brandon, ma'am?" was an enquiry which sprang from the impatience of her mind to have something going on.

"I wrote to him, my love, last week, and rather expect to see than to hear from him again. I earnestly pressed his coming to us, and should not be surprised to see him walk in today or tomorrow, or any day."

This was gaining something, something to look forward to. Colonel Brandon must have some information to give.

Scarcely had she so determined it when the figure of a man on horseback drew her eyes to the window. He stopped at their gate. It was a gentleman—it was Colonel Brandon himself. Now she could hear more, and she trembled in expectation of it. She drew nearer, the cut of the figure on the horse causing her to question her original conclusion. But it was *not* Colonel Brandon—neither his air, nor his height. Were it possible, she must say it must be Edward.

She looked again. She blinked. Her heart pounded and as in days of old, her entire body thrilled at the notion that Edward might draw nigh. She swallowed and gazed anew at the figure. He had just dismounted, she could not be mistaken, it *was* Edward.

She moved away and sat down. *He comes from Mr Pratt's purposely to see us. I will be calm, I will be mistress of myself.*

In a moment she perceived that the others were likewise aware of the mistake. She saw her mother and Marianne change colour, saw them look at herself and whisper a few sentences to each other. She would have given the world to be able to speak and to make them understand that she hoped no coolness, no slight, would appear in their behaviour to him, but she had no utterance and was obliged to leave all to their own discretion.

Not a syllable passed aloud. They all waited in silence for the appearance of their visitor. His footsteps were heard along the gravel path. In a moment he was in the passage, and in another he was before them.

His countenance as he entered the room was not too happy even for Elinor. His complexion was white with agitation, his hair dishevelled as if he had raked it repeatedly while riding, his eyes darted from her mother to her sisters and quickly back to linger on her, and he looked as if fearful of his reception and conscious that he merited no kind one. Mrs Dashwood however, conforming as she trusted to the wishes of that daughter by whom she then meant in the warmth of her heart to be guided in everything, met with a look of forced complacency, gave him her hand and wished him joy.

He coloured and stammered out an unintelligible reply. Elinor's lips had moved with her mother's, and when the moment of action was over, she wished that she had shaken hands with him too. But it was then too late, and with a countenance meaning to be open, she sat down again and talked of the weather.

Marianne had retreated as much as possible out of sight to conceal her distress and her wish to condemn him and show him to the door. Margaret, understanding some part but not the whole of the case, thought it incumbent on her to be dignified, and therefore took a seat as far from him as she could and maintained a strict silence.

When Elinor had ceased to rejoice in the dryness of the season, a very awful pause took place. It was put an end to by Mrs Dashwood, who felt obliged to hope that he had left Mrs Ferrars very well. In a hurried manner, he replied in the affirmative.

Another pause.

Elinor resolving to exert herself, though fearing the sound of her own voice, now said, "Is Mrs Ferrars at Longstaple?"

"At Longstaple!" he replied with an air of surprise. "No, my mother is in town."

"I meant," said Elinor, taking up some work from the table, "to enquire for Mrs *Edward* Ferrars."

She dared not look up, but her mother and Marianne both turned their eyes on him. He coloured, seemed perplexed, looked doubtingly and after some hesitation said, "Perhaps you mean my brother—you mean Mrs—Mrs *Robert* Ferrars."

"Mrs Robert Ferrars!" was repeated by Marianne and her mother in an accent of the utmost amazement, and though Elinor could not speak, even *her* eyes were fixed on him with the same impatient wonder.

He rose from his seat and walked to the window, apparently from not knowing what to do, took up a pair of scissors that lay there and while spoiling both them and their sheath by cutting the latter to pieces as he spoke, said in a hurried voice, "Perhaps you do not know—you may not have heard that my brother is lately married to—to the youngest—to Miss Lucy Steele."

His words were echoed with unspeakable astonishment by all but Elinor, who sat with her head leaning over her work, in a state of such agitation as made her hardly know where she was.

"Yes," said he, "they were married last week, and are now at Dawlish."

Elinor could sit it no longer. She almost ran out of the room, and as soon as the door was closed, burst into tears of joy which at first she thought would never cease.

Edward, who had till then looked anywhere rather than at her, saw her hurry away and perhaps saw—or even heard—her emotion. For immediately afterwards he fell into a reverie which no remarks, no enquiries, no affectionate address of Mrs Dashwood could penetrate. At last, without saying a word, he quitted the room and walked out towards the village—leaving the others in the greatest astonishment and perplexity on a change in his situation so wonderful and so sudden, a perplexity which they had no means of lessening but by their own conjectures.

Elinor, through the veil of her tears, saw him leave the house. Love washed through her body. Understanding dawned that he could not yet find words to proclaim himself. Desire flashed like lightning in her heart, her swelling breasts, her pulsing cunny and she dashed to the front door and down the path.

"Edward! Edward!" She raced towards him.

He whirled around to face her, his expression lax in agony. "Elinor, I came to tell you. But you knew of their marriage?"

"Yes. No." She explained how the mistake had occurred.

"I see." His laughing eyes twinkled. "May I conclude you approve of that match?"

She giggled. "Yes and no. Oh, Edward!" She drew near to him and he opened his arms to her so that she rushed into his embrace. "You did not marry her!"

"How could I? I did not wish to." His voice broke with agony as he clasped her to his warm chest and spread a thousand torrid kisses over her cheeks. "She was not my heart's desire. My boon companion. My very soul. Not as you are."

He had been saved from marrying another by others' actions, all of which she would value because they allowed her to have him. She reached up on her toes, and wrapping her arms around his neck, she gave him kisses that declared her joyous need of him.

He picked her up and carried her to a large rock partially obscured among the trees where he set her down, went to his knees and pushed up her skirts.

Allowing him this meant she risked ruin. Again. But this time, she had greater hopes that ruin would bring infinite rewards.

His eyes twinkled. "Will you let me love you again?"

"You know that you alone make me forget the proprieties."

"All of them," he crooned to her as he threw her a rakish leer. Then he bent and trailed kisses up her thighs. In tantalising licks, he moistened her flesh and parted her. Admiring her, he ran a fingertip along the edges of her cunny lips, tickling her and making her laugh in appreciation and anticipation. Pushing her legs wider, he exclaimed his delight in how lovely she was there and proved his admiration with loud succulent strokes of his talented tongue.

Digging her nails into his frock coat, Elinor rose up to heaven with the touch of his lips to her cunny. This was the very essence of bliss so long denied her. She gushed with wet need and writhed. "Come sink inside me."

"A finger?" he asked, the devil in his gaze as he looked at her.

"Or a larger appendage, please."

Chuckling, he nodded, then went about more of his ardent business. He was avid, persistent, spreading her wider to deliver sweet, brief benedictions to her labia. "You are so pink, so wet, so swollen for me. My God, my dearest, how could I ever have been so foolish as to want another?"

"Do not chastise yourself," she managed as he found a special portion of her flesh and pinched, then bit her. She cried out in delight.

He obliged her with a repetition of this deliciously ribald act. "You are so responsive, so wild for me in an instant."

"Yes, yes. If that affirms how I must have you, Edward, do that again and I shall cry out once more."

He obliged her in a second, making her mewl in thanks. He was such an assertive lover, so quick to make her happy, and she him.

"I wanted you for myself for so long," he said, the sound of his voice almost one of mourning. He pulled down her skirts, stared at her through sorrowful eyes and stood. "Forgive me, dearest, I am undone by your responsiveness and this"—he gestured to how he had caressed her with hands and tongue and teeth—"this must not continue until I make you my own for all to acknowledge."

At that, he yanked at his waistcoat, shot his cuffs, then turned on his heel and left her to watch his fine figure march off down the path.

She prayed he found the right words to approach her, for he had awakened in her an astonishingly ravenous appetite for more of what only he solicited inside her. Brushing down her skirts, she stood, smiled to herself and made her way home in the brightest of dispositions.

Chapter Forty-Nine

Unaccountable however as the circumstances of his release might appear to the whole family, it was certain that Edward was free, and to what purpose that freedom would be employed was easily pre-determined by all. For after experiencing the blessings of *one* imprudent engagement contracted without his mother's consent, as he had already done for more than four years, nothing less could be expected of him in the failure of *that* than the immediate contraction of another.

His errand at Barton, in fact, was a simple one. It was only to ask Elinor to marry him, and considering that he was not altogether inexperienced in such a question, it might be strange that he should feel so uncomfortable in the present case as he really did—so much in need of encouragement and fresh air.

How soon he had walked himself into the proper resolution, however, how soon an opportunity of exercising it occurred, in what manner he expressed himself and how he was received need not be particularly told. This only need be said, that when they all sat down to table at four o'clock, about three hours after his arrival, he had secured his lady, engaged her mother's consent and was not only in the rapturous profession of the lover but in the reality of reason and truth, one of the happiest of men.

His situation indeed was more than commonly joyful. He had more than the ordinary triumph of accepted love to swell his heart and raise his spirits. He was released without any reproach to himself from an entanglement which had long formed his misery, from a woman whom he had long ceased to love, and elevated at once to that security with another which he must have thought of almost with despair as soon as he had learnt to consider it with desire. He was brought not from doubt or suspense, but from misery to happiness, and the change was openly spoken in such a genuine, flowing, grateful cheerfulness as his friends had never witnessed in him before.

His heart was now open to Elinor, all its weaknesses, all its errors confessed, and his first boyish attachment to Lucy treated with all the philosophic dignity of twenty-four.

"I wish to explain myself in regards to my engagement to Lucy," he said to Elinor when her mother and sisters left them alone in the parlour.

Elinor thrust up a hand. "Please, Edward there is no need."

"I proclaim there *is* a need. It is vital to our future happiness. My love for you is a desire, based on the enduring qualities of our mutual attraction."

Elinor gazed at him—dear man!—tears pooling in her eyes.

"It was a foolish, idle inclination on my side," said he, "the consequence of ignorance of the world—and want of employment. Had my brother given me some active profession when I was removed at eighteen from the care of Mr Pratt, I think—nay, I am sure it would never have happened. For though I left Longstaple with what I thought at the time a most unconquerable preference for his niece, yet had I then had any pursuit, any object to engage my time and keep me at a distance from her for a few months, I should very soon have outgrown the fancied attachment. Especially by mixing more with the world, as in such case I must have done.

"But instead of having anything to do, instead of having any profession chosen for me or being allowed to choose any myself, I returned home to be completely idle. And for the first twelvemonth afterwards I had not even the nominal employment which belonging to the university would have given me, for I was not entered at Oxford till I was nineteen. I had therefore nothing in the world to do but to fancy myself in love, and as my mother did not make my home in every respect comfortable, as I had no friend, no companion in my brother and disliked new acquaintance, it was not unnatural for me to be very often at Longstaple, where I always felt myself at home and was always sure of a welcome. And accordingly I spent the greatest part of my time there from eighteen to nineteen.

"Lucy appeared everything that was amiable and obliging. She was pretty too—at least I thought so then. Proximity can induce one to physical intimacy, and I had seen so little of other women that I could make no comparisons and see no defects. Considering everything therefore, I hope, foolish as our engagement was, foolish as it has since in every way been proved, it was not at the time an unnatural or an inexcusable piece of folly."

She rose to him then, taking his hands in her own. She herself had known a certain kind of folly, attracted to Brandon as she had been.

Edward took her silence in stride for a moment then clasped her to him. He kissed her with all the ardour which he now was free to show her. He sank his fingers into her hair, sending her pins flying, as he explored the cavern of her sweet wet mouth. Elinor marvelled at his erection against her mound.

"I daresay," she told him on a giggle, "if we are aroused so easily, I will be with child within the first week of our wedding."

He nibbled at her lips while his hand rucked up her skirts, found her wet cunny and his fingers parted her and stroked her. "Perhaps sooner."

"Now," she breathed the word.

At once, he led her to the settee where he took his leisure kissing her mouth and promising to make all their unions unforgettable. Pushing down her bodice, he gently began to unbutton her chemise so that her engorged breasts popped out of her layers of fabric.

"How I have longed to suck your nipples at my will, my darling Elinor. They are such beauties." He thumbed her hard points, making her sigh and wiggle and want. "I love the rosy colour, their huge size. I shall caress you and make you yearn for my mouth upon these lovelies."

Gripping his arm, she lay down upon the raw satin and pulled her bodice lower, the better for him to access her flesh. "I have hungered for your touch, my Edward. Now these are yours to lave and lick at your pleasure."

He tweaked a nipple. "Let me begin," he said as he bent and pushed her soft breasts together so that he might lick and bite one then the other in quick succession.

She squirmed, eager and hot. "What else will you do, my noble man?"

He pushed up from the settee, undid his flies and with little more than a parting of his breeches, out popped his glorious long red member dripping with his desire for her.

Elinor mewled at the sight. "Oh, how huge he is. May I hold him?"

Hands on his hips, Edward laughed. "Do as you wish, my dearest, he and I are yours."

She reached out, her quim filling with a rush of creamy need between her thighs. She would have this impressive cock inside her and her juices would ease the way for him to ram her over and over again. "Your skin is like silk."

He closed his eyes at her touch. "Yours is finer."

"You are hard beneath."

"To fuck you well and long."

She thumbed his slit. "You give off a luscious drop of love."

"The best way to make you mine is to fill you so full of my cum that every inch of your chat is bathed in my desire for you."

"Oh." She felt faint, overcome with a hot flash of need, her cunny throbbing to be filled and taken by him. "Let me kiss your cock and bathe him in my love, my need."

He inched closer and she bent, taking his member deep inside her mouth to touch the back of her throat. That she could caress all of him thusly stunned her, making her ravenous to enthral him until he spent.

Wicked thought, she knew, but she had to show him her passion for him and impress him with her ingenuity.

He put a hand to her hair, snorting. "My love, you are too much a natural at this!"

"Mmm." She pulled away, allowing her fingers to weigh the heft of his very impressive balls as her gaze found his dreamy one. "And I will have years to perfect other ways to bring you happiness."

"By God, you will," he gruffed.

"You will allow me this pleasure again?" she asked, astonished and delighted, awash in excitement of such a lewd treat.

"You will be my wife and may do to me as you wish."

She kissed the tip of his shaft, admiring the tool that would bring her such joy not only in her pussy but in her mouth. "I wish to have you often like this."

He inserted a fingertip to the corner of her mouth. "You will do it on our wedding day."

She pouted, rolling his balls and making him moan, then licking the angry red crown of his cock and making him groan. "Not now?"

"Now, my pet, I have another treat for you." He slid down to brace himself on the settee and caught her knees up over his forearms. There, with her skirts tossed high and her cunny spread wide for him to see, he angled near to her pussy and grinned. "I will claim you as my love, my bride, my life." Setting his jaw, he nestled nearer to her and with the precision of an artist, he entered her cunny. Slowly, sweetly, with his teeth clenched in raw desire, he drove his way into her waiting, welcoming pussy.

Elinor breathed deeply, revelling in the unexpected girth of his cock, the scalding caress of his member along the swollen yielding desires of her cunt. This love for him, her madness to have him as her mate had so long consumed her that now she screamed as he sank to the hilt.

He froze. "I hurt you!" And he began to pull away.

"No!" She clamped her vaginal walls around his marvellous shaft to hold him, to enchant him.

He arched his back. His eyes drifted shut. "My God, you are talented, witch."

She chuckled, her nails digging into his waist. "Fuck me more. I will show you what trickery a witch can do."

He snorted and arched a brow. "And you have not yet experienced all a warlock might do."

Her eyes flared wide. "But I await his magic with breathless anticipation."

He slid in and out of her, a smooth glide of his cock that enthralled her. "With more than that, my lovely. You purr at my caress."

"Stroke me again, my fine man. I am your cat."

"Let's hear you cry for me," he said and at once began a fluid rhythm to his cock's possession of her. She grabbed at his arms, his waist, his buttocks as he pummelled her, then rammed her with his demand for more and more of her cries, her madness, her need of him. And when she arched up, her eyes squeezed closed, her mind gone, her inner walls pulsing around his cock in volcanic shocks, she knew there on the summit of her joy that waiting for him, believing in him was the best thing she had ever done in her life, and ever would.

Minutes later, as they recovered their senses and straightened their clothes, they laughed together at their rash behaviour and promised that this would be only the first occasion of their indulgence in their natural love for each other. The future, Edward told her, would hold many ribald frolics. In fact, he had a few ideas to ensure she agreed to a quick marriage.

"Dear Edward," she asked him, her mind aquiver with expectation, her body aglow with simmering desire, "what can they be?"

"The day we are married, I will initiate you, my dearest."

"Initiate me? In a cult, a clan?"

"A practice meant for the woman I adore. One meant to take you to the heights of bliss."

She dug her nails into the fabric of his shirt. "I cannot wait."

He struggled to contain his grin. "But you will."

* * * *

The change which a few hours had wrought in the minds and the happiness of the Dashwoods was such — so great — as promised them all the satisfaction of a sleepless night. Mrs Dashwood, too happy to be comfortable, knew not how to love Edward nor praise Elinor enough, how to be enough thankful for his release without wounding his delicacy, nor how at once to give them leisure for unrestrained conversation together and yet enjoy as she wished the sight and society of both.

Marianne could speak her happiness only by tears. Comparisons would occur — regrets would arise, and her joy, though sincere as her love for her sister, was of a kind to give her neither spirits nor language. Turning away from her family's company, she retired to consider the comparisons between Elinor's and her love lives.

Her sister had been restrained, prudent and wise. Moreover, she had kept her fears and frustrations to herself about Edward's courtship, or lack of it. When news of his disastrous marriage had fallen upon her ears, she had managed—though Marianne knew not how she had—to bear the indignities of it with more aplomb than Marianne ever had with Willoughby's desertion of her. Was there a lesson to be learned here from Elinor's forbearance? Could Marianne attempt to emulate her sister—and would that change of heart and change of attitude bring her more happiness than she had yet experienced? Was one connected to the other? Or was she merely hoping for it? Surely, a passionate love in her life was a supreme goal of hers. Could she become a moderately tempered woman and gain the companion she yearned for? No, not Willoughby. Never he. But a man who could love wholly and without restraint to the passions of his mind. Did he exist? Had she met such a man?

She sat in her rocking chair in her room, contemplating this until far into the wee hours of the night. The visage of the man whose name came to mind as answers to each of those last few questions had been known to her for some time. He had shown continued interest in her despite her impulsive behaviour. He had behaved impeccably, with due respect for her and all in her family. He had shown by his own prudence that he was a man of solidity and substance. Which begged the question, why would he find her appealing? Was she a folly to him, a curiosity or a prize to be won, held and coddled? She wished to be a valued spouse, equal in all things, a woman of substance, solid and trustworthy. If he could value her so much as to wait until she had come to her more certain senses, was he not a man she should value and love? Was he not a man to be adored for his constancy and his belief in her basic good nature?

The question remained — could she open her heart to him? And if she did, would he meet her with an equal passion?

She rose, removing her robe, and dared to hope it might be so.

* * * *

But Elinor, as she made her way to her own repose that evening, her mind full of her own new future — how are *her* feelings to be described? From the moment of learning that Lucy was married to another, that Edward was free, to the moment of his justifying the hopes which had so instantly followed, she was everything by turns but tranquil. But when the second moment had passed, when she found every doubt, every solicitude removed, compared her situation with what so lately it had been, saw him honourably released from his former engagement, saw him instantly profiting by the release to address herself and declare an affection as tender, as constant as she had ever supposed it to be, she was oppressed. She was overcome by her own felicity, and happily disposed as is the human mind to be easily familiarised with any change for the better, it required several hours to give sedateness to her spirits or any degree of tranquillity to her heart.

Edward was now fixed at the cottage at least for a week — for whatever other claims might be made on him, it was impossible that less than a week should be given up to the enjoyment of Elinor's company, or suffice to say half that was to be said of the past, the present and the future. Though a very few hours spent in the hard labour of incessant talking will despatch more subjects than can really be in common between any two rational creatures, yet with lovers it is different. Between them no subject is finished, no communication is even made till it has been made at least twenty times over.

Lucy's marriage, the unceasing and reasonable wonder among them all, formed of course one of the earliest discussions of the lovers, and Elinor's particular knowledge of each party made it appear to her in every view as one of the most extraordinary and unaccountable circumstances she had ever heard. How they could be thrown together, and by what attraction Robert could be drawn on to marry a girl of whose beauty she had herself heard him speak without any admiration, a girl too already engaged to his brother and on whose account that brother had been thrown off by his family — it was beyond her comprehension to make out. To her own heart it was a delightful affair, to her imagination it was even a ridiculous one, but to her reason, her judgement, it was completely a puzzle.

Edward could only attempt an explanation by supposing that perhaps at first accidentally meeting, the vanity of the one had been so worked on by the flattery of the other as to lead by degrees to all the rest. Elinor remembered what Robert had told her in Harley Street, of his opinion of what his own mediation in his brother's affairs might have done if applied to in time. She repeated it to Edward.

"That was exactly like Robert," was his immediate observation. "And that," he presently added, "might perhaps be in *his* head when the acquaintance between them first began. And Lucy perhaps at first might think only of procuring his good offices in my favour. Other designs might afterward arise."

How long it had been carrying on between them, however, he was equally at a loss with herself to make out. At Oxford, where he had remained for choice ever since his quitting London, he had had no means of hearing of her but from herself, and her letters to the very last were neither less frequent nor less affectionate than usual. Not the smallest suspicion therefore had ever occurred to prepare him for what followed, and when at last it burst on him in a letter from Lucy herself, he had been for some time, he believed, half stupefied between the wonder, the horror and the joy of such a deliverance. He put the letter into Elinor's hands.

Dear sir,

Being very sure I have long lost your affections, I have thought myself at liberty to bestow my own on another, and have no doubt of being as happy with him as I once used to think I might be with you, but I scorn to accept a hand while the heart was another's. Sincerely wish you happy in your choice, and it shall not be my fault if we are not always good friends, as our near relationship now makes proper. I can safely say I owe you no ill-will, and am sure you will be too generous to do us any ill offices. Your brother has gained my affections entirely, and as we could not live without one another, we are just returned from the altar and are now on our way to Dawlish for a few weeks, which place your dear brother has great curiosity to see. But thought I would first trouble you with these few lines, and shall always remain,

Your sincere well-wisher, friend and sister,
Lucy Ferrars.

I have burnt all your letters, and will return your picture the first opportunity. Please to destroy my scrawls – but the ring with my hair you are very welcome to keep.

Elinor read and returned it without any comment.

"I will not ask your opinion of it as a composition," said Edward. "For worlds would not I have had a letter of hers seen by *you* in former days. In a sister it is bad enough, but in a wife! How I have blushed over the pages of her writing! And I believe I may say that since the first half year of our foolish – business – this is the only letter I ever received from her of which the substance made me any amends for the defect of the style."

"However it may have come about," said Elinor, after a pause, "they are certainly married. And your mother has brought on herself a most appropriate punishment. The independence she settled on Robert through resentment against you has put it in his power to make his own choice, and she has actually been bribing one son with a thousand a year to do the very deed which she disinherited the other for intending to do. She will hardly be less hurt, I suppose, by Robert's marrying Lucy than she would have been by your marrying her."

"She will be more hurt by it, for Robert always was her favourite. She will be more hurt by it, and on the same principle will forgive him much sooner. That is of course if my mother can find any fine qualities in Lucy, which I am sad to say I doubt."

In what state the affair stood at present between them Edward knew not, for no communication with any of his family had yet been attempted by him. He had quitted Oxford within four and twenty hours after Lucy's letter arrived, and with only one object before him—the nearest road to Barton—had had no leisure to form any scheme of conduct with which that road did not hold the most intimate connection.

He could do nothing till he were assured of his fate with Miss Dashwood, and by his rapidity in seeking that fate it is to be supposed—in spite of the jealousy with which he had once thought of Colonel Brandon, in spite of the modesty with which he rated his own deserts and the politeness with which he talked of his doubts—he did not upon the whole expect a very cruel reception. It was his business, however, to say that he did, and he said it very prettily. What he might say on the subject a twelvemonth after must be referred to the imagination of husbands and wives.

That Lucy had certainly meant to deceive, to go off with a flourish of malice against him in her message by Thomas, was perfectly clear to Elinor. Edward himself, now thoroughly enlightened on her character, had no scruple in believing her capable of the utmost meanness of wanton ill-nature. Though his eyes had been long opened even before his acquaintance with Elinor began to her ignorance and a want of liberality in some of her opinions, they had been equally imputed by him to her want of education. Till her last letter reached him, he had always believed her to be a well-disposed, good-hearted girl and thoroughly attached to himself. Nothing but such a persuasion could have prevented his putting an end to an engagement which, long before the discovery of it laid him open to his mother's anger, had been a continual source of disquiet and regret to him.

"I thought it my duty," said he, "independent of my feelings, to give her the option of continuing the engagement or not, when I was renounced by my mother and stood to all appearance without a friend in the world to assist me. In such a situation as that, where there seemed nothing to tempt the avarice or the vanity of any living creature, how could I suppose when she so earnestly, so warmly insisted on sharing my fate, whatever it might be, that anything but the most disinterested affection was her inducement? And even now I cannot comprehend on what motive she acted or what fancied advantage it could be to her to be fettered to a man for whom she had not the smallest regard and who had only two thousand pounds in the world. She could not foresee that Colonel Brandon would give me a living."

"No, but she might suppose that something would occur in your favour, that your own family might in time relent. And at any rate she lost nothing by continuing the engagement, for she has proved that it fettered neither her inclination nor her actions. The connection was certainly a respectable one and probably gained her consideration among her friends, and if nothing more advantageous occurred, it would be better for her to marry you than be single."

Edward was, of course, immediately convinced that nothing could have been more natural than Lucy's conduct, nor more self-evident than the motive of it.

Elinor scolded him, harshly as ladies always scold the imprudence which compliments themselves, for having spent so much time with them at Norland, when he must have felt his own inconstancy.

"Your behaviour was certainly very wrong," said she, "because to say nothing of my own conviction, our relations were all led away by it to fancy and expect what, as you were then situated, could never be."

He could only plead an ignorance of his own heart, and a mistaken confidence in the force of his engagement.

"I was simple enough to think that because my faith was plighted to another, there could be no danger in my being with you, and that the consciousness of my engagement was to keep my heart as safe and sacred as my honour. I felt that I admired you, but I told myself it was only friendship, and till I began to make comparisons between yourself and Lucy, I did not know how far I was got. After that I suppose I *was* wrong in remaining so much in Sussex, and the arguments with which I reconciled myself to the expediency of it were no better than these—The danger is my own, I am doing no injury to anybody but myself."

Elinor smiled, and shook her head.

Edward heard with pleasure of Colonel Brandon's being expected at the Cottage, as he really wished not only to be better acquainted with him, but to have an opportunity of convincing him that he no longer resented his giving him the living of Delaford. "Which, at present," said he, "after thanks so ungraciously delivered as mine were on the occasion, he must think I have never forgiven him for offering."

Now he felt astonished himself that he had never yet been to the place. But so little interest had he taken in the matter that he owed all his knowledge of the house, garden and glebe, extent of the parish, condition of the land and rate of the tithes to Elinor herself, who had heard so much of it from Colonel Brandon and heard it with so much attention as to be entirely mistress of the subject.

One question after this only remained undecided between them, one difficulty only was to be overcome.

They were brought together by mutual affection with the warmest approbation of their real friends. Their intimate knowledge of each other seemed to make their happiness certain—and they only wanted something to live upon. Edward had two thousand pounds and Elinor one, which with Delaford living was all that they could call their own. For it was impossible that Mrs Dashwood should advance anything, and they were neither of them quite enough in love to think that three hundred and fifty pounds a year would supply them with the comforts of life.

Edward was not entirely without hopes of some favourable change in his mother towards him, and on that he rested for the residue of their income. But Elinor had no such dependence, for since Edward would still be unable to marry Miss Morton, and his choosing herself had been spoken of in Mrs Ferrars' flattering language as only a lesser evil than his choosing Lucy Steele, she feared that Robert's offence would serve no other purpose than to enrich Fanny.

About four days after Edward's arrival Colonel Brandon appeared to complete Mrs Dashwood's satisfaction and to give her the dignity of having, for the first time since her living at Barton, more company with her than her house would hold. Edward was allowed to retain the privilege of first comer, and Colonel Brandon therefore walked every night to his old quarters at the Park, from whence he usually returned in the morning early enough to interrupt the lovers' first tête-à-tête before breakfast.

A three weeks' residence at Delaford where, in his evening hours at least, he had little to do but to calculate the disproportion between thirty-six and nineteen brought him to Barton in a temper of mind which needed all the improvement in Marianne's looks, all the kindness of her welcome and all the encouragement of her mother's language to make it cheerful. Among such friends, however, and such flattery, he did revive.

No rumour of Lucy's marriage had yet reached him. He knew nothing of what had passed, and the first hours of his visit were consequently spent in hearing and in wondering. Everything was explained to him by Mrs Dashwood, and he found fresh reason to rejoice in what he had done for Mr Ferrars, since eventually it promoted the interest of Elinor. Marianne too greeted him more warmly than before, conversed more freely and laughed more often with him. Marvelling at his own improved nature when with her, he arrived each succeeding morning at Barton with spirits as high as a man half his age. Chastise himself for such folly as he might, he could not dampen his own joy at his improving relationship with her.

It would be needless to say that the gentlemen advanced in the good opinion of each other as they advanced in each other's acquaintance, for it could not be otherwise. Their resemblance in good principles and good sense, in disposition and manner of thinking, would probably have been sufficient to unite them in friendship without any other attraction. But their being in love with two sisters, and two sisters fond of each other, made that mutual regard inevitable and immediate which might otherwise have waited the effect of time and judgement.

The letters from town which a few days before would have made every nerve in Elinor's body thrill with transport now arrived to be read with less emotion than mirth. Mrs Jennings wrote to tell the wonderful tale, to vent her honest indignation against the jilting girl and pour forth her compassion towards poor Mr Edward who, she was sure, had quite doted upon the worthless hussy, and was now by all accounts almost broken-hearted at Oxford.

'I do think,' she continued, 'nothing was ever carried on so sly, for it was but two days before Lucy called and sat a couple of of hours with me. Not a soul suspected anything of the matter, not even Nancy who, poor soul, came crying to me the day after, in a great fright for fear of Mrs Ferrars, as well as not knowing how to get to Plymouth. For Lucy it seems borrowed all her money before she went off to be married, on purpose we suppose to make a show with, and poor Nancy had not seven shillings in the world. So I was very glad to give her five guineas to take her down to Exeter, where she thinks of staying three or four weeks with Mrs Burgess, in hopes, as I tell her, to fall in with the Doctor again. And I must say that Lucy's crossness not to take them along with them in the chaise is worse than all. Poor Mr Edward! I cannot get him out of my head, but you must send for him to Barton, and Miss Marianne must try to comfort him.'

Mr Dashwood's strains were more solemn. Mrs Ferrars was the most unfortunate of women—poor Fanny had suffered agonies of sensibility—and he considered the existence of each under such a blow with grateful wonder. Robert's offence was unpardonable, but Lucy's was infinitely worse. Neither of them were ever again to be mentioned to Mrs Ferrars, and even if she might hereafter be induced to forgive her son, his wife should never be acknowledged as her daughter, nor be permitted to appear in her presence.

The secrecy with which everything had been carried on between them was rationally treated as enormously heightening the crime, because had any suspicion of it occurred to the others, proper measures would have been taken to prevent the marriage. He called on Elinor to join with him in regretting that Lucy's engagement with Edward had not rather been fulfilled than that she should thus be the means of spreading misery farther in the family. He thus continued.

'Mrs Ferrars has never yet mentioned Edward's name, which does not surprise us, but to our great astonishment, not a line has been received from him on the occasion. Perhaps however he is kept silent by his fear of offending, and I shall therefore give him a hint by a line to Oxford that his sister and I both think a letter of proper submission from him, addressed perhaps to Fanny and by her shown to her mother, might not be taken amiss. For we all know the tenderness of Mrs Ferrars' heart, and that she wishes for nothing so much as to be on good terms with her children.'

This paragraph was of some importance to the prospects and conduct of Edward. It determined him to attempt a reconciliation, though not exactly in the manner pointed out by their brother and sister.

"A letter of proper submission!" repeated he. "Would they have me beg my mother's pardon for Robert's ingratitude to her and breach of honour to me? I can make no submission—I am grown neither humble nor penitent by what has passed. I am grown very happy, but that would not interest. I know of no submission that is proper for me to make."

"You may certainly ask to be forgiven," said Elinor, "because you have offended, and I should think you might now venture so far as to profess some concern for having ever formed the engagement which drew on you your mother's anger."

He agreed that he might.

"And when she has forgiven you, perhaps a little humility may be convenient while acknowledging a second engagement, almost as imprudent in her eyes as the first."

He had nothing to urge against it, but still resisted the idea of a letter of proper submission. Therefore to make it easier to him, as he declared a much greater willingness to make mean concessions by word of mouth than on paper, it was resolved that instead of writing to Fanny he should go to London and personally entreat her good offices in his favour. "And if they really *do* interest themselves," said Marianne in her new character of candour, "in bringing about a reconciliation, I shall think that even John and Fanny are not entirely without merit."

After a visit on Colonel Brandon's side of only three or four days, the two gentlemen quitted Barton together. Elinor was loath to let him go, her status as his betrothed still so new to her as to make her jealous of his time spent with anyone else. Yet she understood his need to leave with Colonel Brandon was for their future happiness as man and wife.

With Marianne by her side, Elinor bid both men goodbye. They were to go immediately to Delaford, that Edward might have some personal knowledge of his future home and assist his patron and friend in deciding on what improvements were needed to it, and from thence after staying there a couple of of nights he was to proceed on his journey to town.

Chapter Fifty

After a proper resistance on the part of Mrs Ferrars, just so violent and so steady as to preserve her from that reproach which she always seemed fearful of incurring, the reproach of being too amiable, Edward was admitted to her presence and pronounced to be again her son.

Her family had of late been exceedingly fluctuating. For many years of her life she had had two sons, but the crime and annihilation of Edward a few weeks ago had robbed her of one, the similar annihilation of Robert had left her for a fortnight without any, and now by the resuscitation of Edward she had one again.

In spite of his being allowed once more to live, however, he did not feel the continuance of his existence secure till he had revealed his present engagement. For the publication of that circumstance he feared might give a sudden turn to his constitution and carry him off as rapidly as before. With apprehensive caution therefore it was revealed, and he was listened to with unexpected calmness.

Mrs Ferrars at first reasonably endeavoured to dissuade him from marrying Miss Dashwood by every argument in her power, told him that in Miss Morton he would have a woman of higher rank and larger fortune, and enforced the assertion by observing that Miss Morton was the daughter of a nobleman with thirty thousand pounds, while Miss Dashwood was only the daughter of a private gentleman with no more than three. But when she found that though perfectly admitting the truth of her representation, he was by no means inclined to be guided by it, she judged it wisest from the experience of the past to submit. Therefore, after such an ungracious delay as she owed to her own dignity and as served to prevent every suspicion of goodwill, she issued her decree of consent to the marriage of Edward and Elinor.

What she would engage to do towards augmenting their income was next to be considered, and here it plainly appeared that though Edward was now her only son he was by no means her eldest, for while Robert was inevitably endowed with a thousand pounds a year, not the smallest objection was made against Edward's taking orders for the sake of two hundred and fifty at the utmost. Nor was anything promised either for the present or in future beyond the ten thousand pounds which had been given with Fanny.

It was as much however as was desired, and more than was expected, by Edward and Elinor. And Mrs Ferrars herself, by her shuffling excuses, seemed the only person surprised at her not giving more.

With an income quite sufficient to their wants thus secured to them, they had nothing to wait for after Edward was in possession of the living but the readiness of the house, to which Colonel Brandon, with an eager desire for the accommodation of Elinor, was making considerable improvements. And after waiting some time for their completion, after experiencing as usual a thousand disappointments and delays from the unaccountable dilatoriness of the workmen, Elinor as usual broke through the first positive resolution of not marrying till everything was ready, and the ceremony took place in Barton church early in the autumn.

Elinor could scarce believe the glory of the golden morning as she made her way to church with Marianne, Margaret and her mother. The sun shone exceedingly bright and hot for October as she climbed into the landau that Colonel Brandon in his generosity had hired from the village to transport the four Dashwoods. Elinor had chosen a deep yellow muslin to celebrate the season but mostly to complement her complexion. Edward, who remained with Brandon in town the evening before, had sent over a nosegay of Chinese chrysanthemums for her to carry.

Marching down the aisle of the little church, Elinor smiled at this one and that who had responded to her hand-written invitations. Among those whom she prized at this celebration were their extended family and friends, especially Mr and Mrs Dashwood, Robert and Lucy, and most esteemed of all, Mrs Ferrars. Nary a disparaging note marred the ceremony. Elinor kept silent but fond hopes to speed the passing minutes quickly so that she might escape the wedding breakfast in that same landau and embark on her wedding journey with her new husband. There in the mansion house that Brandon had given to them both for their honeymoon, Elinor planned to abandon herself to her husband and discover those pleasures he had promised the night he proposed.

The newly united pair arrived at sunset, that witching hour of rich deep shadows when the natural light casts brilliance upon faces wreathed in smiles. Edward scooped her from the plush squabs of the carriage and, laughing at his success, he strode inside. Kicking shut the door, he now took the opportunity he had hungered for all day long. He backed his darling wife to the wall and claimed her willing mouth with all the ardour he had so long suppressed.

"Your lips are my obsession," he whispered to her. "The bow, the fullness. Never have I seen a woman as lovely. Nor as tempting."

"Temptation is a delicacy, my husband," she told him as she flung her arms around his broad shoulders and flattened her chest to his own. "Tonight we dine."

He chuckled, nipping her lower lip and sampling the sweet delights of her mouth once more with a sweep of his tongue. "Dine, hell," he said, seeing how he shocked her. "We feast!" At that, he nibbled his way down her elegant throat. "I would have you naked."

"Here?" The look on her face was stark with surprise and a hint of mischief.

"Now." He arched a brow at her. "Are you game?"

"Are you?"

His gaze locked on hers, he unhooked one button on his frockcoat, then another. Divesting himself of coat, weskit and shoes, letting them drop to the floor, he would have continued but for the sudden shock of her hands on him. Her skin was warm as she stroked his shoulders, his biceps and his ribs. But the enraptured look on her face arrested him. Stole his breath. Quickened his blood, his heart and his very swollen cock. To hurry her would be a sin. But if she continued in this way, he feared he would shame himself before he had done even half a service to her.

"You quiver," she remarked on a wisp of sound, her fingertips brushing his nipples, crumbling his willpower to dust. "I do, too."

He caught her hand and kissed her wrist. "Thank God for that."

"How will we ever get to a bed if neither of us can walk?" she chuckled, her eyes closing as he drew her close and discovered the buttons down the back of her dress.

"We shall find ways." He pushed her dress from her shoulders and pulled at the bodice so that the fabric fell beneath the swell of her breasts. Her porcelain skin was flawless. "You blush, my darling, even here atop these lovely mounds. I shall see all of you tonight. I have hungered to kiss each inch of you."

She shuddered so prettily, his cock twitched.

"I wish to give you the same joy."

"You may. I would have it no other way. Come." He inserted a hand into her bodice and felt the full curve of her breast in his palm. "Let me enjoy all of your charms."

She pressed herself to the wall then and when he startled, fearing she withdrew from him, she did the opposite. She tugged at her bodice so that her luscious breasts sprang free. Her nipples were full and heavy, huge and glistening in the rosy light of the setting sun, hard and pointed in desire. He plucked one and she shivered. He plucked the other and she lolled her head against the wall.

"Your mouth," she said as if in a dream, while reaching out to him and sinking her fingers in the wealth of his hair. "I need your mouth on me here." She cupped a breast and thumbing her own nipple, offered it up to him.

Her risqué act emboldened him. Here was the freedom he had wished for all his life. A woman who gave. A woman who did it without restriction or recrimination. He sank to his knees, gently taking down her gown along with his descent. Tugging at her shift and her petticoat, his wife stood, her milky thighs trembling, attired in only her garters, her white stockings and her pointy little slippers. Now, he faced her frothy bush. He could smell her desire. He could even see a drop of moisture on her curly hair. She did want him as much as all that. He preened. God, he was a lucky man, so right to have wanted her and asked for her. And in a minute, he would have his fill of her. He'd taste her, lick her and nibble on her swollen channel. He shook with the very expectation of her ripe juices on his tongue then he schooled himself to a slow seduction.

With careful hands, he stroked her hips, the outer edges of her shapely legs, her knees and calves. After removing her embroidered shoes, he placed them aside and encouraged her to lift each foot that he might discard the puddle of her gown and undergarments. Then he leaned forward, hands on her perfect ass, and kissed the hollow of her navel. She froze and melted by alternate turns as his fingers kneaded her derrière and he brushed his lips down the curve of her belly to her mound.

Using his thumbs, he tenderly parted her lips and sank his tongue inside along her clitoris. Already she was so entranced with him that her clitoris had grown large and lustrous and oh, so sensitive. She baulked, but in the next second, edged her stance wider.

He smiled, sinking his tongue along her slit to tantalise her more. "I would feast here, my love. Open wider. Let me show you how this man makes a meal of his pretty bride."

Moaning, she complied and he sank to his sensuous work. She tasted of heady musks, her cream thick and rich in texture and form. And as he applied himself even more diligently to exciting her cunt, she gave off more of her milky substance. Her thighs and his chin and lips became drenched in her joy of him.

Beyond much reason now, he encouraged her to let him in and she widened her stance more, tilting up her hips to let him look and lick. To give her greater relief and himself even more pleasure, he thrust a finger in her channel and she groaned her approval. As her hands threaded into his hair, she murmured words of need and urgency. Sitting back on his heels, he drove another finger up inside her drenched core while with his other hand he spread the hood over her clitoris and sucked on her with the most thrilling hunger.

She arched, pushing her mound further against him, encouraging him to have more and more of her. He knew she craved release and by God, so did he. Yet, from years at school and in clubs with his friends, he knew he should give her a strong dose of ecstasy before he claimed her with his cock. For, yes, he would have her yearn for his touch and request it, crave it, need it daily and for that he had to show her the full spectrum of her body's responses.

With a tender kiss to her clitoris, he probed her succulent cunny. The sounds of her liquid response to him were so gratifying, so stimulating that he smiled against her belly.

"Let go of every thought, my pretty wife. Let go. Care only to please me."

"Oh, I want to! As before...yet this feeling, my love, is stronger." She could barely speak, her lips trembling over her words, her eyes limpid with rapture. "Wilder."

"I know. Enjoy it. And me." He flicked a nail over her sensitive nub.

She screamed, her bliss taking her, consuming her and encouraging him to sink another finger high inside her cunny and pump her.

She came—my God, she came!—in a long slow trembling minute.

He knew he could give her even more and let her sink in a puddle before him. With her on her knees, her eyes dazed with delicious fulfilment, he kissed her lips and thrilled to hear her exclaim how she loved the taste of her essence on his lips.

He carefully set her on her back and let her relax in her euphoria. But not for long. He plucked at her nipples and she bucked and begged him to fuck her please. He laved her breasts with swipes of his tongue and she arched her back, then dug her fingernails into his forearms. "Have me," she urged him.

Grinning, he used both his hands to part her hot red lips and found her most sensitive little nub again. He touched it lightly once and made her groan. "Shall I bring you delight once more?"

"Yes, and quickly too."

"A demanding wife?"

"You have made me so. Now do it!"

He chuckled then bent to slide his teeth over the crown of her bulging clitoris. She growled, digging her fingers into the hall rug.

He worked on his buttons, freeing his engorged cock, poor boy, so long confined and so hellishly ready that he dripped with desire.

His rod was no sooner out and ready to romp when his wife circled her hand around it and held on for dear life.

"This is mine," she proclaimed, making them both laugh.

"Of course it is. Although I must say, I think he is more at your service than he is mine."

"How so?" she asked, her expression wily and coy.

"He responds to your touch. Your needs are his."

She tugged on his member. "Show me."

He threw back his head to laugh loudly at that. But deny her, he could not. "Spread your thighs. Lovely. Pink and coated with cream. Here," he said as he scooped rich substance from her lips and coated her mouth with her own juice. Then he took some for himself and sucked long and hard on his index finger, his gaze taunting hers as he devoured every delight from the savoury. "This will allow me to fuck you and make you mine."

"Do it," she said in so low a voice she might have seethed like a female animal in heat.

Gathering her thighs up over his forearms, he smiled at her and inch, by inch, by inch, took possession of his bride. She flowed nearer, encouraging him to be deeper. Then at once frowning in concern, he paused. "I will not hurt you."

"I believe you. Do it."

And so he did, in one swell rage to unite her with him, heart, mind, soul, he slipped himself inside her and held. The moment brought them both to a halt. He froze for fear he'd misjudged her need for pleasure and her capacity for his straining member. But she sent one hand down his chest in a caress that told him she was not only overjoyed but desirous of more. Then when her hand rested above his groin and she tickled the edge of his swollen rod, he knew she wished for more. And when she demanded he take her higher and harder, he was overwhelmed with the knowledge that she was his perfect mate. So he gave her himself in plunging urgency and rabid need. She came, her cunt gripping him and milking him as he gave her his all, and he rejoiced in her sweetness and her love.

Minutes later, he urged her to her feet. She reeled, unsteady.

"Shall I carry you up?" he asked her, as he wrapped his arms around her nude perspiring body, thrilling to the diamond points of her nipples poking his chest.

"No, I can walk," she told him in a husky tone that made his lax cock twitch to get up and inside her once more.

He led her up the stairs, his naked, darling wife.

Leading her to the guest bedroom, he knew the butler and maid of all work had prepared this room for them, as per his instructions. Cold supper was in the kitchen too. Logs ready for a fire in any room of the house. But in the bedroom, he had asked that the bed be turned down—and that a special wooden box be left on the table beside the chaise longue.

He guided his wife towards the bed, encouraging her with a smile to lie upon it. Blushing but allowing him the pleasurable sight of her naked virtues, she cupped her breasts and thumbed her own nipples.

"Am I too forward? Do you wish me not to invite you to me?"

"No, never stop. I would have you do anything you wish that makes your heart sing," he told her as he swept a palm from her ribs to cup her wet core, "and your cunt open to welcome me inside."

She cried out, enfolding him in her embrace and dragging him down to her for an intoxicating kiss. "Make love to me again. Quickly. I fear this fervour will consume me."

"Be consumed," he encouraged her as he sent two fingers up inside her hot drenched core. "Be rabid. God knows I am." And he bent to suck her breasts, one at a time, in lavish declaration of his need of her. "I have gifts for you."

She wended a hand down to his standing shaft and encompassed his heat. "This is what I want. Only this. Besides, your wedding gift of the charming pin for my hat was quite enough, my love."

"What I have for you is for you to wear when you are with me, naked and wanting me."

She coloured then, bright red. "Dare I ask what it is?"

"More than one."

"You are too generous, too kind to me."

"And kind to myself, as well, my pet." He touched the tip of her nose.

"How can that be?" she asked, squirming like a kitten beneath him in her eagerness to see his gifts.

"Do not move."

"No." She lay stiff as a board.

Striding to the table, he opened the box and extracted his trinkets. "Two little birds for you." He held the tiny clamps aloft so that she might inspect them and still, she wondered what they were.

"Lovely and delicate. Birds?" she asked, confused. "Why do they work on that hinge?"

He leaned over, captured a large luscious nipple in his mouth, bringing it up to a high hard point once more then, on a pop, he let her go, only to capture her nipple in one bird...then do the same for the other.

"Oh!" She lay there, gazing at him, her mouth dropped open, her eyes wide, her hands cupping the fullness of her breasts. "That feels stunning. Wonderful. I feel the excitement of the clamps in my —"

"Pussy," he urged her to say the word. "Call it what it is, my pet."

"Yes. I will. My...pussy." She ran a hand through her dishevelled hair. "I like to name it so."

He wrapped her hand around his shaft. "And this?"

"Your cock."

"Quite so." He grinned then pointed his finger at her mound. "Open wide for me there."

"Will you love me again?" she cried, eagerness in her face as she pressed her hands to her breasts.

"I will fuck you here. Fuck you until you laugh with delight."

She giggled.

"And to make it even more delightful?"

"Yes, yes. What will you do?"

He went to his box and extracted two black oddly shaped balls.

"Oh, what can you do with those?" she asked, wetting her lips, her lashes batting in anticipation.

"Roll over, my darling, and put your pretty arse in the air."

She quieted. "You are serious?"

"Never more so."

"Will this aid us?" She was sceptical.

"In our quest to become one over and over again? Never more so."

"How?"

He circled a finger indicating she must present her arse to him. "I will show you."

So she did as she was told.

Her rosy hole was a beautiful pink pucker. He massaged her with ease, and proud of her for allowing him the pleasure of touching her there, he bent and bit her arse cheek. God, she was tasty, firm and fragrant. He flexed his fingers over her derrière and urged her arse higher into the air so that he could roll the plugs in her creamy juice. The delight she gave him with her compliance nearly made him come then and there, and to show her his joy of her, he fingered her slit, found her clitoris and gave her a sweet rub to send her high into her next climax.

"Oh, oh, you do undo me," she exuded her breathy delight. "How can you make me so happy in the space of a few minutes?"

"I want to make you even more so, my pet. Can you relax this pretty hole for me?" He tapped her arse once.

"I...I know not what you mean."

"I mean, dear one, do not be afraid of me, for I would never hurt you. But I do want this plug sitting up inside you so that when I give you your next orgasm, you will scream and spend and do it all again in rapture."

"Is that possible?"

"Ever so, my love. Shall I show you? Will you permit me?"

She turned her head and looked at him, the trust there so apparent. "Anything you say, my husband. I am yours."

"And so shall you become more so as we do this," he assured her with a long caress of her perfect arse cheeks. "Open your little hole for me. That's right. Spread your cheeks and here!" He sank one inside her lovely little ring. "How is that, my pet?"

"Oh, my," she cooed. "I feel full."

"Imagine how you will enjoy another inside you."

"Dare I?"

"Only if you think you might handle the size."

She wiggled her behind at him. "Give it a go, my darling. Give me a go." She chuckled, only to stop abruptly as he tried to get the plug up her ass.

"No, no," she objected, her face in the pillows. "I can't. I can't."

He surrounded her from behind. "There is no hurry, my darling. No rush to do this. We have years and years to have such fun. For now, let me reward you for your sweet acceptance of me and my toys."

"You will have me?" She turned her head up, her eyes expectant.

"Again and again. Forever." He sent his cock along her seam, open to him so charmingly from behind and so damn wet. He glided along like a man on air then he found her cunt, her hot milky pussy, and sank deep inside to his hilt. "Christ, my darling, you feel so good."

"You like making love to me," she said on a sigh.

He bent to nip her shoulder. "My dear wife, say this. 'I like having you fuck me, husband.'"

She repeated his words.

He grinned against her silken skin and fucked her quite thoroughly then.

She cried and pulsed, came and came again, twirling round and taking him to her warm musky body in repletion. Minutes later, she slept.

Smiling at his success, he lay, content that he had begun her education to become his own good submissive wife.

He would love her and keep her and fuck her for the rest of his days, introducing the rest of the toys in his precious box to her as they journeyed through the years. His cuffs, his blindfolds, his chains and whips, he would show her one by one and teach her to love them and crave them as he did. How fortunate a man he was, he had never dared to contemplate. He was now a most happy man and a wickedly happy husband.

The first month after their marriage was spent with their friend at the mansion house, from whence they could superintend the progress of the parsonage and direct everything as they liked on the spot, could choose papers, project shrubberies and invent a sweep. Mrs Jennings' prophecies, though rather jumbled together, were chiefly fulfilled, for she was able to visit Edward and his wife in their parsonage by Michaelmas, and she found in Elinor and her husband, as she really believed, one of the happiest couples in the world. They had in fact nothing to wish for but the marriage of Colonel Brandon and Marianne, and rather better pasturage for their cows.

They were visited on their first settling by almost all their relations and friends. Mrs Ferrars came to inspect the happiness which she was almost ashamed of having authorised, and even the Dashwoods were at the expense of a journey from Sussex to do them honour.

"I will not say that I am disappointed, my dear sister," said John as they were walking together one morning before the gates of Delaford House. "That would be saying too much, for certainly you have been one of the most fortunate young women in the world as it is. But I confess it would give me great pleasure to call Colonel Brandon brother. His property here, his place, his house, everything is in such respectable and excellent condition! And his woods! I have not seen such timber anywhere in Dorsetshire as there is now standing in Delaford Hanger! And though perhaps Marianne may not seem exactly the person to attract him—yet I think it would altogether be advisable for you to have them now frequently staying with you, for as Colonel Brandon seems a great deal at home, nobody can tell what may happen. For when people are much thrown together and see little of anybody else—and it will always be in your power to set her off to advantage, and so forth, in short, you may as well give her a chance—You understand me."

But though Mrs Ferrars did come to see them, and always treated them with the make-believe of decent affection, they were never insulted by her real favour and preference. That was due to the folly of Robert and the cunning of his wife, and it was earned by them before many months had passed away. The selfish sagacity of the latter which had at first drawn Robert into the scrape was the principal instrument of his deliverance from it, for her respectful humility, assiduous attentions and endless flatteries, as soon as the smallest opening was given for their exercise, reconciled Mrs Ferrars to his choice and re-established him completely in her favour.

The whole of Lucy's behaviour in the affair and the prosperity which crowned it, therefore, may be held forth as a most encouraging instance of what an earnest, an unceasing attention to self-interest, however its progress may be apparently obstructed, will do in securing every advantage of fortune with no other sacrifice than that of time and conscience. When Robert first sought her acquaintance and privately visited her in Bartlett's Buildings, it was only with the view imputed to him by his brother. He merely meant to persuade her to give up the engagement, and as there could be nothing to overcome but the affection of both, he naturally expected that one or two interviews would settle the matter.

In that point, however, and that only, he erred. For though Lucy soon gave him hopes that his eloquence would convince her in time, another visit, another conversation was always wanted to produce this conviction. Some doubts always lingered in her mind when they parted which could only be removed by another half hour's discourse with himself.

His attendance was by this means secured, and the rest followed in course. Instead of talking of Edward, they came gradually to talk only of Robert, a subject on which he had always more to say than on any other, and in which she soon betrayed an interest even equal to his own. And in short it became speedily evident to both that he had entirely supplanted his brother. He was proud of his conquest, proud of tricking Edward and very proud of marrying privately without his mother's consent.

What immediately followed is known. They passed some months in great happiness at Dawlish, for she had many relations and old acquaintances to cut. He drew several plans for magnificent cottages, and from thence returning to town, procured the forgiveness of Mrs Ferrars by the simple expedient of asking it, which at Lucy's instigation was adopted. The forgiveness at first, indeed as was reasonable, comprehended only Robert, and Lucy, who had owed his mother no duty and therefore could have transgressed none, still remained some weeks longer unpardoned. But perseverance in humility of conduct and messages, in self-condemnation for Robert's offence and gratitude for the unkindness she was treated with, procured her in time the haughty notice which overcame her by its graciousness, and led soon afterwards by rapid degrees to the highest state of affection and influence.

Lucy became as necessary to Mrs Ferrars as either Robert or Fanny, and while Edward was never cordially forgiven for having once intended to marry her, and Elinor, though superior to her in fortune and birth, was spoken of as an intruder, *she* was in everything considered and always openly acknowledged to be a favourite child. They settled in town, received very liberal assistance from Mrs Ferrars, were on the best terms imaginable with the Dashwoods, and—setting aside the jealousies and ill-will continually subsisting between Fanny and Lucy in which their husbands of course took a part, as well as the frequent domestic disagreements between Robert and Lucy themselves—nothing could exceed the harmony in which they all lived together.

What Edward had done to forfeit the right of eldest son might have puzzled many people to find out, and what Robert had done to succeed to it might have puzzled them still more. It was an arrangement, however, justified in its effects if not in its cause. For nothing ever appeared in Robert's style of living or of talking to give a suspicion of his regretting the extent of his income as either leaving his brother too little or bringing himself too much. And if Edward might be judged from the ready discharge of his duties in every particular, from an increasing attachment to his wife and his home and from the regular cheerfulness of his spirits, he might be supposed no less contented with his lot, no less free from every wish of an exchange.

Elinor's marriage divided her as little from her family as could well be contrived without rendering the cottage at Barton entirely useless, for her mother and sisters spent much more than half their time with her. Mrs Dashwood was acting on motives of policy as well as pleasure in the frequency of her visits at Delaford, for her wish of bringing Marianne and Colonel Brandon together was hardly less earnest, though rather more liberal than what John had expressed. It was now her darling object. Precious as was the company of her daughter to her, she desired nothing so much as to give up its constant enjoyment to her valued friend, and to see Marianne settled at the mansion house was equally the wish of Edward and Elinor. They each felt his sorrows and their own obligations, and Marianne by general consent was to be the reward of all.

With such a confederacy against her — with a knowledge so intimate of his goodness — with a conviction of his fond attachment to herself, which at last, though long after it was observable to everybody else, burst on her — what could she do?

Marianne Dashwood was born to an extraordinary fate. She was born to discover the falsehood of her own opinions and to counteract by her conduct her most favourite maxims. She was born to overcome an affection formed so late in life as at eighteen, and with no sentiment superior to strong esteem and lively friendship, voluntarily to give her hand to another! And that other a man who had suffered no less than herself under the event of a former attachment, whom two years before she had considered too old to be married, and who still sought the constitutional safeguard of a flannel waistcoat!

But so it was. Instead of falling a sacrifice to an irresistible passion, as once she had fondly flattered herself with expecting—instead of remaining even forever with her mother and finding her only pleasures in retirement and study, as afterwards in her more calm and sober judgement she had determined on—she found herself at nineteen submitting to new attachments, entering on new duties, placed in a new home, a wife, the mistress of a family and the patroness of a village.

Social prominence had never been Marianne's goal. But she recognised that in her husband which revelled in others' praise of her. Self-effacing, she used her success to amuse him—and came upon the method quite by accident one afternoon when she walked home from a Women's Relief meeting in the village and he met her halfway.

"Good sir," she greeted him along the path by the woods, "why are you out? To greet me perhaps?"

"I am." He winked at her, took her basket from her hand and offered her his arm so that they might stroll together. "I saw this charming woman making her way towards me and I vowed I must introduce myself to her."

"Ah. I think she knows you well, dear man." She patted his arm, affectionately.

He chuckled and dragged her towards the copse. "Not completely, no, she does not."

"Is that so?" She giggled, not sure what he was about. "Are you taking us home through the woods, sir?"

"Taking you," he corrected her, "*in* the woods."

She laughed heartily, intrigued and complimented, too. Had all her hopes for a man — for *this* man — to learn spontaneity in his daily life come to fruition? "But we shall be a scandal."

"Aye, a ribald tale." He backed her to a tree and there, with gentle hands to her elegant throat, he kissed her lips and pressed his eager body to her own.

"You are definitely up to no good," she cajoled him, chuckling as he led her deeper into the foliage and there, against another broad trunk, he lifted her breasts from her bodice and suckled her nipples until she squealed in delight.

"I would have more of you here in this forest, my pretty maid."

She thought to play along then. "But, sir, I regret to tell you, I am no maid."

"Since when?" he asked with heated ardour, his bold deft hands tugging up her skirts and caressing the soft flesh of her thighs.

"My husband has had me."

"Has he done a thorough job of loving you?"

"He has," she breathed, as his fingers sank inside her seam and filled her body with new ideas of how to enjoy the amorous attentions of her husband. "I think he will soon again, too."

"Will you tell him about us?" he asked as he sank to his knees, parted her wet quim and kissed her there lavishly.

"I will," she gasped. "I will tell him all of this." Why would she not? This ravishing moment deserved a telling. "I will encourage him to have me in similar fashion."

"In the woods?" He licked her clitoris.

She pulsed. "Aye."

"Against a tree?" He caressed her with two fingers up inside her quivering core.

She trembled. "Any one. All of them."

"In the open air?" He stood and undid the buttons of his flies.

"Yes, yes!" She reached for his penis, so thick, so straight, so beautifully ready to fuck her.

He lifted her by the hips and led her to circle her legs around him so that he might pleasure her with his cock.

She lolled her head against the tree trunk as her husband—her darling inventive, spontaneous husband—fucked her until she keened in broad daylight at her fond delight in his loving.

As their bodies cooled and he withdrew from her swollen folds, she sighed against him.

"Shall I take you home to your husband now, madam?"

"Do," she urged him, her lips adoring his. "I want to make love to him in our bed."

"God knows, the man will be thrilled. He cannot ever have enough of you."

"He has told you this?" She smiled at him, his charm growing into a fascination day by day.

"He has. Each day, he hungers for you in his arms."

"And I for him, inside my eager body."

"He asks for nothing more in life than that fond regard for which he pined and yearned to achieve."

"He has," she assured him. "And he shall never lose it."

Colonel Brandon was now as happy as all those who best loved him believed he deserved to be. In Marianne he was consoled for every past affliction. Her regard and her society restored his mind to animation and his spirits to cheerfulness, and that Marianne found her own happiness in forming his was equally the persuasion and delight of each observing friend.

Marianne could never love by halves, and her whole heart became in time as much devoted to her husband as it had once been to Willoughby. She learned that affection breeds more, honesty the same. Her ardent desires for Brandon blossomed a thousandfold and the man who had thought himself unable to love madly discovered he could entice his wife with a look, charm her with a touch and find himself in her bed and her arms and inside her warm, wet cunt within minutes. His joy abounded, for love to him had never promised such amorous vistas. He fucked his wife daily, sometimes twice and three times — and as the years went on, she welcomed him inside her on her garden bench, their parlour rug and even up against their bedroom wall.

Meanwhile, Willoughby could not hear of her marriage without a pang, and his punishment was soon afterwards complete in the voluntary forgiveness of Mrs Smith, who, by stating his marriage with a woman of character as the source of her clemency, gave him reason for believing that had he behaved with honour towards Marianne he might at once have been happy and rich. That his repentance of misconduct which thus brought its own punishment was sincere need not be doubted, nor that he long thought of Colonel Brandon with envy and of Marianne with regret. But that he was forever inconsolable, that he fled from society or contracted a habitual gloom of temper or died of a broken heart must not be depended on — for he did neither. He lived to exert and frequently to enjoy himself. His wife was not always out of humour, nor his home always uncomfortable, and in his breed of horses and dogs and in sporting of every kind he found no inconsiderable degree of domestic felicity.

For Marianne, however — in spite of his incivility in surviving her loss — he always retained that decided regard which interested him in everything that befell her and made her his secret standard of perfection in woman, and many a rising beauty would be slighted by him in after days as bearing no comparison with Mrs Brandon.

Twice he saw her, once at a house party a year or more after her marriage. Polite and conscious of the need to maintain his distance, he bade her hello as if they had met only once. To his eyes, Marianne was more lovely than ever, lovelier still than his own wife. Her fine figure, her style of dress, her laugh, her sighs combined to enshrine her in his mind as the only woman he could ever love. That she was carrying her husband's child and blooming like a hothouse rose only made him more morose.

He pined after her, imaging her in his bed, naked, moaning, his more completely than he had ever dared to make her. His choice of money over love — the one most made for marriage — was now his nemesis. Never did he ask himself if he had chosen well, but drowned his past in a gluttony that the wealth he'd married could afford him.

More than a decade later, his health failing from overindulgence in food and alcohol, he saw her again in the flesh at a friend's hunting party. There, he openly followed her about the house and grounds. Many saw his folly. Some remarked, one to Marianne, who immediately sought the protection and affection of her husband. Brandon himself appeared before the man and with an arch look, warned him off following Marianne. Willoughby retired to his seaside cottage and society learned nothing of him afterward.

Mrs Dashwood was prudent enough to remain at the cottage without attempting a removal to Delaford, and fortunately for Sir John and Mrs Jennings, when Marianne was taken from them, Margaret had reached an age highly suitable for dancing and not very ineligible for being supposed to have a lover.

Between Barton and Delaford there was that constant communication which strong family affection would naturally dictate, and among the merits and the happiness of Elinor and Marianne, let it not be ranked as the least considerable that though sisters, and living almost within sight of each other, they could live without disagreement between themselves or producing coolness between their husbands.

As their broods grew—Elinor with three sons for Edward, Marianne with two for Brandon—the extended families communed weekly together, engendering in their offspring the same gentle affection and honest regard for each other that binds strong families together in love down through the generations.

About the Authors

Jane Austen

Jane Austen (16 December 1775—18 July 1817) was an English novelist whose works of romantic fiction, set among the landed gentry, earned her a place as one of the most widely read writers in English literature. Her realism and biting social commentary have gained her historical importance among scholars and critics.

Cerise DeLand

What's a gal to do to if she lives deep in the heart of Texas, travels often everywhere, and adores Paris, Florence, London, Tokyo and all points east and west?

Ah. She becomes an author who can write about those romantic places. With a passion for cowboys, spies, rakes, knights in shining armour and their gutsy women, Cerise DeLand is an author who adores an alpha male with a tender heart and a need for a smouldering erotic love affair with the right woman!

Cerise is a Top 20 Best Selling author on Amazon with more than three dozen works published in erotic romance, and she is also an award-winning author of mystery, mainstream and romance with St. Martin's Press, Pocket Books and Kensington. Her books are on numerous book clubs, including Featured Selections of The Mystery Guild, Doubleday and Rhapsody. And when she isn't dreaming up fiction or travelling? Cerise is a fabulous cook and an avid history buff.

Busy lady. Happy writer.

Cerise DeLand loves to hear from readers. You can find her contact information, website details and author profile page at http://www.totallybound.com.

Totally Bound Publishing

Home of Erotic Romance

www.ingramcontent.com/pod-product-compliance
Lightning Source LLC
Chambersburg PA
CBHW020458020726
47493CB00001B/83